CRASH SITE

RACHEL GRANT

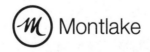 Montlake

Published by Montlake, Seattle

www.apub.com

Amazon, the Amazon logo, and Montlake are trademarks of Amazon.com, Inc., or its affiliates.

ISBN-13: 9781542032377
ISBN-10: 1542032377

Cover design by Caroline Teagle Johnson

Printed in the United States of America

PRAISE FOR RACHEL GRANT

"Rachel Grant's smart, edgy, high-energy romantic thrillers deliver a real rush. The suspense is intense and so is the romance. Fascinating heroines, cool heroes, and intelligent plots. Grant sets a new gold standard for romantic suspense."

—*New York Times* bestselling author Jayne Ann Krentz

PRAISE FOR *DANGEROUS GROUND*

"Grant shines in the heart-pounding romantic thriller that opens her Fiona Carver series . . . This page-turning romance is headed for many a keeper shelf."

—*Publishers Weekly* (starred review)

PRAISE FOR *TINDERBOX*

"Unexpected and intense from the get-go. With irresistible characters, a rare setting, and an inventive, high-powered plot, it's a smartly crafted gem of a story."

—*USA Today*

"This first novel in Grant's Flashpoint series offers a multilayered, suspenseful plot that's strengthened by its appealing characters, strong attention to detail, and a healthy dose of romance . . . An exciting tale that offers an entertaining mix of action and romance."

—*Kirkus Reviews* (starred review)

Named to *Kirkus Reviews'* Best Books of 2017

PRAISE FOR *CATALYST*

"The second novel in Grant's Flashpoint series offers intelligent romantic suspense that moves with the urgency of a thriller."

—*Kirkus Reviews* (starred review)

Named to *Kirkus Reviews*' Best Books of 2018

"From ravaged South Sudan to opulent Morocco, Rachel Grant's *Catalyst* reveals both a sophisticated thriller and a sizzling romance."

—*New York Times* bestselling author Toni Anderson

PRAISE FOR *FIRESTORM*

"Grant expertly braids together action and romance in a propulsive, page-turning suspense thriller."

—*Kirkus Reviews* (starred review)

Named to *Kirkus Reviews*' Best Books of 2018

"Romantic suspense done right and to the max. Don't miss it."

—All About Romance

"An enthralling, heart-pounding masterpiece!"

—*New York Times* bestselling author Annika Martin

CRASH
SITE

DISCOVER OTHER TITLES BY RACHEL GRANT

FIONA CARVER SERIES

Dangerous Ground

FLASHPOINT SERIES

Tinderbox
Catalyst
Firestorm
Inferno

EVIDENCE SERIES

Concrete Evidence
Body of Evidence
Withholding Evidence
Night Owl
Incriminating Evidence
Covert Evidence
Cold Evidence
Poison Evidence
Silent Evidence
Winter Hawk
Tainted Evidence
Broken Falcon

ROMANTIC MYSTERY

Grave Danger

PARANORMAL ROMANCE

Midnight Sun

This book is for
Ruby Bridges
and
Stacey Abrams

A NOTE TO THE READER

Ruby Island and all the cultural, historical, and geological features attributed to it are fictional.

ONE

Ruby Island
Caribbean Sea
June

Fiona Carver had conducted fieldwork in some incredible places in the fifteen years since her archaeological field school, but Ruby Island might be the most unrelentingly perfect. The island had a volcano, rainforest, both sandy and rocky beaches, lore of Spanish gold hidden in unexplored caves, and a 375-year-old star fort. The fort was her destination now as she led a small group up the hillside to the promontory where the massive historic stone structure loomed over the vibrant turquoise Caribbean Sea.

In the 1970s, a wealthy American shipping magnate leased Ruby Island from the Commonwealth of Dominica, an island nation in the Lesser Antilles. The lease had a few years before it was up for renewal, and the leaseholder's grandson, Jude Reynolds, was eager to show Dominica he was a good steward for the land and secure another fifty-year contract.

Fiona didn't blame him. If she had her own private Caribbean paradise, she wouldn't want to give it up either.

They reached the top of the rise, and she could just see the much larger island of Dominica in the distance, while one of the sheer stone walls of the fort loomed above to the southeast.

Laborers had been hard at work last week cleaning up and removing modern-era debris from the site. The view today was quite different from what had greeted her when she'd first hiked here two weeks ago, the day after she arrived on the island.

Dr. Isaac Finch, a retired archaeologist and the world's foremost expert on Dominican history from post-Columbian contact to the present, let out a low whistle at the sight. "It's nice to see the Reynolds family is finally doing something to clean up Fort Domingo. Last time I was here, it was still littered with garbage from the storage structures that were put up in the sixties and then taken out by Hurricane Dean in 2007. They never should have built so close to the fort in the first place. Leaving the collapsed building to rust and rot was insult to injury."

Fiona could only nod in agreement, glad the remaining built environment on the island—a luxurious estate that included a large mansion, servant bungalows, a solar and wind power station, a small runway, plus several outbuildings related to the fleet of boats and fuel dock the estate required—was confined to the opposite end of the island. Ruby Island's previous leaseholder had built too close to the historic fort, which could have had something to do with the man losing the lease in favor of the Reynolds family a decade later.

Her coworker Chad Baylor responded to Finch's valid complaint. "I assure you, Dr. Finch, Jude is not his grandfather or father. He was equally horrified by the state of the fort when he inherited. Clearing out the debris before the film crew arrives was his top priority."

As he spoke, her satellite phone buzzed with an incoming text.

Jude: Helicopter ETA in 10 minutes. Are you at the fort yet?

Fiona: Just reached the flat below.

She looked out over the water, toward Dominica, but didn't see the helicopter. She turned to the group. In addition to Dr. Finch, she and Chad were accompanied by Keili Harris and Gordon Paul, representatives of the Kalinago people.

The Kalinago of Dominica were the last Caribbean community known to be direct descendants of the original, pre-Columbian inhabitants of the region, and they, along with Dr. Finch, were visiting Ruby Island to provide historic and cultural background for the archaeological inventory that Fiona, Chad, and another archaeologist, Sadie Tate, had been hired to do.

In addition to the inventory, Jude Reynolds had also commissioned a documentary for the project, which would begin filming today, as soon as the helicopter transporting the film crew landed next to the star fort, approximately ten minutes from now, according to Jude.

Until they got there, Chad was acting as cameraman. He had a camera capable of filming video in HD at a cinematic aspect ratio. Or something. Fiona didn't actually know much about cameras, still or video.

Last fall, a renowned wildlife photographer had offered her photography lessons, but it had never come to pass, and nine months later, she was kind of making a point of not learning. Any camera that didn't look like a cell phone reminded her of someone she needed to forget.

It was hard to escape, though. Even the name of the hurricane that had destroyed the old warehouse buildings on the site was a reminder.

She was still breathing heavily after the last steep stretch of hillside, and her ego was a little battered when she realized she was alone in being winded, even though she was at least two decades younger than the three guests. "The crew is ten minutes out. We can take a break and wait here."

She pulled water bottles from her pack, figuring she could cut herself some slack—after all, she was hauling water for everyone but Chad. She handed one to each of their three guests.

Keili and Gordon both had bronze skin and dark hair. Keili's was long with soft curls that were tied back so they didn't whip in the wind that buffeted the bluff, while Gordon's hair was close-cropped. Dr. Finch, also from Dominica but not of Kalinago descent, had darker brown skin and a full head of short white hair.

Keili's brown eyes lit with warmth as she accepted the water. "We live in the mountains. This hike is nothing."

"I'm out of shape." Fiona pressed her chilled water bottle to her sweaty forehead, and it felt glorious on her hot skin. It was a good thing she'd slathered on the sunblock today; her Scots-Irish heritage meant her fair complexion didn't hold up well in this much sun. "And we don't get this kind of heat in Seattle."

She took a long drink of water, her gaze on the vibrant blue sea, even bluer sky, and lush green island in the distance. After her breathing settled, she said, "I cannot get over how beautiful Dominica is."

Dominica, not to be confused with the Dominican Republic, had been named by Christopher Columbus after the day of the week he'd spotted the island in 1493. The name was pronounced with the emphasis on the third syllable, more in line with the French name for the island, *Dominique*, but with an *a* added on the end.

Gordon grinned. "You must come see our village. There is nothing like it. And while you are on the island, you can visit Boiling Lake."

Dominica had no less than nine active volcanoes, and one of them was the source of the second-largest hot spring in the world, Boiling Lake, which was, in fact, a lake that was perpetually boiling. It was one of the many wonders she hoped to see, which would depend on how long the survey of Ruby Island took. She'd taken a two-month leave of absence from her job with the US Navy and might need every minute of it to map the island's archaeological resources.

Right now, her plan was to return to her work on the Kitsap Peninsula, but there was a part of her that was seriously tempted to walk away from her Department of Defense archaeology position. Not that she had a plan for what she'd do if she quit, but things in the office had been . . . *awkward*, to say the least, ever since she returned from Chiksook Island last September.

But standing on this bluff overlooking the achingly beautiful blue sea with the world's foremost Dominican historical archaeologist and two Indigenous Dominicans who'd graciously agreed to share their history and culture was not the time to mull over her uncertain future. The time for that was between two and four a.m., when all of life's uncertainties pummeled her anxious brain.

She smiled and said to Gordon, "I'd love to spend a few days on Dominica. I hope I have time before I need to return to Seattle."

"As long as we're killing time here," Chad said, "how about a quick interview?"

Fiona wanted to say no. They'd stopped several times on the hike to record snippets, so it was nice to be able to talk casually—and off-the-record—for a few minutes. Bad enough that she'd need to be mindful of the camera all the time once the real documentary team arrived. Unlike Chad, she wasn't thrilled about being included in the documentary. She'd happily let him and Sadie take the limelight, but Jude had insisted Fiona conduct these interviews, so here she was.

Sadie and Chad would be featured—they were conducting the lidar and underwater surveys, as those were their areas of expertise—but anything to do with the background report or terrestrial survey was Fiona's domain. The couple's part of the documentary would be much more exciting viewing, given the potential to find Spanish treasure and the general beauty of the coral reefs that surrounded Ruby Island. Not to mention the 3D models they'd create with lidar that would strip the canopy from the rainforest and show the land beneath as it had never been seen before.

She scanned the hillside in front of her, her gaze following the rocky path upward to the promontory where the star fort loomed. She studied the steep wall, which was the tip of a bastion, or rather, a point of the star. Dr. Finch would give them a full history of the fort for the cameras when they reached that destination. She turned back to face the volcanic island in the distance.

"We could talk about the relationship between Dominica and Ruby Island during the French colonial period," Fiona suggested. Her phone buzzed again, and she held up a hand. "One second. Might be more information on the helicopter."

She glanced at the screen and felt a rush of surprise and pleasure at seeing the text was from Dylan Slater. Goodness, how she missed him. He'd been on her mind frequently ever since negotiations for this job began. He would love Dominica with its abundance of volcanoes. She'd given in to impulse this morning and emailed him about the job she'd accepted in a whirlwind decision. She'd been avoiding reaching out to him for the last few weeks because he was vacationing with his brother, Dean, on Hawai'i's Big Island.

Her pleasure evaporated the moment she read his message.

Dylan: Just read your email and wanted to warn you. Dean is on a helicopter en route to Ruby Island. Nat Geo sent him to take photos for the wildlife inventory part of the project. We didn't know you would be there or would have reached out to you. Texted Dean, but haven't gotten a received notice. Pretty sure he's in the air already.

A second later, another message popped up.

Dylan: He doesn't know he's about to see you.

A dozen emotions slammed into her. Perhaps three of which were blows to the solar plexus. She couldn't breathe. Sweat broke out on her skin, but this wasn't from heat or exertion. It was the kind of cold sweat that came with shock.

Her hands shook as she hit the button to reply. But she didn't have words. She could barely see the tiny screen.

Fiona: K

The one-letter response was all she was capable of. At least he'd know she'd received his message.

Dylan: I'm sorry.

"Why don't you stand with your back to the sea, Keili, with Dominica behind you?" Chad said. "And I'll film you from over Fiona's shoulder."

Chad's directing jerked her focus from the phone. Chad. Her friend. A man she'd known for a dozen years, ever since she'd attended the underwater archaeology field school in Jamaica that he and Sadie ran together.

Sadie, who wasn't just Chad's work partner; she was his life partner. She'd remained a close friend in the years since Fiona's summer in Jamaica. When Jude Reynolds offered Fiona the principal investigator position for this project, she'd refused because she lacked the expertise. And she'd then turned around and told Jude about Chad and Sadie, who were exactly the experts he needed.

She'd helped him *get* this job.

Chad had been excited for the documentary, this chance to have his work featured. So much so, he'd agreed to act as cameraman today until the real film crew arrived.

"What the *hell*, Chad?"

His eyes widened, and his gaze darted from one person to the next. His pale face flushed red. "Excuse me?"

She knew she wasn't being professional, but she was also certain Chad had been the one behind this blow to the gut. "Why wasn't I told that a photographer from *National Geographic* is arriving with the documentary film crew?"

"How—I mean, what are you talking about? The film crew isn't from *National Geographic*. They're freelance."

"Yeah, and they've got a freelance wildlife photographer with them, and you knew about it. You told Jude, didn't you? You got him to request Dean be assigned to this expedition to give the documentary added drama." It all made sense now. "That's why you were so eager to play cameraman today. You wanted to make sure our surprise reunion was caught on film."

His gaze again darted from their guests to her. "Can we talk in private?"

The whir of rotors had her turning away from him to face the water. She spotted Jude Reynolds's bright orange helicopter zooming toward Ruby Island like a missile.

And Dean Slater was on board. Heading her way.

She hadn't exchanged so much as a text with him since they'd said goodbye in Anchorage nine months ago. But now he was flying through the tropical sea air, coming straight for her.

And he had no idea she was here.

This Caribbean island was so different from the Aleutian one where they'd spent seven harrowing days together, but still, the salt air carried the memory of his scent, reminding her of how it had felt to be held by him as they found themselves in one terrifying situation after another.

She took a deep breath, trying to tap into the cool reserve she relied on in the field and coming up empty. How could Chad do this to her? Had reuniting her and Dean been his idea or Jude's?

What happened on Chiksook had made headlines. Jude had mentioned it when he'd first reached out to offer her this job. Had he planned this from the start or did the idea come later? A way to make the documentary a draw for those who were eager for the salacious details of what had happened on Chiksook?

As the helicopter came ever closer, another thought hit her that made her gasp: *Is Sadie in on it too?*

Her belly fluttered at the idea of seeing Dean. She'd welcome the reunion if it weren't so public. It wasn't fair for either of them to be blindsided in this way.

She'd had doubts about the project after the meeting in Admiral Martinez's office. She'd almost walked away from Jude's offer then. But the lure of two months in the Caribbean had overridden those doubts, and now here she was.

I never should have taken this job.

She *had* tried to say no. She'd suggested Sadie and Chad. But then Jude had insisted he wanted her to run the terrestrial survey. He'd asked her to forget the lousy date they'd shared four years ago and remember the friendship they'd formed when they spent a summer together at archaeological field school fifteen years ago.

He'd claimed he wasn't the jerk who'd spent hours telling her how great he was over a fancy restaurant table, only to be shocked when she refused to sleep with him at the end of the miserable evening. He said the blowhard front had been an act to get over his nervousness at seeing her again after so many years.

He'd reminded her of late nights by the field-school campfire as they looked up at the stars and talked of their dreams. Jude's had been to return to his childhood paradise—Ruby Island—and finally document the archaeology of the island as it deserved.

He'd known he'd go into the family business and dutifully attended MIT so he could design better cranes and boats and whatnot. He'd minored in anthropology and gone to field school against his parents' wishes, all because of his love of exploring this fort when he spent summers on this island as a child.

Fifteen years later, his father was dead and the island was his, and at long last, he could fulfill that dream, and he'd wanted Fiona to run the project.

It had been a heady pitch.

He'd wooed her with the unrelenting perfection of Ruby Island and the proposed project. Housing was in a lavish mansion, built in the 1950s to look like an historic Caribbean plantation home. There was a full-time chef, a maid, and other support staff equipped to see to her every need.

Plus, there would be no budget worries, given that Jude was filthy rich and eager to finance every aspect. He genuinely cared about what would be learned, instead of the work merely serving to check a box to fulfill environmental compliance laws. And the work itself included an historic star fort, lost Spanish treasure, thousand-year-old prehistoric sites, and caves that had provided refuge to enslaved African, Taíno, and Kalinago people fleeing colonizers in the historic period. A full lidar survey *and* underwater survey meant she'd have the opportunity to dive in the Caribbean on a regular basis.

And get paid for all of it.

The project, quite simply, was every archaeologist's dream come true.

The one catch had been the documentary, which he'd tried to frame as a bonus. She'd signed on in spite of the documentary, and now she had to wonder if the reason he'd hired her was to make what happened on Chiksook part of the story.

The helicopter neared the island and skirted along the shore. She could see two people leaning out the open side with cameras. Taking setting shots for the documentary, she supposed. It was a perfect day for it, Ruby Island living up to her name as a jewel in the Caribbean.

She turned to Chad. "Dean is going to be livid when he realizes how you and Jude are using him. And when he tells *National Geographic*, they won't be happy either. Jude will skate by because he can dump more donations their way, but this could blow up in your face if you ever want a grant from them again."

"We need to head up to the fort. The helicopter will be landing soon. We need to be there."

"No."

"Excuse me?"

"No. I won't meet the helicopter."

The whir of the engine faded as the copter rounded the bluff and disappeared from view.

"Our guests have traveled a long way for this. They've hiked halfway across the island and up several steep hills." His gaze turned to the fort on the next rise. "It wouldn't be professional to bag out now."

Dammit. He was right. She was neatly backed in. "You go. Meet the helicopter. Warn Dean that I'm here—off camera—and then I'll join you."

"Fiona—"

"Do it, or I'll walk away now." She wasn't sure if she was bluffing or not.

Chad huffed out a breath. "Fine." He turned to the others. "I'll lead the way up the path. We can do a quick interview at the fort while the helicopter gets more setting shots."

Keili crossed her arms. "I'll wait here with Fiona."

His brow furrowed. "Really?"

Gordon nodded. "Me too." He turned to Dr. Finch. "Isaac?"

"Yes. I think I'll wait too."

Fiona figured it was finally sinking in that this wasn't going to play out as he'd planned and that this stunt had done actual harm to the project. Later she might feel guilty for airing this in front of the others, but right now, she was too angry.

After hesitating for a long moment, Chad turned and trudged up the path, camera in hand.

"I'm—I'm sorry," Fiona said softly. "That was terribly unprofessional."

Keili shrugged. "I don't know what that was about, but I'm glad you didn't back down."

"I think I know," Finch said. "Chiksook?"

She nodded. It made sense that he knew. While the story had made national headlines, archaeologists had shared the story internationally due to the intact prehistoric village site she and Dean had recorded along the way.

"The photographer is on the helicopter?"

She nodded again. "Our history has no place in a documentary about Ruby Island." She looked at the three Dominicans. "This is your story. Not mine."

The helicopter came back into view, rounding the curve of the shoreline. Again, she spotted two people leaning out of the rear cabin behind the pilot.

Dean had to be in his element right now. He was always most comfortable with a camera in his hands. He also was a self-admitted adrenaline junkie, so the helicopter ride, as it tilted to give the cameras the best angle, would probably also thrill him, while Fiona would be tossing her cookies.

Really, there was very little about them that was compatible.

The copter came closer. She could feel the pulse of the engine in her chest. She'd ridden in helicopters many times for her work in the Aleutians, but she'd never ridden in one in the Caribbean, and never for pleasure. It had always been transport to or from work, but she could see the appeal, as the occupants must be treated to a spectacular view.

She was envious, in that moment, of Dean and the others. What a life it must be to get to visit paradise and do nothing more or less than photograph and film it.

Not that they didn't work for the perfect shot. But still, flying as they were over Ruby Island was an experience people would pay good money for.

The helicopter turned and rose higher. It disappeared from view as it crossed over the rainforest behind her, circling toward the fort. It would probably hover over the fort for a few minutes to get aerial shots of the four-pointed star. Then it would land. In a few minutes, Chad would tell Dean she was here.

Should she start up the trail now?

A horrific screeching sound pierced the air, and her gaze jolted up to the fort. A blur of orange slammed into the stone wall, triggering a massive boom that shook the ground.

Fiona collapsed to her knees as flames spurted and the orange helicopter broke into pieces that rained like shrapnel down the hillside and dropped into the sea.

TWO

Impossible. Dean hadn't glimpsed Fiona Carver standing on a bluff above the Caribbean Sea. She was back in Washington, working for the US Navy. Probably dating some man who wasn't worthy of her.

It was simply wishful thinking. After all, she'd mentioned that she'd done underwater archaeology in Jamaica years ago, so she'd been on his mind from the moment he'd accepted this Caribbean assignment to photograph wildlife in conjunction with a documentary about the archaeology and history of Ruby Island.

He'd considered using the job as an excuse to call her. It was so damn tempting. And given the archaeological component, it wasn't even a stretch. But like an addict who counted days since their last hit, he'd quit Fiona cold turkey since she'd boarded that plane in Anchorage, and he couldn't break the streak.

Now here he was in a helicopter flying over paradise, and even as he was snapping pictures of Ruby Island, he was thinking of Fiona. He wished he had time to check the photo he'd taken of the group of people on the bluff, but he needed to focus on the job, like the two-person documentary crew who shared this joyride with him were doing.

Nico was in charge of film while Jenni managed sound. Both were freelancers like himself, and they frequently worked together as a team. Dean had worked with them both before, but they weren't working for *National Geographic* this time around. Their gig was filming content for a soon-to-launch new streaming network, Wild Odysseys. The megarich owner of the island who was funding the archaeological project was also paying for the documentary, making this job a score because Nico and Jenni would get paid and the film would air even if the project didn't find a single artifact. There were plenty of travel shows that talked about history and made a point of searching for treasure, only to find nothing and merely highlight the beautiful vacation spot.

He had no clue if this would be that kind of show, and it didn't really matter to him. He'd photograph the underwater search for the lost convoy's Spanish gold and spend much of the next six weeks photographing wildlife in the rainforest for *National Geographic*. No matter what, he'd have some excellent shots to add to his portfolio, and he'd get to spend weeks on land and underwater in a beautiful place. Added bonus: his brother, Dylan, would be joining the project in a few days.

Life didn't get much better than this.

The helicopter was open on the sides, making it easier to photograph and film. Dean's body pressed against the safety tether as the bird tilted so he and Nico, who sat in the seat facing Dean's, could film the blue water and rocky coastline below.

Fiona would hate this. But he loved every moment. Exhilaration surged through his system. The only thing keeping him from tumbling into the water was the tether.

He got paid to do this.

It wasn't always this fun, and it often was a helluva lot harder, but easy or difficult, every moment on assignment he was living to the fullest. Fulfilling nearly all the promises he'd made to his wife, Violet, in the months before she died.

The copter continued along the shore, flying over the mansion that would be Dean's home for the next six weeks. The house looked like an historic Caribbean plantation home, but he'd been told that Ruby Island never had any kind of plantation, nor had it ever been home to enslaved people. The mansion had been built in the fifties by the island's previous tenant.

It was massive—three stories tall with manicured gardens on one side and a swimming pool on the other. Bungalows—housing for the staff, most likely—were situated behind the main structure. Everything was surrounded by lush, wild greenery.

The helicopter passed over the estate, and he spotted the airfield with a runway long enough for small private planes. Beyond that, on the opposite coast and hidden from view of the house, were the newly installed solar panels and windmills that generated enough electricity to power the estate.

They crossed over the island again and were eye level with the top of the volcano. He snapped several photos for Dylan before they turned and headed back to the shore and the flat where he'd seen the cluster of people upon their first approach. Their destination had to be the star fort, where they would land in the nearby clearing so Nico could film interviews between the archaeologists conducting the fieldwork and two Kalinago people and a Dominican archaeologist.

Dean would stay out of the way during the interviews and get a feel for the landscape. His work would be included in the documentary, but filming today would focus on the history and prehistory of the island. Dean was here for the wildlife, not the culture and history.

He spotted the rocky flat dotted with low shrubs and ferns. The people he'd photographed before were still there, causing him to wonder why they hadn't hiked up the trail to the fort. From this angle, the fort loomed over the flat. He snapped several photos, the people providing excellent scale for the size of the fort and the height of the massive stone wall that was the tip of one point of the star.

"Since the folks haven't reached the fort yet, let's go higher and get aerials of the star." Nico's voice was tinny through the radio headset.

"Roger," the pilot said.

The copter rose like an elevator, then changed direction and followed the ridgeline to the fort, leaving the group on the flat somewhere behind them.

He snapped pictures of the trees. In the coming days, he'd explore and photograph this part of the island extensively. Ruby Island was home to bats, frogs, snakes, and a number of birds, possibly even including the rare sisserou parrot, which was known to live only on Dominica, but there'd been an unconfirmed sighting on Ruby Island several years ago.

The loud whir of the engine sputtered for a second, the sudden gap in sound eerie. Dean's adrenaline pulsed. Across from him, Nico's light-brown face paled with alarm.

A blink later, the engine screeched out a long, high-pitched tone that sent chills up Dean's spine. Through the headset, the pilot shouted, "Shit! We're gonna . . . Hold on!"

The helicopter lurched upward and forward, heading for a clearing, wobbling as if drunk. They cleared the tree line, then dipped down, skimming along the ground, tilting to the left, where Dean and Nico sat behind the pilot.

"Bail! NOW!" the pilot shouted.

Dean snapped the release on his harness and tumbled from the copter. His body slammed into the ground, dropping at least five feet to hard earth covered in cacti and shrubs. Nico landed beside him, and Dean looked up to see Jenni launch herself from the opening as the copter lurched forward.

The pilot bailed last, then the bird swung around and careened into a stone wall. The tail snapped and, like a top spinning out of control, the trajectory of the cab changed, sending it toward the cliff. The bright orange helicopter broke apart as the rotors flailed. Flames spurted, then the shattered pieces of the cab he'd been tethered to just seconds ago dropped over the edge of the cliff.

Dean lay on the ground, his heart pounding as his mind tried to absorb what had just happened. The moments were jumbled and didn't make sense to his shocked brain.

He wanted to check on the others but suffered a moment of paralysis, his body frozen. He couldn't fill his lungs with air, and his hearing was dulled by the screech and roar of the crash. Or maybe his brain just couldn't process sound.

He forced himself to take a long, slow breath. After a moment, his lungs filled. He shifted to face the others, and his vision blurred with each movement of his head. He stilled, giving his eyesight a chance to clear, and there was Jenni, clutching her shoulder, staring at the ledge where the helicopter had been a moment ago with a look of shock on her face that likely resembled his own.

Nico had a cut on his forehead that dripped blood. He looked equally dazed. Farther away, the pilot lay on the ground. Dean couldn't tell if he was breathing.

Suddenly, the man sat up and looked toward his passengers. "Oh, thank God," he said, the relief in his voice piercing even Dean's dulled hearing.

They weren't unscathed, but they were all alive.

Dean flopped back, causing his head to spin again. He'd see what was wrong with Jenni's shoulder in a moment. Right now, he had to get his bearings. His legs were shaky. Probably his hands too.

A few more seconds on that helicopter and he would have been badly injured or dead. He thought of Dylan. His death would devastate his twin brother.

And then there was Fiona. He'd avoided her for nine months. He'd have died without ever having held her again.

If he'd died, how would she remember him as the years went by?

Would the sting of his rejection be her only takeaway?

Minutes ago, he'd been certain he was living his best life . . . but now he recognized there were some aspects he should probably rethink.

Behind him, a woman shrieked, then yelled, "Dean!"

He glanced around to see a tall white man running down the path from the fort. Had he been on the fort during the crash?

18

At the same time, a white woman—the one who'd called his name?—was running full-bore across the scrubby ground. Three darker-skinned people trailed after her, unable to keep up.

He focused on the blur of the woman in motion and blinked to clear his vision. He blinked again. Maybe he had died in the crash, because there was no way what he was seeing was real.

But if I'm dead, then Violet would be the woman I'd see . . .

She drew closer, and her shape became clear even to his swimming brain. All at once he remembered that moment earlier, when he'd spotted the group on the lower bluff, and Fiona had come to mind.

He'd written it off as impossible fantasy, but now here she was. Not a fantasy, and he wasn't dead. Fiona Carver was *here*.

She collapsed to her knees before him. "Oh my God! Dean! I thought you'd . . . I thought I—" She threw her arms around him and burst into tears.

He pulled her tight against him, his hands sliding beneath her backpack, cradling her to his chest as he rested his cheek on the top of her head. His mind had gone helter-skelter at this change in circumstance.

He'd almost died and now had Fiona in his arms.

This wasn't the first time she'd cried as he held her. And it probably wasn't the first time she'd cried because of *him*. But it was the first for both combined. At least these were tears of relief. Joy even.

He felt the same surge of emotion. Dammit, he was alive, and the woman who haunted his dreams was in his arms.

He raised his head to kiss her when Nico said, "Only you, Dean, could pick up a woman immediately after surviving a helicopter crash."

THREE

Fiona wasn't sure if she should laugh or cry, so she did both as she released Dean and rose to her feet. She'd been so focused on him, she'd forgotten that others might need medical attention. It occurred to her that there could have been still more people in the helicopter as it fell in pieces into the sea, and horror rippled through her once again.

"Is—is everyone accounted for?" she asked as Philip limped toward them. She'd met the Hispanic Puerto Rican pilot several times over the last two weeks as Jude and his chief executive, Kosmo Andreas, made frequent trips from Ruby Island to Dominica and elsewhere in the Caribbean. The pilot lived in one of the larger bungalows behind the plantation house but joined the shipping company staff and archaeological survey team for meals in the main house.

"Yes," Dean said as he stood. "Battered, but we all jumped out in time."

Philip knelt in front of the woman who clutched her shoulder. "Dislocated, or do you think it's something worse?"

She moved her arm ever so slightly and sucked in a sharp breath as her face leeched of color. "Not sure. Landed hard. Can't move it."

"Do you have a first aid kit in your pack?" Dean asked, nodding toward the heavy bag on Fiona's back.

"I do. After Chiksook, I'm a little paranoid whenever I set out."

His thumb brushed away a tear that still stained her cheek. His vivid blue eyes held her gaze for a brief but intense moment. There would be energy flaring between them at their sudden reunion even in a normal situation, but he'd just had a near-death experience. The energy that zinged around was off the charts.

All the things she would have said to him today were sidelined. Irrelevant.

A corner of his mouth kicked up in a fleeting and somehow ironic smile. "Never a dull moment with you."

She wanted to laugh and cry again. "Hey. This is all *you*. I'm just here to do my job and interview these kind people." She waved to the entourage behind her.

"What are you—" He cut off his own question. "Never mind. Later. My brain is too jumbled to make sense of anything right now anyway."

"Let's tend your wounds," Keili said, reaching for Fiona's pack, which she still wore.

Fiona slipped off the pack and introduced the others while she dug inside for the first aid kit. Dean then introduced the two-person documentary film crew.

Fiona and Gordon cleaned and bandaged the gash on the cameraman's forehead while Chad and Keili made a sling out of gauze to secure the sound engineer's injured arm and shoulder. Dean used tweezers to pluck cactus spines from the pilot's side, then gave him a cold pack to ice the contusion on his hip. Isaac—who insisted they all stop *Dr. Finch*ing him—assisted by prepping bandages and ointments.

"Fiona, do you have your sat phone?" Philip asked.

"Oh! Of course. I'm so sorry I didn't think to offer it before." After all, they needed to notify someone—or rather, everyone—and Philip's phone had probably gone over the cliff with at least half the helicopter.

Holy hell, the helicopter had *crashed*.

The historic site—Fort Domingo—was now a crash site.

She unlocked, then handed Philip the satellite phone she'd been issued when she'd arrived on the island, because cell phones worked only in the immediate vicinity of the estate, and even then it was spotty.

21

They couldn't get Wi-Fi calling to work with Jude's network, so she'd given up on her personal cell and used only the satellite phone.

Philip paced across the rocky ground, holding the phone to his ear with one hand and ice to his hip with the other as he called Jude Reynolds.

Once Jenni's sling was secured and Nico's head bandaged, Fiona turned to examine Dean's wounds, but he was making a beeline for an object that lay on the ground several meters away.

He bent down and picked up the item, and she realized it was his camera. His soft curse carried the short distance as he scooped up a second item—a long and, presumably, high-powered lens.

She knew what Dean's cameras meant to him, but they were replaceable. He turned and crossed to another item that lay on the ground, this one a much bigger, movie-type camera. "Holy crap, Nico. It's still recording."

"No damn way."

Dean carried it back to the group and handed the camera to Nico.

Nico raised the viewfinder to his eye. "Hot damn. It is." His gaze turned to the gouges in the ground where the helicopter must've hit the earth before it slammed into the side of the old stone fort. The tail of the helicopter rested against the high stone wall, along with other pieces of bright orange debris.

"If the lens was pointed toward the fort . . . it might have recorded everything."

Dean nodded. "I think it was."

Chad cleared his throat. "I was up on the fort wall, filming. I caught almost everything, except when it hit the wall. I jumped back, and it was below my line of sight."

Fiona's gaze jerked to his camera, which was on the ground, near where he'd sat as he made the sling for Jenni. Had he been filming when she'd hugged Dean? Had he caught their reunion after all?

Oh, hell. The crash will be part of the documentary. But then, maybe everyone involved will want it to be?

"I presume Dominica will send a team to investigate?" Jenni said.

"Reynolds will probably ask the United States to send someone from the NTSB. His helicopter. American pilot. All American passengers," Chad said.

Fiona nodded to the two working cameras. "They'll want both recordings." At least the videos might hold some answers. Had it been a mechanical error? Pilot error? An unlucky combination of both?

The helicopter belonged to Jude Reynolds. Fiona had no clue what the guy's net worth was, but he controlled a rather sizable island in the Caribbean. Leased or not, it was technically his, and the cost had to be exorbitant. And the family business was a shipping line that had started in the early twentieth century and expanded into an empire over the decades. Reynolds American Marine Freight—better known as RAM Freight—was worth billions upon billions, and a large portion of that belonged to Jude.

Had someone sabotaged his helicopter in an attempt on his life?

She turned to Dean, wanting to read his take on the situation, but it was too soon and everyone was too raw. It was a terrible time to make assumptions about anything.

And whatever had happened, the pilot had been able to save everyone by making it possible for them to bail before the crash. Even himself. That's all that mattered in this moment.

Her gaze traveled down Dean's body. He still hadn't been checked for wounds. His shirt was torn at the left shoulder, and his slacks had a large rip down the left side. A couple of small, flat bulbs from a prickly pear cactus had attached to his hip, and she spotted more spines piercing his upper shoulder.

It was entirely possible he hadn't even noticed the hitchhikers yet. Adrenaline was a potent drug.

He could have died.

For a few minutes there, she'd believed he *had* died. She didn't even remember running up the path, but her cheek stung, telling her she'd charged into some whipping branches along the way. She'd been fueled by shock and terror, and her feet had moved of their own accord.

Her brain hadn't started working again until she'd spotted him. *Alive.*

She wanted to call Dylan and share the joy with him, while at the same time she was glad Dylan hadn't witnessed the crash. Hadn't experienced the horror of watching the helicopter break apart and fall into the sea, knowing his brother was on it.

Would she be able to handle watching the video Chad had recorded if it was included in the documentary?

Her belly clenched. She didn't think she could view it, even though she knew how it ended.

She cleared her throat as she grabbed her tweezers, then approached Dean. "We need to get those spines out of your skin."

He glanced down at his side, and his face registered surprise at the skinny needles that projected from his arm. She plucked them with the tweezers and dropped the spines on the ground. She removed the prickly pears from his hip, then scanned him from head to toe. "Take off your shirt so I can see if there are more."

He flashed a grin. "Already trying to undress me, Fiona?"

She laughed even as tears rose again, so utterly grateful that he could turn on the cocky charm now, even if it was some sort of autopilot reaction. "You know it, Hot Bird Man."

"I'm getting the feeling you two know each other," Nico said with a snicker and a wink.

"What gave it away?" Fiona asked.

The man laughed as Dean unbuttoned the top two buttons of his Aloha shirt, then pulled it over his head.

Fiona eyed his chest—her reasons were noble, truly—but she couldn't stop the pleasurable jolt at seeing his perfectly sculpted torso, complete with violet tattoo over his heart.

She wanted to reach out, run her hands over his skin, and feel the beat of his heart. Confirm he was here. Alive. And perfect.

But they had an audience. This wasn't the time.

She spotted a small spine protruding from his biceps and plucked it with the tweezers, then circled to check out his back. Four long red welts ran in parallel lines across his left shoulder blade. "Ouch," she murmured as she gently touched the healthy skin below the scrapes.

"What's there? I don't even feel it."

"You scraped pretty badly on some rocks, I'd guess. Looks like you tangled with a very big cat."

She dabbed antiseptic ointment on the welts and used the tweezers to pluck bits of dirt and gravel from the wound, remembering the night on Chiksook when Dean had tended her injured knee.

What a wild turn of events this was.

Another isolated island. Another disaster. Hell, they were even on the lower slope of another volcano.

All they needed was a map and a quest.

Instead, her quest was to make the map.

FOUR

Chad led the group down the path to the beach, where Jude had sent a boat to pick them up. The decision to skip the interviews today had been unanimous. Dean couldn't take photos without his camera, Nico wasn't in the mood to film, and Jenni's sound equipment had tumbled into the sea.

Dean had eavesdropped on the discussion among Fiona and the three interviewees, and they all agreed to return to the fort tomorrow. It would mean they'd skip visiting the caves and a few of the interior sites, but Keili and Isaac said they could stay an extra day if more time was needed to finish the interviews.

Fiona took the rear of the long chain of hikers heading down the hillside. Dean took the penultimate spot in the lineup, giving him the opportunity to slow his pace so they could talk in semiprivate. The initial shock of seeing her was wearing off, and now he had questions.

After allowing the distance between them and the rest of the group to expand, he said, "You knew I was on the helicopter." His gut clenched at the idea that she'd known he was coming and hadn't warned him.

"Dylan texted me minutes before you arrived."

He stopped in his tracks and faced her. "Dylan knew? How? When?"

"I emailed him this morning to tell him about the project. I'd avoided emailing him because I knew you were on Hawai'i together, but knowing I was going to hike the lower slopes of the volcano today, I was thinking of him and wanted to tell him about the project."

She hadn't emailed Dylan sooner simply because he was with Dean?

Dylan had never hinted at that. But then, Dean had made it clear months ago that he didn't want Fiona updates. Sounded like she was just as happy to avoid hearing about him.

And there was Dylan, stuck in the middle.

Dean was a crappy brother.

He looked at Fiona, a woman who meant more to him than he could say, and acknowledged he was a shitty friend too.

She stood before him, sweaty and disheveled, with her honey-brown hair pulled back in a messy french braid, exactly as she'd worn it in the field on Chiksook the first day. In the shadows of the rainforest, the reddish hues in her hair were muted, but even in the dim light, with streaks of dirt on her freckled skin and a welt across one flushed cheek, she was more beautiful than he'd allowed himself to remember.

His gaze fixed on the freckle on her full bottom lip. He wanted to pull that lip between his teeth and kiss her senseless.

He'd almost done exactly that in the first moments after the crash, but thankfully Nico had yanked him back to earth with a quip about Dean's well-known promiscuity.

Now her brow furrowed and she pulled that plump lip between her teeth, biting the freckle that never failed to fascinate him. She cleared her throat and said, "Anyway, I guess he didn't read the email until you were already in the air. He said he tried to text you, but he didn't get a received notification."

Her words pulled his attention away from her mouth and back into the moment. His brain was still scattered after surviving a helicopter crash. He shouldn't be thinking about kissing Fiona. Ever.

"Dylan didn't open your email earlier because he was on a flight to LA. He returned there to handle a few things and gather gear for both of us. He's flying to Dominica in a few days."

"Dylan's coming here?"

He nodded. "Reynolds hired him to set up monitors and evaluate volcanic activity. Mount Asilo has been dormant for over four hundred years, but it's far from extinct."

Her jaw set in an angry line. "Jude is using us. For his documentary."

"You and me, yeah. But Dylan . . . that one's my fault. When *Nat Geo* called me about the job, they said something about taking pictures of the volcano because Reynolds wanted to include volcano monitoring as part of his environmental study to impress the government of Dominica. The volcanology and geology of Ruby Island would be part of the article for the magazine. So when I got on the phone with Reynolds, I suggested Dylan for the job."

He grimaced. "It felt like a gift. He's been looking for work and feeling discouraged." He met her gaze again. "And now we know why you and Dylan didn't compare notes. The offer came in just a few days ago. We decided to cut our vacation short to take it. I flew directly from Kona. Dylan stayed to close up our rental before heading to LA to collect our gear."

"I was offered the job nearly five weeks ago," she said, "right as you were leaving for vacation. The navy fast-tracked my request for leave." She made a face he couldn't interpret, then shrugged. "Signed the contract and next thing I know, I've been here two weeks already." She nodded toward the trail where the others had disappeared. "I recommended Sadie and Chad to Jude. Sadie's brilliant with lidar, and they have an underwater archaeology consulting business. The project is perfect for them. They arrived with their boat the day after I got here."

His brain was still fogged from the crash—or maybe it was jet lag. He'd arrived on Dominica yesterday afternoon, and had spent the evening and this morning exploring the tropical paradise. He'd always wanted to visit Dominica. This assignment had felt like a godsend. A bucket list destination and a job for Dylan, who was literally back on his feet now after surgery nine months ago to repair a busted femur that had gone without medical attention for weeks.

"So . . . if it's a fluke that Dylan's going to be here too, is there any chance it was a coincidence that you were tapped for this assignment?" she asked. "I kind of made a big accusation to Chad, and I'm wondering if I need to apologize."

He shook his head. "I was told Reynolds specifically requested me."

"That's what I thought. I think Chad's in on it. He probably suggested Jude request you." She ran a hand over her face. "If I find out Sadie was involved, I'm going to lose it."

"I'm sorry. I'm still a little confused. Who is Sadie exactly? Besides an expert at lidar?"

"Sorry! I'm a bit out of sorts too. Sadie is Chad's girlfriend. More than that really—they're all but married, and they have a remote-sensing and underwater archaeology consulting company that bears the same name as their boat, *Tempus Machina*."

"Time machine? Good name for an archaeological-research vessel."

"Yeah." She let out a soft sigh. "We've been friends for years, ever since I attended their underwater archaeology field school in Jamaica."

"Why wasn't Sadie at the fort today?"

"She's at the estate, crunching the lidar data she got yesterday." She paused and leaned in. "Do you have any sort of . . . feeling about the crash? Was it mechanical? Do you think it could have been deliberate?"

He hadn't begun to wrap his brain around the cause of the crash, but given that the copter was owned by shipping magnate Jude Reynolds, it wasn't outrageous to think sabotage could have been the cause.

"I have no idea. There was a noise, and the helicopter lurched. We cleared the tree line, then . . . next thing I knew the pilot shouted for us to bail. It all happened so fast. I don't know anything about helicopters, but I've never heard anything like that before. It sounded like death."

"Dean? Fiona?" Chad's voice carried through the trees. They'd stopped for too long, causing the others to worry.

He turned back to the path and resumed walking. "We're fine!" he shouted back.

"Sorry!" Fiona added.

They caught up with the others, who waited at the base of a steep slope. Dean tackled the descent with long strides, glad he'd worn hiking boots and pants in the helicopter, as thorny branches encroached on the path and brushed against his legs.

It took a half hour to hike down the hillside to the beach, where they were met with a boat sent by the magnate to ferry them to the estate they'd flown over earlier.

The boat ride over turquoise-blue water with fresh salt air whipping around helped clear Dean's fogged mind after the shock of the crash and jolt at seeing Fiona.

In the distance, he spotted a pod of whales. Dominica was known for being home to several whale species, one of which resided in the area year-round, and he itched to photograph this first of what should be many sightings, but for the first time in years, he found himself without a camera. He still carried the busted one—his only possession here, as his bag had gone over the cliff in a rain of fire. He would have to ask Reynolds for clothing and other items to tide him over until Dylan arrived in a few days.

He felt strangely naked without a camera. He imagined it was how someone who relied on glasses felt when they were lost. He always saw things differently—clearer—through a lens. After Violet died, he'd only found peace when he was outside, with a camera to his eye.

Plus, a camera gave him an excuse not to participate. He was an observer.

Even when he attended parties with people in the entertainment industry in LA that—until last year—he had so enjoyed, he'd had his camera in his hands. It gave him the distance he needed. When he took the pictures, he didn't have to be in them.

He gripped his broken camera now like a former smoker might grip an unlit cigarette. He wasn't getting his fix, but the ritual helped as the boat cut across the turquoise water.

He risked a glance at Fiona, her hair now glowing red in the bright afternoon sun. Her expression was pensive.

She wasn't happy to see him.

It crossed his mind that she might be dating someone. And that person might be here on Ruby Island. He could, in fact, be the billionaire who'd possibly been the target of the helicopter crash.

———

Fiona visited her room to drop off the heavy backpack. The moment she was inside, she slumped to the floor, back to the door, and breathed deeply to hold back the tears. She needed to face Jude and didn't want to have puffy eyes. Never show weakness.

No. Jude would see only her righteous anger. *Livid* didn't begin to describe her feelings. Her body vibrated with the emotion. He'd played the *old friend* card to get her here, but what kind of friend pulled a stunt like this? Worse, he didn't even have the decency to meet them at the dock after a helicopter crash that would trigger nightmares for everyone involved for years to come.

She took several deep breaths. Control was key. Always.

She closed her eyes and relived the moment when she'd spotted Dean's light hair—blonder now than it had been nine months ago, thanks to his weeks on the Big Island—across the flat and realized he was *alive*.

She didn't want him to know how rattled she was by his arrival. How seeing his stunning blue eyes that matched the sea just a few dozen feet away was a desperate pleasure that triggered shattering pain.

What was *wrong* with her?

He'd rejected her, sure. But he'd had good reason. The best reason, really. But even so, it *hurt*.

And she was still so damn elated to see him.

Focus on that.

She unbuckled the heavy pack and left it on the floor as she rose to her feet. She headed to the bathroom, intending to clean up before facing Jude, but took one look at her disheveled appearance with the red welt on her cheek—which she must've gotten when she'd charged through the forest to get to the crash site—and changed her mind.

She didn't care how she looked in front of her *old friend*.

After one more deep breath, she shoved the backpack out of the way and opened her door. She marched down the hallway and descended the stairs to Jude's first-floor office.

She paused outside the open french doors when she spotted Philip inside. The cause of the crash and investigation took priority.

As she waited, she found her center. That calm place she relied on to see her through the worst of times.

She *hated* that she knew how to find that place within her, but really she knew she should be grateful to know coping mechanisms that kept her together during stressful moments.

Her sister, Regan, had been a huge advocate of imposing a sunny outlook on the darkest of times. Fiona would never reach that level of optimism, but she could aim for composed and call it good. Plus, memories of Regan's efforts to cheer her up always brought a smile.

Not for the first time, Fiona wondered what Regan would have thought of Dean. But really, she knew. Regan would have told her to pursue the man with all she was worth, or she'd regret it for the rest of her life.

Did she regret boarding that airplane in Anchorage?

Sometimes.

Often.

Every damn day, to be honest.

She was so wrapped in her spiral of thoughts, she didn't realize Philip was done until he nodded to her as he passed her in the hall.

She straightened her shoulders and took her ten thousandth calming breath since watching the helicopter break apart and erupt into flames.

Not surprisingly, breathing failed to soothe as the images flashed through her mind.

Good. She needed her anger and fear to get through this meeting with her temporary boss.

She'd been a fool to trust him and take this job. She'd been wrong thinking he was the man she'd known in field school and not the entitled prick she'd gone on a single date with four years ago.

Note to self: if a job appears to be too good to be true, it probably is.

Jude smiled in greeting as she approached. "Fiona, my dear, I was just going to search you out."

At thirty-eight, Jude Reynolds was young for his position of CEO of RAM Freight, although more likely than not, he'd inherited the role, making age irrelevant. He had the looks and polish of a trust-fund kid—white, well-dressed, and always perfectly groomed—but she'd known him when he was a rebellious twenty-three-year-old, desperate to shake off the shackles of his family's legacy and to live the life he wanted for himself.

He'd been sweet and awkward and desperate to fit in at the archaeological field school that had leaned much harder on the hippy end of the spectrum than MIT-educated engineering types.

One didn't find a lot of MIT types in archaeology field camp.

Fiona had liked him while, at the same time, she'd had sympathy for his awkwardness. She could relate. She was a nerd too, just not so far on the technical end.

They'd become fast field-school friends, but lost touch when he returned to MIT's graduate program and she enrolled in grad school in the Pacific Northwest. She'd been stunned when he'd reached out to her four years ago and asked her on a date.

She hadn't even been certain it was a *date*, given that they'd been friends once upon a time. But that night at Canlis, he'd made it more than clear that he expected her to be impressed with the man he'd become in the years since field school, and he anticipated sex as a reward for his transformation from sweet, awkward guy to key player in his family's business.

He'd been filthy rich before, but with his role in the business, he'd become the heir apparent, and he'd made sure she knew every excruciating detail. She gathered that tactic had worked for him in the past, but she'd mourned the loss of the nice guy she'd once known.

Before she accepted this job, he'd managed to convince her that the guy she'd spent an evening with four years ago was the aberration, and he really was the Jude she'd spent a summer with when she was twenty-one. And for the last two weeks, she'd believed him.

But today changed everything.

He sat behind his imposing desk, looking handsome with his tanned skin and dark hair slicked back as if he'd just stepped out of the pool.

After learning that his helicopter had crashed, had he opted to do a few laps in the pool? Was that why he hadn't greeted them at the dock?

She crossed her arms. "I trust you had a nice swim?"

His dark brows furrowed. "I was testing my drone prototype. Is that a problem?"

She frowned. Fine. Technically, that meant he'd been working. His giant MIT brain was developing an underwater drone that he planned to incorporate into the family shipping business. But still. Playing with his new toy could have waited. The helicopter had *crashed*.

Plus, he owed her an explanation for why Dean was here.

"I hope you're wrapping up, Ms. Carver. I need to speak to Jude in private."

Fiona turned to face one of RAM Freight's executive vice presidents, Kosmo Andreas. Kosmo was a white man with a deep tan worthy of his Greek heritage. He was only a few years older than Jude, but too much time in the sun had aged his skin another decade. That same heritage was evident in his thick, dark hair and bushy eyebrows. He would be attractive if he wasn't a condescending prick 90 percent of the time.

He'd made it clear within hours of her arrival on Ruby Island that he believed the archaeological project was a waste of time and he thought she was taking advantage of the CEO and their old friendship. She'd worked on plenty of projects that turned up nothing and *were* a waste of time. But the Ruby Island Archaeological Inventory—RIAI was the official acronym—wasn't that kind of project. Hell, the star fort alone was worthy of a report.

She remained thankful Kosmo wasn't her boss, even though he acted as if he were. Her contract was with Jude Reynolds, not RAM Freight.

She pasted on her least genuine smile. "I haven't even started yet, Kosmo, thank you very much." She turned and planted her fists on the desk and leaned in toward Jude. "I thought we were supposed to be *friends*."

He cocked his head. "I thought you would be pleased to see Slater."

At least he didn't pretend to be confused.

"You're using me. My life. My *trauma* to build your entertainment brand. My life outside the archaeological inventory is off-limits for the documentary."

"You signed the release," Kosmo said, his voice dripping with schadenfreude. "Everything that happens while you're working on Ruby Island is fair game for filming."

"Then I'll quit." Of course, that would make Kosmo happy, but she couldn't base her decisions on that.

Jude rose from his seat behind the desk. "Kosmo, leave us."

"We need to discuss—"

"I said leave."

The man turned on his heel and marched angrily from the room. Once the french doors clicked closed, Jude circled his desk and sat on the edge, next to where she stood. He raised a hand as if to cup her cheek, and she stepped back.

"What do you think you're doing?"

"You have a welt on your cheek."

"I'll survive." Her tone was clipped.

He let out a soft sigh. "If you quit, I can sue you for breach of contract."

She locked her emotions down tight so he wouldn't see fear. She couldn't afford a lawsuit. "That would be a dick move, when you're messing with *my life* for your documentary."

"I honestly thought the surprise would be welcome."

"You want us to talk about Chiksook on camera. You attempted to blindside us both so our reunion would be recorded after I signed a release."

"Chad called me when you sent him to meet the helicopter alone and convinced the others to strike with you. That, too, was in breach of contract."

"You've got to be kidding me. You're going to complain about that after you set us up then the helicopter *crashed!*" She turned on her heel. "Sue me, then. I'm out of here."

"Fiona! Wait. Please. I'm sorry. I screwed up. I really thought you'd be happy to see him."

"How I feel about seeing him is irrelevant. You're using the nightmare Dean and I went through to spice up your documentary—a documentary on an unrelated subject, I might add. I won't have it. I will quit first."

"No. I'll call *National Geographic* and ask them to send someone else. I can get a different volcanologist too. The Slater brothers can be replaced. You can't."

That brought her up short. She was certain it wouldn't matter to Dean. He could cherry-pick his assignments and didn't need the income. Dylan was a different story. He'd been out of work since Chiksook. His recovery had been long and painful, and he'd told her he was eager to return to the field. This job was perfect for him, and he'd have his brother here to make sure he didn't push himself beyond his limits as he regained strength in his leg.

And Fiona would be here too. The idea of spending the next six weeks with Dylan made her chest bloom with warmth.

"No," she said, realizing Jude had neatly backed her into a corner. "You can't fire Dylan."

One corner of his mouth turned up. "No?"

She glared at him, irritated that he'd outmaneuvered her before she'd even stepped into his office. She should have guessed he was a skilled businessman. It wasn't all hot air and inheritance.

Who was this man? She tried to reconcile the guy she'd known from field school with the man she'd had dinner with at Canlis. He'd been careful to show her only his field-school face these last two weeks, but now the arrogant, entitled executive had joined the party.

And that man had just threatened to sue her.

He was hard to read in moments like this, when his deep dimples cut into both cheeks, making even the fakest of smiles look warm.

How much had he played her when he'd apologized for his behavior four years ago and asked for a reset? Had he only wanted her for this project because she'd made headlines after the Chiksook story broke?

The press had hounded her for details for weeks, and now it appeared Jude wanted to exploit that curiosity to sell his documentary and launch his personal venture, a streaming TV channel, Historic Odysseys or Odyssey Escapes—she could never remember the name, just that it had buzzwords that signified travel and adventure—but if she balked now, her action would hurt someone very important to her.

And Jude knew it.

She cleared her throat. "Dylan will be great for this project. You need him."

"You want me to keep Dylan on the project?"

"Yes."

"So it's just Dean Slater you object to?"

"No. If Dylan stays, so does Dean."

Jude put both dimples on full display. "So what's the issue with Dean, then?"

She kept her face carefully blank. "Nothing. I just don't like having my personal life being made public."

"What happened on Chiksook was all over the news. You can't blame me for that."

"No, but I can blame you for trying to use it to launch your travel channel."

Jude gave her a skeptical look. "But this is your chance to get your version of the story out there. Set the record straight."

"I've never had a shortage of options for telling my story. I've chosen not to."

"Listen, Fi . . . I have it on good authority your work situation is . . . uncomfortable."

That was an understatement. It was also a reminder that she needed to email Admiral Martinez and tell him about the crash. She should have done that already, but she'd been too upset to think straight.

Would the admiral be alarmed by Dean's arrival? Martinez knew as much as anyone about what really happened on Chiksook. It would help if she knew exactly what the navy was after when it came to her work on Ruby Island.

"My work for the navy is not part of the documentary. I will not jeopardize my security clearance by talking about my job." That was relevant in more ways than Jude would ever know.

He broke eye contact and glanced toward the window, which had a magnificent view of the beach and sea. A blue helicopter crossed in front, then disappeared from view as it headed for the landing pad by the runway to the west. "Fine. If you aren't quitting, and you don't want me to fire the Slater brothers, we're done. There's a medical team on that helicopter; they're here to examine everyone, make sure no injuries go untreated."

At least he'd made arrangements for that. "Is Dominica sending a team to investigate the crash?"

"Dominica has agreed to allow the NTSB to investigate. Team should arrive in a day or two."

She guessed that the lack of fatalities contributed to the lack of urgency. "I'm sure it will mean a lot to everyone to know what caused it."

Did Jude think it had been an attempt on his life? It must've crossed his mind, but he came across as unruffled by the day's events.

In his shoes, she'd be rattled. And seriously considering having food tested before eating.

His gaze scanned her from head to toe, and she realized he was reading her body language. She was locked up tight, from crossed arms to stiff shoulders. She tried to force herself to relax, but that just meant now her arms were stiff at her sides.

"You saw it happen. What's your guess for the cause? Sabotage?" His eyes narrowed. "Pilot error?"

She closed her eyes and remembered the loud screech followed by the flash of flame and the shattered pieces tumbling over the cliff. "I didn't see most of it. Just the last part when it hit the fort and the pieces fell." She considered mentioning that Nico might have gotten footage and Chad certainly did, but he'd find out soon enough and would probably be eager to put it in the documentary. No point in introducing that idea sooner than necessary. She snapped her jaw closed and turned for the door.

She was committed now. She'd be spending the next six weeks in paradise with Dean and Dylan Slater, and she'd signed a release that allowed the producers to use any footage of her taken in relation to the project. Included in that broad description was the black-tie party Jude was hosting in a few days' time for the uber-rich yacht set that included Fortune 500 CEOs, celebrities, and politicians who enjoyed vacationing on big donors' yachts when they couldn't afford their own.

Odds were, some of the guests would have read the stories about Chiksook and would be eager to hear details that hadn't made the news, offering up another motive for Jude to bring her, Dean, and Dylan together.

Jude was big in shipping circles, but he was trying to make inroads in the entertainment industry with his new streaming travel channel. Dean had connections in Hollywood and deep respect in the travel industry, as his photos accompanied articles that were free advertising for remote and beautiful places.

Jude could be playing an especially long game as he attempted to impress his billionaire cronies with the scintillating opportunity to pump her and the Slater brothers for details about Chiksook.

FIVE

Dean leaned against the closed door of his suite. It was as luxurious as any five-star hotel room he'd ever stayed in, which, come to think of it, was a sample of . . . one? More often than not, when he was on assignment, accommodations were more in line with the tents they'd had on Chiksook, but without the electricity.

He closed his eyes and took a deep breath, keeping his back pressed to the door. He still had dinner to get through, and between jet lag and a near-death experience, his body was ready to shut down. But the moment his lids closed, he was assaulted by memories of the crash.

With the safety of having survived and knowing the others were all relatively unscathed—Jenni would be in a sling for a bit, and Philip had fresh stitches on a cut they hadn't known about when they assessed triage by the fort—there was an added but not entirely unpleasant adrenaline rush that came with the memory.

That he felt a buzz from it was probably a bad sign.

But still, it was there. The shock of realizing they were in danger. The dip of the copter as it plunged and tilted toward the earth. The millisecond between the pilot telling them to bail and hitting the release on the safety harness.

Watching the others slam to the ground followed by the helicopter careening into a centuries-old stone fort.

His heart raced with the memory. Should it scare him that he got a little thrill from it?

Yeah. Probably.

He wasn't about to go seeking out more near-death crashes, but the rush was still there. His reaction reminded him of the first years after Violet died, when he actively sought dangerous assignments and situations, anything that would make him *feel.*

Dylan had reminded him that he wasn't alone in the world and urged him to dial back his recklessness. He'd made a promise to his twin before boarding the plane to Tanzania the day after Violet's funeral: he would return in one piece.

And he'd repeated that promise with every expedition until it no longer needed to be said.

His gaze landed on the stack of clothes and toiletries on the dresser, generic tropical wear that would suffice until Dylan arrived with Dean's clothing and photography equipment. He wouldn't be surprised if these were hand-me-downs from the billionaire himself, as they had a similar height and build, but more likely they were clothing provided to house staff, as he'd noticed that they generally wore Hawai'ian-style shirts and cotton slacks. It didn't matter. He was just glad he'd had something to change into before cocktail hour on the beach. Fiona had been traumatized enough without seeing him in his torn shirt and pants again.

He pushed off the hallway door and crossed the room to the second-floor balcony, which faced the water. The sky was clear of clouds, and the blazing orange disk of the sun hovered an inch above the dark-blue water on the horizon.

He pulled the door inward and stepped onto the balcony, the salty evening breeze washing over him with a calming touch. Down below on the sandy beach, next to the long dock that extended into the sheltered bay, a cluster of people had gathered for the nightly show of the sun descending into the sea.

He'd be down there too, continuing to enjoy his first sunset cocktail hour on Ruby Island with the rest of the team, but he didn't want to watch Jude Reynolds follow Fiona with his eyes one minute longer.

The billionaire had a thing for her. He was smooth, but anyone who was watching for it would pick up on the subtle differences in his behavior when Fiona was around.

It wasn't like Dean could blame the guy—Fiona was, without a doubt, exceptional—but that didn't mean he wanted front-row seats to watching Reynolds make his case with her.

It was going to be a long-ass six weeks.

Thank goodness Dylan would be here in a few days. Dean would have his brother and photography to focus on. Fiona wouldn't—and couldn't—be central to his every waking moment.

The sound of a door on the far end of the balcony turned his attention away from the setting sun. And there she was, twenty feet away. Her hair was loose around her shoulders, and she wore the airy sundress she'd donned for cocktail hour. The breeze whipped her hair and skirt, and she appeared utterly at ease in the tropical environment. She held a glass of red wine in one hand as she stepped forward and leaned on the railing, her gaze on the setting sun.

He considered slipping back inside and letting her have the long wraparound deck all to herself, but he wasn't a coward. Instead, he crossed the distance between them.

Alerted by the sound of his steps, she turned and faced him. She hesitated a moment, and then her face broke into a wide, warm smile, the one she couldn't give him in front of the others. She set her glass on the railing and opened her arms.

He pulled her to his chest, wrapping his arms around her. Her tall form fit against him perfectly, just the right height for him to bury his face in her neck. Her body molded to his, and he remembered so many moments on Chiksook when holding her had been the only thing that kept him sane.

She smelled of seawater and sunshine. The scent of paradise. And holding her was the most natural, wonderful thing in the world.

The sun was halfway below the horizon before he raised his head. He tucked a lock of her hair behind her ear and brushed his lips over hers in the kiss hello he hadn't gotten hours ago on the mountainside. "It's good to see you, Fi."

She stroked his cheek, her forefinger touching a scar—a souvenir from Chiksook—as her other fingers threaded through the bristles of his beard. Her eyes were warm. Calm. "It's good to see you too, Dean."

He could lower his mouth and kiss her again. She would probably let him spread her lips with his tongue and invite him to explore. From there, he could lift her over his shoulder and march through the door and drop her on what was certain to be a king-size bed with a luxury mattress. There, he could make love to her for hours.

It was a fantasy he'd replayed in his mind a thousand times in the last nine months, and that's where it needed to stay. In his fantasies. Only in his mind. Because in reality, he could never give Fiona what she deserved.

And after the way he'd ghosted her since Chiksook, it was entirely possible she wouldn't welcome his kisses or want him in her bed.

"You okay?" he asked softly.

Her mouth twisted in a smile that was also a grimace. "I am now. It's . . . been a day."

His hold on her loosened so they could both face the sunset. He draped his arm around her waist and watched the sun disappear into the Caribbean, feeling calm and content in a way that had eluded him for months. Possibly even years.

And the feeling terrified him as much as it had that last time he saw her in Anchorage.

———

Jude backed up the video again and watched the moment Fiona ran across the field and dropped to her knees in front of Dean Slater. It was natural for her emotions to run high after the crash, but the look on her face when Dean tilted her head back to kiss her revealed something deeper Jude hadn't counted on.

He'd been assured she hadn't been in touch with the guy since Chiksook. He'd assumed that meant there was nothing between them. When photos of the photographer and yet another supermodel showed up on the gossip sites in the spring, he'd figured that sealed it. Dean Slater and Fiona Carver had shared an experience on Chiksook, but no lasting friendship or bond had formed.

He'd thought it would make interesting fodder for the documentary to bring the Slater brothers on board, but that was all. Hell, if anything, he'd figured it was the twin, Dylan Slater, who was the bigger threat. Fiona had worked with him in the field for weeks, and Jude was well aware how appealing she was in a field situation. Plus, she and Dylan had remained in touch. Jude had hesitated to hire him, but when Dean offered him up, it was too good an opportunity to let pass by.

Today, that gamble had paid off. Fiona would have quit if not for Dylan's job hanging in the balance.

Fiona. It would be so much simpler if he could let the fantasy of her go. If he could cherish those field-school memories for what they were and move on. But fifteen years of believing—*knowing*—he'd made the biggest mistake of his life when he left field school without telling her how he felt made it impossible for him to give up now.

He'd come this far. He'd gotten her to his island. He'd given her the project of her dreams—*his* dreams, *their* dreams—and had the perfect opportunity to gently woo her as he should have done when he blew his shot four years ago.

He'd nearly blown it again when he threatened to sue her tonight, but he'd been desperate to keep her here. It had been a massive screwup to let Chad convince him to bring Slater on board as a surprise to spice up the documentary.

Was she in love with the photographer?

He rewound the video and watched the embrace and almost-kiss for the nth time. He paused and studied her mouth as her eyelids lowered in anticipation of a kiss.

He'd give anything to see that look on Fiona's face when she was in his arms.

He covered Slater's head with a hand.

He should be glad Slater didn't die in the crash—after all, Fiona would have been so distraught, she'd probably have quit the project—but it was hard to muster joy at having brought a rival to his paradise.

He backed up the video again and this time watched Slater drop from the helicopter and slam into the ground, followed by the other three survivors.

It would be a hell of an opening for the documentary. He supposed that made Slater's presence on the island worth it.

He reached the almost-kiss again. How could she like a prick like that? The guy had a different woman on his arm every week. And hadn't there been some kind of scandal with the most recent model?

His fingers drummed the table. How would Fiona feel about Slater when faced with the womanizer he really was?

He remembered the model's name. Paige Vance. He searched his memory. He knew people in the industry. He must know someone who knew the beautiful cover girl.

———

Fiona knocked on the interior hallway door to Sadie and Chad's quarters. The couple had been given the corner suite on the second floor, with a view of both the water and the gardens. The room was two doors down from Fiona's suite and closest to the exterior staircase that led from the ground floor to the wraparound balcony.

She heard the soft pad of footsteps on the hardwood floor, and the door swung wide to reveal Sadie, a petite woman with dark ebony skin. Sadie was stunning, with an elegant beauty that literally stopped people in their tracks when they saw her. Fiona had witnessed it more than once when she'd visited her friend in Southern California, where Sadie's mother lived. They would be in a restaurant or simply walking down a street, and another pedestrian would pause, do a double take, then ask if Sadie had been in one movie or another or a perfume or cosmetics commercial. They were always certain they'd seen her somewhere before, and it was LA, where people expected to run into famous people on the street.

She wore her long black hair in hundreds of thin braids. Tonight, the braids were piled on top of her head with a hair tie. The style highlighted the long slope of her neck and her elegant cheekbones and did nothing to hide the puffiness around her wide, brown, and, tonight, bloodshot eyes. She'd been crying.

She grimaced as she pulled the door open wider, inviting Fiona in. "Shit, Fi. I am so damn sorry."

Before she entered, Fiona scanned the room. "Is Chad here?"

"No. I told him to sleep on the boat tonight."

That explained the crying. She stepped into the room and followed Sadie to the couch and easy chair in the corner. Sadie sat in the chair, so Fiona settled on the couch. "I take that to mean he definitely knew Dean was coming."

Sadie nodded. "He lied at first, got pissed when I didn't believe him, then when I told him I found his emails—he sent Jude info on Dean from the company account, which we both have full access to—he couldn't deny it any longer." Another tear spilled, and she swiped at it. "I think I'm just as pissed that he hoped to lie his way out of it as I am for the scheming. He said some nasty things to me when I told him I knew he was lying."

She took a deep breath. "We've been . . . having problems. Financially at first, but it's bled over into the relationship. Overspent on new equipment, and there was a big balloon payment. I thought this project might fix everything—Jude gave us a hefty advance that covered the balloon with money leftover—and once we got the business on track, the relationship would follow."

Sadie's slight Jamaican accent was more pronounced than usual. She'd been born on the island, but grew up in LA, having moved there with her mother after her father died when she was four years old. She'd retained a slight accent over the years due to her mother's influence, but it always grew more pronounced when she was in the Caribbean, and it was even heavier tonight after her fight with Chad.

"Is that why Chad is so eager for the documentary? He thinks it will make him a star and solve all the money issues?"

Sadie nodded. "He has dreams of being the host of a nautical archaeology reality TV show and thinks this is his big break."

Of the two of them, Sadie was far more suited to have her own show. She had a PhD in archaeology specializing in lidar and remote sensing *and* was almost certainly a descendant of an enslaved woman who'd escaped, then turned to piracy to free her fellow captives.

Sadie's life goal was to find one of Ruby Hawthorne's ships. Some believed Ruby Island was named for the woman pirate who'd rescued enslaved African, Taíno, and Kalinago people, then brought them to this very island for refuge. But no one was certain if that's where the name came from.

If anyone should be the star of a documentary about this archaeological project, it was Sadie, which made Chad's actions all the more baffling.

SIX

They took a speedboat to Fort Domingo for their second visit. The boat was the fastest route, and they were behind schedule with the interviews because they hadn't recorded any after the crash. Gordon needed to return to Dominica that night, but Keili and Isaac had both agreed to stay an extra day.

Dean captained the boat as Nico recorded Fiona interviewing Keili, Gordon, and Isaac, as they pointed out features along the eastern coastline, including the littoral caves that were accessible only at low tide.

On the east side of the promontory where the fort was situated, there was a sheltered cove with a long dock. The dock was the only modern construction that was permitted in the vicinity of the fort, and it was a lengthy boat ride almost exactly halfway around the island from the estate. Dean piloted the boat into the cove and reduced the speed as they eased up to the dock.

A gentle, but noticeable, reserve had settled between Fiona and Dean. It was necessary for them to work together, as they were mindful of Nico's camera, which made her glad they'd had a few minutes alone last night to be themselves.

She dropped the bumper, then reached for the piling as Nico tied on to a cleat. Within minutes, they had their gear and were climbing the wooden stairs—also permitted construction—up to the fort.

They reached the top, bringing them to the opposite side of the fort from where the helicopter had struck the day before. This side of the fort was heavy with vegetation all around the bastion that pointed toward the sea, but there was a wide, clear path that led to the top of the crenelated walls of the structure.

As they neared the top, Fiona noted both Dean and Nico paused and took deep breaths, and was reminded they were not far from the flat where they could have died yesterday.

It hadn't even been twenty-four hours.

The wall where the helicopter had struck was on the far side, not within their line of sight, and they weren't here to relive the crash, so they got straight to work, walking upslope to the heart of the fort, treading on stone pavement that had been hewn from this very island 375 years ago.

Isaac gave a brief history of the fort's construction and the role it played in the ever-shifting claims of ownership made by France, Spain, the Netherlands, and Great Britain in the 1600s, before the island became a refuge for African, Taíno, and Kalinago people who'd escaped from their enslavers in the early 1700s.

Sadie really should be here. Fiona found it frustrating that Jude insisted she be the one to conduct these interviews, but at least Sadie would be on camera with Keili and Isaac tomorrow, when she would do a lidar demonstration and then they'd discuss what secrets the island interior may hold.

Today, Keili and Gordon gave the Indigenous history of the relationship the Kalinago had with the European invaders. After Spanish colonizers abandoned Fort Domingo and the local population claimed the island, the fort had become the first line of defense for the island's refugee population to repel Europeans who sought to recapture the formerly enslaved residents.

Fiona checked her list of questions, which she'd composed with feedback from Isaac via email in the days leading up to their visit to the island. One item they'd agreed not to address were the vile claims of cannibalism that had been applied to the Kalinago by colonizers in an effort to justify mass slaughter of all Indigenous people.

It was a tactic as old as war—dehumanize the enemy to justify genocide.

Fiona would not dishonor their guests by asking them on camera about the rumors that still accompanied the last remaining Indigenous people of the Caribbean. Instead, at a later date, she would record a segment in which she would make it clear the allegations were part of a five-hundred-year-old smear campaign and not supported by archaeological evidence.

She was glad for the information this documentary would provide. Columbus was no hero, and his actions would not be lauded. He'd personally inflicted suffering, enslaved people, and initiated genocide.

As much as she wasn't happy to be in front of the camera, she also recognized the documentary itself was an opportunity to fill gaps and highlight biases inherent in the American—and European—education systems. These were the same biases she'd been taught as a child and had to work as an adult to identify and change. It was an ongoing process of learning, and she needed to support Keili, Gordon, and Sadie, who were giving extra emotional labor in sharing their personal and ancestral stories.

She'd been put off by Jude's plan to center her as the host of the show and was determined to make certain that the people who needed to be centered were the focus. Nico was on board with this in a way that Chad hadn't been—but then, Chad wanted the fame of being a TV personality, so maybe it was best that she conducted these interviews after all—and this morning, Nico had promised her she would be peripheral in these vital interview scenes.

With Nico's promises and the gut-wrenching first-person testimony delivered by Keili and Gordon, Fiona felt her heart surge at the realization that the documentary would be meaningful. Viewers would face several hard truths from history—facts many sought to bury or deny. More than five hundred years might have passed since that first voyage, but the pain and suffering inflicted on Africans stolen from their homes and on the Indigenous people of the New World still lived on. Entire cultures had been lost. Racism remained rampant.

Jude had vowed nothing would be glorified or whitewashed in the documentary, and as Keili and Gordon shared stories of atrocities their ancestors faced and what it was like to be the last of their kind today, she felt a surge of thankfulness for her boss and his desire to use this project to educate. She'd buried all kind thoughts of him in her anger yesterday, and needed to remember that there were other important aspects to this job and she shouldn't center herself in this.

If using what happened on Chiksook in the documentary drew in more viewers, who then would learn the truth of what happened in the Caribbean—and all over the New World—during colonization, that was a good thing, right?

The wind whipped across the top of the fort, requiring several takes for the interviews. When everyone was satisfied, they all let out a collective sigh, but the energy was positive overall. It had been intense, but good. Nico was skilled at giving subtle direction that put interviewees at ease.

Fiona needed a moment to regroup and walked across the fort to the high wall that had been struck by the helicopter yesterday. On another day, she'd return to record damage done to the fort by the crash. Today, she would do nothing more than take a peek from this perspective.

She climbed up the four-foot-high crenelated parapet. The wall was capped with wide merlons—the solid upright sections of wall—separated by narrow embrasures, which were the open spaces between merlons, just wide enough for a cannon to nose through. These gaps were called crenels, a series of which made a crenelation. It was this part of the battlement that gave the old fort the classic look of a castle.

She climbed from the gap of the crenel to the top of the thick, wide merlon. Not being a fan of sheer drops and high wind—and from the top of the merlon to the flat below, the wall was nearly thirty feet high—she remained on her knees and crawled to the edge, the humid wind buffeting her sun hat, which would have gone flying into the sea if not for the tight chin strap.

Before she reached the edge, she sat back on her heels, looked up, and closed her eyes. The warm sun and sultry wind kissed her cheeks. She was on top of the crenelated parapet of a 375-year-old fort in the Caribbean as part of her job. The interviews just recorded were *good*. Documentary-worthy, even.

Archaeology—heck, *life*—didn't get any better than this.

"Fiona, turn for the camera," Dean said.

Not wanting a picture of herself with her butt in the air as she crawled across the merlon, she complied, twisting and sitting, leaning on her hand, her back to the sea and thirty-foot drop. This was more posed than she liked, but it would be too precarious if she got to her feet.

He snapped photos with a camera he'd borrowed from Jude. She smiled as she watched him, not for the photos he was taking but because he was comfortable once more with a camera in his hands, and in spite of how it had come about, seeing him again gave her a warm glow.

They would figure out how to be friends, and it would be enough.

"Got what you need?" she asked.

"For now."

She turned back to face the water and crawled the last two feet to the edge of the wall, lying flat on the sun-warmed stone so there was no way the wind could upset her balance. She looked down. What she saw—or rather didn't see—made her dizzy, and it had nothing to do with vertigo.

She closed her eyes and pressed her forehead to the rough but warm rock, trying to regain her equilibrium as the meaning sank in.

She needed to update her report to the admiral and let him know the tail of the helicopter and every bit of orange debris that had littered the flat below were gone.

———

Dean stared at the gouge marks the helicopter tail had made on a fort that had taken over a decade to build and was over 375 years old. The scars in the stone would still be visible well into the next millennium.

He remembered being with Fiona in the Unangax̂ house, being the first people inside the structure in fifteen hundred years, and the wonder of experiencing that glimpse into the past. Fifteen hundred years from now, would someone stand in this spot and wonder what had damaged the star fort's wall in antiquity?

What other marks would his life leave on this world?

Next to him, Nico filmed the damage to wall and earth, documenting what they could. Fiona had called Reynolds and been informed that as far as he knew, no one from Dominica or the United States's National Transportation Safety Board had made it to Ruby Island since yesterday's crash.

Not a single piece of the helicopter remained on the ground. If it weren't for the gouge marks in the wall and the scrapes on his back, he might believe the crash had never happened.

Keili stood near the edge of the cliff, looking down at the sea below. "I don't see any orange in the water, but most of it could have been washed out with the tide."

Fiona stood nearby, but a bit farther back from the steep drop, reminding Dean she didn't do heights if she didn't have to, for good reason. "Sadie and Chad need to use *Tempus Machina* to map the floor and look for the rest of the helicopter. Even if most of it washed away, there should be something here. I'll give her the heads-up." She pulled out her phone and paced across the field with it pressed to her ear.

Dean strode to the edge and looked down at the vertigo-inducing drop. She'd been closer to the edge than he realized, probably because she'd needed to see the truth for herself.

Her courage never failed to impress him. She might gripe about a situation, but she always found a way to buck up and never backed down.

It looked like she'd need that courage now, because there was only one conclusion to be drawn from the missing helicopter parts: the cause of the crash had been sabotage.

SEVEN

The field day started with Sadie doing a demonstration of the capabilities of lidar, ostensibly for Keili and Isaac, but really it was for Nico to film for the documentary. Both Gordon and Jenni had left the island on Jude's private ferry the night before. Gordon because he couldn't stay an extra day, and Jenni because her shoulder ached to the degree that she couldn't perform several tasks. She'd decided to return home for X-rays and to recuperate.

Fiona knew Jenni had told Nico that the crash had her on edge. Her position in the cab had meant she couldn't bail until after both Nico and Dean had cleared the opening, and those extra seconds in the helicopter haunted her. Nico had shared that she'd chosen to return home to address her mental health as much as physical.

Jude had assigned two men from his staff—one a Dominican who maintained the gardens and pool and the other an American RAM Freight employee who had transferred to the island to maintain the various boats required to keep the Ruby Island estate running smoothly—to accompany them in the field. The men were tasked with clearing brush in addition to holding the boom mic and other duties as needed.

Everyone gathered on the front veranda for Sadie's lidar demonstration after the morning breakfast buffet had been cleared. It was a good day for it, as the wind was light. There was speculation a tropical storm could be forming in the Atlantic, but it was days out if it did gather and not a concern yet. Jude's party the following evening would not be affected. The guests would arrive tomorrow and be well on their way the following day before anyone would see a drop of rain or an uptick in the wind. It was still early in hurricane season, which was why the party was planned for June and not later in the summer, when the archaeological project was further along.

For the morning demonstration, the veranda had been cleared of all furniture except a table for Sadie's computer. Nico borrowed Chad's tripod for his camera and again borrowed the dive company's boom mic. Replacement equipment for both Nico and Dean would be arriving the following day along with Dylan. Until then, they were making do with borrowed equipment and even borrowed clothes.

Dean opted to hang around for the lidar demonstration, but when they discussed their field plans for the day, he'd stated he intended to do a scouting mission of the rainforest for the best places to photograph birds, which were the primary photogenic fauna that could be found on Ruby Island. He wouldn't be joining them in the field this afternoon, which was just as well for Fiona.

She needed to adjust to his casual presence on this project. He couldn't be the focal point in her mind. To that end, she studied the rest of the group gathered. Everyone involved with the project plus Kosmo—who was not, but always found a reason to lurk—was here. He expressed a strong interest in seeing what Sadie's high-tech toys could do.

Even Philip, the helicopter pilot, was there. He'd been enjoying breakfast with the group as they discussed the morning shoot and had chosen to stay and watch.

All in all, filming this morning would be a solid setup for the documentary, and Fiona was relieved Sadie would be front and center. She was brilliant at her job and knew how to break down the technical details in an engaging way. She'd set up a mapping drone in the center of the cleared veranda, and now it powered up and lifted for Nico's camera. Smooth and effortless, piloted by Sadie.

This drone would fly over sections of the island in transects, mapping with lidar. As the drone flew toward the water, she gave her rehearsed explanation. "This drone is equipped with topographic lidar, which is for mapping land." She sent the drone over the water. "I will use bathymetric lidar, which uses water-penetrating green light to measure seafloor elevations, to map Cannon Bay."

She spread her arm, indicating the sheltered bay that fronted the mansion, with its sandy beach and long, low pier with multiple boat slips along one side. To the very far right was the fueling dock, but the pumps and maintenance shed were out of sight from the veranda and balconies, keeping the view pretty for the billionaire owner and his guests. The estate was situated midway up the hillside, with a sweeping view of the bay and sea beyond.

Sadie sent the drone to fly to the left of the house and gardens, gliding above a wide flat dotted with palm trees that stretched over the bay below. "For over two hundred years, this flat and the one facing it on the opposite side—above the current fueling dock—provided protection for the north end of Ruby Island. There was never a fort here, but there were cannons—a battery of six guns on each flat, aimed at the mouth of the bay.

"From historic photos and written accounts, we know that both landforms had a furnace for heating shot—to propel hotshot cannonballs into wooden ships, setting fire to any vessel that dared enter this bay. As Dr. Finch shared yesterday, in the 1700s and 1800s, well over a dozen vessels ran afoul of those cannons. Some managed to escape, but several sank not far from the end of the current pier. Unfortunately, the cannons and hotshot furnaces that protected the bay were dumped into the water in the 1950s by the island's then leaseholder, American oilman Fedor Mallet, when this house was under construction."

Dr. Finch jumped in to provide more context as planned. "It's worth noting that historically speaking, we're not sure when this port was dubbed Cannon Bay, or if the name was bestowed by those who lost their vessels to cannon fire or the American who had the cannons dumped in the bay, but the name stuck, partly because we do know there are at least twenty cannons and likely the remains of several ships in the harbor."

"One of my goals," Sadie said, picking up the thread, "for this archaeological inventory is to use bathymetric lidar to find all the cannons—be they from sunken ships or the ones that protected the island—resting in Cannon Bay."

"If possible," Jude said, drawing Nico's camera, "the ones that once sat on the flat above the bay will be restored to their previous position, a reminder for all who visit of the role Ruby Island played in Caribbean history."

"To make it interesting," Chad said, "we should place bets on how many cannons are really in Cannon Bay."

"Bet against Dr. Finch, a man who has spent his life studying the maritime history of Dominica? That's a no from me," Fiona said with a laugh.

"I'll take that bet," Jude said. He faced the Dominican archaeologist. "I'm not foolish enough to bet against your research, Dr. Finch, so we can structure the wager based on it. If your guess is within three cannons of the final tally—plus or minus—I'll make a donation to the historical museum on Dominica in the amount of one thousand dollars per cannon."

Fiona smiled. It was a clever bit of staging, and she wondered if he and Chad had planned it. After all, now everyone would be rooting for the archaeologist to win the bet.

For Jude's part, he looked handsome in his casual, tropical billionaire wear. She figured he'd expected to be filmed today but hadn't gone so far as to put on makeup for his cameo appearance in his own documentary. But then, for most of the filming, there wouldn't be makeup. Scuba and makeup didn't play well together, nor did fieldwork in a rainforest.

Wager settled, the billionaire and the archaeologist shook hands for the camera as Finch said he'd consult his notes before making his official guess.

Sadie brought the drone back so it flew along the shoreline, staying within view of the spectators on the veranda and Nico's camera. "For today's demonstration, I'm going to give a simple example of what lidar can do."

She directed the drone to the low bluff on the northwest corner of the house, where the second battery of cannons had once sat but which now was covered with thick, wild, overgrown vegetation, hiding the fuel dock and maintenance structures from view of the mansion.

"On my computer screen, you can see what the camera on the drone sees."

Nico's main camera followed the drone, while Chad's camera focused on the computer screen. They'd split the image in the editing room, splicing in the drone footage.

Sadie's screen showed greenery and more greenery. Vines and thorns and broad leaves, all low shrubbery, no large trees, in an effort to keep the view of the water from the house intact as one stood on any of the upper balconies and gazed over the low but thick vegetation.

"All *we* see here are plants, but when I turn on the lidar and run transects, I get a very different image."

Fiona knew Sadie had already mapped the area yesterday in preparation for this demonstration, so she'd have processed images and 3D models prepared for viewing today. These would be spliced into the video as well; for now, they looked at the screen as Sadie pulled up digital images of the patch of green between house and water.

"With lidar, I can strip away the layers of plants. In some instances, I can even identify the differences between plants and isolate layers of different types. But for this, I'm going to remove all the layers and show what's hiding beneath all that greenery."

Crash Site

With a few keystrokes, the plants disappeared. Large underground fuel tanks appeared as if she were showing an X-ray of the island's skeleton. "This, of course, is easy. Large metal fuel tanks for the fueling dock on the far side of the bay, but it's a good example of how large something can be and still be utterly obscured by vegetation.

"This area isn't nearly as grown over as the mature rainforest in the middle of the island. As Keili has shared, there are likely structures in the middle of the island. Oral history tells us her ancestors—and mine—took refuge here and used the tools and materials left behind by colonizers who built the fort to make hideouts in the rainforest in case their defenses were breached." She smiled for the camera. "There is much we can find on Ruby Island."

"Perhaps you can find the pirate gold hidden in the lake." This comment came from Oliver, the Dominican maintenance worker who would help them in the field.

"Which lake is that?" Sadie asked.

The young man shrugged. "I don't know. You know the story, don't you, Keili?"

Keili nodded. "Yes. It is rumored that a pirate who sought to hide on Ruby Island paid the refugee occupants in stolen Spanish gold. The Spanish came after it, and the locals dumped it in one of the lakes in the center of the island for safekeeping. Some say it is still there, lost in the silt at the deepest part of the lake, or that the volcano opened up a crevasse in the middle of the lake and swallowed the gold as tribute."

"Well, I'll be sure to map around all three lakes in the central part of the island, and if we have time, we can use the bathymetric lidar to map the lake floor," Sadie said. "It won't pick up individual coins, but a pile or chest could be identified, and fresh water is good for wood preservation."

Sadie flew the drone around a bit longer, and there were more questions and answers, but Fiona doubted any of it would end up in

61

the documentary, as the story about hidden gold would surely end the segment.

People loved anything to do with pirates, especially cannons and treasure—which was the reason for recording this segment by Cannon Bay, even though Sadie didn't have time to include water-penetrating bathymetric lidar in the demonstration.

After filming was wrapped up, Philip dropped into the seat next to Sadie and studied the image on the screen. "So you can just click on these layers on the side and make the ground cover disappear?"

Sadie nodded. She tapped the keys and toggled between showing the northwest corner of the island with vegetation and without.

"I never would have guessed those fuel tanks were that big."

"It's one reason why it was the perfect demonstration," Sadie said. "It's easy to forget how much the jungle can hide. Not long ago, in Mexico, a massive three-thousand-year-old Mayan pyramid complex was found with lidar."

"You think you'll find a pyramid in the jungle on Ruby Island?" Kosmo asked, his voice dripping with condescension. "Is that how you convinced Jude to finance this project?"

Jude flashed his executive VP a glare, but Sadie was the one who answered the snide question. "You might remember that Jude approached me. And no. There is no oral history of Kalinago constructing pyramids, as Keili can attest."

The other woman nodded in agreement. "But we did build other structures. While homes made out of wood will have decomposed, stone features will have survived."

"In addition," Sadie added, "there are areas around Fort Domingo that are heavily overgrown, and some outbuildings may well be extant under all that vegetation. There is likely to be a larger cistern than the one already located. Don't fool yourself into believing we know everything that's here just because nobody bothered to look before now."

Dean stepped forward and studied the image on the screen. "When was the last time your fuel tanks were inspected?" he asked Jude. "As big as they are, a leak would be devastating to the reef and wildlife."

"I assure you, Mr. Slater, we make sure our fuel tanks are sealed tight and don't threaten my island paradise." Jude's stress on the word *my* was subtle, but intentional. Fiona caught it and was certain Dean did too.

Keili and Sadie both bristled, but neither said a word to the financier of the project.

Jude might have taken some anthropology classes, but he had a lot to learn about respecting cultural identity and history. It might be over five hundred years since Columbus invaded, but he, as lessee of the island, was still a colonizer. Yes, it was *his* island technically, but the history and culture belonged to Keili and even to Sadie.

He'd been aiming his jab at Dean, but his assertion of ownership had been a direct microaggression toward the women.

"Glad to hear it," Dean said. "Is there a reason you need such large fuel tanks? Seems like an unnecessary risk to the ecosystem."

"Our location on the edge between the Caribbean and the Atlantic means we sometimes are the first island vessels in trouble can reach. My father was committed to always having enough to provide aid when needed, and he upgraded our fuel reserves about ten years ago. As the head of a shipping company, he knew it's good policy to treat all seafaring vessels with the same care we'd like our ships to receive. Since taking over the company and island, I have chosen to carry on that tradition. We keep plenty of fuel on hand and never charge those in need."

"That's very generous," Dean said.

He was right; it was generous, and yet the way he said it . . . it was pretty clear Dean felt there was a catch.

Dean didn't like Jude, and now she was certain the feeling was mutual. Certainly, after Jude withheld that Fiona was part of the archaeological team, Dean had reason to be angry. But what was Jude's problem?

After all, he was the one who'd insisted on hiring the wildlife photographer.

———

It was a relief for Sadie to be in the jungle with a small team and away from Chad for the afternoon. It didn't bother her that Jude and Kosmo were nowhere to be seen either.

There were some weird dynamics brewing on this project that she wanted nothing to do with, and at least here she could do her job and enjoy talking to Keili and Isaac. She'd never met Keili before this week, but she'd been in touch with Isaac many times over the years. She reminded herself to be thankful Jude Reynolds was paying them all very well to be here.

This was a great project and opportunity. She needed to set her annoyance at Kosmo aside.

Unfortunately, her problem with Chad wasn't quite so easy to ignore.

She focused on the drone that was flying over the canopy as they stood in a small clearing. "I'm going to do some passes over the three lakes," she announced. "So we can look for your gold, Oliver."

He laughed. "Will I get a cut if you find it?"

"Only if cameras aren't rolling and no one tells the Commonwealth of Dominica."

"Too bad I'm recording now," Nico said with a chuckle.

"Damn," Oliver said, winking for the camera.

Oliver was supposed to be off camera, but given his local knowledge and the fact that he'd worked on Ruby Island for the last few years, he was a natural to interview. He'd searched the jungle, hiked the volcano, and explored the fort.

He'd even researched the history of the house and its original builder, Fedor Mallet, and this afternoon they'd recorded a short interview in which he'd described the American oilman's ties to the Soviet Union and how he'd increased his wealth selling fuel to the Soviets during the Cold War.

Isaac had expanded on that, noting that in the wake of the Cuban Missile Crisis and Mallet's disregard for the island's historic properties, the Commonwealth of Dominica hadn't been keen to renew his lease, which was when the Reynolds family had stepped in.

It was a good segment. Two Dominican men talking, one gray-haired with dark-brown skin, his manner that of a teacher at heart. The other several decades younger with light-brown skin and dark hair cropped close to the scalp, displaying loads of enthusiasm for local history.

She had little doubt some of the interview would be included but wondered how deeply they'd delve into Mallet's background. Had he been allied with Fidel Castro in the sixties, or was his alliance with the Soviet Union about the family ties he had with the communist nation? Whether he was a communist ally or not, it wasn't difficult to understand why Dominica could have grown uneasy with Mallet's continued stewardship of their pristine jewel of an island.

Also, she couldn't help but wonder if Jude was nervous about lease renewal because of the country's past record of not renewing the fifty-year lease.

Dominica had been hit by a devastating hurricane a few years ago. The money Jude would pay for lease renewal was desperately needed in their ongoing efforts to rebuild lost infrastructure. But was the government of Dominica entertaining other offers?

The drone flew its preprogrammed transects, giving Sadie a moment to sit back and enjoy a tiny mental break. It was sweltering in the shade of the high canopy, and the forest was alive with the sounds of insects, frogs, and birds.

Walker, the RAM Freight mechanic who'd also been tasked with helping in the field, shifted as a brown-and-orange butterfly with dark spots that looked like eyes landed on the arm that held the boom mic. "Nico," he whispered softly, holding his arm still. "Check it."

Nico turned the camera on the insect. "Too bad Dean isn't here."

Sadie agreed, but then, he didn't have a macro lens, so he wouldn't be able to capture the shot he wanted.

The butterfly flew off, and Walker's arm relaxed. He'd seemed a bit disgruntled at Oliver's elevated status. She'd gathered that the house and grounds staff—all from Dominica and most with skin in varying shades of brown—and the RAM Freight employees who'd relocated to the island with Jude just a few months ago—mostly white and from the US mainland—were still figuring out how to work together.

She'd been surprised Kosmo had permitted a RAM Freight employee to be assigned to the documentary and fieldwork crew but figured this was his way of keeping an eye on the project. As long as Walker did his job and held the boom mic as needed, Sadie wouldn't complain.

Fiona engaged Keili and Isaac in light conversation, while Nico kept the camera rolling in case something interesting came up, but for the most part, it was a break for everyone except the drone that flew in transects around the lakes.

The equipment worked beautifully. Investing in the latest technology, as Chad had urged, had been a good call. She needed to remember that as her temper threatened to boil over in other areas. Their state-of-the-art equipment was already paying off with this contract.

She'd been terrified it would take years to earn out the cost of the upgrades, but Jude hadn't balked at the upcharge, considering what he'd be getting in return.

Walker moved to stand beside her as she stared at the computer screen. "You really can peel away all the trees and see everything? Like, can you find caves and shit?"

"I can peel away vegetation, but I can't peel away rock. So while I might be able to find a cave opening—a blank space with greater depth than the area next to it—I can't map the extent of the cave underground, as it would be capped by rock. For that, we'd need to take the lidar into the cave."

"Bummer. I hear the caves can be pretty extensive."

"They are," Keili said. "My ancestors hid in those caves three hundred years ago, escaping colonizers."

"As, it is believed, did mine," Sadie said.

Nico had shifted to stand behind his camera, as the conversation had just turned documentary-worthy. And Walker was the one who made it happen, making Sadie wonder if he'd been seeking to create a cameo moment. The butterfly had only whetted his appetite.

Not that she cared; it was a good conversation for her and Keili to have and better that it flowed naturally.

Keili shared a story about the caves that had passed down through generations, and then, with prompting from Isaac, Sadie shared a story of Ruby Hawthorne, the Black woman pirate who the island might be named after.

As she spoke for the camera, she was again reminded why this job was a dream come true. She wouldn't let her frustration with Chad ruin this opportunity.

EIGHT

The morning sun shone bright on the water as Dean watched the boat enter the sheltered harbor. He stood on the second-floor balcony overlooking the beach so he could watch his brother's arrival from a distance. Fiona was down on the beach with the rest of the team.

Nico was there with his camera. He'd promised Dean he wouldn't film Fiona and Dylan's first greeting, but his job was to film the rest. Dean had opted to avoid this moment. The three of them on camera together would happen, but not in this first emotional moment of Dylan and Fiona's reunion. It would be too much for a documentary filmmaker, even a friend like Nico, to resist.

The bumper buoys were tied on as the boat nudged the dock. Dylan emerged from the yacht's interior. He jumped over the gunwale and landed on two firm feet and strode down the dock with the merest hint of a limp that would be noticeable only to someone like Dean, who was looking for it.

Fiona burst from the group onshore and ran down the dock. She launched herself at Dylan. He caught her and cupped her face. He paused and glanced up, his gaze meeting Dean's across the distance. Then he turned and bent Fiona over his arm and kissed her.

Dean's belly twisted as he watched Fiona open her mouth and kiss his brother back. A hundred yards separated him from the scene below, but somehow, he could see every nuance as if he were looking through a zoom lens.

His heart thudded. He wanted more than anything to look away but was frozen in place. His grip on the railing might shatter the wood beam. He managed to shift his gaze to the left and realized Nico's camera had swung around to capture his reaction.

A low, pained groan came from deep in his throat, causing him to bolt upright. He was drenched in sweat in a darkened room. In bed.

Oh, hell. It had been a nightmare. And his own groan of pain at seeing Dylan and Fiona kissing had woken him. The feeling of being frozen in place had been nothing more than a brief sleep paralysis.

The irony that the subject of his nightmare was also the thing he'd wanted most for Dylan and Fiona last fall wasn't lost on him. He'd wanted them to be happy, and he'd been certain Dylan was in love with her.

He dropped back on the bed and huffed out a breath as his heart slowed.

Maybe he should leave the project after Dylan was settled. He could finance his own expedition. Go to Thailand or Malaysia or New Zealand. Some place far away where he could immerse himself in the work he loved.

Maybe, if he were halfway around the world, Fiona and Dylan would discover they had feelings for each other after all. Or she could fall in love with the shipping magnate and live happily ever after.

Whoever she ended up with, it was certain they would have more heart to give her than he could, and that's all that mattered. Dean wasn't capable of loving again. Not after losing Violet.

He'd given his wife every ounce of his heart and would never risk losing like that again. Not even for Fiona.

Whatever he decided to do after Dylan was settled, he had to face Fiona for the next few days. He had to lock his feelings down tight and be a professional, so his brother and his . . . *friend* could both have this incredible opportunity that had fallen into their laps.

Dylan desperately wanted to work in his field again, and Fiona was looking for a change in employment. Dean wouldn't screw this up for them.

———

Sadie brought her laptop to the morning breakfast meeting, an excited smile lighting her face. She set the computer on the table and lifted the screen.

"Wow, we're looking at data before you even get coffee?" Fiona asked. "You must've found something good."

Sadie's smile widened. "I mean, it's not a pyramid, but I'm pretty jazzed."

Fiona rolled her eyes. She would never understand the point of that jab by Kosmo. Or why he resented the project so much. What did he care? It was Jude's money, not RAM Freight's, that was funding their work. But still, the shipping company would look good in the documentary that would highlight Jude's care for the environment, culture, and history of Ruby Island.

Even so, she had the distinct feeling Kosmo wanted Jude's travel channel endeavor to fail.

She shook off the thought. Not her problem, and Sadie had something exciting to share. "What've you got?"

Dean and Nico chose that moment to step out on the veranda. "Oh, you got something, Sadie? Should I get my camera?"

"No cameras at breakfast," Fiona said firmly. "We made a deal." She did *not* want to be "on" before she'd had coffee. That was just cruel.

Nico huffed out a sigh. "Fine. But breakfast is when the good conversations happen."

"Because there aren't any cameras," Sadie said. She rose from her seat. "I may as well get coffee before I start."

A moment later, she was back in her seat next to Fiona, with Dean and Nico standing behind looking at the screen. "Okay, so I crunched the data last night on the transects I ran around the three lakes."

The first images she showed on the screen were satellite photos of the three small lakes that were connected in a chain in the central portion of Ruby Island. The middle lake was the largest. In the photos on the screen, it was all lush greenery with three irregular dark-green ovals.

She flipped the image to the lidar-generated map. "Here's where it gets interesting. Check this out."

She zoomed in on the center lake, then kept zooming until the screen was filled with the southern edge of the lake. She clicked off layers of vegetation one by one, and slowly, almost like a drawing showing movement as a stack of pages was flipped with a thumb, a series of perfect rectangles near the lakeshore appeared.

"Each of the rectangles has an outline that is over a foot thick. They vary in size from ten to fourteen feet long and eight to twelve feet wide. All of them have one long wall that is three feet thick in one section; the length of the thicker expanse is generally about four feet."

"You think these are brick or stone structures?" Fiona said.

"I think so. At least, the footprint of structures for all but one, and I believe the thick section of wall is a hearth and chimney. But here's the really cool part—"

"It all looks pretty cool to me," Nico said.

Sadie looked over her shoulder at him and smiled. "Me too." She faced the screen again. "So lidar measures the distance to the ground, and the rectangle is higher than the immediately adjacent ground surface. But one of the rectangles shows a significant difference between the top of the wall and the ground, so that one structure is likely to be extant. There may be more to the others as well, but I'm confident we will find one fully walled building.

"These structures were a hidden refuge next to a freshwater lake. We might be able to find metal and stone tools in situ inside—even outside, as they likely utilized the whole area. The extant house—or whatever it was used for—can tell us a lot about how this island was used in the 1700s and 1800s by the island's occupants."

"Okay, that is extra cool," Nico said.

"I want to go out there today," Sadie said.

"No way," Nico said. "Not until I get more equipment for filming. Dean will need his good cameras too. This will be a *moment* for the documentary, and it's worthy of a two-page spread in *National Geo*."

"I hate to say it, but Nico's right," Fiona said. "Plus, there's the party tonight. We're supposed to cut out early today so we have time to clean up and look pretty."

"And Dylan is arriving this afternoon with our equipment," Dean added. "We need to be here for that, and I'm guessing it's going to take some big machete action to get to those structures from what you showed us before you stripped off the vegetation."

Sadie sighed. "Damn. And curse you *all* for being right."

"Maybe we can hike out there tomorrow?" Fiona suggested.

Sadie shook her head. "There's some guest who will be at the party tonight who's investing in the documentary and travel channel. Tomorrow he wants us all out on *Tempus Machina* to film an underwater segment before he leaves in the evening. It's a dog and pony show I can't skip if I want *Tempus* to stay afloat. Pun intended."

"Do you need me for that?" Fiona asked.

"Nope, you and Dean are free to do your own thing, but Nico and Oliver will be with us."

Fiona glanced at Dean. She'd bet the last thing he wanted was to spend a day in the field alone with her, but for where she intended to go tomorrow, she'd need a partner. She hadn't stepped foot inside a cave since Chiksook. In truth, she'd been avoiding it since she arrived on Ruby Island.

How would he react if she asked him to accompany her as she explored the large, unmapped littoral caves on the eastern shore of the island?

But then, while Oliver was needed for the demonstration for the investor, Sadie hadn't mentioned Walker. It would probably be better for both her and Dean if she explored the caves for the first time with the boat mechanic and all-around handyman. Dean would have his cameras tomorrow and could finally begin his part of the project in earnest.

———

Fiona stood on the far end of the dock as Jude's private ferry was tied up and the gangplank lowered. Anticipation filled her. She turned toward the house and spotted Dean watching from the balcony. He'd chosen to remain there to give less fodder for the cameras, which she appreciated.

There were several yachts in Cannon Bay. Party guests had been arriving all day while the team worked on the archaeological inventory. More would be arriving over the next two hours. For now, Nico was there with his camera to film Dylan's arrival and the backdrop of arriving mega yachts, but he promised to delay filming until after Fiona and Dylan's initial greeting. Chad and his camera were nowhere to be seen, thank goodness.

Jude's personal yacht was, as always, moored at the end of the dock, nose to nose with the ferry. The rounded animal horns of the company logo were on both boats—thus ensuring the documentary would have some plugs for RAM Freight in the mix.

Dylan stepped onto the gangway, and her heart squeezed at seeing him walk down the long bridge on two solid legs. The slight rocking of the gangway hid any sign of a limp, but then, maybe he didn't have a limp at all.

Femur fractures could take four to six months to heal. Dylan's had taken longer because of the time he'd gone without treatment, but nine months after his surgery, he looked as healthy as he'd been on their first Chiksook expedition over a year ago.

He was halfway down the dock when she couldn't help herself and darted forward. Dylan opened his arms, and she launched herself at him. He surprised her by scooping her up and spinning her around in a circle as if she were nothing more substantial than a rag doll.

Given her height and addiction to carbs, she was significantly more substantial. "Dylan!" she squealed even as she laughed. "Put me down! You're going to hurt your leg!"

He laughed. "I'm fine, Fi." He set her on her feet and grinned down at her, his hand cupping her cheek. "Damn, it's good to see you."

She rose on her toes and kissed his cheek. "It's good to see you too. And I appreciate you making a less dramatic entrance than your brother."

He winked at her. "I would never try to upstage Dean."

She chuckled and leaned into him for a last squeeze, then let him go and faced the gangway. She nodded to Nico that he could start filming. Her gaze strayed to the balcony, but Dean was no longer there. He was probably heading down to the dock now that Fiona and Dylan had had their moment.

Dylan grabbed the suitcase he'd set down when he picked her up, and they strolled down the dock, passing Nico, who continued filming as another boat entered Cannon Bay.

When they reached the cobblestone path to the house, Dylan paused and pressed the suitcase handle to her palm. "Give this to Dean for me, will you?"

"What? I mean, sure, but you can—"

"I'm not staying. I'm taking the ferry back to Dominica when it departs in a few minutes."

"What? Why?"

He smiled and leaned down, pressing his lips to her forehead. Damn, it was *so good* to see him upright and towering over her, his face filled out and a healthy glow about him. "I'm going to hang out on Dominica and explore all nine volcanoes for a few weeks. It's going to be amazing."

"But you're supposed to monitor Mount Asilo."

"Mount Asilo has sensors in place already, and it's sleeping like a baby. I can monitor the sensors from Dominica and will come back if something interesting happens. We all know Reynolds just brought me on board because he wanted a story for his documentary. I'm not interested in that role."

"If you're leaving, I should go too. You're the reason I decided to stay."

"Don't you dare. This job is perfect for you. And frankly, it's perfect for Dean. But if I'm here, Dean is going to use me as an excuse to . . ." He shook his head. "Just give him a chance, Fi. We didn't plan for this reunion, but it's past time. He's ready. I'm hoping you are too."

Dylan didn't want to speak with Dean before he left Ruby Island, but the ferry needed time to off-load the photography and filmmaking equipment Dean and Nico required, along with supplies for tonight's party, before he could board again and depart.

He spotted Dean heading down the path from the mansion that loomed on the hill and decided to duck down to the beach to avoid his brother. He wasn't going to change his mind and didn't want to hear Dean's arguments for why he should stay.

Besides, spending the next few weeks on Dominica wouldn't be a hardship. Lodging would be pricey, but he'd pay Dean back as soon as he landed a new job. Odds were, Dean wouldn't take his money, but Dylan would insist, or at least donate it to a wildlife charity. He'd mooched off his twin enough these last nine months.

The Ruby Island job would have fixed that, but it was better this way. He'd been trying to figure out how he was going to get Fiona and Dean together again anyway. How it had come about was shitty, but part of him wanted to thank the scheming shipping magnate for making it happen.

He slipped off his shoes and let his feet sink into the warm sand. Neither this island nor Dominica had many sandy beaches, so this was a treat. He walked along the swath of sand until he was tucked at the base of an overgrown steep bank where Dean wouldn't spot him. He couldn't go far, needing to be ready to return to the boat when the signal horn blew. The captain knew not to leave without him, but that didn't mean he'd wait long if Dylan wandered too far.

The thick plants and shrubs encroached on the beach, and he debated continuing around them when he heard voices—low, angry whispers—and paused.

"Everything I've done is for *us*." A male voice laced with desperation.

"No, Chad. It's for *you*. You weren't thinking about me at all when you signed that contract." A woman's voice. She had a slight Jamaican accent.

"Not true! I used the money to pay off the equipment! I saved us thousands on the loan. And now we have the documentary . . . it will be the start of something big. We'll be amazing as a team. We'll have our own show on the network—just think, Sadie, a whole series devoted to finding one of Ruby Hawthorne's ships. Isn't that what you've always wanted?"

"Not like this! I don't want my research—my *boat*—owned by some corporation. What were you thinking?"

"*Please—*"

"Enough. You had no right to sign for me. I'm calling my lawyer. When the project is over, we're through, and you're either giving me the boat or buying me out."

"Don't do this, Sadie. You know I can't afford—"

"I want all your belongings removed from our suite in the house."

"I can't ask Jude for my own room. He'll want to know why."

"Then live on the boat until this is over. I don't care where you sleep as long as you're not in my bed."

Dylan was about to turn around and head back. He had no interest in these two people knowing he'd overheard their breakup, but before he took a step, Sadie said, "Let. Me. Go."

Dylan charged around the shrubbery that separated him from the couple. His leg ached as he sprinted across the sandy ground. He stopped two yards short of the pair: a tall, beefy white man with his large hand wrapped around the biceps of a petite, slender Black woman.

He glared at the man. "She said let her go."

"Who the fuck are you?"

"Doesn't matter. Let her go."

The woman—Sadie—shrugged out of the man's grip and stepped back. "Leave, Chad. Before you get yourself fired from the project."

Chad's gaze darted from her to Dylan and back. He was puffed up. Angry. Was he likely to turn violent?

The woman didn't appear to be afraid of him, but she'd been alarmed enough to demand he release her.

Finally, he said, "I'll get my stuff from our suite, but we're not done with this conversation."

Sadie didn't say a word as he stomped down the beach, heading in the direction of the house, giving Dylan a wide berth as he passed.

Long after Chad was out of earshot, Sadie murmured, "Well, that wasn't humiliating or anything." Then in a louder voice, she said, "Thank you." She took a step toward him with her hand out. "You must be Dylan Slater."

He closed the distance and shook her hand. "I am. And you must be Sadie Tate."

She nodded. "I'd say it's great to meet you, but I'm feeling a bit mortified right now. I want you to know, Chad wouldn't have hurt me." She paused and looked down. "At least, I don't think so."

"I'm glad we didn't have a chance to find out otherwise." He debated if he could say more. She was already embarrassed. He didn't want to make it worse. But really, how could he not say it? "It sounds like you'll still be working together for the next few weeks. Be careful. If you can avoid being alone with him, do it. And as far as the mortified part . . . I've been through an ugly divorce. I know how nasty things can get. I worked in the same office with my ex and the guy she cheated on me with, which was a whole other level of humiliation. There's no reason to ever be embarrassed with me."

She raised her head and met his gaze. She was at least nine inches shorter than he was, and utterly exquisite with flawless dark skin, wide brown eyes, rounded cheeks, and a pointed chin. He could see sadness and sympathy in her beautiful eyes. "I'm sorry you went through that."

"And I'm sorry you're going through . . . what you're going through." She glanced in the direction Chad had gone. "We've been together since grad school. I . . . We share joint ownership of the business . . . I don't even know how we're going to do this."

Knowing that, he wondered if this abrupt breakup would stick. He wouldn't be surprised if they attempted a reconciliation or two before it was truly over. It was rare to make a clean break on the first try, and they had a business to divide in addition to dishes and furniture.

"Listen, if you find yourself needing someone to talk to—who doesn't know squat about your situation—you can call me. Get my number from Fiona."

"But . . . you'll be here, right? No need for your number when you're right down the hall."

He shook his head. "I'm going back to Dominica on the boat in a few minutes." He glanced at his watch. "Actually, any second now."

"But why? I know Fiona is thrilled you've joined the project."

He smiled. "Watch Fiona and Dean together, and you'll know why. In fact, get my number from her and report back to me. I want to know how long it takes for my brother to get over himself and finally make a move."

She raised a dubious brow. "You want me to spy on your brother and Fiona?"

"Absolutely. Neither of them will tell me anything. Dean still thinks I'm in love with her."

"Are you? In love with her?"

He gave her a pointed look. "No. Don't get me wrong, I think she's amazing. In fact, she'd make a great sister. In-law."

Sadie smiled, and it was more beautiful than the sandy beach and turquoise Caribbean. It was the kind of smile to make a man's heart beat faster when it was directed at him.

Down, boy. She literally just broke up with her boyfriend.

Or husband. He didn't really know, but after several years that included a shared business, it was the same thing.

"Okay. I'll do it."

"Good. And if you can, make them work together alone."

She laughed. "That'll be easy. Fiona's got to ground-truth my lidar data."

"Perfect."

The horn on the boat sounded, causing them both to jolt.

"That's my signal. It was nice meeting you, Sadie Tate."

"Thank you for coming to my rescue, Dylan Slater."

He turned and headed up the beach to take the short flight of stairs to the long wooden pier. He felt a twinge of regret that he wouldn't be spending the next weeks on the island with the beautiful Ms. Tate. But then, she had a man she needed to divest herself of, so it was good he wouldn't be around to muddy that water.

She was in no place to start something new when the old wasn't finished, and unlike his brother, Dylan didn't casually date.

Truth was, he didn't date at all. He'd gone on a few in the early days following the divorce, but quickly realized that was a bad idea. But maybe, just maybe, he was ready to try again.

NINE

Dylan had slipped out of sight before Dean could greet him. He'd been busy overseeing the off-loading of his and Nico's gear, making sure the items were sorted and sent to the proper rooms, when he looked up to see the ferry leaving. In the same moment, his phone buzzed with a text notification.

Dylan: See you on Dominica in a few weeks. Until then, don't blow this opportunity. She's worth it.

Dean hit the button to call, but it didn't go through. Dylan must have turned off his phone right after sending. He'd call his brother a bastard, but since they were twins, it was a self-inflicted insult.

But then, Dean *was* a bastard. Worse, really. Dean had avoided Fiona for nine months. Total dick move.

Once again, he regretted the night on the Big Island in which he and Dylan had gone out and had far too many drinks. Instead of picking up a fellow tourist for a little vacation fun, he'd confessed to thinking about Fiona more than he should. Or wanted to.

It appeared Dylan was seizing on this chance to play matchmaker, as he'd said he wanted to do when he first met Fiona and figured she was perfect for his brother who had sworn off relationships.

Dylan always conveniently forgot there was a damn good reason Dean would never fall in love again. Of course, Dylan would say he didn't forget—he just believed enough time had passed.

Fiona approached, a large suitcase in her hand. "Dylan told me to give you this."

Dean kept his eyes on the departing ferry. He didn't want to meet Fiona's gaze. She knew exactly why Dylan had skipped out. His brother had just planted a big elephant between them.

"That'll be my tux for tonight and my favorite camera."

"How many favorite cameras do you have?"

"Whichever one is in my hands in the moment," he said without emotion. His true favorite camera had broken when the helicopter crashed. He would choose a new favorite.

It was easy to be fickle when it came to cameras. To move on. He could always find another that could make him happy. Tell himself the new one took superior pictures. They were just tools, after all. Interchangeable in the long run.

"Will you be taking pictures at the party tonight?" she asked.

"No. I'll be off duty." He regretted the words as soon as he said them. He was always more comfortable with a camera in his hands. But at the same time, he wasn't being paid to be an event photographer, and he knew damn well that's what Reynolds would demand if he had a camera around his neck.

He didn't want to give Reynolds power over him tonight.

Damn, he'd been looking forward to sitting in a corner and catching up with Fiona and Dylan tonight, but his bastard brother had run away. Worse, he'd been counting on Dylan's presence to help him avoid one-on-one time with Fiona in the field and after hours.

He picked up the bag from the cobblestones. "Thank you for the bag. I better see what I can do to get the wrinkles out before the party."

She smiled. "Now I'm trying to imagine you ironing."

He laughed. "I bet I iron more than you do."

"If you iron at all, then you iron more than I do."

"See? Well then, if you have trouble with your gown tonight, bring it by."

"Will you iron shirtless?"

He shook his head.

"Too bad. But thank you for the offer."

He laughed and turned for the path to the outside stairs to the second-floor balcony. As he passed the room on the corner, he heard banging and cursing. He stopped. It sounded like Chad's voice.

He debated moving on. Was Sadie in the room with him? Was Chad a threat to her?

He didn't hear any sounds that indicated another person was in the room. The guy could be having a temper tantrum.

But if he walked by and later found out Sadie had been hurt . . .

He set down the bag and knocked on the door. A moment later, it was yanked open. Chad was puffed up, red-faced, his eyes practically feral. *"What?"* The word was more shout than question.

"Is everything okay?"

His eyes narrowed. "That was your brother down at the beach, wasn't it?"

Dean shrugged. "Maybe? I don't really know what you're talking about."

"You and your nosy brother need to stay out of people's business." The door slammed in Dean's face.

He stood there for a moment and debated what he should do. He didn't give a damn that Chad had behaved like an ass—although working with him in the coming weeks would suck—he was more concerned about Sadie. He needed to be certain she wasn't in the room with him.

He scanned the beach and dock below, not seeing her, but Fiona was still down there and had a better view. He pulled out the satellite phone Reynolds had given him after he'd lost his own when the helicopter went over the cliff. He sent a quick text to Fiona, asking if she had eyes on Sadie.

Fiona: I see her on the beach. Why?

Dean: Will explain later.

So much for avoiding one-on-one time with Fiona. He needed to know what the deal was with Chad Baylor.

He reached his room on the far end of the row of doors flanked by storm shutters. Before going inside, he paused and turned. Maybe from this angle, he'd spot Sadie. He didn't see her, but he did see Reynolds talking to Fiona as he looked out over Cannon Bay, which was filling with luxury yachts as party guests arrived.

As Dean watched, Jude gestured broadly, hands waving. He pulled his arms in and moved closer to Fiona and planted a hand on the small of her back.

Dean took a deep breath. He should leave. Join Dylan on Dominica and finish their tropical vacation on a different volcanic island than the one they'd started on. He didn't need to be tortured by watching the billionaire try to win her over.

Fiona took a step to the side, shaking off Reynolds's hand.

All at once, he remembered that last night on Chiksook, when he'd held her and she told him about her sister, Regan. Regan, whose death was ruled an accident, but Fiona believed her sister's boss—who Regan had been involved with at the time—had killed her.

Dean would bet anything Fiona was deeply uncomfortable right now. His need to protect her ran deep. He wanted to get violent . . . and he'd never been a violent person.

He had no doubt Fiona could deal with Reynolds's advances by herself. But she didn't have to. Not when he was here to back her up. He'd pay for her return ticket to the United States if the man crossed the line. He'd beat the crap out of him if it was warranted. Whatever it took.

Plus, the idea of leaving her alone after the helicopter debris had disappeared made him uneasy. They still had far too many questions about that crash, and not a single answer.

There was no way Dean was leaving Ruby Island, not without Fiona.

TEN

Fiona straightened the emerald-green beaded gown over her hips and checked her appearance in the mirror. This might be the most gorgeous dress she'd ever worn, and she loved it to pieces. It was full length with a sheer green organza skirt with a godet flare, according to the saleswoman. She'd had to look up *godet* on her phone when the woman was helping another customer. At the time, she'd wondered if skirt types was something most women knew or if it was a secret language of the fashion-oriented.

All that mattered, though, was she loved the way the dress looked on her, and the fit was perfect. The bodice had a deep V cut at the front and back, with crisscrossing lines of sparkling emerald-green beads that hugged her hips and trailed off into points as the organza flared out. The sheer organza sleeves were decorated with the same crisscrossing ribbons of emerald from shoulder to just above the wrist.

The gown was shimmery, flowy, and utterly feminine. All she needed was a tiara and she'd know she had finally achieved full princess-hood.

Jude had given her a budget to purchase the gown because attending the party was part of her contract. The event would be a little glitz and glamour to add to the documentary. She'd had fun going dress shopping with a girlfriend in Seattle before setting out for this trip, and that had been before she'd known Dean would be here to see her wearing it, which added a little extra spice to the pleasure of donning such a beautiful piece of clothing.

She didn't have to wonder how he'd look dressed up. A few months ago, she'd broken down and googled him. She'd seen the photos of him on a red carpet with supermodel Paige Vance at two separate events. As handsome as he'd looked, the pain was such that she'd closed the browser and vowed never to google him again.

On the one hand, she was glad that he was living the life he wanted. He deserved happiness. But it still hurt to see another woman beaming as she clung to his arm.

Now she studied her face in the mirror, knowing she could never measure up to a woman like Paige, whose makeup was as flawless as her bone structure, while Fiona's was . . . as adequate as her bone structure. Makeup skill was another thing she'd missed out on in addition to a particular sense of fashion.

Functional was her general style, but she also dabbled in bland.

This dress—the entire trip, really, as she'd purchased lots of airy beach clothes with a friend's guidance during that Seattle shopping spree—reminded her it was fun to dress up and look pretty. She ought to try it more. Get out more. She needed to make changes when she returned to the Pacific Northwest.

Her phone chimed. She checked the screen.

Sadie: Where are you?

Fiona: On my way down now.

She'd delayed long enough. She pulled on the three-inch stilettos that made her an even six feet tall. At least she could match Paige Vance in height.

She exited her room through the balcony, choosing to take the outside stairs to head down to the party. She wanted to feel the salt air on her skin and the flow of the breeze through the sheer godet skirt. Plus, this way she could cross through the garden and sneak into the ballroom via the back way.

The bay in front of the house was littered with luxury yachts. It was quite a sight to see nearly two dozen boats—which ranged in size from large to mega—filling the private harbor. Guests had been arriving all day. They would enjoy Jude's hospitality for the next few hours and then would return to their vessels to sleep. According to Jude, many would depart with the first light of dawn. It was a convenient way to host an extravagant affair in a remote place, given that Jude wouldn't be saddled with guests in the house or even on the island once the party ended.

The formal garden at the south side of the house was circular and divided into twelve pie-piece sections, like the face of a clock. At the center of the clock sat an elaborate fountain complete with cascading waterfalls lit with red lights so the water shimmered like rubies in a nod to the island's name.

The posh estate had been constructed in the fifties by the previous lessee, the American oilman with ties to the Soviet Union. She had to wonder at the man's communist sympathies, considering he'd spared no expense on his vacation home. The water-facing front facade had been designed to look like a Caribbean plantation house from the early 1700s, but the interior was modern for 1950s standards.

Jude had gutted and further modernized the kitchen and upgraded the electrical, cable, and internet wiring when he inherited the lease after his father's passing. He'd put in solar panels and windmills and a large satellite dish. He intended for the island to be fully self-sufficient for power, water, and communications.

The garden still had the brickwork and fountain put in by the original owner, but Jude was slowly having the vegetation replaced with native plants, with a few pieces of the pie full of lush greenery and fragrant tropical flowers. Native birds had begun frequenting those areas, and even now she could hear the chirps of locals as she passed by.

Nerves fluttered through her as she crossed the brick path, her gaze fixed on the four sets of open french doors, which gave her a view of the elegantly dressed guests within the ballroom.

She spotted Nico with his camera. He wore a suit that indicated he was staff at this event and not a guest. She'd asked him if it bothered him that Dean was off for the night while he had to work, and he'd said he preferred being behind the camera at events like this, as it gave him an opportunity to observe without engaging. Dean was the one who enjoyed fancy parties and rubbing elbows with celebrities.

She spotted Sadie at the center of the gathering, chatting with three white men and a Hispanic woman, while Chad stood off in a corner, watching Sadie.

She didn't know what had happened between them today, but suspected it was big. It would be good when this party was behind them so she could catch up with her friend, who clearly needed a shoulder to cry on.

It was easy to spot Jude, who stood by the arched interior entrance to the room, greeting guests as they entered from the front of the house.

Last, but oh so very far from least, she searched for Dean and found him as he crossed the room, heading in Sadie's direction. He glanced Fiona's way and came to a dead stop as he took her in. Somehow, even from this distance, she could feel his appreciative stare.

Warmth bloomed from her belly, spreading outward until she could feel it flushing her skin. The beads at her hips swayed as she stepped through the doors and entered the ballroom, her eyes fixed on his.

He wove his way through the crowd to meet her by the door, then took her hand and raised it to his lips. His warm blue eyes swept over her as he murmured, "You look amazing."

She experienced another flush of heat, a reaction to his gaze, words, and the press of his lips on her skin. Maybe this party thing wouldn't be so bad after all.

He released her hand. Instead of pulling away, she touched the lapel of his tuxedo, tracing a line down the fine fabric. She knew even less about men's suits than she did about women's fashion, but she could tell this was quality. Armani, maybe? Whatever it was, it had been tailored to fit him and was worth every penny.

Plus, she would never understand why bow ties were sexy, but they were. She itched to tug on the end of Dean's so he'd have that rumpled, post-party look, but it was too darn early for that. Maybe later she'd get a chance . . .

She managed to find her voice, which just might have been a little breathy. "You look hot."

He grinned. They faced each other nearly eye to eye thanks to her heels. She liked matching his height. Or almost matching. He still had two inches on her. "Can I get you a drink?"

"Please," she said.

She turned to accompany him on the walk across the room to the bar, but one of the staff approached and said, "Ms. Carver, Mr. Reynolds would like to speak to you."

She gave Dean an apologetic look, and he nodded in response. "I'll bring a drink to you. What would you like?"

"Something tropical and fruity and very boozy."

He laughed. "You got it."

She turned and headed to greet her boss in the entryway.

He gave her a wide smile, his gaze scanning her from head to toe. As with Dean, she was eye to eye with Jude and again appreciated the vantage point. She really should consider wearing heels more.

"You look beautiful," he said.

She wouldn't return the compliment, even though he did look handsome in his tailored tux. Instead she said, "Thank you, *boss*."

He didn't fail to notice her stress on the word *boss*, making their roles clear.

"I wanted to introduce you to Ned Hanson, an old friend and investor in the adventure travel channel." He placed a hand on the small of her back and steered her toward a group of white men who stood in a cluster several feet away.

She felt that hand like a brand and didn't like it one bit, but could hardly call him out in the middle of his big party. She gritted her teeth as she crossed the short distance and tried to figure out the best way to handle Jude.

She was introduced to the men, and tried to remember names and faces, which was not her strong suit. They were all within a few years of Jude's age, give or take, and she gathered that they were also sons of the wealthy elite and were making their own forays into the business world. One was a politician, newly elected to the House of Representatives from New York. Another was a venture capitalist in Silicon Valley. Ned Hanson's family, it turned out, had started in telecommunications. His parents had built their wealth in cellular technology, starting with car phones in the early 1980s, but now the company was deep in the internet streaming market. Ned, she learned, would be providing one of the platforms over which Jude's new network would stream.

Dean arrived, carrying a *very* fruity drink. The garnish looked like a fruit salad. She laughed as he handed it to her. "I said very *boozy*."

"You also said fruity. I took you at your word. Don't worry, there is a lot of booze in there too."

Dean was then introduced around the circle, and Fiona braced for the coming questions. Sure enough, Ned dove right into that forbidden pool. "Wait a minute, weren't you both stuck on that island in the Aleutians?"

"Yes," Fiona said, "but we cannot offer any details. Not while the trial is still pending." It was true enough and the kind of statement most people would accept.

The politician's gaze landed on Dean. He cocked his head. "Where's your brother? I thought he was going to be here."

That statement dispelled any doubt Fiona might have clung to that Jude hadn't spread the word that all three of them would attend the party.

"He doesn't like parties," Dean said, his voice clipped, his gaze on Jude.

She guessed he was seething inside, same as she was. The happy buzz she'd felt after having that moment with Dean had popped like a balloon landing on a cactus.

"Is it true he survived for six weeks with a broken leg by eating rats?" the venture capitalist asked.

"If you'll excuse me, gentlemen, I need to get some air," Fiona said and left the group without meeting Jude's gaze.

Dean was right beside her. She could feel the tension in him. The exchange had been abrupt to the point of whiplash. Neither of them had a chance to brace for it.

Is that what the whole evening would be like?

Kosmo intercepted them on the way to the open garden doors. "Mr. Slater, I have some questions for you about your brother's contract, since he didn't see fit to speak with anyone involved with the business end personally."

Fiona grimaced, but Dean nodded for her to continue to the garden. She was grateful for the escape. The only person she wanted to talk to less than Jude's friends was Kosmo.

She had almost made it to the french doors and freedom when Nico and his camera stopped her. "Can I get some shots of you mingling?" He nodded toward the glass in her hand and added, "That drink alone is quite photogenic."

She tried to shake off her tension. She grimaced at the drink and said, "Makes sense, considering it was created by a photographer."

Nico's gaze caught on something over her shoulder. He let out a low whistle and muttered, "This is almost too good to be true," then raised the viewfinder to his eye. She turned to see what he was recording. Her stomach dropped.

An exceedingly tall, gorgeous Black woman—she had to be the most beautiful woman Fiona had ever seen in the flesh—approached Dean from behind as he spoke to Kosmo.

The woman placed her hands over Dean's eyes as she whispered something in his ear.

———

Dean recognized the feminine whisper and her accompanying perfume instantly. Pleasure and pain hit him with equal force. He was genuinely pleased to cross paths with Paige Vance, but he was well aware that her presence could—almost certainly would—hurt Fiona.

"We'll finish this conversation later," Kosmo said while Dean's eyes were still covered. Telling him that stopping him had been a ruse to make sure Dean was in the ballroom for his reunion with Paige.

He pulled her hands from his eyes and gently lowered them as he turned to face her. He clasped her hands low, keeping contact, but making no move to lean in and kiss her cheek or hug her.

This reserved greeting was unusual, especially after her request in March to let the world believe they were still an item. Given that Nico was almost certainly filming this moment, it would signify to the tabloids that he and Paige had split once again. Not that they'd ever really been together beyond a brief liaison over three years ago.

It was time to end the charade anyway.

"It's good to see you, Paige. What brings you to Ruby Island?" He knew the answer, of course. Jude Reynolds had made a move in the bizarre game he was playing to win over Fiona. But how did he expect this strategy to play out?

Paige studied his face. Her keen eyes acknowledged the limits he was placing between them. She gave him a wry smile and said, "To my great surprise and delight, a few days ago I received an invitation from my friend Thaddeus to join him on his yacht and attend this party. I had no idea you'd be here, but from your reaction, I'm guessing the decision to invite me was deliberate. The question is why? Is someone trying to ferret out my secret, or is this about you?"

Dean turned to see Fiona's back as she stepped through the open french doors and out into the garden. "See the woman leaving? That's Fiona Carver."

"The woman from Chiksook Island." She grimaced. "Hoo boy. I think I get it. Is this an attempt to make her jealous?"

"To drive a wedge between her and me would be my guess. Make her see who I really am." He leaned down and whispered in her ear. "Jude Reynolds has a thing for her and believes I'm standing in his way."

"Are you? Standing in his way?"

"No. Fiona knows my limits. I've always been honest with her. But seeing you here is still likely to hurt her, if she believes the tabloids. I need to go talk to her, alone. But then I need you to talk to her, too, and tell her our arrangement."

Paige smiled and nodded. "Go after her. Now. Before Reynolds does." She tipped her head toward their host, who was also eyeing the door through which Fiona had disappeared.

Dean didn't hesitate and bolted for the door, passing Reynolds as the billionaire strode in the same direction but at a more respectable pace.

———

Fiona nearly tripped when her heel caught in the groove between loose bricks. She couldn't get out of the ballroom fast enough. She needed time to collect herself so she could go back in and meet Dean's girlfriend.

She took the path straight to the fountain, then circled it and took an offshoot path that disappeared into a lush, overgrown part of the garden. There was a bench hidden in the tiny forest where she could sit and eat the fruit from her cocktail. Maybe she could return to her room. She could then text Sadie and ask her to let everyone know she wasn't feeling well. That would allow her to avoid returning to the party altogether.

Moments after she was seated and nibbling on a pineapple ring, she heard Dean's voice. "Fiona? Where are you?"

She debated answering. She could hide here and nurse her broken heart. Except she didn't have the right to have a broken heart. Dean wasn't hers, and never would be. He'd always been clear on that.

What hurt was that he'd then turned around and gotten involved with someone else—proving the reason for his rejection had been a lie. Intended to ease her heartache, no doubt, but still a lie.

"Fiona?" he repeated. "Please talk to me."

"I'm here," she said.

"Can you be a little more specific? It's kind of a jungle out here."

Even in her heartache, she was able to find a soft laugh. "With north being twelve, I took the path at seven o'clock. I'm on the iron bench, if you know where that is."

A moment later, he appeared, his shoes tapping on the bricks. When he reached her, he took her hand. She set her drink on the seat and let him pull her to her feet. His arms enfolded her. She molded against him, needing the feel of his arms as tears threatened. If she cried, it would ruin her makeup and she definitely wouldn't be able to return to the ballroom.

She hated this feeling. This weakness. She had no right to this jealousy. And it was embarrassing. But there was no hiding it now, so she might as well face it head-on. "Your girlfriend is quite beautiful."

"Paige Vance is an astonishingly beautiful woman, inside and out, and she is a good friend, but she's not my girlfriend."

"My bad. I should have said your lover."

Dean's arms loosened, and he leaned back so he could look into her eyes. "She *was* my lover, but that ended years ago. We're just friends."

She closed her eyes, hating what she was about to admit, but she needed the truth. "You don't have to lie to me anymore, Dean. I can take it. I saw the photos. I know you were with her in March and again in April."

His eyes narrowed. "I realize you're hurting right now and so I won't take offense that you just accused me of lying. But know this: I would never lie to you about anything. Except maybe being an ornithologist."

She couldn't help but snicker. Even when her emotions were in turmoil, this man could make her laugh.

"In March and April, Paige had a couple of important events to attend. She was in a difficult place and needed a date. I agreed. I also agreed to let her fans believe we'd resumed dating, as it helped her situation. She can tell you more about it. It's not my story to share." His lips brushed across her forehead. "The truth is, Fiona, I haven't been with anyone since before Dylan disappeared last summer."

His admission caught her by surprise. It wasn't something he needed to share. It was none of her business. And yet, he'd said it and it did ease her mind, pleased her even, to know he hadn't slept with anyone in the months since they'd met.

"Thank you. I appreciate knowing that."

His gaze held hers, and once again there was a powerful, intense flow of energy that always seemed to fill the air between them. She would tell him how long it had been since she had slept with anyone, except she was fairly certain he'd already guessed her last encounter predated Chiksook—by quite a while, actually.

And really, this was a dangerous conversation to have between two people who were avoiding getting involved.

"Will you come back to the party with me? I'd like you to meet my friend Paige."

She nodded. "I'd like that. But first I'd like to sit for a minute and finish eating my drink."

He laughed.

She sat on the bench and picked up her glass and nibbled on an orange wedge, then offered him a strawberry. He bit into the berry, sending juice dribbling down her fingers. For a moment, she thought he would lick the juice from her skin, but he pulled back. She popped the remainder of the berry into her mouth, then licked the side of her thumb clean.

"Remind me not to let you get creative with the drink order in the future."

"Awww, come on, you got a meal *and* a drink."

"I haven't even gotten to the alcohol yet and let me tell you, I feel like I'm gonna need a lot of booze to get through tonight. And not because Paige is here, but because of Jude and the way he's behaving. And then there are his cronies." She huffed out a sigh. "Sometimes I wonder what I'm even doing here."

"You're here because Jude Reynolds was right about one thing: you are an excellent person for the job you've been tasked with. You care about the resource, you care about the culture, you care about the island and the plants and animals—everything connected to the ecosystem and how each element ties in with the past.

"It's one of my favorite things about you, Fiona, that this—and Chiksook—were never just a job for you. You're trying to do your part to preserve something that can and will be lost. And Sadie was the absolute best person to bring into the project because she cares in the same way you do. Her knowledge and experience ensure the work will be done right. This is an amazing island, and small though it is, it has an important place in the history of the Caribbean. A history that needs to be known and shared.

"History books often don't delve any deeper into Dominica than the fact that Christopher Columbus named the island on a Sunday. But people need to know what colonizers did to this part of the world and the people who inhabited it. They need to know what Columbus and those who came after him did to make it necessary that this island become a refuge. The Kalinago and Taíno stories need to be told. That's why Keili and Gordon were here. That's why Sadie is here. And that's why you're here. All of you working together to get the complexities of the story to the world. I'm damn proud to be a part of this project and have the opportunity to document the wildlife that has survived the centuries since colonization."

She stared at him, completely caught off guard by his speech and the emotion behind it. After a long pause, she said, "I really like you, Dean Slater."

"And I think you're magnificent, Fiona Carver."

She gave him a kiwi, then said, "I finally got to see some of your wildlife photos. I'm no expert or anything, but I think you're pretty good."

He laughed, then almost choked, as he'd been midswallow of the kiwi. He cleared his throat and said, "So they tell me."

She leaned against him. "Your pictures are stunning. I was blown away over and over again."

He draped an arm around her. "Thank you. It means a lot that you appreciate my work."

The photos, no matter the subject—spider on a flower petal or hippo in the mud—were vibrant and *alive*. His work was awe-inspiring, and he was a master of his craft.

"It's a shame that Ruby Island doesn't have any big fauna to photograph."

"Birds always have their own story to tell. Honestly, I really just love the process, getting the feel for the place. Sinking into the natural landscape. There is always something interesting to capture."

They'd eaten enough fruit that she could now take a drink without getting stabbed in the eye by a fruit-bearing plastic sword. At last, she took a sip. "Oh, that's good. What is it?"

"Goombay Smash. It's popular in the Bahamas."

"It's delicious."

"And very boozy. Four kinds of rum."

"Perfect." She handed him the drink and stood, taking a moment to detangle strands of beads that had crossed. Low, covered lamps dotted the path, and the emerald beads sparkled and flashed in the soft glow. She couldn't help but give a little twirl to play with the light.

He chuckled. "That really is a gorgeous dress. I'm glad I got to see you in it."

"I'm glad I got to wear it, even if it means I have to find a way to get through the next two hours. At least I have a pretty dress that makes me feel feminine."

He stood and returned the cocktail to her, then placed his hand at the small of her back, and they walked down the path. It wasn't lost on her that his touch was welcome, whereas Jude's hand in the same spot had set her on edge.

They entered the ballroom, and that hand on her back steered her toward the tall, gorgeous woman who had been featured on the cover of every major fashion magazine at some point in the last few years.

Paige Vance was an honest-to-goodness supermodel, at the very top of her profession. For all of Fiona's teasing about Dean's playboy lifestyle, the truth was that he really did move in high circles in the entertainment and fashion industries and had been associated romantically with more than a few models and actresses.

And here she was, getting her first glimpse into Dean's life when he wasn't behind the camera. He'd told her that he very much enjoyed his life in LA. She needed to remember that he really was a playboy of sorts. It wasn't all a joke. The man she met on Chiksook had been his field persona and not the man he was at home.

Fiona knew Nico's camera would be trained on her and Dean as they approached Paige. Nico had agreed to do his best to keep their personal lives out of the documentary, but his orders tonight were to film everything he could, and this juicy scene was too good to pass up. Hard to beat footage of the woman Dean had been stranded with on Chiksook meeting the famous woman the world believed he was in love with.

Paige took Fiona's hand in both of hers and smiled warmly as she said, "It is truly a pleasure to meet you, Fiona."

Fiona smiled, feeling the warmth emanating from this woman, and said, "Same."

"Let's sit down, have a drink, and talk." Paige nodded toward two empty chairs facing each other against the back wall with a small round table in between.

Dean raised a brow. "Only two seats?"

"But of course," Paige said. "How can we talk about you if you're sitting right there?"

She linked her arm through Fiona's and led her to the empty seats, leaving Dean to find his own entertainment.

"I think we're going to become friends," Fiona said.

"I'm absolutely sure of it."

ELEVEN

Sadie approached Dean from behind and handed him a drink. "You look like you could use one of these."

He turned away from the two women chatting by the back wall and met Sadie's forthright gaze. "Thank you."

"You don't have anything to worry about," Sadie said as she faced the women as well.

"I know. It's just all a bit much. I came here to take some photos, and I find myself at the center of a billionaire's games to win Fiona."

"I don't think she realizes how much Jude wants her. She thinks he's her old friend from field school and his priority is making the documentary a smash. Even when he pisses her off, she wants to see the best in him. I'm not sure that what she wants to see is there."

"You're brave to be saying that here."

She downed her drink in one gulp. "After what happened tonight, I'm fresh out of fucks to give."

"Something happened with Chad?"

She nodded. "I'm still not entirely sure how it happened or if it's even legal, but . . . see that white guy in the black tux?"

"I'm afraid you're going to have to narrow it down a bit. Present company included."

She laughed. "Yeah. I meant to add *talking with Jude*."

"Ahh, him. He's the guy with the streaming platform, right?"

"No. He's the one who's investing in the travel channel. He's been tapped to head it, in fact."

"Oh. I don't think I've met him, then, but he looks like the other guy."

"Frankly, I can only tell them apart because that dude, apparently, now owns *Tempus Machina*."

Dean startled and looked at her. "Um, *what?*"

She stared down into her empty glass. "Damn, I drank that too fast, and I need to pace myself or I'll have regrets and I won't be able to dive tomorrow."

"You want me to get you some water?"

She sighed. "I'll get some in a minute."

"So what's the deal with your boat?" Dean prodded. Chad's anger earlier was starting to make sense.

"He cut some sort of deal that mortgages the boat to pay off the new lidar equipment. But the problem is, we didn't *need* to pay off the lidar right now. The loan had good terms, and we'd made a sizable payment with the advance from Jude. So there must be something he's not telling me." She paused, then added under her breath, "I'm afraid to think of where the advance money really went." She cleared her throat and resumed speaking to Dean. "And then there's that thing about mortgaging a property we both own without my consent, but since it's in the business name and we both have signing privileges, somehow that's legal?"

"It sounds like you need a lawyer."

"Yeah. I called our lawyer tonight right after I found out. And he told me that since he represents the business, he can't represent me *against* the business. So now I need to find an attorney." She stared down at the ice cubes in her glass. "I'm working on the best project that's come our way in a long time, getting to do work I've dreamed of doing for years, and my decade-plus business partnership with the man I loved has just been destroyed. Needless to say, the relationship is toast too."

He noticed the past tense on the verb *love*. "I'm so sorry, Sadie. You're based out of California, right?"

She nodded. "We have property in Jamaica too, but California is where the business is registered."

"I have a good attorney there. If she can't help you, I'm sure she can recommend someone who could."

"Thank you. I will take you up on that."

A waiter passed by with a tray for empty glasses, and Sadie took the opportunity to get rid of hers. "I think I'm going to bolt. I know Jude expects us to be here for the whole party, but I haven't got it in me tonight to be in the same room with Chad any longer."

Dean nodded and pulled out his phone, then grimaced. "I was going to text you my attorney's number now, but my address book couldn't transfer to the new satellite phone."

"I wish Jude could get Wi-Fi calling to work. I miss my cell phone."

"Paradise always comes with a price."

She grimaced. "I was born in Jamaica. I feel that to my bones." Then she smiled. "But even in Jamaica, we have better cellular coverage than this."

"I'll send you the number when I'm at my computer later."

"Thanks. I'm going to head upstairs. Night, Dean."

"Night, Sadie."

Her path to the arched entrance to the ballroom took her past Fiona and Paige. Fiona called out, and Sadie veered in their direction. After a moment of chatting, Fiona jumped up and pulled over another chair, and Sadie sat down. Within minutes, she was belly laughing at something Paige had said, and his fondness for Paige bloomed.

He liked the idea of Paige and Fiona becoming friends. Except, when this was over, he'd be shutting Fiona out of his life again. He didn't see how he could have her in his orbit and maintain his distance. But if the women were friends, it would probably be best for him to give up

Paige too. It was hard enough knowing Dylan checked in with Fiona on a regular basis.

———

Sadie dabbed the tears of laughter from her eyes and smiled. She twirled the cocktail glass in her hand and said, "Okay, I'm officially glad I decided to stay."

Fiona felt a rush of happiness. She still had no idea why Sadie was upset, but they'd spent the last twenty minutes laughing with Paige, and it felt . . . *good*. The most relaxed she'd been since the helicopter crash, really.

So maybe all she'd needed was a night off. Well, plus incredible food and drinks being delivered by unobtrusive waiters, as she sat on the edge of a black-tie party chatting with one of her closest friends and a supermodel.

Yeah, that was the *totally normal* recipe for relaxation she'd been looking for.

Fiona studied the wine in her glass. She'd switched to wine because another Goombay Smash had the potential to put her under the table. "Sadie, this is the best job we've ever landed, so why does it feel so . . . *off?*"

"Well, personal reasons for me aside, I think we aren't used to having money dumped our way and being told we can have free rein to do what's best for the resource."

"That must be it. It's kind of surreal, having a client who *wants* us to spend more. Do more. Well, except for Kosmo, but he's not the client, thank goodness."

"Yeah. That would suck."

"Kosmo gives me the creeps," Paige said. "And believe me, in my line of work, I have a very good creep radar." She leaned forward and lowered her voice. "So Thaddeus told me when we were on the yacht on the way here that Kosmo is driving Jude batty. He usually only comes to the island for a few days, then returns to corporate headquarters. He's always here for the parties like this one, but then he's gone the next day with everyone else. But now he's decided to stay for the full two months of the archaeological inventory and documentary filming."

"Why doesn't Jude send him away?" Fiona asked, equally quiet. "Ruby Island is a personal holding, not part of the company."

"I asked Thaddeus the same thing. He just shrugged. It's got something to do with the business and the family trust, I think. Jude probably isn't the all-powerful CEO he wants everyone to think he is."

That wouldn't surprise Fiona. There was definitely an odd power dynamic between the two men.

"So," Sadie said, leaning in, "you never mentioned that the volcanologist was a hottie, Fiona."

Paige's eyes lit up. "Are you talking about Dylan? I finally got to meet him this spring and . . . wooo. It's really criminal how hot both Slater brothers are, and they're not even identical."

Fiona was midsip when Sadie said, "Says the *actual* supermodel," causing Fiona to spew out a laugh.

Paige snorted, something Fiona didn't think women that flawlessly beautiful could *do*.

"Fine, but you know I'm right," Paige said. "They've got this rugged-manly thing about them. I mean, come on. Volcanologist and wildlife photographer? Did someone read my hot-guy fantasy journal I kept when I was twenty-two?"

"Or when I was thirty-six," Fiona muttered.

"Thirty-nine," Sadie added. She grabbed a mushroom appetizer from the plate a waiter had delivered some time ago and nibbled on the edge. "So what do you think of Dylan Slater, Fi?"

"He's one of my favorite people in the world. And yes, I'm saying that because we went through something together. But also, I really genuinely think he's great."

She remembered his words on Chiksook, proclaiming her family now, and how deeply she'd felt it in her bones.

"You interested in him?" Sadie asked. "I figured it was the other brother you wanted." She nodded to the side of the room where, presumably, Dean was mingling with Jude's guests.

"Dylan is an important friend. I love him like a brother." She grimaced. Sadie was one of the few who knew about Fiona's messed-up relationship with her brother, Aidan. Sadie had even met him when he'd visited Jamaica for a week while Fiona was there for Sadie and Chad's underwater archaeology field school.

"So it *is* the photographer you want." She nodded again to Fiona's left. "Not surprisingly, he's taking photos of us—of *you*."

"But he doesn't have his camera on him tonight. He said he was off duty."

"He must've gotten bored and went upstairs to grab it, because he's snapping away now."

She turned and saw him, not participating in the party but photographing it. Her. She gave him her profile and sipped her wine. Let the wildlife photographer capture her in her natural habitat, doing what came naturally.

Except the Caribbean and fancy dresses were not her natural habitat. These days, she had trouble figuring out what was, though.

She loved her home state of Washington, but since Regan's death, it felt . . . inhospitable. There were no jobs for her in the private sector thanks to her serious problems with Regan's former boss, who owned a consulting firm and was extremely well connected in the region.

And then there was her job, which was miserable with the fallout from Chiksook. But maybe her spying while she was on Ruby Island would help there.

Except she was a tad upset the admiral had asked her to spy.

She'd really hoped Ruby Island would be the escape she needed, but instead it had only brought more complications. Chad and Sadie's

relationship had fallen apart, and Jude wasn't keeping things professional as he'd promised.

And then there was Dean Slater, a man who filled her with longing
for something that would never be.

———

Paige stood and picked up her cocktail from the table. "I'm feeling
guilty. I promised Thaddeus I would mingle and make him look good.
He's got some business deal in the works with Jude. I might have
screwed it up for him by *not* mucking things up between you and
Dean." She covered her mouth with her hands, her long, pearly white–
painted fingernails a striking contrast to her dark skin as she grinned,
her eyes lit with mischief. *"Oops."*

Sadie stood too. "I'm going to turn in. I'm glad I stayed to hang
with you both, but I am not up for circulating the room any longer."

Fiona was about to rise and mingle after they left, but instead she
took a deep breath and appreciated the quiet of being alone in a room
full of people. She was good at extroverting, but she was an introvert at
heart and needed to recharge.

Even though it had been a private conversation with just the three
of them, it had been in a public place that brimmed with public energy,
which had drained her social batteries.

She was in the process of mustering the energy to stand and social-
ize when Jude dropped down in the seat next to her. He set a glass of
something bubbly on the table.

"A soda or cocktail of some sort?" she asked.

"Fizzy water. I notice that most evenings on the beach, you have a
cocktail or two, then switch to sparkling."

She picked up the glass and took a sip. "That's very thoughtful.
Thank you."

"Have you enjoyed the party?"

"It has been lovely." Not that she'd participated much, but she refused to feel guilty about that. He was the one with voyeuristic friends and who'd invited Paige to hurt her.

She did not understand him even a little bit. He had more money than any person—or even a thousand people—needed to live comfortably for the rest of his life. He'd inherited his wealth, sure, but he was successful and smart in his own right. He'd designed his own prototype submarine drone that was going to be the next great thing, making the shipping business more profitable than ever, according to him.

He was handsome and, she knew from their past friendship, perfectly capable of being charming.

He also knew her number one rule—even above *no field flings*—was absolutely no sexual or romantic involvement with a boss, ever.

When he'd offered her this job, she'd reiterated that rule, and he'd agreed to abide by it.

Given his looks, brains, charm, and wealth, there were *literally* thousands of women in the world who would welcome his attention. Fiona had to be among a very finite minority of single women who weren't interested—and even she had happily agreed to that one date.

It made no sense that he was interested in her, yet after tonight's scene with Paige, she could no longer ignore the clues he'd been dropping since she'd arrived on Ruby Island.

Days ago, he'd indicated he wanted her to play the role of hostess of this event, but she was nothing more than a dig bum on the job. And then there was the hand on her back earlier, as they stood on the beach before the party even started. It had been a signal of possession, and she'd known damn well he'd been aware Dean could see the gesture from the balcony. Then Jude had done it again as he led her to meet his awful friends.

Truth was, he'd behaved oddly since Dean arrived, and from what Paige had said, he'd arranged for her to show up at the party that very first evening.

That thought reminded Fiona she was supposed to be keeping track of the names of the guests, but she hadn't even circulated the room. She was a terrible spy, when it came right down to it. She drank her fizzy water, delivered by none other than the billionaire host, and mustered the courage to begin circulating the room so she could memorize names.

She wished she'd never been asked—let alone grudgingly agreed—to report what she observed on Ruby Island, but later tonight, she'd send an email to the admiral like a good little navy employee.

"Is everything okay, Fiona?" Jude asked.

She gave him a bright, fake smile and said in a low voice, "You really have the nerve to ask me that, after bringing Paige here?"

He frowned. "I'm sorry. I shouldn't have done it."

"No kidding. Also, not a fan of you putting your hand on me. Twice tonight."

"Did you tell Slater the same thing?"

She merely cocked her head.

"It felt natural. Both times. I'm sorry."

She didn't believe him, but this was hardly the place to get into it. "Just make sure it doesn't happen again. I'm your employee, and it made me uncomfortable."

"C'mon, Fiona, at field school we went skinny-dipping in the quarry together with the rest of the students. You cried on my shoulder when you got that letter from your mom on the anniversary of your dad's accident. Hell, you took a nap with your head on my belly during our lunch breaks more than once. We're friends, and friends touch each other without it meaning anything."

His words were true. She *had* cried on his shoulder. They had seen each other naked more than once, and it hadn't been a big deal, and there'd been a lot of casual touches back then. But that didn't change how his touch felt *now*.

"We *were* friends. We were also equal—students who would return to separate schools at the end of the summer—but fifteen years changes a lot."

"Duly noted. I'm sorry."

He said the words with sincerity, and frankly, the reminder of skinny-dipping and naps that included nonsexual cuddling did frame things differently. Was she too wrapped in ego believing he was attracted to her to realize his behavior was based on a friendship she'd largely forgotten?

Kosmo approached, and Fiona had no interest in trading barbs with the executive tonight.

She sighed. "I've spent the last two and a half weeks trying to figure out if the man I knew fifteen years ago is still there. But there's something equally important you should know about me. I'm *not* the woman I was then. That makes us barely more than strangers; we just have a few extra shared memories. And you are my boss."

He gave her a wry smile. "It sounds like we need to get to know each other again. We should have dinner together. Just the two of us. We can take my boat out tomorrow for a sunset cruise. I'll have the chef prepare us a special dinner. All my guests will be gone by then."

"That sounds an awful lot like a date."

"It wouldn't be. Just friends. Talking about old times. Taking the boat out is the only way we can guarantee we'll be alone, unless you want to have dinner in my suite?"

"Yeah. That's a no."

"Then the boat it is." He gave her an admittedly charming smile, dimples and all. But then, she figured tuxedos and bow ties made everything look charming. "Pretty please?"

She thought back to field school and campfires and lunchtime naps and swimming in the quarry and reminded herself how much this man had meant to her once. Had he meant as much to her then as Dylan did now? It was hard to remember. She sighed. "Fine."

She realized she should have gotten up and walked away when she had the chance, because Kosmo joined them, taking the empty third chair. "Ms. Carver, you should be mingling with our guests and not monopolizing the host."

"Shut it, Kosmo," Jude said.

She flashed a grin. "You heard the boss." She nodded to Jude. "On that note, I think I'll get another drink."

She left the executive with the CEO without looking back. But she could hear Jude scolding his VP. What was Kosmo's agenda? Did he view her as some sort of threat? Did he think she was going to use her womanly wiles to manipulate his boss?

She ordered another fizzy water from the bartender, then crossed to the open doors to the garden and stepped outside. They were on a hill, above the beach, and the open part of the garden meant she could feel the Caribbean breeze on her skin. It was time to get over herself and enjoy this project.

Contrary to Kosmo's opinion, she was off the clock in paradise.

Except, even now, she was composing her email to the admiral in her head, with the list of guests she could name and asking again if he'd learned anything about the helicopter crash. Had someone from Dominica investigated and cleaned up the site without informing Jude?

It was marginally possible.

While Jude's lease covered the entire island, the government of Dominica retained unlimited access rights to the fort. It was a protected historic property. Same with the portion of the island that was a nature preserve. After the fiasco of the previous lessee constructing warehouses on the fort promontory and dumping cannons into the bay, Jude was not allowed to alter or develop the historic sites or nature preserve. He could limit access, nothing more.

It was one reason for Fiona's survey—to identify all the historic and prehistoric sites that were off-limits to any kind of development. She imagined it was the same for Dean's wildlife photography. Set a baseline for what was present on the island. There was sure to be an environmental survey to follow, but best to get the photos now while the film crew was here for the documentary.

Given that the government of Dominica retained access to the fort, there was a slim chance there was no great mystery behind what had happened to the helicopter pieces. It was even conceivable they'd cleaned the wreckage to prevent it from being a blight on the landscape for decades, as the hurricane-destroyed warehouses had been.

But deep down, Fiona didn't think so.

TWELVE

Fiona met with Sadie on the front terrace where the breakfast buffet was served every morning starting at six thirty, roughly an hour after sunrise. It was just before seven when Fiona was filling her plate with eggs, bacon, and fresh-baked pastries, marveling, as she did every morning, that this was field food.

Really, no project could ever live up after this one.

She sat next to Sadie at a round table with seats for four. A server delivered fresh orange juice, then retreated inside. The house, pool, and gardens were maintained by a staff of ten, who divided their time between Ruby Island and Dominica, as only a skeleton crew remained on the estate when Jude wasn't in residence. Extra staff had been brought in to work the party, but as far as Fiona could tell, they'd cleaned up when the event was over and left with the dawn.

She sat facing Cannon Bay, in which only seven mega yachts remained and one was just now pulling anchor.

"I knew they'd be leaving early, but not this early."

"The tropical storm in the Atlantic is making them nervous," Sadie said. "It's two days out at least—if it even heads this way—but I'm guessing they want to get as big a head start as possible in case it does."

"Should we be worried?" Fiona asked.

"It's hard to say anymore, with how intense hurricane season has gotten with global warming, but from the looks of it, I doubt we'd get more than the edge of the storm." She nodded to the bay. "We'll probably moor *Tempus Machina* in the cove by the fort, though. It has better protection than Cannon Bay. Jude says that's what he does with *Rum Runner* when it looks like a storm is heading this way."

Fiona nodded. Worry over damage to the boat from a storm was definitely a headache Sadie didn't need.

"You taking the boat out for the dog and pony show for the investor today?"

Sadie grimaced. "Yes. We'll do some filming and show off what the side scan sonar and multibeam profiler can do." Sadie's face was pinched, and Fiona wondered what had happened with Chad once again, but since they were likely to be joined by others at any moment, she didn't ask. Sadie would tell her when they had time and privacy. "What are you going to do today?"

"Low tide is at ten thirty a.m., which is perfect for me to scout the littoral caves."

"You need a field buddy for that."

"I was thinking I could see if Walker is available—unless you're willing to give up Oliver?"

"Nope. We definitely need Oliver. And I think Walker is needed at the dock, given that boats are still fueling up before leaving." Sadie gave her a knowing smile. "I can think of someone who's perfect for the job. Plus he can take pictures."

So Sadie had signed on to Dylan's matchmaking scheme.

"Et tu, Brute?"

"Not my fault you didn't hire an assistant for the field."

Fiona had wanted to, but Jude had insisted the laborers he'd hired to clean up the fort could accompany her in the field and wield machetes to clear the path. And while that would work well for expedited filming, it wasn't needed for scouting days like today, when the filming would happen elsewhere.

Dean and Nico stepped out onto the terrace. As always, Fiona felt that familiar frisson at the sight of Hot Bird Man's Paul Newman blue eyes. She wondered if she'd ever get used to seeing him like this, away from Chiksook and danger. Dylan safe and whereabouts known.

Could they do this? Work together? Be friends?

Last night in the garden, something had shifted between them. But perhaps not in a direction that allowed for friendship, because one thing she knew she couldn't do was hope for more. And whenever she was near him, she wanted more.

Dean had been clear on his limits, and she understood why. He'd loved Violet with all of his heart, and he'd watched her die over the course of two and a half years. He'd been a widower at the age of twenty-five, having lost the love of his life.

She understood why he wasn't capable of loving again. And she also knew she didn't want anything less from him.

She didn't do flings in general. She'd considered making an exception for Dean, but in the end, he'd been the one to say no.

So now here they were. She was full of feelings that had nowhere to go, and he was . . . fond of her.

She cleared her throat. "Dean, I need a field buddy today. And you know how I feel about the buddy system when it comes to fieldwork."

His eyes warmed as his mouth curved in a smug smile. "I seem to remember you weren't a fan until things went sideways."

"That just means I'm capable of growth and open to new ideas."

Nico snorted, while Dean let out a full-on laugh. "You mean you realized a broken leg while alone in the wilderness is potentially deadly."

She smiled. "That too." Her smile faltered as she realized what she had to share next. She took a deep breath. "But fair warning. My job today is to scout the littoral caves. There are three we know of that might be quite extensive. Places where enslaved African, Kalinago, and Taíno people might have hidden. Today, I need to determine how accessible they are and what equipment will be needed for survey and excavation—if that's even deemed possible."

Dean's eyes turned serious, and she knew exactly what he was thinking. "We're going spelunking?"

"Yes."

The last time they'd entered a cave together . . . well, it had been harrowing, to say the least.

His blue, blue eyes probed her face as his nostrils flared. Then his mouth curved in the slightest of smiles, and his voice dropped to just above a whisper. "There is no one I'd rather explore a cave with than you."

She bit her bottom lip and gave him a crooked smile back. "We're all set, then."

"There is one caveat. Same as when we worked together before, I also have work I need to complete now that I finally have my equipment, and I need a buddy because Nico will be on *Tempus Machina*."

"What's the task?" she asked.

"It's the fun stuff," Nico said. "Slingshotting lines into the rainforest canopy, setting up ropes to climb trees."

"You want to set up photography blinds in the canopy?" she asked.

Dean nodded.

She kept her face carefully blank. He was aware of her fear of heights and aversion to climbing cliff faces. Did her fear extend to ropes run up trees? She hoped she wouldn't need to find out.

The boat dropped into the swell as Dean steered the sixteen-foot Boston Whaler over the crest of the low wave. Fiona sat on the side seat next to the console, in front of and to the left of him, while he stood at the helm, ignoring the cushioned seat behind him and enjoying the warm breeze on his face as the sporty boat made quick work of the distance.

He took the next wave at an angle, and Fiona let out an exhilarated laugh as she gripped the railing mounted to the inside of the hull and water sprayed over the side, splashing her lightly.

He wished he had his camera out to capture the moment, but steering required both hands and concentration, so instead he would just enjoy the view of Fiona in a carefree moment as her ponytail of damp curls captured the sun and glowed red and the salty seawater drenched her top, too much for the moisture-wicking fabric to combat all at once. It clung to her, highlighting the curves he'd had few opportunities to appreciate when they were dressed in layers upon layers in Alaska.

The Caribbean sun and sea looked good on her.

But then, the North Pacific cold and ocean had looked good on her too. He'd been infatuated with her from pretty much the moment of their meeting, and everything that transpired after only increased the attraction.

But still, no amount of attraction would change his mind. It wasn't a matter of him not being ready, as Dylan believed. It was a fact of not being able or willing.

He'd enjoyed plenty of sex in the years since Violet died, but his liaisons never included messy emotions. They were always flings enjoyed by both parties with no strings attached. Paige was a perfect example.

He'd met her when he was on assignment and she'd volunteered to do a shoot at a wildlife preserve in Kenya to raise money to fight poaching and preserve habitats. They'd hit it off immediately, enjoyed their week together, and when he returned to LA, they'd remained friends. Her friendship had opened doors, leading to invitations to red-carpet affairs and private parties hosted by people at the pinnacle of the entertainment industry.

He enjoyed the events because they were so vastly different from his day job, and also completely unconnected to his life with Violet. It wasn't anything his dead wife had ever wanted or imagined, and so he didn't feel the pang of loss that she didn't share it with him.

The black-tie events were a balm against loneliness, especially after Dylan moved north, so he made a habit of saying yes to everything when he was in town. As a result, his photo appeared in a lot of tabloids, often linked to women he may or may not have slept with. And he'd never cared in the least.

The only people who were likely to care were Violet's parents, who'd always despised him. But he didn't give a damn what they thought. There was a reason Violet chose to spend her last years with Dean and not her dear old mom and dad.

It was the same reason she'd left her vast trust fund to Dean.

But after Chiksook, he'd reconnected with Violet's sister, Becca, and it had been important to him to tell her his heart had always been with Violet, that the tabloid stories were only partially true.

He hadn't considered how the pictures of him on the red carpet with Paige and the rumors of their relationship would hurt Fiona. He supposed he should thank Reynolds for bringing it all out in the open so he could remove any pain the articles might have caused her.

And now he was piloting Reynolds's very nice speedboat around the eastern shore of Reynolds's leased island paradise, as the tropical sun lit Fiona's smile and the boat bounced on the waves. She appeared happier and more relaxed than he'd ever seen her.

Thank you, Jude.

She said something he couldn't hear over the roar of the motor and pointed to the open ocean to the east.

He followed the line of her finger and spotted a dark fin in the distance. A moment later, the whale breached, and his heart surged.

The beauty and majesty of the massive mammal leaping from the sea. There was nothing like it.

He checked the fuel gauge. The tank was full—more than enough to do a side expedition before visiting the caves. He turned the small craft and headed out into deeper water. He'd just get close enough to take photos of the pod of sperm whales.

He cut the engine a fair distance from the pod and pulled out his camera. He adjusted the settings to make sure the light and focal point were right, then settled in and snapped pictures as the pod moved through the bright blue water.

Fiona gasped and laughed as the whales breached and swam and splashed, and pleasure settled in his belly at the sheer joy of the moment. He was with a woman whose mere presence made his heart beat a little stronger, doing the thing that gave his life meaning.

Wildlife photography had given him purpose after Violet died. His first expedition had lasted nine months, spanning a half-dozen countries in central and south Africa. It was on that trip that he really learned his craft. He'd met up with a seasoned photographer in Kenya who'd taken him under his wing and taught him survival skills, tracking, camouflage, creating blinds. Everything a man with Dean's ambition and drive needed to know.

He'd returned home a changed man.

And when he'd entered his house, clutching his battered expedition bag that had traveled thousands of miles of jungle, desert, mountains, and rainforest and faced his living room that was empty of both hospital bed and wife, he'd immediately wanted to turn right around and set out again.

But he'd promised Dylan he'd stay and get to know his brother's latest girlfriend. He'd ended up staying for two months before the quiet inside his small Southern California home became too much, and an invitation from his newly acquired mentor had him packing his bags for Brazil.

That became his pattern, how he'd passed time for the first several years after Violet's death. Except late in the second year, thanks to doors opened by his mentor, who freelanced for *National Geographic*, some of Dean's expeditions had begun to be financed by wildlife protection organizations, and Dean was earning enough to live off his income from selling photos.

Now, as the bright morning sun warmed his skin and the gray body of a whale glided through the pale-blue water in the foreground while another breached behind, with Fiona next to him, gasping at the sight as he snapped the perfect photo, he knew this might be the single most harmonious moment he'd ever had on the job—and he'd had some damn spectacular moments for this to compete with.

"Wow," Fiona said for probably the fifth time.

He laughed, then lowered his camera. Only the sound of waves lapping at the sides broke the serenity of the moment as they drifted in the warm sea wind. "I'm glad to be here with you," he said. "I wouldn't want to share this moment with anyone else."

She turned, meeting his gaze, her face radiant with a smile. After a moment's hesitation, she climbed over her seat and settled on the padded bench next to him. She faced the whales as she said, "Me too. I know neither of us wanted this. But I'm really glad to see you again. I hope . . ." She paused, took a deep breath, and said, "I hope after this, we can figure out a way to be friends. I want to know you. I want to see Dylan. And I don't want any of it to be awkward."

He leaned over and kissed her temple. She leaned into him, resting her head on his shoulder as he draped an arm around her waist and pulled her to his side. Together, they faced the pod of whales playing in the deep-blue sea.

He didn't touch his camera as the boat rocked in the waves and a whale tail flapped in the water. He just held Fiona to his side and enjoyed a peace he hadn't known in a very, very long time.

———

There were three known littoral caves on the eastern side of the island. It was highly likely there were even more caves—both inland and on the water, because Ruby Island had never been officially mapped, having been basically off-limits for one reason or another through the centuries.

Very little was known about the first enslaved Africans who escaped and made their way to the island, taking refuge with the Kalinago and Taíno, who had also fled to Ruby Island. But experts in the region's history all agreed the coastal caves might have been key to the refugees' ability to remain hidden.

The caves were extensive and could well contain artifacts from those first explorers who hid inside. Fiona had dug in rockshelters in Washington State and explored lava tubes on Chiksook and was well aware of the incredible preservation to be found in such environments. But it was also possible that even the deepest parts of Ruby Island's caves were flooded regularly by tidal activity, leaving nothing for anyone to find.

Her job today was to determine if the caves could be explored and mapped by humans or drones. And if humans could do the work, she needed to determine if it was likely the caves had intact cultural deposits. It was also rumored that loot from the 1567 lost Spanish convoy had been hidden by the Kalinago in caves on Dominica or possibly Ruby Island.

Whether any gold would remain over 450 years later seemed unlikely, but the story would add romance to the documentary. Just like the stories of pirate gold in the lake, no matter how flimsy the evidence, historic coins would always be worthy of screen time. The rumors of lost gold would probably get more coverage than several more important research questions.

Dean piloted the boat like a pro as they approached the first cave. The openings of all three caves were small enough that they could be accessed only at the lowest part of low tide in a vessel as large as the Boston Whaler. They would have taken a smaller boat—a Zodiac, or even a canoe—except they had a lot of ground to cover today and a lot of equipment to haul for Dean. They'd opted for speed and capacity.

She eyed the entrance. "Looks like the window on entering and exiting this one with a boat of this size can't be much longer than an hour before and an hour after low tide. But we can't give this one more than thirty minutes if we want to have time to explore the other caves before the tide rises too high."

He nodded and dialed back the throttle to a crawl as he aligned the boat for the low and narrow opening. "We'll give it twenty minutes, just to be sure."

They glided through the tight slot, engine noise bouncing off the cave walls. Dean cut the engine, allowing them to drift as he grabbed a paddle to maintain their forward momentum.

She grabbed another paddle but kept her head low as she dipped it in the water. There was only a scant five inches of clearance in height and just a foot on either side of the vessel.

Dean had threaded the needle perfectly, but they were entering the unknown and could run aground quickly. She heard the mechanical noise of the propeller being raised just in case.

He flicked on a spotlight mounted in front of the helm, and she could see there were no obstacles in their immediate path as the cavern opened up, widening all around as the ceiling rose.

The cave had been hollowed out by wave action, and it was uneven with large boulders that had been cut from above and dropped into the sea. The spotlight illuminated a series of dark shapes adhered to the ceiling. One after another, they released from the stone and swarmed.

Bats.

Thousands and thousands of bats.

She held her breath against a yelp—not wanting the wildlife photographer who shared the boat to see her behaving so squeamishly—as she dropped her paddle inside the boat and ducked, her arms going up to protect her head from the onslaught of flapping wings.

The air in the cavern shifted as several thousand bats took flight at once, most heading for the opening they'd just navigated.

Just below the sound of beating wings, she heard the shutter of Dean's camera as he snapped away, capturing the swarm.

"I don't know if I should be freaked out by this or not," she said. "I've never seen so many bats."

The cave reeked of the creatures, which Fiona had always found to be mysteriously beautiful when she'd spot them flying solo at dusk in the Pacific Northwest. But a swarm definitely had a more ominous feel.

"Well, we did invade their home," Dean said.

"I'm not blaming *them* for the swarm; I'm questioning my life choices that brought me here."

He let out a soft laugh as the flying mammals continued to race to the exit by the hundreds. "Oh, the number of times I've asked myself that as I sought the perfect shot."

"Yeah, well, you're an adrenaline junkie."

"You feeling adrenaline now, Fi?" he asked, his voice seductively low as the swift movement of thousands of wings caused the air to buffet her skin.

It took her a moment to realize the feeling swirling through her was the not-entirely-unpleasant sensation of an adrenaline spike. Was it the fear of rabid bats? The narrow opening that didn't offer escape for the boat now as it was clogged with exiting bats? The dark, unexplored cave? Being with Dean?

Of course, the answer was all of the above contributed to her pounding heart. And she didn't hate it. Didn't love it, either, but it wasn't standing on a cliff's edge and looking down as thoughts of her father and sister swirled through her mind.

She came by her fear of heights honestly, and Chiksook had served to both exacerbate and excise that fear. The end result was that she feared nature less and people more.

With the crash four days ago, she had a new potential phobia to add to her list, and she hadn't even been on that particular helicopter.

Watching it break apart in flames was a trauma in and of itself.

The boat scraped against a gravelly bottom just as the swarm was beginning to settle down. "Okay. Twenty minutes starts now," Dean said.

"We won't get far with so little time," she responded.

She grabbed her pack, then crawled forward and climbed over the gunwale, getting her legs wet to midcalf. She held the boat in place as Dean did the same. Once he was in the water, he reached into the bow and grabbed the anchor. She released the boat, and they both walked the last feet to rocky shore that was slick with seaweed and bat guano. He wedged the anchor behind a boulder to secure the boat against wave action that could dislodge it from the slimy, rocky beach.

They each donned their headlamps—just like old times—and set out over the uneven ground to see how far back the cave extended and estimate how much time exploration would take and the likelihood of success in finding archaeological resources.

The cavern was divided by boulders they had to climb around—they were too slick to go over—and the air was thick with the scent of guano. They'd expected this, though, and had each donned masks with filters they carried in their packs.

They made it around the first and biggest boulder obstacle to see the cave branching off in different directions.

There weren't stalactites or stalagmites here, as this cave had been formed by waves cutting into the island's rocky base. Water reached all the way back here, and when the tide rose and storms surged, the waves would continue their eons-long work of eroding and undermining the rock that was Ruby Island's foundation.

Dean snapped pictures as they went, Fiona shining her light as directed. Since they couldn't be in here long, she would rely on studying the photos in great detail to decide on her research plan.

Her light glanced off one rock at an angle, and parallel grooves jumped out at her. She moved closer, shining the light head-on, but the markings disappeared. She moved sideways so her headlamp would project at an angle, spreading the beam across the surface of the stone, and there it was, an image etched in the rock face.

A petroglyph, so faint she could have missed it. A spiral, a bird, and a face in a triangle.

She dropped to her knees, bringing herself nearly nose to nose with the human etching. She no longer smelled the rank cave or feared the bats. She didn't even hear the lapping of the water on the rocks as she took in the artwork that had very likely been drawn by humans who had hidden in this cave as a desperate refuge.

Their story needed to be told, and she would do everything in her power to make sure the right people—the descendants of those who'd suffered—were the ones to tell it.

THIRTEEN

The second and third littoral caves were just as bat-filled as the first, but neither offered up more petroglyphs for Fiona to find. With the cave-scouting task completed, Dean piloted the boat around the island to a rocky beach centrally located on the western shore. This small cove was the best access point for the mature rainforest where he wanted to set up cameras.

As before, they pulled the boat as far as they could onto the shore and wedged the anchor between the trunks of two palm trees that grew side by side in the intertidal zone. The tide was coming in now, and, given enough time, they'd have to wade—or even swim—to collect the boat, so they weren't taking chances that it could become unmoored in their absence.

Before setting out, they ate a quick lunch while sitting on rocks looking out over the sea. The day was cloudy with warm breezes. It would likely rain in the afternoon, but the showers would be brief. Current models were predicting that the edge of the storm brewing in the Atlantic might cross over Ruby Island in two or three days.

After the devastation of Hurricane Maria in 2017, no one would dare be blasé about the potential damage of any storm. To that end, several of the locals, including Oliver, had expressed an interest in going to Dominica if it looked like the storm was coming this way. Oliver had family on the island and wished to be there to help batten down their houses.

Ruby Island, with her limited structures that had been upgraded over the years and were as stormproof as possible, was relatively safe, so there wasn't talk of needing to evacuate everyone. Just the staff who wished to ride out the storm with their families.

While Dean could join Dylan in the vacation rental he'd managed to secure for six weeks, he wouldn't leave Fiona and doubted she'd be willing to leave the island. So here he would stay.

Besides, Dylan would probably kick Dean's ass right back to Ruby Island if he showed up without Fiona. Last night, after the stunt with Paige had played out, Dean had called Dylan. His brother had shared his anger over the manipulation but was steadfast that Dean needed to stay by Fiona's side. If nothing else, he needed to be there to protect her against further manipulations.

That had been Dean's thought as well. He hadn't needed any convincing.

He did wonder why Fiona had opted to stay, but guessed she was taking it one day at a time. He'd seen her talking to Jude at the party and hoped she'd called their boss out on his behavior.

Lunch finished, they slathered on a DEET-free insect repellant before they each donned heavy packs loaded with the photography equipment he would install in a tree deep in the forest. "At least the packs will be lighter on the way back to the boat," he said by way of apology to Fiona, who hadn't really signed up for the job of equipment porter. "Of course, that's the downhill part of the hike, unfortunately."

The estate and all associated infrastructure were situated on the north end of the island, while the fort filled the southern end. In between, on the central eastern side, sat Mount Asilo, which rose up 2,800 feet above sea level. Between the estate and Fort Domingo, the island was primarily lush rainforest, the canopy of which covered much of the lower slopes of Mount Asilo. The exception being patches of ground where wind and rain scoured the rocks, preventing soil from collecting and plants from germinating.

They were now situated on the central western shore, directly opposite the highest point of the island, and would be hiking east into the heart of the rainforest, meaning their path would be a steady uphill grind across the lower slopes of the mountain to the center of the island.

She smiled. "It's fine. I'm no stranger to hauling gear uphill."

He couldn't help himself and grabbed the clips for her padded waist belt. He clipped the ends together, then cinched it tight. "How does that feel? If this pack isn't comfortable, we can switch it out for yours."

"My pack isn't big enough to carry all this gear." She adjusted the hip belt, seating it slightly higher, then pulling on the shoulder straps to fix the position.

Dean snapped the breastbone strap together, then loosened it to accommodate her full bust. Of course, she could do all these things herself, but he liked attending to her.

And damn, he'd never realized how hot it was to see a woman in full hiking gear like this. On Chiksook, they'd been bundled in layers upon layers. But now she wore lightweight moisture-wicking hiking clothes. With the chest and hip straps cinched tight, her hourglass shape was well defined.

Her hair was pulled back in a high ponytail, and her skin glistened with sweat. He raised the camera that hung around his neck and snapped a photo.

She smiled, then rolled her eyes and said, "I feel I should point out that this pack is *heavy*."

He chuckled and took a step forward to kiss her forehead. "Sorry. Couldn't resist." He cinched his own pack at his hips, and they entered the rainforest together.

It was slow going with the heavy packs uphill, combined with the need to weave their way through the forest, but thirty minutes after they'd set out, Dean spotted the branch he'd selected on his scouting mission two days ago. He dropped his heavy pack on the ground and started rummaging through the supplies. Beside him, Fiona dropped hers, then plucked the water bottle from the side pocket and took a long drink.

He paused to enjoy the view as sweat and her lightweight top clung to her skin in a very attractive way.

She and Sadie were both photogenic women. Their looks would be a huge marketing feature for the documentary. They were both eminently qualified for their roles, but he was all too aware that more often than not, women in the entertainment industry were held to higher attractiveness standards than men if they were expected to carry a program.

Many in the industry believed viewers only wanted male hosts to speak with authority on science, nature, and history, and wouldn't watch a show with a female host at all.

It was a sexist industry, and Dean was glad this assignment had been given to Nico and Jenni, because it was important to have women on both sides of the camera. He hoped Jenni would be able to return to the project, but even if she didn't, she'd be with Nico in the editing room.

He had no doubt Nico would do his part to make Fiona come across as knowledgeable and compelling in the interviews and monologues that would be required. Once the documentary released, Fiona would likely become a star in her field, and Dean would find himself lost in her sea of fans.

He looked forward to that for her. She'd see how amazing she was.

She nudged the bag with her toe. "So what did I haul for you? Bricks?"

He laughed and reached into a side pocket of the pack. "No bricks, but one bar." He held out a chocolate peppermint LUNA bar, which he had on good authority was her favorite.

"Oooh. That almost makes my aching shoulders worth it." She ripped open the wrapper and took a bite, then let out that soft humming sound she made when she enjoyed what she was eating. He knew she exaggerated the reaction for his benefit, and it brought him back to Chiksook, when they'd eaten ramen noodles and chicken that tasted like heaven after a brutal day.

It had been the scariest time of his life, being stranded and searching for Dylan, and yet those quiet moments with her had also been strangely—even intensely—gratifying.

And now here he was, alone with her in the jungle, and danger wasn't ever-present, but the moment still hummed with that intense pleasure.

But then, that was a danger too.

She held out the half-eaten bar. "Bite?"

He held a hand to his chest. "You'd give up a bite for me?"

"Well, only one."

He laughed and took a very small taste, then returned to sorting through the items in the pack he'd need to set up a line and climb into the canopy.

Today he would place high-tech game cameras—surveillance cameras, really—that he'd been wanting to test in the field for a long time. This was the perfect project to test the motion-activated cameras with satellite hookup and portable solar panels.

He'd be able to monitor activity in the canopy remotely and would return in a few days to take photos if this tree proved promising.

In the rainforest, the majority of wildlife activity happened in the canopy. To photograph it, one needed to be in the trees, where the action was.

The two cameras he'd set up today would give him a solid preview of the best places to devote his energy later, as he would likely spend hours in a blind, waiting for the perfect shot. Over the course of the next five weeks, he could move the cameras to different locations, ensuring he had a chance to capture the widest variety of birds that inhabited the island.

Ideally, he'd be diving right in today, settling in with his DSLR in the leafy camouflage of the tree, but given that he was dividing his time with Fiona's priorities, he didn't have that luxury.

He would, however, return with Nico tomorrow at the crack of dawn for some early filming. Nico would capture setup and climbing shots for the documentary, and then Nico would be free to join the archaeologists.

Dean would then see if Walker or Oliver could accompany him while he explored the rainforest, taking macro shots of butterflies and other fauna that could be found closer to the forest floor.

Dylan had been slated to act as Dean's field partner and vice versa. It would have been the first time they'd ever worked together in that capacity, and he'd been looking forward to it.

His brother had left him in the lurch in more ways than one, and he'd have to figure out how he felt about it. As it was, Oliver or Walker was the only solution, because Nico couldn't get up at five thirty every morning to assist, and Dean and Fiona couldn't keep splitting their days like this. She had too much work to do for her to be his field buddy.

Which was for the best.

He pulled out the spool that held the thin line that would be shot up into the tree and over the thick branch he'd selected. He would use that line to pull up heavier lines until finally he had a rope that could bear his weight rigged to the sturdy branch. Once he had the rope, he would use ascenders to climb a hundred feet straight up into the canopy.

He studied his target, then moved back, ensuring he had enough room to make the shot, then planted the spool.

"Is there anything I can do to help?"

"Not really. Just compliment me when I impress you."

She snorted. "I'll do my best." She eyed his equipment and picked up the slingshot. "What is this for?"

"For sending a line up into the canopy. The wrist rocket is usually fast and easy, but the branch I want is pretty high. I'm going to go with the bow and arrow for this one." He nodded toward the pack where the unassembled recurve bow poked out the top.

"You're a good shot with an arrow?"

"Better than I am with the slingshot, actually, which is why I use it for the higher shots."

He reached into his kit and grabbed the bow, quickly attaching the upper and lower limbs to the riser, then stringing it so it was ready to fire. He pulled an arrow from the small quiver hooked to the outside of his pack and tied on the spool line.

"What happens if you miss?"

"It can be a pain. Sometimes the arrow can't be retrieved, and I have to cut the line. I've only got four arrows, so I can't make too many mistakes."

"You don't take practice shots?"

"Without a line attached, I'd definitely lose the arrow in this, so I don't bother. The slingshot is easier, because I can always test with a rock first. Dial in my aim."

He nocked the arrow and aimed upward, lining up his shot. It looked good. The branch he wanted was easily a hundred feet up, but there was a good-size window for him to aim for. He pulled the bowstring back to the limit and let loose.

The arrow shot upward and arced through the opening above his target branch, then it curved downward for the return to earth. The line unfurled from the spool at lightning speed, draping over the branch he'd targeted.

A perfect shot.

Fiona let out a low whistle. "Okay, I'm officially impressed."

"Thank you," he said, feeling inordinately pleased she'd witnessed the shot.

He retrieved the arrow and then set about attaching a slightly heavier line to the lightweight one and hoisting it up and over the branch. He couldn't be certain the branch would support his weight, but it looked to be sturdy, and he'd managed to get it in the V where branch met thick trunk.

It was a long process, but finally the rigging was ready, and he donned his climbing harness and clipped on the ascenders. Fiona checked his knots and carabiners. With her focus locked on the center of his chest, she asked, "You sure they're solid?"

It wasn't until the danger had passed on Chiksook that he'd learned her father had died in a climbing accident when she was in her teens. She hadn't elaborated beyond that, but he'd gathered she'd done some climbing with her father before his death but not in the two decades since, and he wondered if it had been equipment failure that had caused the accident.

Unfortunately, now was not the time to ask.

He placed a finger below her chin and nudged her to raise her gaze to meet his. His belly clenched when he glimpsed the stark fear in her eyes. He should have realized this would scare her. He touched her cheek. "I had Nico double-check the equipment before we packed up this morning. He's the most experienced climber I know. I'll be fine."

"Promise?"

He nodded, then dipped his head to kiss her lips, but at the last moment redirected to her forehead. They were coworkers—for real this time—and he needed to behave as such. No matter how natural it felt to move in for a kiss.

He had to ignore the memories of how good she'd felt in his arms and needed to keep this platonic if they were going to find a way to be friends, as she'd requested.

Time to redirect.

He flashed his most cocky grin. "Prepare to be impressed again as I conquer this tree. You might want to set a stopwatch to record my time to the top."

She smiled as she rolled her eyes, and he knew he'd achieved his goal of chasing the shadows from her eyes. "I finally get to see Hot Bird Man fly up a tree."

Of course, the ascender jammed when he was five feet up.

"Don't hold back for me, honey. Soar, baby bird, soar!"

He started laughing, which shook the leaves as he hung in the air. "No fair making me laugh."

"Hey, at least we know the branch can hold your weight."

"Yeah. That's why I stopped. To test the branch."

"Uh-huh."

He freed the ascender and didn't run into more snags as he made his way up the rope at a safe and steady speed. He reached the branch where he wanted to set up the camera and satellite modem, then hooked himself to the trunk so he could free his hands to haul up the gear.

He rigged a pulley to the branch and sent a line down. Fiona clipped his gear to the line and sent it up. They worked in tandem like this as first he set up the waterproof camera, then the satellite modem, which would sit beneath a small camouflage rain cover.

Last, he climbed to the highest point and had Fiona send up the small solar panels that would supplement the power pack. He placed the panels as far out on the branch as he could reach, in a patch of sunlight that sliced through the highest canopy. The camera battery was fully charged and would last at least four days, as would the modem battery pack—which, come to think of it, was a whole lot like a brick and had been in Fiona's pack. He owed her more than a LUNA bar for hauling that.

The solar panels served to extend battery life to a week or more depending on how much sun made it through the gap in the leaves on any given day. He had backup battery packs and would change out for fresh batteries when he could, but this would be an excellent test of a system he'd been eager to try for some time.

This morning, he'd woken Dylan at the crack of dawn to recruit him to monitor the camera feed. After all, if the guy was going to abandon him in the field without warning, the least he could do was keep an eye on the data collected by the cameras from the comfort of his vacation rental.

Dean ran lines from solar panels to modem to camera, a jumble of cables that were mostly green and brown to blend in with the environment. The two-lens camera was a special order, because usually it only came in white, but he'd requested forest camouflage. It looked like a mottled green-and-brown owl face and blended well when mounted to the trunk.

Once everything was set, he powered it on and called down to Fiona to check the feed on the laptop it was connected to via a very long LAN cable, because the laptop wouldn't be able to connect to Wi-Fi out here.

"How does it look?"

"Crystal clear." After a moment, she added, "Wow, for a game camera, this is pretty spiffy."

"It's actually a surveillance camera, not a game camera. Draws a lot more power, uses more memory, and costs a heck of a lot more, but if you want to find bigfoot, this is the camera that could do it, and it wouldn't be a fuzzy blob."

"I'm guessing you'd be able to determine sasquatch eye color with this."

He laughed. "Probably. These photos won't be *National Geo*–worthy, but for an inventory of birds on Ruby Island, it could be amazing. Focal length can be adjusted remotely and independently between the two lenses. I'm going to make one focus close and the other distant and play with the settings when we're back at the house."

Dean checked all the lights, and it appeared everything was in working order. He had one more of these to set up today, so didn't have time to linger. Unfortunately, they had to hike back to the boat to retrieve the second set of packs, as there'd been too much to carry in one trip.

He used the descenders to zip down the line. His body was stiff from the awkward position he'd held for the hour he'd been at the top of the tree. He rolled his shoulders and cricked his neck.

"Let's pack up the computer and other equipment but leave it here. No point in carrying it back to the boat just to bring it right back this way."

"You sure you want to come back this way? We could take a different path."

"I was thinking we should set up the second camera closer to the central lake, where Sadie may have found a structure. Nothing is a straight line in a rainforest, but this spot is definitely on the straightest route between the boat and the lake."

"Oh. I like the idea of the camera being near the overgrown structure. Sadie will too. We can get a peek at the rainforest day and night. Given the conditions, it's not likely to be much different from what you'd see two hundred years ago."

"Exactly."

They walked in companionable silence back to the boat, which went much faster without heavy packs. Even the return went faster, and forty minutes after they'd left Dean's gear at the foot of the roped tree, they were retrieving it and continuing on. Thirty minutes after that, Dean spotted a branch that would be ideal for the second camera mount. Good thing, too, because they were running out of time if they wanted to be out of the rainforest before sunset.

It took two tries with the bow to get the line over the branch, but thankfully he was able to retrieve the arrow, and the rest of the setup went smoothly—taking less time than the first round, given that they both knew what to do.

After the equipment checked out, he sighed with relief that he'd been able to achieve this much today. He'd been doubtful. He glanced at his watch and saw it wasn't yet four o'clock.

He clipped the descenders on the line and worked his way down. When he was halfway, he said, "Sun doesn't set until six thirty, giving us a little time if you want to check out the lake—see how close we can get to it."

"Sorry. I . . . need to get back to the house. I have . . . a meeting with Jude later."

"Surely he'd understand if you're making progress on the inventory."

"Yeah. I still think it would be better if we head back." She sounded uneasy.

The moment his feet hit the rainforest floor, he asked the question that had been bothering him since last night, but which he'd put aside as none of his business until now. "So what's the deal with you and Reynolds?"

"Deal?"

"Last night, Sadie said something that indicated you and he have some sort of history." *But it doesn't stop with the past. He obviously wants a future with you.*

Dean kept that last thought to himself.

"We do."

As they strapped on the much-lighter packs for the final return trip and set out, she told him about how the MIT graduate student took a summer off and attended an archaeological field school as a lark, and a friendship had formed between them.

"He's not the guy Regan slept with, is he?"

She startled. "I'm surprised you remember that detail."

"I remember everything you told me that week." He'd played every conversation they'd shared over and over in his mind.

"Well then, you might remember the story I told about the important executive who took me to dinner at Canlis."

"The guy who expected sex as his due because he bought you an expensive dinner?"

She nodded. "Yeah. Jude wasn't the guy Regan slept with during my field school—which is good because she was barely eighteen and he was twenty-three, nothing illegal, but I'd have been concerned—but he *was* the guy who took me to dinner at Canlis."

"You didn't mention you knew him before the date."

"It wasn't germane to the conversation. And also, I didn't *feel* like I knew him. We'd lost touch after field school. It had been eleven years since I'd spoken to him when we went out to dinner and he behaved like a jerk."

"How long has it been since that date?"

Her steps slowed to a full stop. "Four years. Honestly, when he first called about this job, I hung up on him. He reached out again—through a mutual friend—and explained the project." She raised her arms expansively to encompass the rainforest. "Before you judge me, ask yourself how I could say no to this."

He stepped before her and placed a finger under her chin, again nudging her to meet his gaze. "Fiona, I would never judge you. You could be sharing Reynolds's bed and I wouldn't judge. All I want is for you to be happy."

Truth was, he wouldn't judge, but he'd definitely ache.

"I'm not sharing his bed."

"He wants you to, though."

She nodded. "I'm sure that's part of it, but also, it's important you understand that Ruby Island and this project are deeply special to him. He's not doing this *for me*. If that were the case, I wouldn't be here. During field school, he talked about Ruby Island a lot. It was the only place he was happy when he was growing up. His family was extremely

137

wealthy, and his parents had rules and expectations but no . . . affection for him. He was the heir and next CEO to them.

"He spent his summers on Ruby Island—with and without his parents present—and he loved hiking to the fort and up the volcano. Along the way, he'd find artifacts—both historic and prehistoric—and became fascinated with the subject. He'd wanted to go into archaeology, but that was never gonna be allowed, not if he wanted to remain in the family. And he didn't necessarily care about the family, but he didn't want to give up Ruby Island. So he followed the path laid out for him, and in one summer of rebellion attended archaeological field school in Washington State.

"When he offered me this job, he reminded me of all this. What Ruby Island means to him and all the stories we'd shared fifteen years ago. He could lose the island. It's valuable to Dominica, and they have no obligation to renew the fifty-year lease. So he's pulling out all the stops to show them he's a good tenant. He tried to hire Dr. Finch for the work, but he declined. So he turned to me. I pointed him toward Sadie and Chad, whose expertise is more in line, but they can't do everything, so I signed on."

She frowned and dropped her gaze to her feet. "The navy was eager to grant me leave, for a few reasons, not the least of which is things have been awkward on the job since Chiksook."

Her words shouldn't have surprised him. He should have expected fallout with the navy given the circumstances, but he didn't really consider it. And he'd forbidden Dylan from talking about Fiona.

He'd basically abandoned her when she was going through a difficult time, and he was the one person who would have understood. Hell, it was his fault she'd been in that situation at all. It was a wonder she wanted to be friends with him, considering how lousy he was at it.

"You didn't have to justify taking the job with Reynolds to me. As I said, I'm not judging you."

"But I wanted you to know that there is more to Jude than the arrogant businessman. I'm trying to remember that myself, to reconcile the man he was at field school, the man he was four years ago, and who he is today." She stepped back, putting a few feet of distance between them. "Tonight, he and I are having dinner together on his yacht. A sunset cruise. That's why I need to be back before six o'clock." She crossed her arms, telegraphing her defensiveness. "It's not a date, if that's what you're thinking."

It was absolutely a date, but he wouldn't be the one to break that news to her. She'd figure it out when they were anchored offshore, and Reynolds found an excuse to get her into his cabin.

But then, maybe she wanted that but didn't want to admit it to Dean. She was very defensive when it came to Jude Reynolds.

"Fiona, if you like him, you should go for it. Don't . . . not give him a chance because of me." *Because we aren't going to happen.*

Pain flared in her eyes, and she took another step back. After a pause, she cleared her throat and said, "Maybe I will," then continued down the path.

FOURTEEN

It was ridiculous to fuss over what she would wear to dinner with Jude, but Fiona did it anyway. Part of her did it because she wanted to feel desirable after the stinging rejection from Dean. He'd more than made it clear he was physically attracted to her, and another part of her wanted him to see what he was missing. And the last but not to be ignored part of her ego wondered if he was right and she had written Jude off because of her feelings for Dean. Maybe she was hiding behind her rules about bosses because she was hung up on someone she'd never get to have?

Regardless, she wanted to look hot tonight. She wanted Dean to regret his words. Her ego had taken a blow, and she needed a bandage to staunch the wound.

She tried on outfit after outfit, and finally settled on a coral-colored tight halter top with a built-in bra. The deep V neckline showed off her cleavage without being over-the-top. Her back and shoulders remained bare, as the garment tied in a bow behind her neck. The color of the shirt would bring out the orange lights in her hair, which she decided to wear up in a messy bun. She paired the top with pale-blue capri pants that hugged her hips and would wear girlie beaded flip-flop sandals for the walk from house to dock.

She stared at her toes and wondered if Sadie had any nail polish she could use. When was the last time she'd polished her nails?

Tonight she wanted to feel pretty and feminine and that required polish. And lipstick. She would even—gasp—put on eye makeup. And this wasn't even a black-tie party.

Screw Dean Slater and his most recent rejection. She was a desirable woman with a lot to offer.

She texted Sadie, and minutes later her friend was at her door with a makeup bag and a bottle of wine. "So you've got a date with the boss tonight?" she asked as she pushed her way into Fiona's room.

"It's not a date."

"Riiight."

Fiona sighed. "Fine. It might be a date."

Sadie scanned her from head to toe. "I approve. Sexy but casual. He'll be so distracted, the boat will run aground."

Fiona hesitated. The goal was to make Dean regret his words, not to entice Jude. "Maybe I should change."

"Nonsense. You look good."

"But Jude will get the wrong idea."

Sadie cocked her head. "It's okay for you to dress for you, you know. If Jude thinks you did it for him, set him straight. Or flirt with him and figure out if you like him after all. He's your boss, sure, but he's not your long-term employer. He doesn't hold any real power over you. From the way his eyes follow you, I'd say the power is yours to wield."

Sadie was right. Fiona *could* quit this job tomorrow and suffer no repercussions. She didn't for a moment believe Jude would sue her for breach of contract. But if he tried, she would fight it, and Sadie would back her.

"You deserve some fun," Sadie added, "and it's a good opportunity for you and Jude to connect without Kosmo around. Don't overthink it." She pushed the bottle into Fiona's hands. "Open this and pour two glasses. Meet me in the bathroom and I'll do your makeup. I'm going to make your skin glow and eyes pop."

Fiona headed to the wet bar to grab the corkscrew and wineglasses. Her chest bloomed as her heart lifted. This was exactly what she needed tonight. "Have I mentioned lately how much I love you, Sadie?"

"You haven't. But don't worry. I know."

———

He should be in his suite, going over the photos he took today, checking the feeds for the game cameras . . . basically doing anything to take his mind off how much he'd screwed up today in practically baiting Fiona to go for it with the billionaire.

But no. Dean wasn't doing those things. Instead, he was on the beach for cocktail hour, wondering when Fiona and Boss Man would stroll by on the way to their romantic sunset dinner cruise.

What had he been thinking? The day had been perfect up to that point, and he could have said nothing, or, better yet, pulled her into his arms and kissed her like he wanted to do every time he was within twenty feet of her. Send her off on her date with his taste on her lips.

But no, he had to go and tell her to go for it.

He'd seen the pain that flashed across her face. Pain he'd caused a person who mattered more to him than he had words for.

But that wasn't the worst of it. His real problem was, he didn't want to care this much. Didn't want to feel this much. His life had been ideal last July before Dylan disappeared. He'd been happy in his emotional isolation.

He had a career he loved, a social life he enjoyed, and women in his bed when he wanted. Life had been goddamn *perfection*.

Now he looked back, and all he saw was the loneliness that had lurked beneath the surface. After his brother—his closest friend— moved to Seattle, life in LA had become hollow. Happiness was found only when he was on assignment, traveling the world with a camera in his hands.

His life in LA, no matter how much he'd thought it was great, had been empty. The joy he took in socializing with famous friends had been thin, a veneer that fooled even himself until he'd had a life-changing glimpse of something more.

In the first weeks—months, really—after Chiksook, he'd told himself he'd return to and enjoy his pre-Chiksook lifestyle as much as before, once Dylan recovered. It was fear for his brother that kept his heart heavy and muted his pleasure in the day-to-day. Once he was able to travel again, he'd feel the thrum of excitement that coursed through him when he was on assignment.

On the Big Island, he'd had both his brother—who was healthy again—and travel, and it hadn't been enough. He'd found himself in a bar one night, confessing to missing Fiona and seeing—or at least admitting—for the first time how incomplete his life had been over the last several years.

He'd had a taste of emotional connection. Worse, that taste had *reminded* him of the emotional connection he'd once shared with Violet, a feeling he'd managed to bury for ten years. Buried was good. Buried meant he couldn't miss the feeling. But now that he remembered, he feared he'd never experience true joy again without it. The dull ache that had settled in over the last nine months might eventually consume him.

And today he'd told the one woman who eased that ache that she should go for the accomplished, highly intelligent billionaire who was obviously in love with her. Jude Reynolds could give her everything she'd ever dreamed of—including a sweet Caribbean island with archaeological sites she could study to her heart's content.

Dean was a complete and utter dipshit.

And yet . . . he hadn't been wrong. He couldn't give her the relationship she deserved, but there was a chance Jude Reynolds could. Just as he'd once thought Dylan might be the man for her.

Footsteps on the path caught his attention, and he turned to see an absolute vision descending the outer stairs from the upper terrace.

Fiona and Sadie were side by side, leaning toward each other in deep conversation.

Mesmerized, he stepped back from the cobblestone path to let them pass. He got a whiff of soap and shampoo as Fiona breezed by. She and her friend made a beeline for the outdoor wet bar that was staffed by a bartender at the end of every day.

His gaze followed her as she strode with a relaxed, sexy gait, her hips swaying as the breeze caught the loose hem of her halter top. The top was a masterpiece of fashion—the deep V of the front showed off her ample, soft cleavage, and the back . . . *hot damn*, her lightly freckled skin was bare from the tie at her nape to the small of her back, except for a ribbon of fabric that secured the top tight midway down her back.

He'd appreciate her fashion choice even more if not for the fact that she'd donned it for Jude Reynolds's benefit. The capri pants hugged her ass, and even her shoes—low-heeled, girlie sandals—were utterly feminine. Her toenails were painted a cheerful pink.

He'd never imagined Fiona like this. Not even last night, when he'd seen her in a couture gown at a black-tie affair.

During their time together on Chiksook, he'd seen her stripped down to a sports bra and underwear and knew she had lush curves that he ached to explore, but his brain had never considered how she would look in pretty, feminine clothes. With makeup, even. After all, she'd been hot in long underwear, hiking boots, and a polyfill coat, so there had been no need for him to imagine her like this in his far-too-frequent fantasies.

But now that he got to enjoy the view . . . well, it would be harder to bury this attraction that could only interfere with the friendship she wanted.

He circled back to the truth of it. He might regret telling her to go for it with Jude, but he hadn't been wrong to do so.

Jude could give her everything she wanted—and everything she deserved.

It wasn't that Dean couldn't compete financially—he might not be anywhere close to being a billionaire, but he had more than enough money to live comfortably for the rest of his life—but unlike Reynolds, Dean couldn't give Fiona anything more than material goods.

So he was left devouring her with his eyes as she ordered a drink from the young Dominican bartender on duty.

Unable to help himself, he stepped up beside her and said, "The Caribbean looks good on you."

She gave him a bright but clearly forced smile. "Thank you."

Her smile tightened as she glanced over his shoulder. "Jude! Before we set out, I think you need to talk to Sadie about what she and Chad found today when they used the side-scan sonar near the fort."

Reynolds joined them at the bar and ordered his own drink, then turned to Fiona. "Of course. Let's sit on the terrace and talk." He turned to Sadie. "Will Chad be joining us?"

She tilted her head to *Tempus Machina*, anchored in the bay. "He's still on the boat, crunching data."

Drinks mixed, they all moved to the terrace. Dean and Nico joined them as well. They all had a vested interest in knowing if Sadie and Chad had found parts of the helicopter in the sea. Dean glanced around, looking for Philip, and realized he hadn't seen the pilot since . . . yesterday? The day before?

As they sat at the circular table, everyone's least favorite RAM Freight resident executive VP stepped onto the terrace. His mouth pinched in the usual tight line.

Kosmo Andreas never failed to make it clear he was not a fan of the project to document the historic and ecological resources of Ruby Island. The only thing he disliked more was the documentary.

Curious as to why the man would join the discussion, Dean stood and waved to offer his seat. He raised his camera in excuse for removing himself from the inner circle. He would take photos and stay close and listen. He didn't need a seat at the table, and he'd learned long ago that assuming the photographer's mantle often meant people were conscious of the camera but not so much the person operating it. It was convenient at times.

Sadie pulled out an iPad and placed it in front of Reynolds. "We used the multibeam sub-bottom profiler to map the seafloor all around the peninsula where the fort is situated. We didn't find anything that looked like helicopter debris—which we'll confirm tomorrow when we dive in the area—but we did find something odd. It's a spoil pile, which in itself might not be odd—after all, fort construction happened off and on for two decades, and soil and rocks were removed during each remodel—but slow removal of dirt and bedrock would result in a well-sifted and well-sorted spoil pile, and given that it's been over three hundred and fifty years since construction, the pile should be *very* well sorted. What we found today has the stratigraphy of hydraulic dredging."

"So you think there was dredging in or around the fort recently?" Jude asked.

"From the looks of it, my guess is anytime post–World War II."

"Why would someone dredge near the fort?" Nico asked.

Sadie looked to Fiona, who, Dean had gathered, was in charge of researching everything there was to know about Fort Domingo.

Fiona shrugged. "Beats me. I haven't found any reference to attempts to restore or do anything with the fort in the last century."

"Tomorrow," Sadie said, "we'll scuba dive around the dredge piles and look for datable materials that might give context to the deposition." She looked up, her gaze meeting Fiona's across the table. "We need all eyes underwater, so, Fiona, I want you to dive with us. We can film a bunch of shots for the documentary while we're at it."

Nico chimed in. "Dean and I were going to get some rainforest footage in the morning."

"Skip that," Jude said. "You can film in the forest another day. I want you and Slater in the water as well. I'll suit up too. I'm certified."

146

Was this Reynolds's ultimate goal? To star in his own documentary? Did he think that would impress Fiona?

Would it?

"Jude," Kosmo said, "our insurance doesn't cover—"

"I don't really care. I'm diving with the team tomorrow."

———

Jude's seventy-five-foot yacht, *Rum Runner*, was an interesting combination of luxury boat and work vessel. The luxury part was obvious in the sleek design with large upper deck that included an extended seating/cocktail area lined with weatherproof couches behind the exterior helm. Below the upper deck was another outdoor seating area, open on three sides with the deck above acting as a partial roof overhang. Tinted glass doors on the lower deck led to the interior, which Fiona had yet to see.

A big metal cage that housed what looked like a torpedo hung over the stern, extending out from the upper deck. This was the jarring note that didn't fit with the yacht's otherwise luxury design. If she remembered correctly, there had been no torpedo cage this morning when she'd looked down on the yacht from the breakfast terrace as the vessels belonging to party guests departed.

She wanted to ask about the item in the cage—which, she presumed, was the unmanned underwater vehicle—a.k.a. UUV, a.k.a. the submarine drone he'd been developing for several years—but decided to wait. It was likely he planned a demonstration of some sort, and frankly, she was relieved. She'd harbored suspicions that he just wanted to take her out on the boat to romance her, but if he wanted to do a test drive of his invention, well, that changed things.

She focused, instead, on the boat name painted on the stern as they passed the rear of the vessel. "Your family's shipping business began with rum running during Prohibition, didn't it?"

"Correct. It's not exactly an original boat name, but fitting in this instance, I think."

She smiled. To think Jude owed all his wealth and success to a business that had started a hundred years ago in response to the banning of alcohol.

"Your great-grandfather ran rum from the Bahamas to Florida?"

"That's where it started. Two years into Prohibition, he moved the operation to Cuba and added more routes up the East Coast of the United States, smuggling British whiskey and other European goods in addition to Cuban rum. They hid the contraband among legitimate goods, and Reynolds American Marine Freight was born."

"He conveniently left 'Cuba' out of the name."

"He was no dummy, my great-grandfather."

Fiona boarded the vessel, stepping on the rear platform, and Jude followed behind.

"When Prohibition ended," Jude continued, "he focused on the legitimate end of the shipping business. At that point, he'd built up a sizable fleet, and it didn't take much restructuring to make it profitable without the need to smuggle."

"And RAM Freight has been clean ever since, I presume."

"As a whistle. Each generation has done their part to grow the business to the point where we now employ over thirty thousand people worldwide." He waved to the torpedo-looking device hanging above their heads. "And that there is my innovation to further expand our profit margins. But that show-and-tell will happen later. Right now, head to the upper deck and pour yourself a glass of wine. I'll be up after I untie the bowline."

She glanced around, realizing there was no staff to help with the lines. "You're captaining the boat? No crew?"

He narrowed his eyes. "I'm CEO of a major shipping company and grew up on boats big and small my entire life. I also have a graduate degree in mechanical engineering from MIT. Believe it or not, I can captain my own yacht."

She winced, realizing how her question had sounded. "Sorry. I just . . . haven't seen you at the helm before. I can handle the lines if you want to go up and start the engine."

He shook his head. "I have a strange need to show you I can do it all by myself now."

Chagrined, she climbed the steps to the upper deck. There she saw the uncorked bottle of white wine chilling in a bucket, two wineglasses, and a platter of appetizers under a screen dome to protect the food from the many insects that dared to mar the perfection that was Ruby Island. She dropped onto the thickly cushioned seat and poured both glasses, noting the stemless and shatterproof wineglasses had a rubber base to keep them from sliding on the table when the boat rocked. Elegant and functional.

A moment later, she felt the boat drift away from the dock, the bow swinging out to face the open sea, and Jude emerged from the stairs and crossed to the helm, where he started the engine with the touch of a button.

He took the boat out slowly, keeping the wake down in the sheltered bay, but once they cleared the mouth, he dialed up the speed. The engine purred as the sleek hull cut through the water, barely rocking as it sliced through low-breaking waves.

She sipped her wine and leaned back, breathing in the salt air.

Enjoy this moment. Enjoy this moment. Enjoy this moment.

The thought repeated like a mantra, and she wondered when she'd lost the ability to simply relax and have fun. When did she have to start telling herself it was okay to be happy?

She couldn't blame that on Chiksook or unrequited feelings.

No. This tension that always hummed through her stretched much further back.

She was certain it predated the moment when her mother could no longer remember any of her children's names.

Was it when Regan died? Or when Aidan turned on her?

Or was it when her father's line snapped, and he plunged over a hundred feet to his death?

It could be any of those, but it was Regan's death that had tainted her feelings toward her profession and the loss of Aidan that had shattered her trust in people she loved. She'd built up barriers after that, probably because she expected people to disappoint her.

Moments like this, with old friends, were often fraught with doubt and fear. She needed to let that go and just enjoy. It was a beautiful night in a beautiful place, and she was with a man who cared about her as a friend.

She needed to sink in and enjoy that. Forget Dean. Forget all her nagging doubts.

The luxurious estate on the northwestern edge of Ruby Island was but a dot on the shoreline when Jude dropped anchor and cut the engine. The anchor bit, and the drifting boat halted, then settled in, bobbing on the turquoise sea. Dominica was just visible in the far distance off the bow. Port of *Rum Runner* sat Ruby Island. To starboard was the pinkening sky of the lowering sun.

Jude's mouth curved in a smile as he dropped down in the seat next to her and lifted his wineglass. "I asked Slater to take some pictures of the boat as the sun sets behind us. Should be spectacular images."

She frowned. "He's not an event photographer, you know." Had he seriously asked Dean to spy on them with a zoom lens as they enjoyed a romantic sunset dinner?

"What's the problem? He's got a camera, and he was on the beach. It'll be a great shot."

"The problem is it was a dick move." So much for enjoying the moment.

"Why? What's the deal with you and Slater?"

She took a deep breath. "Funny. Dean asked me the same question about you earlier today."

Jude shrugged, then lifted the dome from the appetizer platter and set it aside. "What did you tell him?"

"The truth."

"And what is that?"

"Stop with the games, Jude. You said this wasn't a date, yet you're doing everything you can to make it look like one and then specifically instructed Dean to watch with his zoom lens and take pictures."

"Are you in love with him?"

She rose from the seat. "My feelings for Dean or anyone else are nobody's business but mine." She circled the table. She wanted to pace, but the area was too small. What had she gotten herself into?

"Fi, it's an honest question between friends. I care about you. And I worry about you. And I don't see him behaving as though he shares your feelings."

She took a deep breath. He wasn't wrong, *dammit*.

"Please," Jude continued. "Give me twenty minutes. I mean, there's an amazing dinner baking in the galley. You don't want to miss it. I *do* want to be friends. I screwed up, but only because I'm worried about you getting hurt. Slater seems like a good guy. I'm not knocking him."

He sighed. "Truth is, I respect the hell out of him. I've followed his work for years. Having him on this project . . . it's a kind of . . . validation for me. I want you to understand, my appreciation for his work, more than anything, is why I asked *National Geographic* if he was available."

She looked at him and remembered the young man who was so desperate for his parents to value the things he valued, and his words rang true.

She sighed and sat down again, this time across from him. "Fine. But I won't be caught in a pissing contest between you two. You both are friends. Nothing more."

A shadow crossed over his face, telling her he wasn't happy with being placed firmly in the friend zone. But that was where he would stay.

Dean had said to go for it if she were genuinely attracted to Jude, and the thing was . . . she was in pretty much the most romantic setting possible with the guy, and not a single romantic feeling stirred in her heart.

She just wasn't into him. As simple as that.

She grabbed a cracker and smeared goat cheese on top, then added a dollop of fig jam. With the first taste, she let out a low hum of pleasure. "Really, I think the most amazing thing about this project has been the food. I'm now spoiled for all other fieldwork."

Jude let out a soft laugh. "Well, that was one of my goals. I mean, this doesn't have to end with Ruby Island, Fi."

"But it does. I have a job I'm going back to in"—she did the math in her head—"a little more than five weeks."

"But you don't have to. You can stay on my payroll. Work for me. I can give you full bennies, everything you need. And you won't have to worry about budgets or government bureaucrats or anything like that again."

"Exactly what would you be paying me for? I'm not in the market for a sugar daddy."

"Nothing like that. You can be the host of my archaeology adventure travel series. Just think, Fiona, a whole show—ten episodes a year—where you get to travel the world, explore history and archaeology, educate people, and also have gourmet meals three times a day."

Fiona let out a hoarse laugh. "Three gourmet meals a day is too much. It wouldn't be special." She waved her arm around, indicating the perfect evening, perfect weather, perfect water, perfect island, and perfect food. "*All* of this is too much for every day. It's amazing for an escape—eight weeks in paradise is more than most people get in a lifetime—and I'm thankful for that. But this . . . it isn't my dream. I don't want to host your show. Find someone who does want it. They'll appreciate it more."

She faced the descending sun. They were at least fifteen minutes from sunset, and the low clouds were taking on ever more orange and pink hues. It was stunning.

"Fine, we'll shelve that discussion for now." He plucked a loaded slice of bruschetta from the tray, then gestured with the bread in his hand toward the cage hanging from the back of the vessel. "Tonight, I'm giving you a demonstration of the unmanned underwater vehicle I've designed. Because it, too, has archaeological implications. A reason you might want to sign on with RAM Freight."

She gave him a skeptical look. He'd never once suggested RAM Freight might have a job for her, and she had a hard time believing Kosmo would be on board with such a hire. As executive VP, Kosmo appeared to be much more involved with the day-to-day operations than Jude. He was a step below the CEO and, like an executive officer in the military, was the interface between commander and troops.

Or something. She really couldn't be sure, but the one thing she did know was Kosmo had been Jude's father's right hand, and likely knew the business far better than the current CEO. And Kosmo definitely seemed bitter about that.

"Isn't your UUV technology supposed to be super top secret?" The question brought her back to her conversation in the admiral's office. Was *this* what they'd been after when they asked her to report any unusual people or happenings on the island?

She would not play a role in industrial espionage. Not even for her government. *Especially* not for her government. Sure, the admiral's request had been confirmed, but unless there was something blatantly illegal about Jude's technical development, she would keep mum.

"The battery technology and programming are proprietary, because those are the heart of what makes this UUV so efficient. This baby can go over twelve hundred nautical miles—the distance from here to Miami—without a recharge. So it's proprietary, but not top secret. If you want, I can have you sign an NDA, but I have a feeling you won't understand the coding anyway." He popped the last bite of bruschetta in his mouth.

She laughed. "Hardly."

Part of her wanted to sign an NDA, though. That would take care of any decisions to be made on what to share with the admiral and his FBI and NSA cronies.

After Jude swallowed, he reached for a laptop tucked away in a cubbyhole built into the table. "It's best if I show you it now, before the sun sets. After dark, there won't be much to see. At least, not on the surface; we'll see everything below water just fine."

He booted up the laptop, which ran both face and fingerprint recognition before giving access to the home screen.

As expected, when he opened his UUV program, all she saw was gibberish lines of code on a dark screen. It was like the DOS interface she'd had to use for some programs in her teen years.

"Yep. Your technology is safe from me."

He laughed. With a few keystrokes, another window opened, this one showing a live video feed—the camera embedded in the UUV. The cage turned, directing the camera at the upper deck of the boat where she and Jude looked at the computer, and she was greeted by her own profile as she leaned toward the screen.

"Wow, that's a high-quality image for something that's going to be underwater." It reminded her of Dean's game cameras, which weren't game cameras at all but something far more technical.

"Nothing but the best for my baby. And it's only the start. It's equipped with the best bathymetric lidar available. This little sub will be able to scout ahead of RAM Freight ships and track water current, temperature, weather—all the things that affect fuel efficiency. Once my ships are cruising in tandem with drone scouts, we should be able to decrease fuel costs by five percent. That might not sound like much, but fuel is our highest operating expense. It will save us millions—a whole lot of millions—per year."

She laughed at his less-than-technical speech. It was so not Jude to be imprecise.

"But even more exciting, these babies can dive down and map the ocean floor in areas where it's not super deep. I figure, they're going to be out there anyway, may as well gather as much scientific data as we can in the process, right?"

"Ohh. I like that idea," she said, meaning it.

He flashed a satisfied smile. "My dad didn't want me to do archaeology at all. He was so mad when he discovered I'd sneaked off to field school that summer. Now he's gone, and I've found a way to run RAM Freight *and* pursue my real dream. Mapping the ocean floor will be a benefit for our shipping routes and science. We can make our data available to NOAA and USGS. We're on the cutting edge of what this technology can do, and I'm going to push it to the next level, with a UUV that has the most efficient battery ever designed, so the cost of powering it will have minimal impact on the environment."

This was the man she'd so enjoyed knowing during field school. All the other stuff was stripped away; he was the eager scientist. Genuine.

And she was *so* glad he'd found a way to show this side to her.

She loved everything about his project. Cutting fuel consumption might be better for RAM Freight's bottom line, but it was also better for the environment and therefore everyone. It was pure win-win. And the idea they could also casually map the seafloor—well, that was an incalculable benefit to science. Only a tiny fraction of the ocean floor had been mapped, and each new study that charted more led to a deeper understanding of the earth and the delicate balance of all her ecosystems. "This is really amazing, Jude."

"Want to see it in action?"

"Absolutely."

"Prepare to be impressed."

She placed her fingers to her lips to hide her smile. He was the second man to say that to her today.

Jude crossed to the stern of the upper deck, where the rigging was attached to the boat and the cage dangled in the air. He hit a button, and the arm holding the cage flexed, swinging out over the water.

Once it was fully extended, he hit another button, and the metal cables unreeled, gently lowering the cage into the water.

"When I say so, hit the red button on the touch screen," Jude instructed.

"You sure?"

"Positive."

It was a simple request, but it somehow scared the heck out of her. Was it possible to hit a button wrong? This prototype had to have cost hundreds of thousands of dollars to build. Possibly millions?

On the laptop screen, Fiona followed the progress, watching the video feed as the camera dipped below water. The bars of the cage rose until there was nothing to see but open sea.

"Release the kraken!" Jude said with a laugh.

She couldn't help but laugh too, and, with shaking fingers, pressed the red dot on the screen.

The UUV launched, gliding silently from the cage as it zoomed out to chase the setting sun.

Jude returned to her side, and his fingers flew across the keyboard. Two more windows opened. One showed a radar screen; another was fed sonar data. "Not bringing lidar online tonight. It'd slow the demo as it collects massive data."

"You've impressed me enough as is."

"Good." He pointed to the windows on the laptop screen. "Ordinarily, each element would be displayed on its own monitor."

He hit another button. "This is what it sounds like underwater."

There was a faint sloshing of water through a propeller, but that was it.

"It's almost silent," she said with awe.

"I designed it to have minimal impact on sea life. I mean, it has sonar, and I've read the studies on the effects of sonar on marine mammals and navigation, but we're doing everything we can to minimize the frequency and impact. It's a mixed bag because anything we do to reduce fuel costs is better for everyone, but we don't want to do it at the expense of wildlife. I'm trying to make a difference at RAM Freight now that I'm CEO. Kosmo and others aren't thrilled, but for now, I'm in charge."

"If you don't get along with him, why is Kosmo here? Why not have some other executive VP assist you on Ruby Island?" She remembered Paige's comment about how Kosmo was irritating Jude with his continued presence.

"Kosmo's been with the company for a long time. Since before you and I met. He was my father's right-hand man for the last decade. He knows the players better than I do. I need him for the transition. I won't earn the trust of the board until after the UUV is fully integrated and saving us *literal* boatloads of money. Once that happens, if Kosmo is still a problem, I'll have him removed."

A timer beeped, and he rose from the seat. "That's dinner. My chef put it in the oven three hours ago."

"Three hours? What is it?"

"A traditional French cassoulet."

A frisson ran through her. "Cassoulet? But that's . . ."

"The entrée you ordered at Canlis. Yes." He held her gaze. "I was an ass that night. I ruined your dinner. I've been waiting for four years to make that up to you."

Something stirred in her chest. For the first time, she believed he really wasn't the guy she'd had dinner with at Canlis. That guy wouldn't have remembered what she ordered.

She followed him down the staircase to the lower deck. She stared out over the water, toward the setting sun, where the UUV was silently swimming along, while he turned to enter the main cabin through the tinted sliding glass door.

A loud, screeching alarm split the air, and she turned to see Jude at the door with his hand on the latch.

She covered her ears to protect against the piercing wail. "What is that?" she yelled, but the moment the words were out of her mouth, she realized the dark glass wasn't only due to the tint. The interior was filled with black smoke. There was just enough light seeping from the galley below to see a swirling dark plume.

"Jude! Don't—"

He slid open the door, and the acrid scent of burning plastic and electronics billowed out with the dark smoke. Behind the plume, she caught a flash of orange flame.

He slammed the slider shut, but it bounced back open. "Holy fuck! Jump overboard!"

As he said the words, he ran for the railing. Fiona was already halfway there. She grabbed the rail and swung her legs over like it was a vault, plunging into the turquoise sea.

The eighty-degree water was cool to the skin, but not jarringly so as she sprinted away from the boat, determined to put as much distance as she could between herself and the yacht. Her sandals slipped from her feet as she swam freestyle for Ruby Island, which was too far away for her to make it without a float of some kind. But she'd try.

She must've gone fifty meters when she slowed up to search for Jude. One of them might need to return to the boat to get life vests.

Gasping for breath, she paused, treading water as she got her bearings. Jude had stopped ten meters behind her. Beyond him, black smoke poured from the open sliding glass door. The alarm wailed, the shriek carrying across the water. Through the galley windows, she could see a glimmer of orange flame at the heart of the dark smoke.

As she watched, treading water and wanting to cover her ears against the siren, the vessel split apart, exploding with a brilliant flash of orange and black, accompanied by a deafening roar.

FIFTEEN

Dean wasn't spying. No. He'd been told to take photos by the big prick himself. It was the perfect shot with the boat against the backdrop of the setting sun. With his zoom lens, he could just make out Fiona's dark, perfect silhouette on the lower deck as she looked out over the sea.

He snapped away until the piercing wail of an alarm traveled across the water.

What the hell?

A moment later, Fiona vaulted the railing.

Dean dropped his camera on the dock and ran for the Zodiac tied only twenty feet away. He undid the bowline, then jumped in. One hard pull on the cord and the engine purred to life. He released the stern line and set out.

As he zoomed toward the yacht at maximum speed, the vessel exploded with a roar that would be heard for miles.

He searched for Fiona in the bobbing waves but didn't see her. Had she cleared the blast zone? Had the resulting wave upended her?

His heart went cold. No.

No.

No.

She must've cleared the blast zone. There was no other option.

She'd told him she wasn't a fast swimmer, but she was proficient. Strong. She scuba dived and was comfortable in water.

The boat rocked as the wave from the blast threatened to toss him. He gripped the handhold and steered over the crest, dropping into the swell.

And there she was, her pale-peach skin and coral top a splash of color in the darkening sea as night fell in the Caribbean.

He turned the boat in her direction, slowing when he got close. The boat bobbed in the waves as the sea tried to right itself after the blast.

Fiona swam toward him. "Dean! Thank God!"

She grabbed at the inflated hull. He reached down and caught her arm, pulling her into the boat. He fell backward, and her wet body slid over his, pressing him to the bottom of the boat.

He wrapped his arms around her and held her to him, hearing her panting breaths, feeling her trembling limbs.

His Fiona. She was okay. Alive.

He cupped her face and looked into her eyes. He lifted his head to press his mouth to hers, but she pulled back. "We need to find Jude."

———

Fiona leaned against Jude as Dean steered the boat toward the group of people gathered on the dock. Jude appeared unhurt, but dazed. Like he couldn't quite wrap his brain around the magnitude of what had just happened. Which was totally reasonable to Fiona's jumbled brain. She couldn't grasp it either.

The boat was . . . gone. Utterly decimated. Had they been farther out to sea—out of sight of the island—she'd likely still be treading water and her strength would give out and she'd drown before she had any chance of rescue.

And that was only if she'd managed to leap from the vessel before the explosion in that alternate reality.

She'd come close to dying in several different ways. Smoke inhalation. Explosion. Drowning. Too many options.

Had the explosion been an accident? Or had it been an attempt on Jude's life?

A second attempt, if the helicopter crash had also been deliberate.

All of a sudden, Jude sat bolt upright. "Fuck. The UUV!"

Fiona jolted. "Can you . . . get it back?"

He ran a hand over his face. "I . . . I . . . don't think so. It's out of range of the computers on the island. The prototype is short-range. The computer is supposed to send a signal to call it back when it nears the limit. I never factored in that the computer and backup systems might all blow up while it was in motion."

"Is there any chance it would just . . . stop?"

"I don't know. Sadie and Chad can take *Tempus* out tomorrow and search the wreckage for it."

They reached the dock, and Chad took the bowline while Kosmo took the stern.

Fiona climbed from the boat first, with Jude second and Dean last. Jude faced Kosmo. "I want Walker to take a boat out with a crew and get GPS on the debris on the surface and collect what they can."

"The sun has set. It's getting darker by the minute."

"Then they'd better hurry." He turned and stalked, dripping wet, up the dock without a word to any of the employees who'd gathered to help in the wake of the explosion. He didn't bother to look up or back as he disappeared into his mansion.

Fiona started after him but then stopped short. She didn't have to follow him. It wasn't her job to tend to his emotional needs.

She'd almost died too, and he hadn't even said so much as a thank-you to Dean for pulling him out of the water. He was a wreck, like her, but that didn't mean she had to take care of him instead of tending to herself.

She'd just undergone a terrifying experience. Maybe she should pause and nurse her own wounds instead of chasing after her boss? Or friend. Once again, she wasn't sure. After all, he hadn't shown an ounce of concern for her.

Strong arms surrounded her, and she leaned back to feel Dean's firm chest against her shoulder blades. She closed her eyes as trembling overtook her. She'd been swamped by water as the explosion sounded, and she wasn't sure if her hearing was muted because of water in her ears or the pulse of the blast. The explosion replayed in her mind, and she let out a low cry. Or maybe it was a whimper.

She hated being weak and berated herself for letting others see it.

All at once, Dean scooped her up. With one arm behind her back and the other beneath her knees, he carried her up the cobblestone path.

He didn't enter the house through the front door. Instead, he went to the outer stairs that led to the second-floor balcony.

"I can walk."

"Shhh," he said as he ascended the stairs.

Fiona wasn't petite like Sadie. She was tall and solidly built. Dean shouldn't even attempt to carry her up a flight of stairs. But somehow, he succeeded. He took her straight to the door to her suite, pressed down on the latch with her still in his arms, then carried her inside, making a beeline for the bed.

"I'm soaking wet."

He set her on her feet. "I don't care. Strip if you want. You're shaking and need to get warm."

She noticed the goose bumps on her arms and wondered if she was going into shock. It wasn't cold here in the least. The water hadn't even been that cold.

She peeled off her pants as he closed the door, then returned to pull back the duvet. She decided to keep her top and underwear on. The shirt was synthetic fabric that would dry quickly.

"Get under and scoot over."

She complied, and he climbed in behind her, pulling her body to his, spooning her and wrapping her in his warmth.

They'd slept like this several times on Chiksook, and it felt wonderful to be wrapped in his arms again. Just what she needed. She closed her eyes and sank into his warmth. The feel of his body pressed to hers. The smell of him mixed with the seawater that soaked her shirt and hair. She shivered for a long time until the heat finally won out and the shaking stopped. Not long after that, she drifted into a deep, dreamless sleep.

———

Dean jolted awake sometime in the middle of the night to find his body still pressed tight to Fiona's. Her breathing was slow and steady, the soft cadence of a deep sleep.

She would be okay. Was okay. She had to be. He didn't know what he would do if something happened to her.

It was a chilling thought. He'd avoided her for nine months because he couldn't risk caring, and now here he was facing the truth: harm to Fiona would hurt whether he was with her or not. He could be thousands of miles away in Indonesia, and he would still lose it if he got word she wasn't well.

He cared. He needed.

Far too much.

The explosion tonight had triggered a fear far greater than even the helicopter crash.

But then, within hours of the crash, he'd been considering the adrenaline high.

There was no high to be found in the nightmare of watching Fiona flee a burning boat.

His arm had gone numb from the weight of her shoulder pressing on it. Another reminder of Chiksook, and how they'd found ways to sleep cuddled up on hard ground.

And how much he'd enjoyed it, because he was with her.

He debated moving his arm. Unlike Chiksook, they weren't confined to one sleeping bag. In fact, he could remove his pants and crawl back in beside her in his underwear. Might as well get comfortable.

The one thing he wouldn't do was leave her and sleep in another bed. If she woke up with a nightmare, or just plain disoriented, he would be here for her.

He eased from her side, and she mumbled something in her sleep.

"Shhh," he said softly.

"Please don't go," she said, her voice clearer.

"Never. Just getting more comfortable. You want to take off your wet top?"

"S'pose."

He smiled. "I'll grab you a T-shirt. Which drawer?"

"Top left."

He found her an extra-large shirt and grabbed one for himself. It would be more comfortable than the button-down Aloha shirt.

He slipped into the bathroom to use the facilities, then stripped down and donned the shirt.

When he returned to the bed, Fiona was back asleep. He debated what to do but decided to let her be. The halter top was mostly dry anyway.

He crawled into bed beside her again and settled on the right side, not touching her. No need to sleep cuddled up when she wasn't shaking anymore and there was plenty of room. But no sooner was he under the covers than Fiona had turned over and reached for him. He scooted forward and kissed her forehead. "Sleep, Fi. I'm not going anywhere."

He closed his eyes and breathed in the scent of her warm breath and soft skin. It was a heady aroma that sent him back in time.

He'd once vowed never to hold her like this again. And just as he'd wondered then, he questioned how in the world he was going to find the strength to let her go in the morning.

The breeze flowed through the open jalousies, and the morning bird chorus was close to reaching full crescendo when Fiona opened her eyes. Waking up in Dean's arms with a tropical breeze salting the air and birds singing felt like the most natural thing in the world.

His eyes were closed and his breathing soft and even, so she took the opportunity to study him. She itched to run her fingers through his blond hair. To touch the scar on his cheek. To feel the bristly texture of his beard with her fingertips.

After weeks on Hawai'i and nearly a week on Ruby Island, his skin was tanned and his hair blonder than it had been last fall. He was as devastatingly handsome as ever.

Once upon a time, he'd kissed her and promised to possess her. His sexy, dirty whispers had played over and over in her mind for the last nine months.

She scooted close and whispered in his ear. "Have you ever been utterly *possessed*, Dean? Ever been reduced to nothing but nerve endings demanding *more, more, now*?"

A soft smile overtook his features. He'd heard her. He was badly feigning sleep so he didn't have to respond. That was fine with her. She'd planted the elephant in the room. Let him photograph it.

All at once, he sprang into action; grabbing her hips, he flipped her to her back and spread his body over hers. She opened her thighs, and his hips pressed between them even as he took her wrists and pulled them above her head. "What do you think you're doing?"

His heavy morning erection pressed to her center. She wrapped her legs around his hips, locking him in place as best she could.

"Reminding you of a promise you made but didn't keep."

His lips found her neck and trailed along her skin. It was glorious, the feel of his whiskers against her throat, his lips at the sensitive spot below her ear.

"You said you want to be friends," he murmured as his lips brushed over her skin. "We can't do this and remain friends afterward."

Her hands were still held together above her head. She itched to run her fingers through his hair, but also didn't fight against the restraint because she wanted him to keep kissing her, keep rocking his hips so she could enjoy the exquisite torture of his erection against her clit, separated only by panties and boxer briefs.

"I'd like to point out you've remained friends with Paige."

He paused, his lips pressed to her collarbone. He let out a slow breath and said, "That's different. I care about Paige, but not in the same way I care about you."

Her belly tingled with the admission. She tightened her thighs around him, preventing him from escaping should he make the effort. "Well, in that case, we haven't exactly been good at being friends, so if I have a choice between no sex and no friendship or sex and no friendship, I'm going to choose the sex."

"You want to have a fling while we're on Ruby Island? But you don't do field flings, and this time, I'm definitely a colleague."

"Don't throw my rules back at me. You know you're more than a colleague."

He brushed his lips over hers in the lightest of kisses, then released her wrists. He shifted his weight to press against her legs locked around his hips, and she released him. He rolled to his back. With his gaze fixed on the ceiling, he said, "Let's give it a few days before we do anything rash. I want nothing more than to be deep inside you. To give you everything I promised when I talked about possessing you on Chiksook."

"But?"

"But you had a traumatic experience last night. This isn't a time to be making decisions that will have long-term consequences." He swallowed and rolled to his side again, his gaze probing hers. "Because I promise you, if we become lovers, I will end it when we leave Ruby Island. I don't have the capacity for more. I can't do a relationship. My career will always come first. I usually travel nine months out of the year—this year was different because of Dylan, but now that he's back on his feet, I'm already looking at lining up my next assignment. Indonesia, I think.

"I won't dial back on work because . . . it's the only thing that keeps me going. Makes me feel alive. And I won't do long-distance, because I won't do a relationship at all. So take a few days to think carefully about what you're asking. I've already admitted I care about you, Fiona, and that means if we become lovers, it will be short-term and end any shot at the friendship you said you wanted yesterday."

She was about to say she knew all that already and wanted the sex . . . but his earnest tone stopped her. Did she believe deep down that once they became lovers, she'd be able to change his mind?

That was a road to heartbreak.

She'd be gambling their friendship on something that probably wasn't possible. And truly, she'd take a weak, few-days-a-year friendship with him over nothing any day.

Plus, there was Dylan to consider. She and Dylan would remain close. How awkward would it be if they had to continue this game of not talking about Dean because she'd done something foolish like sleeping with him, falling in love with him, and then being devastated because he would never love her in return.

She threw back the covers. "Okay. I'll think about it. Now, I need a shower. I'm still salty from my swim last night. I'll see you at breakfast." She darted for the bathroom and closed the door.

She leaned against it and took several deep breaths. She tried to figure out how she felt. Strangely, she wasn't hurt or sad.

She found a smile on her lips, filling her heart.

Dean Slater wanted her. He cared about her.

And it terrified him.

Maybe, just maybe, that was a good thing.

SIXTEEN

Before she could join the team on the breakfast terrace, Fiona needed to send an email to the admiral. She logged in to the encrypted server and composed the email there. Not even a draft would save on her laptop. Not that she thought anyone would snoop on her computer, but it was important to the admiral, and she'd informed Jude when she took the job that she was required to check a navy email account on a regular basis, so the URL wouldn't be blocked or questioned—Jude's Ruby Island network server was locked tight because his proprietary technology and RAM Freight's entire business network needed to be accessible.

She quickly drafted a message informing Admiral Martinez that Jude's boat had blown up and the prototype UUV had been lost.

This had to be the kind of information the admiral, the FBI agent, and the other man—she assumed he was from the National Security Agency or maybe the Defense Intelligence Agency, because he'd been cagey about his affiliation—had been seeking when they told her to report back on anything "unusual." An exploding boat ranked right up there with crashing helicopters in the unusual department.

Even as she typed, she wondered if she was doing the right thing. The information was important, clearly, but she was also, possibly, acting as a spy. It had felt a lot like espionage when she emailed the admiral with party guest names and attached a photo of the yachts anchored in Cannon Bay that she'd taken from the balcony before the party began.

But was it spying when it was at the behest of the US Navy and basically part of the agreement that had granted her this leave of absence?

Still, she couldn't help but wonder who, exactly, she was working for. The US Navy, certainly. The FBI, confirmed. But the other guy remained a mystery. No one had even hinted at which agency Chris Richards belonged to. She'd tried to google him but, not surprisingly, hadn't found anything that connected to the man she'd met in the admiral's office.

Given what she *did* know, she was certain she wasn't unwittingly spying for an enemy of the US government.

But that left the question . . . who *was* the enemy? RAM Freight?

She couldn't imagine the government of Dominica was involved. The island nation wasn't a player in espionage games.

She'd looked into drug trafficking and knew smuggling cocaine from Venezuela was always a possibility. But that didn't make sense. RAM Freight was a massive shipping company with revenues in the billions. The Reynolds family's rum runner days had ended with Prohibition.

She sent her message and stayed online for a full ten minutes after hitting "Send," to see if the admiral, the FBI agent, or mystery man Richards would respond with follow-up questions. When no reply came, she shut down her computer and put it in the safe in her room, as instructed by the admiral, agent, and mystery man.

She wasn't entirely sure who the safe was supposed to protect her device from, because it wasn't the staff, who most certainly knew the override to unlock it if she forgot her code. But still, she went through the motions because she was at heart a rule follower and always would be.

As she snapped the safe closed, she thought about the explosion, and it crossed her mind again that she could—and probably should—leave the project.

A helicopter crash and a boat explosion were enough to make even the most trusting person question things. But at the same time, it was possible both had been accidents. The chef had put the cassoulet in the oven three hours before, and neither she nor Jude had checked the galley when they'd first boarded.

It could have been an electrical problem that ignited the gas oven—she'd have to ask Jude if the oven on the boat was gas—or something could have happened when the boat left the dock. Perhaps the chef had left something flammable unsecured on the counter or stove top, and the rocking motion of the boat had upended things.

The cynical side of her remained aware that the prototype UUV cage had been loaded onto the back of the yacht at some point that afternoon, and everyone who was part of that process, or anyone who looked at the boat at any point after that time, would have seen it and known Jude intended to do a drone demonstration that evening.

Could the explosion have been part of a plan to steal the drone?

Who had motive for that?

Everyone on the island worked for Jude in one capacity or another—either as staff for the house; maintenance for the grounds, fleet of vessels, or power station; employees of RAM Freight; archaeologists surveying historic and prehistoric resources; and documentarians and a photographer to highlight the environmental and historic preservation work Jude had initiated.

Again, she didn't think anyone in the government of Dominica was looking to get in the espionage game and hijack the drone, which limited the suspects to those on the island.

The more she thought about it, the more questions she had, but she was entirely without answers.

Life wasn't a damn Agatha Christie novel.

She grabbed her pack with her dive gear. Even if she did decide to quit, she wasn't leaving today, so she might as well do her job. Today she'd go scuba diving in the crystal-blue Caribbean and look for answers to the past and present on the seafloor as they'd planned last night, before she almost died in an explosion.

Bonus, she'd get to see Dean in a wet suit. That was bound to be a treat.

———

Just watching Fiona step onto the terrace sent pleasure rippling through Dean. How many times had he seen this woman face a dangerous situation and rise to the challenge of tackling it head-on? And now here she was, twelve hours after she could have blown up or drowned, and she carried a bag with fins and snorkel sticking out as if this were just another workday.

He wouldn't have blamed her if she'd decided to leave Ruby Island on the next boat . . . or opted for a plane, as that was the only mode of transportation that hadn't failed so far. He searched around for wood to knock on, but the table was wrought iron and glass and the patio terrace brick and cobblestone.

She dropped her swim bag next to a chair and headed to the buffet to fill a plate. A minute later, she was back with a slice of quiche, fresh fruit, a cherry danish, a pile of bacon, and a steaming mug of coffee. "I didn't realize how hungry I was until I smelled the food. I missed dinner last night."

Dean pointed to his empty plate—a smattering of crumbs hinted at the quantity he'd eaten already—and said, "Same."

"I'm sorry I made you miss dinner. I just . . . shut down, I guess."

"I'm not sorry. You needed me. Glad I could be there." He smiled. "It's what friends do."

She leaned over and kissed him, her lips brushing the scar he'd received when a bullet triggered a spall that grazed his cheek on Chiksook. He could shift his head just a few inches and make it a real kiss. She wouldn't object.

But he didn't. If he kissed her again—a real kiss—he wouldn't do it in front of an audience.

Instead, he followed up by brushing his lips over her forehead. It would have to do for now.

Sadie stepped out on the veranda, her demeanor lacking the energy and joy she'd brought to the project on previous days.

The explosion had a way of taking the wind out of everyone's sails. Dean suspected she had spent the night wondering if it was time to quit. He sure as hell knew he had.

"So what's the plan for today?" Nico asked as he dropped into the last empty seat at the table.

"Chad will bring the boat to the dock in twenty minutes. We're going to dive on *Rum Runner*'s wreckage—looking for the drone. Are you going to be okay to do that, Fi?"

Fiona leaned back in her chair and drummed her fingers on the table—a nervous gesture and one of her tells, Dean knew. She took a deep breath and said, "I can do it."

He smiled. "Of course you can. Because you're amazing." His words were yet another echo from Chiksook.

Her nostrils flared as she met his gaze. "I'd better get the good LUNA bar."

"Also of course."

Today, he'd be in the water with her. A first for them. He hoped she'd be able to focus on the corals and fish and wonders of the sea, and not on the wreck that could have killed her. But it would be damn hard, considering she'd be diving on that very same wreck.

———

"You know, Fiona, viewers won't complain if you pull the wet suit on over your bathing suit on camera," Nico said with a wink.

"Yeah, that's not going to happen." She gave him a scheming grin. "You know what would set this documentary apart?"

"What?"

"If you objectify the men. Get shots of Dean in his Speedo before he pulls on his wet suit."

"No one wants to see that," Chad said.

"Yes, they do," Dean, Fiona, and Sadie all said in unison.

Fiona busted out laughing that Dean had joined the conversation on the side of objectifying himself. She'd missed his abundant ego.

"You'll do it?" she asked him.

"Why not? I mean, I work hard for this body. It's nice to get some appreciation."

She could almost swear he'd said something like that on Chiksook, when, just like now, she'd been in need of a pick-me-up. She was more than a little scared of diving on the *Rum Runner* wreckage so soon.

She shouldn't have said yes, but then, she didn't really know how to say no.

She glanced around the deck. "Jude's not here. He was supposed to dive with us today." She didn't blame him. She wasn't exactly eager herself. But still, it might be easier if he were here too.

"I'm pretty sure after last night, Kosmo convinced him not to take chances," Nico said.

Chad fired up the engine, and *Tempus Machina* pulled away from the dock. She gripped the rail, her gaze fixed on the water.

Dean stepped up beside her and placed an arm around her waist. She leaned against him, resting her head on his shoulder. No words needed to be said, so they rode in silence as the boat cut across the water.

When they reached the coordinates, Chad cut the engine and dropped anchor.

"If you don't want to do this," Dean whispered, "that's okay."

She took a deep breath and stared at the sea that hid all evidence of what had happened last night.

"No, I need to do it, I think." She turned to Nico. "But I don't want to be interviewed and no footage of me diving here. This is *not* part of the documentary. It has nothing to do with my research into Ruby Island. You can film me when we're diving by the fort."

Nico nodded. "Got it."

"Same for me," Dean said. "I'll keep an eye out for fish to photograph, but this isn't a wildlife dive for me."

"Okay," Nico said. "I won't film anything unless Chad and Sadie are in the water. Agreed?"

Everyone nodded.

They decided Dean and Fiona would dive first, alone. They entered the cool blue water together, and he followed behind as she kicked hard, driving herself down the twenty feet to the seafloor. They didn't have the kind of masks that allowed them to talk, so they communicated with hand signals as she examined bits of debris that were scattered across a large area.

Dean had a camera, which he directed at the seafloor in the clear water. Visibility was excellent, and currents hadn't had a chance to disguise much of the wreckage.

They'd swum a fair distance from *Tempus Machina* when she found *Rum Runner*'s anchor.

Dean photographed both the anchor and a school of fish that swarmed nearby.

They'd reached the limit of the distance they should roam from the boat without any sign of the drone, so they returned to the anchor line and surfaced.

"There's not much we can do here," Sadie said as she reached out to pull Fiona onto the dive platform. "I think we should head to the spoil pile. As you said, this isn't part of the documentary."

Dean took Nico's hand and climbed to the platform. Fiona dried her face with a towel, then said, "I was thinking the same thing. But I'm glad I dived here. It . . . helped to see it."

She felt calmer after diving on the wreckage. She wasn't even sure why, but she did.

Maybe it was because it hadn't killed her. She saw the end result, and she didn't have to wonder if it was truly as bad as it had seemed.

If anything, it was worse.

She imagined Jude had reached out to US authorities, and they would send an investigator. It was a private vessel with no deaths, but they needed an investigation to determine if it was an accident or sabotage. She wondered how long it would take for investigators to arrive.

One thing Fiona felt certain about: Jude wasn't behind it. He'd been shocked and in just as much danger as she was. And he'd lost his prototype.

They pulled anchor and set out for the fort. Thirty minutes later, they were in position.

Sadie gave a brief interview, sitting on the dive platform with the fort high on the hill behind her, as she outlined the history of fort construction and explained why evidence of mechanical dredging raised a lot of questions: Where had the deposits come from? And why had the area been dredged sometime post–World War II?

Then it was Fiona's turn to be interviewed, but she didn't really have much to add. It was ridiculous for her to even be in this part of the documentary, but she imagined they wanted some wet-suit shots of her.

But seriously, Dean in a wet suit was far more enticing for the camera. He did that thing where, while on deck, he doffed the top half, which hung down around his waist, showing off his wide shoulders, thick biceps, and sculpted pecs with blond chest hair that did nothing to hide the violet tattoo over his heart.

And when he pulled on the shorty wet suit that was all that was required in the warm Caribbean and zipped it tight, he looked just as good as he did bare-chested. The neoprene bulged over his upper arms and chest, highlighting the taper of his waist that gave way to a tight ass and muscular thighs.

The guy could be on the cover of a comic book. She'd added several layers of detail to her fantasies after their morning swim.

Token interview done, she donned her scuba tank. Once again, Dean would be her dive partner, but this time, Nico would join them and take documentary footage while they were underwater.

They started with the spoil pile—which had been in place long enough for corals to grow and fish to frequent.

Her expertise underwater was weak—that's why Sadie and Chad were here—but she could see right away what Sadie had meant about the spoil pile having stratigraphy that indicated machine dredging. Materials had been dumped in large chunks—which wasn't possible without a hydraulic dredge. Over time, the debris had sifted and sorted by size, but it was clear that it hadn't been deposited one small bucket at a time, as would have happened if the spoil pile had been created during fort construction in the mid-1600s.

After Nico filmed her diving on the pile and exploring, attention shifted to Dean, who had staked out a reef that took over a large mound of dumped rocks and gravel.

He took photos using a macro lens, and a calmness settled over her as she watched him work. It was like the calmness she felt when staring at a fish tank.

She coveted a saltwater tank but lived alone and traveled too often to commit to fish.

Dean waved her closer, and she swam forward to see what he'd found. He pointed to a gap in the rocks, and she peered inside. She didn't see anything at first, then all at once, she realized the dark shape was an octopus that had filled the space like liquid fills a glass.

She would have squealed in delight if that were possible with a regulator in her mouth. Instead, she placed a hand on his biceps and squeezed.

She stared for another minute, then left the creature to study other gaps for more surprises. The corals were shades of yellow, green, and orange, and the fish that made the reef home came in all colors, from silvery, shimmering rainbows to bright yellows, blues, and neon red.

Small, dark crabs crawled sideways across the rocks, and anemones swayed in the current, all while Dean swam slowly over the top, camera pointing straight down.

Once again, she was envious of his line of work. She loved archaeology, but excavation was destructive. To gather data meant destroying the site.

He got to take pictures and leave the reef exactly as he found it.

He'd promised to give her photography lessons at one point. If she couldn't collect on his sex promise, maybe she'd collect on that one.

"I will instruct the chef to make another one."

She held up a hand. "No. Please don't. I don't think I could eat it. The thought actually turns my stomach." She gave him a weak smile. "See? Not rational."

"Do you want to leave Ruby Island?"

"I've considered it. Right now, I plan to take each day as it comes."

"I really hope you'll stay. We'd have to scrap the documentary without you."

"Not really. We've barely started. My interviews can still be spliced in, and Sadie should be the star of the show anyway."

"But my hope was the documentary would . . . elevate you from your government job."

She bristled at that. Elevate? As if working for the DoD were something lowly? "I'm proud of my work for the military."

He shook his head. "I didn't mean it that way. I meant give you a new opportunity. Fiona, I . . . I just . . . I want you to know that if . . . by any chance you would wish to spend more time on Ruby Island, there are opportunities for you here."

"What do you mean, Jude?"

"You could live here. Enjoy this paradise, but also, it wouldn't be lonely because you could still travel and work. But this could be home. I want you to consider staying on Ruby Island. With me."

She reared back. "Is this some kind of proposal?"

"Not yet. But maybe eventually. Yes."

There were so many things off about this conversation. She'd never even kissed the guy, and certainly hadn't ever led him to believe she wanted to.

She put her head in her hands and let out a pained laugh. "If you think I'd be happy living on an isolated island with Kosmo Andreas constantly sniping at me, well, you definitely don't know me at all."

"I'll send him away. Hell, fire him if I must."

She shook her head. "Jude, Kosmo isn't really the problem and you know it."

SEVENTEEN

As she stepped out of the shower, Fiona heard a knock on her bedroom door. She wrapped a towel around her hair and pulled on the thick terry cloth robe that hung in the bathroom like an amenity at a nice hotel.

She opened the door to see Jude. His face flushed as he took in her attire. "Sorry! I should have realized you'd want to rinse off after diving today. I didn't mean to pull you out of the shower."

"It's fine. I just finished. Come in." She opened the door wide. Chatting with him while wearing a robe with a towel on her head wasn't ideal, but it didn't really matter. She tightened the sash of the robe and sat on the love seat, pulling the split at the front of the garment tightly closed.

Jude eyed the plush chair but then dropped onto the love seat next to her.

"I wanted to apologize for my behavior last night—"

"There's no need. We were both rattled. It was . . . terrifying."

"Yes, but I showed more concern for the damn drone than for you. I'm . . . mortified. And deeply sorry."

"Please don't give it another thought. I had planned to check on how you were doing after my shower." She hesitated, then placed a hand on his thigh just above the knee. "We went through something awful last night. Our responses were not going to be logical or rational." She squeezed, then released him and leaned back. "For example, while you were upset about the drone, it crossed my mind that the cassoulet was destroyed." She shrugged. "Shallow, I know, but the thought was there."

"Give me a chance, Fi. That's all I'm asking. I know . . ." He cleared his throat. "I know you've got feelings for Slater that you need to work through first, and if I thought for a second he returned your feelings, I'd never have come here tonight."

That stung.

And yet, he wasn't wrong. Dean might care about her, but clearly not enough.

"Please, Fiona. Just . . . think about it. I never would have asked this now but—" He let out a harsh laugh. "Nearly blowing up has a way of putting things in perspective. Knowing you might choose to leave, I figured I had to go for it, even though you aren't in the same space emotionally. I can't let you go without telling you what my end goal is. You. Here. With me. I care about you. I think I could love you, and I'm just asking that you give me a chance."

———

Dean loaded a bag with camping gear. Tomorrow, after a full day in the field, he would camp in the heart of the rainforest, near the second camera he'd set up with Fiona. He'd get night shots and be in position to work with the first light of dawn. It would rain tomorrow, but with the high canopy of the forest and his tent, he'd be fine. And really, he worked better when he was uncomfortable in some way. He also worked best when immersed, and he had yet to get a feel for the heart of Ruby Island. Too many distractions. Too much comfort.

Too much temptation.

A knock on the door interrupted his packing. He opened it to face temptation head-on.

She barreled into the room, visibly agitated. Her hair was loose and slightly damp from her shower. She wore another halter top, but this one wasn't as low-cut as the one she'd worn last night.

"What's wrong?"

"Nothing."

"Liar."

She crossed to his dresser and studied his array of cameras and lenses. He was short one lens after last night—he'd dropped the camera with his best zoom attached on the dock before jumping in the Zodiac. The camera survived; the lens had not. No regrets. Lenses were replaceable. Cameras too.

She ran a hand over a macro lens. "I came to collect on the photography lessons you promised me on Chiksook."

That might be the reason she'd come to him, but there was clearly something else on her mind. "What's going on, Fiona?"

She huffed out a deep breath. "I finally had a chance to catch up with Sadie and found out what Chad did. She said you know about it."

"Yeah. I've recommended a lawyer."

"Thank you."

He waited. He didn't think Chad and Sadie's problems were the only thing that was bugging her. But then, there were a lot of options, including one exploded yacht.

Finally, she said, "Jude asked me to stay on Ruby Island."

"It's reasonable for him to be worried you'd quit after last night."

"Yeah. He's worried about that too, but he meant forever. With him."

Dean wasn't close to being surprised—after all, almost dying had a way of pushing a man to take chances—but at the same time, he felt the words in his gut. One thing was certain: if Fiona ended up choosing Jude, any thought of keeping a friendship alive was pretty much shot.

Jude wouldn't want Dean around, and Dean sure as hell wouldn't want to see the happy couple. "What did you say?"

She shrugged. "I didn't really say anything. He asked me to think about it and left. I'm trying to figure out why he wants me. It doesn't make sense."

"He's in love with you."

She met his gaze. Her green eyes were angry. "But how could he love me? He barely knows me."

He let out a pained laugh. "Believe me, Fiona, it doesn't take long to develop feelings for you." Truth be told, he'd been a goner by the second night on Chiksook.

She looked at him sharply, then shook her head. "Yeah. That's why you called me every week for the last nine months."

"It's exactly why I didn't call you, and you know it." He crossed to the dresser and grabbed two camera bags that each had multiple lenses. "But you're right, I promised you lessons and never delivered. We'll start with tropical flowers and Caribbean sunsets."

——

Jude watched Fiona from the balcony. She looked beautiful with her hair whipping in the breeze and lit by the setting sun.

He turned his attention back to the weather forecast. They'd get a glancing blow from the storm late tomorrow. They'd button up the house tight in the morning, but it really shouldn't be much worse than a heavy rain.

Fiona's laugh floated up to the balcony, and the hand that held the phone tightened into a fist-like grip.

Slater was standing behind her with his arms around her, as if teaching her how to use his camera required full-body contact and positioning.

And he'd made Fiona laugh.

Bringing Dean Slater to Ruby Island had been the biggest mistake of his life. He should have fired Chad on the spot once he found out the archaeologist's assurances that there was nothing between the two had been complete bullshit.

But dammit, he needed Chad and Sadie for the survey. Fiona never would have signed on without them.

His phone vibrated, and he checked the text. Ned Hanson had run into a snag with customs in the US Virgin Islands, questions about clearance from Dominica or some such.

Jude frowned. That was the second guest to mention having issues when they reached their next port.

Jude had signed all the clearance papers and passed them on to Kosmo's assistant to make sure each yacht had what they needed. Had the guy—Erik, if he remembered correctly—screwed up somehow? Mixed up the paperwork?

He sent a text to Kosmo alerting him to the issue, then returned his focus to the couple on the beach below.

As long as Fiona stayed on his island, he had a chance to convince her. But he needed to find a way to get rid of Slater. Once the photographer was gone, she'd fall in love with him, and they'd live happily ever after in paradise.

EIGHTEEN

Chad hadn't slept well in days. It wasn't sleeping on the boat that was the problem. He and Sadie lived on the boat for several months every year. He was used to the sounds of the water against the hull, the rigging on the decks slapping, even the lighter sleep necessary to spring awake at the first sign of a dragging anchor.

No. *Tempus Machina* wasn't the problem. The problem was Sadie's side of the bed was empty. He'd screwed up, and now she was living in Reynolds's mansion, enjoying breakfast every morning with the team, while he lived in exile on their dive boat.

He should claim his space at the breakfast table. After all, that was where the team planned each workday, but he couldn't deal with Fiona's disdain, Dean's and Nico's curious and pitying stares, and Sadie's bitter indifference.

It was the indifference that gutted him. After a dozen years together, she was prepared to walk away from him and everything they'd built without a care. Sure, he'd fucked up. He knew that. He'd expected anger, which was why he'd been trying to pay off the debt before she found out about it. But still, didn't their years together mean something? Had it all been nothing more than a business arrangement for her?

He threw off the covers and climbed from the half-empty bed. If he wasn't going to sleep, he might as well work. Maybe, just maybe, if he did a fantastic job on this project, Jude would hire him again. He could earn enough to get the boat unmortgaged and win Sadie back.

He booted up the computer and opened the GIS program. He plugged in the drive that had the data from Sadie's lidar survey of Fort Domingo to feed into the system. She had her own computer and data with her; he'd insisted on having a backup so he could stitch her work to the maps he was creating of the seafloor using the multibeam sub-bottom profiler and side-scan sonar.

Sadie was more skilled at crunching the lidar data—his expertise was with underwater remote sensing—but no time like the present to learn, when he couldn't sleep and he had a wealth of data that hadn't been looked at.

Sadie had shown him how to manipulate the layers to strip away vegetation. He'd load satellite images first to look at the scale and over-view, then he'd load Sadie's drone survey sections on top of that. With Sadie's data, he should be able to strip away the thick jungle vegetation that encroached upon—completely covered, really—the north and east faces of the four-pointed star.

Lidar could see beneath vegetation to the solid earth, stone, or metal beneath. When combined with satellite imagery, the technology had been used by archaeologists to find footprints of ancient cities in the Mayan jungle and even identify the street maps of ancient Roman cities. Telltale traces of ancient roads scarred the earth even as modern civilization covered the wounds with new roads and structures.

That Chad might be able to find secrets hidden in or around Fort Domingo wasn't even a stretch.

The mechanical dredging spoil pile was odd, and the placement of the pile raised even more questions. It was just outside the cove on the southeastern side of the fort, where Chad was currently moored.

Better outside than inside, as the piles would have filled in the small bay, but still it was close, running along the southern tip of both fort and island. They'd spotted smaller spoil piles on the west side—but those were the kind that had been created one bucket at a time in the 1640s and 1650s, when Fort Domingo had been constructed.

The mechanical pile was so close to the tip, it had to be related to the fort somehow. Where else could the piles have come from?

Chad believed work must've been done to expand hidden, interior chambers of the fort. Perhaps it wasn't littoral caves that had offered refuge to enslaved African and Caribbean people. Maybe they'd hidden inside the fort—and someone had later come along and expanded those passages.

Not all forts had an interior, and there was no reason—except for the modern spoil piles—to think Fort Domingo had chambers that had been cut into the earth.

Forget the sinking of the 1567 Spanish treasure fleet: if there were hidden chambers in Fort Domingo, they would be the true treasure of Ruby Island—a refuge. Freedom. A place where people who'd been stolen from their homes and lives in Africa and the Caribbean could make a new home, creating a new community of free people.

This piece of Ruby Island history was what they'd all been hired to find, document, and share with the world. This was what Sadie had been searching for her entire adult life. Maybe he could win her back by finding it. For her. With her.

The dredge piles told a different, more modern story. If someone had expanded the escape tunnels after World War II, wouldn't the Reynolds family know about it? But then, they hadn't acquired the island until the early 1970s, and the dredging could have occurred as early as the late 1940s. Today's dive had produced no artifacts or debris to narrow down the date of the dredging.

He loaded the sub-bottom profile data and manipulated the maps to look at 3D images next to plan views and cross sections. If he could find an underwater sally port, that would be something.

He focused on the water south of the fort, between spoil pile and land. The tip of one bastion jutted out, pointing toward the vast Atlantic Ocean. There were no islands due east of Ruby Island, which sat on the cusp of the Atlantic. From Ruby Island onward, there was nothing but sunrise and disappointment.

The submerged edges of the coastline were particularly rocky. He studied the deposition of boulders that had, over the course of centuries, broken from the cliffs of Ruby Island and descended into the sea. Tomorrow, weather permitting, he would dive along that shore and explore the boulders, looking for gaps. A path into the heart of the fort. He would scout at both high tide and low tide to see how accessible and exposed the shoreline was.

He closed the program and returned to the lidar data, focusing in on the eastern side of the fort, where thick vegetation encroached right up to the walls of the bastion. Beneath the cobblestone surface he'd walked upon days ago, as he filmed a helicopter crashing into the side of the historic structure, he'd known there was a cistern. The entrance to the cistern was well known, and sometime in decades past, it had been mapped and explored, but now it was closed off, as far as he knew. On the lidar map, it was easy to see the rectangular entrance.

With a few keystrokes, he ran the program that stripped the vegetation from the fort to see what had been hidden by hundreds of years of growth.

One anomaly stood out that he tried to make sense of. Could that be an opening hidden in the thick shrubs? It would be good placement for a sally port or a postern gate.

Part of him itched to explore the structure right *now*.

He brushed off the idea, then asked himself, *What's stopping you?*

He was alone, bored, and there was no way he'd sleep anytime in the next few hours. He couldn't go scuba diving by himself, but he could take a machete to the vegetation on the east side. It would work out a little frustration, and if he found something, maybe Sadie would be impressed.

His field pack was ready to go. All he had to do was throw on hiking clothes.

Without really thinking, he found himself dressing, grabbing his pack, and jumping from the boat to the dock. It was just after ten p.m. and peak low tide. It was the night of the new moon, and between the lack of moon and the clouds blocking the stars, when looking toward the Atlantic he saw nothing but inky darkness, punctuated with the sound of breaking waves. To the south, lights on Dominica were the only disruption in the endless black night.

Wind whipped waves up, and they crashed with gusto on the rocky point. He used to love nights like these on the boat with Sadie. All alone in the world with the woman who made every day better.

He turned on his headlamp to light his path. It was far too dark to navigate the dock or steep stairs mounted to the cliff without artificial light.

As he climbed the path, he thought of the men who'd attempted the same journey on dark nights hundreds of years ago. The approach was protected by the sheer wall of a high bastion. Back then, when invaders attempted to breach the fort from this direction, they could have been met with boiling oil, but there was no record of any such thing happening at Fort Domingo.

Tonight as well, no such assault came his way. He reached the top of the staircase, winded by the steep climb while wearing a heavy backpack. He was fit and usually had better stamina, but not sleeping for days had taken a toll.

Before he began, he climbed to the top of the crenelated wall above where the helicopter had crashed and looked down.

It had all been so surreal. Why did it happen? And who cleaned it up?

He should have packed up and gone home that night. Taken Sadie with him. But this project was too good to be true, so Sadie hadn't wanted to leave. And then there was the fact they'd fought that night over how he'd convinced Jude to bring in the Slater brothers, and she'd been so angry, she wouldn't have gone anywhere with him.

Chad was on Jude's shit list for that move too.

Truth was, he'd had no idea Fiona had a thing for the photographer. She'd never mentioned him at all, and she told Sadie everything.

He sat down and leaned against the merlon, then pulled his water bottle from his pack and took a long drink. He'd spent half of the last dozen years in the Caribbean, six months here, three months there. Disjointed, but long enough that the islands felt like home. Still, in all that time, this was a first, exploring a fort by himself on a nearly moonless night. It was just windy enough to give him a chill as the sweat from the climb dried on his skin.

With a sigh, he rose to his feet. He was both wired and exhausted. But that's what happened when one screwed up every aspect of their life at once, he supposed.

He traipsed back to the east side of the fort. Time to tackle the overgrown jungle that threatened to consume the stonework like it was a Mayan pyramid. He pulled out the machete he kept nice and sharp. He paused and studied the thick and thorny vines and branches that engulfed the east bastion.

He took a swing, and the plants separated like butter. Anger and frustration had built up over the last several days, and there was something satisfying about wielding a long blade and hacking through vines.

He entered a mental zone where his arms moved, his muscles burned, and plants died. He had no idea how long he spent chopping his way deep into the vegetation. He just kept swinging and striking.

All at once, the blade hit a rock. The pain of the strike reverberated through his wrist and arm. A jolt to the system.

He looked around, almost as if he were coming out of a trance. He was soaked with sweat, and welts covered his skin from branches that had sliced at him, fighting back against his onslaught.

He lowered the machete and shone a light into the darkness for which he'd been aiming and found a pile of stones that must have come from the fort. The partial collapse of a hidden wall? This was what the lidar had picked up; he was sure of it. It wasn't plants, it wasn't a wall, and it wasn't solid, rocky ground.

With gloved hands, he pulled at the vines to uncover the rocks and get a better sense of the scale of the collapse.

He changed tactics and did targeted clearing, making sure to keep the blade away from the stone. He cut the vines like a chef carving meat from bone, and used his hands to shove the greenery aside. He was almost certain this was the outer edge of a collapsed tunnel or entryway of some sort. The cobbles were far too big for him to move—nor would he, given that they were part of an archaeological site and needed to be documented first—but if he kept hacking, it was possible he'd find an opening he could crawl through without destroying anything.

———

Dean lay in bed, flipping through images taken by the game cameras, a conversation with Dylan open in the chat window. As promised, his brother had sorted through the first twenty-four hours of data and compiled the best images for Dean to peruse.

Dean: Damn. At least sixteen species passed by camera 2.

Dylan: I caught that. There were several dozen more bird pics, but many were the same bird, or possibly the same species. I'm not the bird man you are.

Hot Bird Man, Dean wanted to add, but that joke was for Fiona. And Dylan would only take that as another opportunity to tell Dean to get his head out of his ass.

What would Dylan think of Jude Reynolds's proposition to Fiona?

Dylan wanted her to be happy as much as Dean did. He'd probably tell her to go for it, as Dean had yesterday, before he'd held her in his arms all night and remembered how good it felt to have her body pressed tight to his.

And now he was alone in his luxurious suite while she slept two doors down, and he missed her. On Chiksook, after the first time they'd had to share a sleeping bag, they'd spent every night together, wrapped in each other's arms. But he had no such excuse to do that here.

It was one of the reasons he was camping out tomorrow night. One less temptation.

A new message popped up on the screen.

Dylan: You going to spend time in one of the tree blinds tomorrow?

Dean: Yeah. Camera 2.

Dylan: I'll watch out for you.

Dean: I'll be behind the camera, not in front of it. But will try to remember to moon you if I can do it without falling.

Dylan: Dare you.

Dean sniggered. It was the kind of dumb crap they'd done when they were teens. It was tempting to show his brother he could still be ridiculous. Things had been far too serious between them since Dylan had gone missing. Hell, probably since the divorce.

Dean: I wish you were here. Fiona wishes you were here too.

Dylan: I'm glad I'm not. Have fun tomorrow and give Fiona a kiss from me.

He remembered his nightmare of Dylan kissing Fiona in a way that was anything other than brotherly. He could handle losing Fiona to Dylan, because it would mean his two favorite people in the world would be happy, no matter how much it hurt.

But Jude Reynolds?

He didn't think he could ever be happy about that.

———

The opening was small, really just big enough for Chad to climb through with his shoulders brushing the sides. It was risky and dangerous, and he could well end up regretting his rash decision. But no guts, no glory, right?

When he told Sadie about this, she'd be thrilled. Jude would be thrilled. The project would take on a whole new angle. They'd need Sadie to use her lidar to map the inside of the fort. She might find hidden tunnels that led to the island's interior.

Tonight, he'd be careful. He'd turn back if the ceiling looked unstable. As it was, he was sure the top of this archway he'd exposed was the top of a postern gate. The bottom of the opening was filled with jumbled rocks, effectively closing off the gate for decades, possibly centuries.

But he'd found it and made a hole big enough to crawl through.

In the end, he was able to go much deeper into the fort than he'd imagined—and when he gazed upon what had been tucked away in the vast underground chamber, he knew he'd found the solution to all his problems.

He'd be able to buy his boat back, pay off the equipment, and Sadie would love him again.

NINETEEN

As they did every morning, the team met on the veranda for breakfast to plan the day. Nico no longer tried to suggest they let him film the meetings, even though it was clear to Fiona that it drove him batty that he couldn't capture their casual planning sessions.

Sadie looked up at the sky and said, "We're looking at a short day, folks. I bet the rain will hit in earnest by late afternoon."

"I thought the storm was going to miss us completely?" Fiona said. She didn't doubt Sadie's knowledge of Caribbean weather patterns; she was curious why the prediction Kosmo had sent out with the morning tide and weather report was off.

Sadie rolled her eyes. "Kosmo gets the tide right, because we can easily look that up ourselves, but his consolidation of weather reports needs work from someone who knows the region."

"I wonder why he does that himself," Fiona said. "Isn't it beneath him?" It behooved everyone here to know the weather and tide. It mattered. But Kosmo definitely viewed some tasks as lowly.

"Oh, c'mon. I'm sure he has Erik do that crap," Sadie said. "Then he just puts his name on it."

"Which one is Erik?" Nico asked.

"He's the beefy guy who always looks pissed off," Sadie answered.

Fiona laughed, guessing exactly who Sadie meant from that description. She hadn't known the guy's name either. He looked more bodyguard than executive assistant. But what did she know about the shipping business?

"So what's the plan for today?" Nico asked.

Sadie looked up. "Given the weather, I was thinking it'd be good to stick close to Cannon Bay. I want to do the bathymetric survey. We need a cannon count for the bet between Dr. Finch and Jude."

"I want to spend a few hours in one of the tree blinds," Dean said, joining the conversation. "I plan to spend the night in the forest so I can take pictures in the morning—birds in the rainforest at dawn after a storm."

"Ohh," Sadie said. "I like that."

Dean smiled. He looked all handsome and confident this morning, and Fiona wanted to climb on his lap and whisper dirty suggestions in his ear.

She'd missed having his body wrapped around hers last night.

"Sounds like Oliver and I should shadow Sadie today," Nico said. "I can film the Cannon Bay/cannon bet survey and get shots of the bay as the storm rolls in." He smiled at Dean. "Sorry, dude. You look great in a wet suit, but there's not much to see when you're in camouflage in a tree."

"That's kind of the point," Dean said. He met Fiona's gaze. "I checked with Kosmo this morning, and he said he needs Walker to secure the boats and dock for the storm, should we get hit by more than a glancing blow. Looks like we're field buddies again today, if you have work you can do in the rainforest?"

Fiona had known this was coming, but still the thought of another day alone with Dean sent a frisson through her. "I can do a preliminary survey of the lakeshore, see if we can find Sadie's structures."

"It'd be good to scout that," Nico said. "So we can plan the shoot for the big reveal if you find anything."

"If?" Sadie said, clearly affronted.

"Pardon me. *When,*" Nico corrected.

"It's settled, then," Dean said.

"Well, except for one thing," Fiona said. "I'm not excited by sleeping in the rain when I have a perfectly good memory foam mattress and a roof waiting for me."

"No problem. At the end of the workday, before the rain starts, I'll hike with you back to the boat, so you can return to the estate, then I'll head deeper into the forest and find a good camping spot."

She nodded. "Okay, then. To be clear, I'm not made of sugar and have done plenty of camping in the rain."

Dean smiled, and his eyes flared with warmth. "I'm well aware of that."

"I just don't see the point in being miserable when I don't have to be."

His grin seemed to say, *You wouldn't be miserable if you were with me.* But she supposed that thought was just wishful thinking.

———

Before they set out, Fiona returned to her room to pack her gear. A day in the rainforest was very different from a day on the beach or diving, and she hadn't been sure where she'd be today or who she'd be teamed with. She should probably set up a calendar with goals, but everything had been so disjointed from the day of Dean's arrival, between equipment being lost and not having another person on the team without Dylan.

Jude had been focused on the party, but once that was behind him, his boat blew up, so planning had been . . . nonexistent. Not that she blamed him.

It was what it was for a reason.

She really needed to decide if she was going to stay or go. Jude's proposition last night had only served to make her eager to leave.

And then she questioned whether he was right and, deep down, she wasn't giving him a chance because of her feelings for Dean.

196

Was she being a fool to pass up Jude's offer?

If it wasn't for her muddled feelings for Dean, could she fall for Jude?

She didn't think so. But she wasn't exactly clearheaded at the moment.

She decided to head down to his office before setting out for the day. It seemed like the right thing to do when a man fell short of proposing but basically asked her to spend the next phase of her life with him . . . right before she set out to spend the day with the man she really wanted.

Her life had gotten seriously wacked in the last few days.

A true and bona fide billionaire wanted her to share his private island with him. He'd even get rid of the ogre who haunted the place at her request, yet there was no part of her that was excited by the offer.

That right there was her answer, but she wouldn't be so cruel as to tell Jude now. She owed her friend, the guy she'd cared for so much fifteen years ago, a gentle and heartfelt *no*.

She paced in front of his office, as the french doors were closed, and through the windows, she could see a man sitting across from Jude in the visitor's chair.

He must've arrived on Jude's private ferry, because no helicopters or yachts had arrived this morning, and the man hadn't been here last night.

Finally, the man stood and crossed to the closed french doors. The mullioned windows allowed her to see him from head to toe. He strode with confidence, and she noted his lightly tanned skin and short brown hair specked with gray before she met his gaze through the glass, and it took everything in her to not jolt in recognition as he opened the door and exited the room with nothing more than a polite nod.

Christopher Richards. The mystery man from her meeting in the admiral's office. What the hell was he doing here?

Dean paced impatiently by the dock, waiting for Fiona.

Field buddies again. He'd known it would happen, and he tried not to be happy about it. But dammit, he was. He'd even gotten the treat from the chef that he'd surprise her with at the end of the day.

He shouldn't do it. He was acting like a damn suitor, and that was the last thing in the world he wanted to be.

But at the same time, he couldn't wait to see her smile when she saw what he had for her.

Hell, he wanted to give it to her first thing, but he reminded himself that patience was one of his key skills.

He should wait until lunch, at minimum.

His satellite phone buzzed with a text, and he pulled it out, expecting to see a message from Dylan. Maybe he had more game-camera bird news to share.

But the text wasn't from his brother.

Paige: I forgot to send you this the other night.

The next message was a photo of Fiona, Sadie, and Paige with their faces pressed together in a selfie. He didn't know if he'd ever seen a photo of three more beautiful women. And the spark of joy in all three sets of eyes warmed him. Sadie had been having a shit night, and Fiona . . . well, things were confused there. But in this instant captured by Paige, all three women were happy. Sharing a moment of fun.

Dean: Thank you. I'm glad you three hit it off.

Paige: Oh, we're besties now. I'm going to drunk text Fiona and tell her all your secrets. Sorry, but I warned you I'm a drunk texter.

He laughed.

Dean: Just be sure to include the fact that the water was VERY cold.

Paige: LOL. That made me spew. Seriously, she's great, Dean. I'm happy for you.

His heart clenched. Even Paige assumed he could give more than he had.

Dean: Where are you?

Paige: Change the subject much?

He waited. He didn't have anything to say to that. Finally, another text posted.

Paige: We made port in Puerto Rico early this morning. I have a flight out later today. But we're being detained by customs for some reason. Thaddeus says they want to search the entire boat. Funny thing, we were in a convoy with two other boats from the party, and they're in the same sitch. Hope it doesn't interfere with my flight. I've got a shoot in two days.

Dean: Weird.

Paige: Yeah. Will keep you posted. Have fun today. Hope the storm doesn't bite you.

He signed off from the conversation and tucked the phone away as Walker finally emerged from the boat office. "Sorry, man. Just got word from the big house that we can't let anyone use the motorboats today. We're pulling them all up into the shed in case the storm is worse than predicted. We'd usually be moving *Rum Runner* to the fort dock, but . . ."

Yeah, no need to move an exploded boat.

"The storm isn't supposed to do more than glance by, and it won't be here until afternoon. Can we at least take a canoe?" Dean did not want to spend extra hours hacking through the jungle when a boat would be faster, and he also didn't want to haul his camping gear on his back the extra distance if he didn't have to.

"Sure. Canoes are no problem. Just make sure you pull it way up onshore and tuck it in the trees. High tide in a storm can wreck your day if it takes your boat."

Dean nodded. He knew the drill. This wasn't his first tropical storm.

He turned to see Fiona heading down the dock. He'd have her all to himself today. He shouldn't be excited by the prospect, but he was.

TWENTY

It was quiet, paddling across the water with Dean. Even more pleasant than the whale sighting from two days ago, Fiona supposed. There was a kind of harmony to paddling, and it was nice to share the rhythm and peace with him.

She didn't know what to think of crossing paths with Richards this morning. He'd walked right past her with nary a sign, which, of course, was to be expected.

But why was he there? What was his business with Jude?

She hadn't told the admiral about Jude's . . . proposition. How could she? Lord, what if the man urged her to accept? Live on Ruby Island and spy for the infinite future?

No. No way. Never.

She shouldn't have accepted the assignment for eight weeks.

There were actual, codified rules against this sort of thing for archaeologists. They signed on to a pact not to spy, because it endangered others, endangered the profession.

It didn't help that T. E. Lawrence, when working as an archaeologist prior to World War I, had spied for British intelligence. It set the stage, putting future archaeologists at risk. And now, wasn't she doing the same thing?

Except, it was Americans she was spying on, not foreigners or foreign governments. Ruby Island might be part of Dominica, but it had deep American ties, including an American billionaire and an American shipping company.

She wasn't violating her archaeologist oath, was she?

She was just doing her job. The one her true employer, the US Navy, had asked her to do.

"What's wrong, Fi?" Dean asked from the rear seat of the canoe.

"Nothing."

"Riiiight. Um, you're paddling at twice my speed. In a hurry?"

Am I?

She took a deep breath and tried to center herself. "Just eager to get away from the estate, I guess."

"Did you give Jude an answer this morning?"

"No. But I told him we'd talk tonight. I can't draw this out."

"Good call."

The rocky beach where they'd parked the Boston Whaler two days ago came into view, and Dean steered them toward shore while Fiona tried to paddle at a more even pace. They were more than two hours out from low tide and paddled as close as they could to the tree line.

Once they were aground, they both climbed from the boat and carried it the rest of the way to the thick forest. It was heavy, loaded with their gear, but not as bad as the packs last time, when they'd set up the cameras. Even with Dean's camping gear, this was a breeze compared to that.

They tucked the boat safely in the trees well above the high-tide line and prepped for their hike. It was past ten a.m. by the time they set out in earnest, heading uphill into the rainforest to where Dean had set up the second game camera. Loaded as they were, it was almost eleven by the time they reached it.

They paused for a snack. Bird chatter was lively, as were frogs and other forest critters. Fiona leaned against the thick roots of a tall tree as she ate her pepperoni stick, taking in the sounds and earthy, flowery scent of the rainforest. "You know what this forest is missing?" she asked.

"Missing? It's perfect. What could be missing?"

"Golf balls."

"Golf balls?"

"Yeah. I've never worked on a project where I didn't find a golf ball. Well, except maybe Chiksook, and even then, there might have been some in the World War II site? I don't remember. Plus, I know I found one on Japonski Island, in Sitka, Alaska, during a survey there. Golf balls are everywhere. But not here. The other thing that's missing is litter. I've spent hours upon hours in this rainforest, and I've never seen even one piece of garbage." She smiled. "Not even a stray LUNA bar wrapper."

He grinned at that. "Dylan will never live that down." He glanced around the trees, with their thick buttress roots. "I've seen trash in the most remote places—and yeah, golf balls too."

She smiled. "No litter. No golf balls. Ruby Island really is a paradise."

He nodded toward the rigging. "If you want to climb . . . the view of the forest is pretty spectacular from above too."

"Yeah. No. Your pictures are good enough for me." Two days ago, when she'd stood below the ropes Dean had rigged and climbed, she'd known the truth: there was no way she could climb that high straight up a rope. It didn't matter that it wasn't a rock face, like where her dad died, nor was it a cliff to fall from like Regan. It was the height that was the problem.

He finished his apple and tucked the core in his pack—pack in, pack out anything that wasn't native was the rule, even if it was biodegradable—then stood. "Time for me to get climbing. You going to be bored down here?" They'd agreed he'd sit in his tree blind for at least two hours so he could get shots of birds in the canopy before the rain came in.

"I'll be fine. I'm going to walk some transects and take notes. I loaded my Kindle with research material to go over if I run out of things to do. I'll stay within shouting distance."

"Fine, but only shout if absolutely necessary or you'll scare the birds."

She nodded. "I'll tread lightly too, for the same reason."

This wasn't the most ideal field pairing, as they were both limited in their work, but it was better than working alone and, truthfully, there was no one else she wanted with her today.

After an hour, she had explored as far as her leash would allow, then returned to the area where they'd enjoyed their snack and plopped down to lean against a buttress root and work. They were close to the freshwater lake, but not close enough for her to search for Sadie's structures.

She pulled out the map Sadie had printed and compared it to the topo map that was based on decades-old data. The lake appeared on both maps, but it looked larger now than it had been in the past. Were the houses—or whatever they were—right on the lakeshore now?

She leaned back to gaze up at where Dean was perched in a tree. If she didn't know he was there, she'd never have spotted him. He'd rigged a blind and dressed in camouflage. He blended in almost perfectly. A sharp contrast to her in her bright orange field shirt.

She stared up at him, and something shifted inside.

She didn't want Jude or this island. The only thing she was certain she wanted was Dean Slater. And she would have him.

Even if it was only for one night.

———

Dean's muscles were cramping from being in one position too long. But a small, blue-crowned with deep-yellow underparts Antillean Euphonia was singing on a branch ten feet away, and the bright afternoon sun that lit the high canopy was perfect. Antillean Euphonia were rare for the Lesser Antilles, and this was the bird he'd been hoping to photograph when he saw the second game camera had captured both a male and a female of the species.

He held his position, ignoring the discomfort, as he waited for the tiny male to turn and show off his yellow underparts.

The male's twittering song paused, and Dean heard a female sing. The bird turned, and Dean got his photo and a half dozen more as the bird picked up his song again.

It was near the end of mating season, but not too late for the little guy to make a match. The female landed on a nearby branch and sang some more.

These birds could nest anywhere from floor to canopy, but they bred at high elevation. They tended to remain among dense foliage and flew around treetops, which was why it was so important for him to place blinds high in the canopy. Given the height at which they lived and their tiny bodies, they were hard to spot even with their bright plumage.

The female twittered and moved closer to the male.

Dean cheered on the little guy, who was singing his heart out for the pretty lady.

He snapped several shots of the birds moving closer together. These images would be magazine-worthy, just for their bright colors, but it was also a moment rarely seen as two elusive birds flirted with song. He had another camera that was recording video, and he'd hooked up a mic to capture their song.

He snapped photos, in his mind sharing the moment with Violet, as he'd done in nearly all moments like this over the last ten years. His gaze dropped to the woman sitting on the ground below him, and he realized he was sharing the moment with her in a very real way, even if she wasn't in the tree with him.

Guilt washed over him. It wasn't right. This was his one remaining connection to Violet.

He returned his attention to the birds. The female had taken a step back, and the male was upping his game, making more noise.

Even as he watched their foreplay, he saw Violet in his mind.

She whispered, *It's time. Let me go.* And then she faded away.

Dean gripped his camera, his heart thrumming, no longer taking pictures.

Tears dampened his cheeks, and his body shook with the suppressed sob; this, in turn, shook the branches and startled the birds.

The female flew to a neighboring branch. Dean swiped at his cheek and mentally apologized to the male bird. *Sorry, dude. My bad.*

The female let out a soft, twittering call, and the male followed her to the next branch, landing beside her and starting over with his song. Branches were in the way now. Dean didn't have a good shot.

He'd gotten what he wanted, though. It was enough.

He leaned back in his perch, moving slowly so as not to make another noise that would startle them. He'd give the little guy time to do his thing before descending. He needed to collect himself before he faced Fiona anyway.

———

Fiona was on her feet the moment she realized Dean was descending. She got nervous every time he ascended or descended. At least when he was in the blind, his weight was supported by both ropes and branches, so if one failed, the other would still be there. Ascent and descent had no such backup.

"Did you get some good shots?" she asked when he was a third of the way down.

"I got some incredible ones. I can't wait to share them with you."

There was a note to his voice on the last sentence that struck her as . . . different, triggering a sweet burst of anticipation.

She gazed up at him, his muscles moving as he controlled his descent. He abruptly dropped a few feet, then came to a stop with a curse.

"What's wrong?"

As she watched, he slipped down another foot. Jolting, uncontrolled.

Her heart lurched and hammered. He had to be more than sixty feet up.

"One of my descenders gave up. Won't clamp the rope." His voice was strained. As far as she could see, he was hanging on with one gloved hand and sliding down.

His next words sent a chill straight to her heart. "And the other one is failing."

TWENTY-ONE

Dean yanked his emergency Prusik cord from his pocket and looped it around the line once, twice, three times. It cinched tight enough to hold his weight. He tied a figure eight with the ends of the Prusik line and clipped a carabiner to it, which he then clipped to his harness. He was now attached to a new brake, halting his jerky, uncontrolled slide down the rope.

No longer in imminent danger of plunging sixty feet, he took a deep breath, then got to work on a second Prusik line, which he attached below the first. He took his last emergency section of rope from his pocket and looped it over his foot, securing it like a stirrup. He then looped a quick knot at knee height and clipped it to the second, lower Prusik knot.

He now had a mechanism he could work to descend the rope, resting his weight on one friction knot while he lowered the other.

It was slow going. Prusiking was much better suited to ascension. Attempting to go too fast on the descent could be a fatal mistake.

As eager as he was to set his feet upon the ground, he wouldn't rush.

In the back of his mind was the knowledge that Fiona was watching, and her father had died in a climbing accident. He needed to focus on the ropes, but the thought wouldn't go away.

He pulled himself up straight on the rope, legs fully extended, then lowered the top knot to meet the lower foot knot. His knee bent level with his chest now, he then took his weight off the foot in the rope stirrup and lowered the knot. He extended his legs again to standing height and repeated the process. Sweat soaked his clothing as he worked his way down, inch by slow inch, foot by slow foot.

Climbing down to Fiona.

For her part, she said nothing. Didn't shout questions or do anything to distract him. She was silent, and, he imagined, utterly terrified.

His arms ached with the stress of the slow manual descent. His leg muscles, already strained from being strapped in the blind and supporting his weight for nearly two hours with little to no movement, burned like fire now. His need to be on the ground wasn't just mental; it was a physical agony.

At last, he was mere feet from the forest floor. As much as he wanted to unhook himself and jump the last bit, that would be foolish with his shaking limbs. If his foot remained tangled, he could seriously hurt himself.

His free foot—the left one—reached the ground, and he did one last maneuver, releasing the slack at the middle carabiner, standing straight, lowering the top knot, bending his knee, and lowering the bottom. His right foot touched the ground without fanfare.

Fiona let out a gasp of pent-up breath, and he unclipped the carabiner on his harness, releasing the rope.

He stood on the ground, drenched in sweat, breathing heavily, his legs shaking. Fiona stood back, as if afraid to touch him, tears streaming down her cheeks.

In two steps, he had her in his arms. He covered her mouth with his, sliding his tongue between her lips. She opened for him, taking his tongue inside and stroking it with her own. At last he was kissing her as he'd wanted to for nine long months.

Her body molded to his, and while he'd barely been able to support his own weight on shaky legs, holding her was no problem. She stabilized him. Grounded him.

Made him whole.

He kissed her deep. Couldn't get enough of her hot, stroking tongue as his adrenaline surged. She gave as much as she got, tasting him and making soft pleasure sounds that he remembered too well from the few kisses they'd shared far too long ago.

He released her mouth and buried his face in her neck, his arms wrapped tight around her.

He didn't for a moment think the ghost of his wife had visited him in the tree blind. He knew damn well his subconscious produced those words. A way to take what he wanted. But then, it had never been Violet who held him back from relationships; it was the sheer terror of loving again. And losing again.

But this thing with Fiona, it might be worth the risk. The agony. The hope.

Reluctantly, he let her go. There would be time to explore this later. Right now, he needed to take a good look at his descenders . . . because odds were, someone had tampered with them.

———

Fiona stared at the piece of hardware, her belly churning at what she saw. "Someone deliberately filed down the grips that locked on to the rope, then replaced the raised edges with epoxy or something?"

Dean nodded. "I'm not sure what they used to rebuild the ridges that grip the rope, but whatever it was, it wore down with friction created when the rope slid through on my descent. This one gave out first—completely wore off, which is why the ridges are nearly flat like a worn-down tire tread." He showed her the second descender. "This one still has some teeth left, which is the only way I was able to catch myself. If they had given out at the same rate, I'd have fallen in an instant."

Fiona shuddered. She wanted to vomit. She wanted to hold Dean all night long, as he'd held her the night before last.

She met his gaze. "We need to get off this island. Now. Yesterday."

The helicopter, the boat, and now the rope. None had been an accident.

But who would do these things? The targets were so varied.

Only Dean had been targeted twice, unless Jude had been the intended target of the helicopter crash.

But this targeting of Dean was deliberate. No one else would have used those descenders. Even Jude knew about Fiona's fear of heights. Plus, the ascenders were just fine. Whoever did this wanted to make sure Dean could climb high before he fell.

"I'm so glad you had the Prusik knots on you." She paused, remembering her dad's lessons from a lifetime ago. "My dad always said a Prusik cord could save your life."

Dean held her gaze, and she knew he had questions about her father's accident, but all he said was, "He was a wise man. I always have them in my pockets when I climb, old-school backup. I've practiced using them in an emergency, but this was the first time I had to do it for real."

She cupped his face and pulled him to her, giving him a fierce, deep kiss, then said, "Thank you for not dying today."

He dropped the attempted murder weapons and held her tight against him. Being in his arms was exactly what she needed. She pressed her ear to his chest, taking in the strong thump of his heart. Alive and beating.

He placed a finger under her chin and turned her head up. He kissed her again, holding nothing back in a carnal kiss that celebrated his survival. Deep and hot, his tongue took her mouth, devouring her. Possessing her.

They'd crossed a new threshold, traversed by terror, but there was no going back. This thing between them would happen.

She'd worry later about how long it could last.

He released her mouth and pressed his forehead to hers. His breath was uneven. Panting. Not from exertion but from the intensity of the kiss. "The only way off this island is through Jude, unless we can get a call to my brother. Sat phones don't work in the rainforest—not without being up in the canopy. And I'm not climbing again today. Not with only Prusik knots to descend."

She pulled out her phone and confirmed that there was no signal this deep in the rainforest.

"If we take the canoe to *Tempus Machina*, which should be moored by the fort for the storm, Chad could take us to Dominica. We could circle the island and pick up Sadie. She'll want to leave once she hears what happened. Nico too."

Dean shook his head. "I don't think Chad would cross Jude that way. I don't trust him. Also, fuel is an issue. Odds are, he'd have to fuel up with Walker, and that would lead to questions. Don't forget, a storm is going to hit in a few hours. It may not be possible to make the crossing tonight."

"Do you think Jude is really behind this?" She felt another ripple of nausea. Jude saw Dean as a rival. Could this be about *her*?

"I don't know, but someone who works on this island is behind it, and they have access to everything. My gear. Jude's boat. Hell, they even cleared the helicopter debris without anyone spotting them."

"It stands to reason that Jude was the intended target for the boat explosion. Hard to see why he'd risk his own death."

"I agree, but I don't want to rule anyone out yet. You had lead time to get off the boat."

This was true, but still, it was hard to fathom. Jude had seemed devastated by the loss of the drone. Maybe even more than he'd been afraid he could have died.

But then, it was all in reaction to trauma. There wasn't a lot that would be *normal* in that situation.

"So what do we do?"

Dean bit his bottom lip. His gaze unfocused. Finally he said, "We head back to the house. Show Jude the sabotaged descenders and insist on leaving. I'll call Dylan and have him arrange for a boat from Dominica, leaving Reynolds out of it so there's no chance for sabotage on his end. I'll pay for everything so there is no need for his involvement."

"So we hike back to the canoe, then."

He nodded and began collecting his scattered gear and shoving it in his pack. "If we hurry and contact Dylan the minute we're out from under the canopy, he might be able to send a boat before the storm hits. Then we wait out the storm and leave the moment it passes."

She wanted to believe it would be that simple. Fear thrummed through her, like there was a ticking clock that warned her every second they spent on this island would make it harder to leave. They needed to be on a boat *now*. No passing go.

But they could hardly canoe to Dominica. Not without food and lots of fresh water, and not with a storm coming.

But when they reached the shore forty-five minutes later, they discovered they couldn't paddle to Jude's estate either. Their canoe was gone.

TWENTY-TWO

Dean pulled out his satellite phone. Free of the rainforest, he should be able to call Dylan. The rain clouds were beginning to roll in, but the cloud cover wasn't thick yet. The screen lit, and the welcome screen glowed bright. He entered his passcode to unlock the phone. A box popped up with the text No Service Provider.

"What does that mean?" Fiona asked. She glanced at the sky. "It usually just says 'No Service' when it can't connect."

"See what your phone says."

She pulled out her phone and went through the same powering-up process. The same message appeared on her screen.

"Did Reynolds give you that phone?" he asked.

"Yes. He gave everyone a sat phone when we got here because Wi-Fi calling doesn't work with the island's network."

"My guess is, someone cut off our phone service at the source. The employee who handles all the technical stuff—Erik—could have shut down our phones with the provider." He looked out over the rocky beach. It was getting darker as the storm neared. "It looks like someone wants me dead and you stranded."

"But that doesn't make sense. It's not like we can't just walk through the forest to the house. The canoe was a shortcut, not a necessity."

"If that's what they're expecting, we can't give it to them."

"So what do we do?"

"I've got a tent and sleeping bag. We camp. Regroup. Tomorrow, we hike to *Tempus Machina* at the fort. The boat has a radio."

She grimaced. "One sleeping bag and a tiny tent. And it's going to rain."

"Hey, at least we have a tent this time."

"But not much in the way of food."

"I packed a little extra."

She rubbed her arms, and he noticed goose bumps had risen, in spite of the humid air, but then the wind kicked up, and fat raindrops started to fall, plopping on the rocky beach as the tide slowly came in.

She shivered. Dean didn't think it was wind or rain that triggered that reaction any more than they'd been the cause of goose bumps. She was scared, with good reason.

They had a few hours before sunset and a storm to weather. Maybe they could do something constructive to kill time that would also provide better shelter than his tiny tent.

He placed a finger under her chin and turned her to face him. "Hey. Let's head back into the forest. Maybe we can find Sadie's structure and sleep in there tonight."

———

Raindrops filtered through the canopy and misted the air as they once again traversed the rainforest. Fiona found herself shivering as they approached the ropes where Dean had barely managed to hang on sixty feet up and rig a slow but safe descent.

Dean took her hand as they passed and squeezed. He was here. By her side. Walking and breathing.

Why had she hesitated to quit after the boat explosion? In hindsight, the decision to stay even one day defied logic.

Had she hoped the admiral would make sense of it? The man had yet to respond to the email she'd sent yesterday morning about the explosion. But then, Richards was here, so maybe he had?

Richards. She'd managed to forget about him in the midst of everything else. What was he doing here?

As they neared the lake, the trees got shorter and the vegetation thicker. They were no longer under the canopy and instead faced the thick vines and thorny branches of an overgrown jungle.

Without tall trees to protect them from the storm, it wasn't long before they were both soaked through as the rain had picked up considerably during the long uphill hike from beach to lake in the central part of the island.

Rain dumped down on her head as she studied the thick vegetation that separated them from the lake. Her compass and map told her both water and Sadie's structures were near, but all she saw was a solid mass of thorny plants that grew in copious tangles, as impenetrable as the vines that grew for a hundred years as Sleeping Beauty slumbered, waiting for a prince to wake her.

They each carried a machete, thankfully, because there was no way to move forward without it. The work was hard and slow, and it didn't take long for Fiona's arms to begin to ache. After a half hour of chopping at the vines, they'd made little progress.

Fiona paused to take a drink of water, then turned her face up to the drenching rain. At least the downpour kept her from building up a sweat, but it made the machete handle slippery in her wet work gloves.

"We can stop if you want," Dean offered.

Frankly, she'd considered it. But they probably had two hours before they were without light, and the idea of maybe getting to find an historic structure to use as shelter for the night was appealing. It wasn't like they had anything else to do.

Plus, she'd be leaving this island and project tomorrow and would never return to finish her work. Might as well determine if Sadie's structure was extant or not.

They kept at it. The sky drew ever darker thanks to the heavy rain and lowering sun. Even though the air temperature was warm, soaked through as she was, Fiona began to get chilled.

Her arms were tired from a combination of canoe paddling and machete wielding, and her legs were sore from hiking miles uphill, twice. She couldn't even imagine how much Dean's muscles must burn, considering he'd climbed a hundred-foot rope and then had a slow, intense climb down.

"You look tired, Fi. We can stop for the night. Build the tent. Eat dinner."

"How would you feel if tomorrow, in daylight, we discovered we were only ten feet away from being able to build a fire?"

As had been happening for the last hour, rain hit the broadleaf plant next to her head and splattered into her face. She was being rained on from all directions. If there was a drop of water in this forest that hadn't found its way to her skin somehow, she didn't believe it.

"But we might not be ten feet away. Or the wall measurements could be off and it's just a footprint, like the others."

"It's here. Sadie knows what she's doing and has the best equipment."

He nodded and faced the thick plants again. He swung his machete, taking out a vine and stepping forward. She did the same on her side. Together they were clearing a narrow path, aiming directly for structure and lake.

If anyone was tracking them, they were leaving a neon trail, but odds were, anyone tracking them would also have access to Sadie's map, so they'd start looking in this area anyway.

"You plan to record the structure, don't you? Even though you're quitting the project."

"Absolutely. Isn't that why we're doing this?"

"I was thinking more in terms of shelter for the night."

She couldn't help but laugh. He was far more pragmatic than she was. She remembered how on Chiksook they'd also recorded archaeological remains after the project had combusted. It was in her nature, she guessed.

But there was more to it. Fifteen years ago, a young man she had befriended told her amazing tales of this island and all she had to offer. Ruby Island was likely named for a pirate—a woman who'd claimed freedom when it was stolen from her before she was even born. She'd then used that freedom to strike back at her enslavers and free her fellow victims. Survivors.

Fiona wanted Ruby Hawthorne's story to be told. And she wanted Sadie to do it. Sadie had found something in this jungle with lidar. This was Sadie's find. Fiona—and Dean—were simply ground-truthing.

"I won't write Jude's report, and I'm done as far as the documentary, but Sadie might be able to do something with the data."

"Do you ever wonder if all this is just . . . a massive and dangerous hoax to make the documentary a big deal? Nico told me he was filming the yacht when it exploded. He'd been on the upper balcony. Like me, Jude had told him to get footage of the boat in the sunset."

"I didn't know that, but yeah, I admit that did cross my mind once or twice, but I discarded it because how messed up—and desperate—would Jude have to be to blow up his own yacht while he was on it? And the guy is loaded. He doesn't *need* the documentary to be a success."

"Is he? I've started to wonder. Maybe he's got the kind of investors who end up owning you, like Russian mafia with their *kompromat*. On paper he has money, but his life isn't his."

She shook her head. "I don't see it. I mean, for Kosmo, sure. But not Jude."

"Well, Kosmo is basically second-in-command. And he's not loaded like Jude. I mean, he's loaded for sure, but not to the tune of billions. A guy in that situation can cause a lot of problems.

"Look at it this way—Chad mortgaged the boat without Sadie's approval. Imagine what Kosmo could do if he brought in unsavory investors and they've wormed their way into the business. It's a shipping company, which is basically a smuggler's wet dream. Do you know how much Triads, Yakuza, Bratva, Colombian cartels, or good old-fashioned US Mafia would love to get their hooks into RAM Freight?"

"RAM did get its start smuggling booze during Prohibition."

"Yeah. What if they never stopped? What if the majority of Jude Reynolds's massive wealth is dirty? The business is just a laundry, or a front. Most of Reynolds's fleet runs Caribbean routes, and the Caribbean is the major transportation route for cocaine smuggled into the United States."

Fiona's machete hit stone at the same time Dean's words registered. In a flash, she was back in the admiral's office and it all made sense.

She was such a fool.

Richards wasn't NSA or DIA. He was DEA.

The US Navy—which worked in conjunction with the Drug Enforcement Agency in the Caribbean to track and capture drug smugglers on the water—wanted to know if Ruby Island was a smugglers' haven.

TWENTY-THREE

The ring of blade on rock stopped all conversation. Dean slipped his long machete into the sheath as Fiona did the same with hers. With gloved hands, he pulled at the vines that covered the stone.

He hoped this was it, because Fiona was soaked and shivering. They'd have to give up and get her dry in his tent if they didn't find the shelter soon.

It was dark enough to need flashlights now, and she shone hers where he'd cleared the cut vegetation, revealing a rock clad in rotting vines, moss, lichen—a web of life coating lifeless stone.

The light shifted, and she gasped, pointing to a darker-colored stripe that crossed the surface. She yanked off a glove and ran a finger down the groove, tracing it as it bent around a lighter patch of rock. "This is mortar. These are separate rocks mortared together to build a wall. We found it!"

He let out a full, joyful yelp and pulled her to him. And because he could, he kissed her.

She kissed him back, matching his exuberance. The rain poured down on their heads, finding where their lips met, seeping inside.

All hint of chill left his body as he had Fiona hot against him, her tongue sliding along his.

How had he resisted her this long?

He forced himself to end the kiss. They still had work to do before they could celebrate in earnest. He released her and began ripping at the vines with his gloved hands, following the wall, searching for an opening.

Rain thundered down, and the wall went on forever. Finally, they found a corner and rounded it, thorny vines ripping at their skin, as they didn't pause to hack a path with machetes anymore. Five feet down the second wall, he reached for a vine, and his hand punched through. He tugged with both hands, and a dark gap opened up.

Window or door?

He didn't care much either way, so long as there was an inside they could get to.

Fiona's flashlight pierced the gap and revealed the dark went deep.

They put their heads together to look through the hole. It appeared to be a window opening, with the sill about a foot thick, just as Sadie had said it would be. Fiona aimed the beam downward, and he saw the floor. Insects and rodents had made use of the structure. He spotted fungi and plants that survived with limited light in the cracks between the mortarless brick floor.

Fiona's light hit the far wall, and he guessed the stone structure was eight by twelve feet. A perfect refuge from the downpour.

"The door is on the next wall," she observed.

"I vote we go through this window." He placed his hands low on her hips and picked her up, setting her on the ledge facing him. She squealed at his sudden act, and he planted his mouth on hers, kissing her as she sat in the hole in the wall and rain poured down on his head.

He released her. She smiled, gripped his soaking wet shirt, and brushed her lips over his, then released him and lifted her legs, tucking them to her chest as she pivoted in the opening. With her back to him, she pushed off the ledge and jumped into the stone structure.

He followed her through the window. Inside, he immediately dropped his pack, glad to be rid of the heavy weight for the first time in hours. She did the same.

He looked up, shining his headlamp at the ceiling, revealing a thick network of branches and more branches, topped by leaves. The roof had to be several feet thick. With the right vantage point, from the outside, the stone structure would look like nothing more than an overgrown hill.

"Those branches are hardwood," Fiona said, tracing the arms with the beam of her light.

She crossed to the wall, where the branches grew down the sides in a tangle. "It's likely this structure was built in the early 1700s, after the fort was abandoned and the island became a refuge. When enslaved, they'd been forced to build structures like this on other islands, so it makes sense that they would make one here, in the heart of the island next to a freshwater lake. A place they could hide using materials left behind by the Spanish and Dutch fort builders."

She pointed to the vine- and fungi-covered brick floor. "They probably salvaged the bricks for the floor, hearth, and chimney from Fort Domingo. There are several structures that were on the original maps of the fort but which now are completely gone." She pointed back to the ceiling. "I'm guessing they used simple broad leaves over wood-branch beams for the roof, but eventually the forest took over."

She knelt before the hearth, which was centered in the wall opposite the overgrown doorway. They'd probably been near the exterior of the hearth when her machete hit stone the first time.

She peeked her head up into the chimney. "It's full of vines and such, but it will probably draw."

He reached up and touched a low-hanging branch. It was dry enough. Very little rain made it through the layers of vegetation, even in the heavy storm. "We can cut some branches and burn them for heat and a cooking fire."

She winced.

"It's wood growing naturally here and not several hundred years old. It's not part of the original structure. Plus, I'd like to point out we're both soaking wet, and you're shivering. This might not be Alaska, but hypothermia can still happen if you don't get dry. A fire is a good idea about now."

She nodded. "I know. I was just . . . hoping we could find something to burn outside?"

"You mean in the rainforest? Where it's pouring rain?"

"I suppose that isn't likely, huh?"

"Nope." He crossed to stand before her. "You get the hearth ready, I'll cut the wood."

"Photograph it first, before you cut? Just so we can have a record of what it looked like undisturbed."

He brushed his lips over hers. "Of course."

He photographed the entire interior of the structure, then took a short video in which he rotated in a circle. He'd make another video in the morning when light would maybe penetrate the leaves and branches and provide better illumination, but this at least would be a baseline before they left their own mark on this shelter.

He photographed the hearth as Fiona took scrapings of the black soot that stained the bricks and stone.

"There isn't any charcoal or ash left after decades—centuries?—of rodent and insect activity," she said as she wrapped the scrapings and a few rocks that were stained black in aluminum foil and slipped the bundle into a zipper-top bag. She then pulled out a Sharpie and wrote the location and date on the bag. "But maybe there's enough here to date it using AMS—accelerator mass spectrometry—dating. It was important that I at least try to get a sample before we contaminate it." Her tone was defensive.

"You know you'll get no judgment from me."

She nodded. "I know. This structure has seen a lot of fires in the hearth; ours won't change the integrity. But still. It feels wrong."

He pulled her to him and cupped her cheek. Now that he was touching her freely, he couldn't seem to stop. Didn't want to stop. "I told you on Chiksook and I'll repeat it here. Lives are more valuable than any site, and we'll do everything we can to preserve the integrity."

They were back to only seeing each other in the light of their head-lamps. It was a strangely comfortable feeling.

She smiled up at him in the glow of his light. "Here we are again."

"Here we are. But this time, I'm not going to make the same mistake."

"Oh yeah, what mistake aren't you going to make?"

"I'm not going to let you go without making love to you first."

———

It wasn't lost on Fiona that Dean had said *"making love"* and not *"having sex."* She'd have accepted the latter without regrets. But it appeared she didn't have to and felt a rush of emotion that rocked her on her feet.

He smiled and kissed her softly. "But first we need fire. And food."

She looked up at the ceiling that would provide fuel for the fire. "You got a saw or hatchet in your field kit? The machete won't do much good here."

He nodded. "I've got a wire saw."

She set a small flashlight that converted to a lantern on the mantel. It shed a cheery yellow glow across the vine-covered bricks. Dean pulled out a thin wire embedded with sharp metal teeth and set to work. After draping it over a branch, he placed his index fingers in the rings on the ends and pulled back and forth in a seesaw motion, quickly cutting through the two-inch-diameter limb.

The storm howled outside, and even though they were protected from wind and rain, her shivering increased. He was right about her need to get dry.

He must've noticed her increased quaking because he said, "I've got dry clothes in my pack if you want to change."

His words jogged her memory. "I might have something."

She dug through her pack and there, at the bottom, were shorts and a T-shirt she'd tossed in that first week, after she got caught in a sudden downpour and didn't have anything dry to change into.

She crossed to the darkest corner of the stone structure and stripped, even removing her bra and underwear, which were hopelessly soaked.

As she lowered the panties, she dropped down in a squat to pick up the dry clothes. She noticed the sawing sound behind her had ceased and glanced over her shoulder to see Dean's eyes on her. His gaze smoldering in the dim light.

She rose and started to turn and face him.

"No," he said, his voice husky. "Not yet. I want to savor this."

She turned back, her grin wide and goose bumps disappearing. His words and gaze had been hot enough to raise her body temperature.

She pulled on the shorts and shirt, then returned to the hearth to prepare it for its first fire in decades, or even centuries. Rain thrummed even harder, but few drops made it through the layers of leaves, vines, and branches.

Their cozy hideaway smelled of earth and rain and green foliage. The structure fairly pulsed with life, from its living roof to vine-covered walls—interior and exterior. So very different from the volcano on Chiksook, which had been void of any kind of vegetation.

Once he had a decent-size pile of sticks, he joined her at the hearth. He piled thin strips of dried vines and leaves he'd gathered from the rafters—for lack of a better term—over a two-inch chunk of fire-starter brick. Then he propped larger sticks over the mound like a house of cards.

"Got any paper we can use to set it off with?" he asked.

She nodded and grabbed her notebook and ripped out blank pages from the back.

He tucked them in the bottom of the pile next to the wax-coated brick and used a lighter to set it aflame.

The brick caught quickly, a small yellow blaze latched on to the corner. The dried leaves flared, then smoky flames spread across the mound and licked at the hardwood card-like structure.

She watched, mesmerized almost, as the wood gave in to the inevitable and became one with the flame.

Once the fire was steady, Dean said, "I'll get changed, then we can relax for a bit before we eat." He dug through his pack, pulling out his sleeping pad and bag before he found his clothes. He nodded to the items. "Set up a seating area while I change? The brick floor is cold."

She nodded and opened the valve on the sleeping pad and blew into it, her eyes on him as he gathered dry clothes from his pack.

Catching her gaze, he grinned and faced her, not bothering to retreat to a dark corner as she had. He pulled his soaking wet shirt over his head, revealing that muscular torso she itched to explore with hands and mouth. The violet tattoo over his heart was but a dim shadow in the firelight.

He paused with his hands at his waistband, then turned and presented his back to her. Apparently, she, too, would have to wait.

She was fine with that. His muscled back was a work of art, which she was ready to appreciate with the enthusiasm of an aficionado of the medium. Today she'd seen those muscles in action as he paddled, hiked, climbed, and macheted.

The man was fit in the extreme, and today had demonstrated why he worked so hard to maintain his body when he wasn't on assignment.

She'd managed to keep up with him for the most part, but she highly doubted she could have climbed that rope—and not because she had a deep-seated fear of steep drops. Plus, her arms were utterly exhausted after the machete workout, but he still seemed to have energy to spare.

He dropped his shorts and underwear, presenting her with her first view of his perfect bare ass, and she let out a blissful sigh.

He was so damn beautiful.

It was surreal to be this . . . *happy* at this moment. Someone had tried to kill him today. But right now, they were safe, drying out, and gloriously alone. And with Dean, that was all she needed to be happy.

The pad was quality—extra-wide and over two inches thick when inflated. She set it on the floor in front of the hearth. She then set both their packs side by side next to the long edge to provide a backrest. After unzipping the sleeping bag, she draped it over both packs and the thick pad. Their "couch" was about the size of a love seat without legs.

She fed a few larger pieces of wood to the fire as she settled onto her seat. He joined her, draping his arm around her and pulling her tight to his side. She leaned her head on his shoulder and let out a content sigh. "This is so much better than being at the estate."

"To think Reynolds thought he could impress you with fancy meals, a massive tropical beach estate, a giant luxury yacht, and a pretty sunset. I know your tastes run more toward ramen cooked over an open fire, dank historic structures, and a fierce storm raging outside."

She snorted out a laugh, then said, "To be fair, I was quite excited to try cassoulet again, but then the boat blew up, which was sort of a bummer."

He snickered. "I bet."

"Yeah. Ramen isn't *quite* in the same league."

"Duly noted. So you're saying Reynolds is still in the running?"

"Oh, hell no." She threaded her fingers through his, resting her hand on his thigh. "He was never in the running. I considered him a friend, nothing more, and sometimes not even that."

"And now?"

"I don't know what to think, given all that's happened." She lifted their joined hands and pressed the back of his to her lips. "But right now, I don't want to talk about Jude."

"Fair enough. Want me to start dinner?"

"You cut the wood and built the fire. The least I can do is make ramen."

She poured water from her hydration pack into a small metal pan and set it propped on a brick in the fire. She found a pouch of cooked chicken in his food supplies and added it with the noodles to the boiling water. Three minutes later, she split the small meal between their two coffee mugs, and they clinked vessels and started eating.

She hadn't realized how hungry she was until she took the first bite, and suddenly she was ravenous. She forced herself to eat slowly because there would be no seconds. Dean had packed enough food for only one person for two days. They would head back to the estate tomorrow, but it wouldn't be wise to blow through their supplies all at once, just in case they had other issues.

She paused between bites, noting that Dean, too, was pacing himself. They both knew this drill. "When you get back from an expedition, what's the first restaurant you go to?" she asked.

"It's not restaurants I miss when I'm away, it's my kitchen. My bathtub. My personal comforts. What about you?"

"I'm never gone for more than two or three weeks. Not long enough to develop a real longing for anything except plumbing. And this trip—well, until tonight—plumbing hasn't been lacking, and the food has been better than any restaurant I frequent at home."

"This trip was going to be two months, though. Surely you'd have ended up missing some home comforts?"

"We'll never know, because I'm heading home after three weeks."

"I'm sorry for that. I know this was a dream project for you."

She shrugged, brushing aside the jab of pain. She was *happy*, dammit. And wanted to stay that way. For a few hours, at least.

He cleared his throat, probably reading her mind. "I think I'll hang out on Dominica with Dylan for a few weeks, since we cut our Big Island vacation short. What do you think you'll want to do?"

She noticed he didn't invite her to join them, but that was hardly a surprise. She was under no illusions that tonight would be anything other than singular. He'd said it himself when they'd first entered this oasis. *"I'm not going to let you go without making love to you first."*

Yes, he'd said *"making love,"* but he'd also made it clear he had every intention of letting her go.

His rules were clear, and she would abide by them.

———

Dean winced as soon as the words were out of his mouth. He should have invited her to join them. But he *couldn't.* When he made love to her tonight, he'd be breaking one of the most important vows he'd made ten years ago. He'd accepted that. It was inevitable, really. But he wouldn't break the final vow.

He twisted and reached behind him to dig in his pack. He pulled out a square plastic food container and a small, insulated pouch and held them up. "I forgot about this earlier. In the wake of . . . well, everything. But I asked the chef if he would make a treat for you. I planned to break it out at the end of the day, before I walked you back to the canoe."

Her eyes lit with delight. "Ohh. What is it?"

He grinned and opened the container, his heart pounding a bit with anticipation of her reaction.

She gasped. "Is that . . . pavlova?"

He nodded.

"How did you know I love pavlova?"

"You mentioned it on Chiksook."

Her eyes widened, and he could see the moment she remembered, the exact conversation.

He set the open container and the insulated bag on the floor, cupped her face in his hands, and kissed her softly. "I remember *everything* from that week. Relived every conversation." He cleared his throat. "Now, if

I remember correctly, and we've just established that I do . . . you said you like your pavlova with strawberries and cream."

He released her and reached for the insulated bag, pulling out a container of sliced strawberries and a plastic jar of whipped cream.

He spread the whipped cream over the pavlova, then placed the strawberries on top. Last, he pulled two spoons from his utensils and handed her one.

"This is the sweetest thing ever," she said as she sliced into the dessert with the side of her spoon. She tasted it and let out a soft moan. "I can't believe I'm eating pavlova in the middle of a rainforest." She took another bite and turned over the spoon in her mouth, sliding it out slowly with her eyes closed. "So. Good."

The look of pleasure on her face was a complete turn-on. A drop of cream stuck to her bottom lip, covering that distracting freckle. He leaned forward and licked the spot clean, fulfilling a long-held fantasy.

She laughed. "There's enough in the container for you to have your own dessert."

"Tastes better this way."

She gave him a wicked grin and took a messy bite, letting the meringue and cream cover her lips. He took her bait and licked the sweetness away.

She scooped another bite from the dish, but on the way to her mouth, for some mysterious reason, it fell and landed on the bare skin in the V of her top. The cream dripped down, falling into the valley of her cleavage.

Pavlova would never be the same for him again.

He set the dessert aside and leaned in, nudging her back until she was leaning slightly arched over her backpack. The tight T-shirt hugged her full breasts and hid nothing from his gaze, her peaked nipples spots of pink beneath the thin white fabric.

He leaned down and traced the line of cream from her cleavage upward, licking slowly, thoroughly, being sure not to miss a drop of sweetness. He scooped up the dollop of meringue and strawberries with his tongue and savored the flavor before returning to lick her some more.

Once her skin had been cleaned of all traces of dessert, he rocked back on his heels to take her in.

Her face was flushed, her eyes hot with desire. Her nipples tempted him. He very much wanted to taste them, with and without whipped cream.

She must've read his mind because her hands found the hem of her shirt and she lifted it, rising from the pack she leaned on just long enough to pull the top over her head.

She lay before him, a bare-chested feast in the firelight. He leaned forward to indulge, but she placed a hand on his chest. "This is tit for tat. As in, you see my"—she waved a hand in front of her chest—"and I get to see your tat."

He laughed and whipped his shirt over his head faster than that guy on YouTube, then sat back on his heels so she could look her fill. She raised her hand and gave him a questioning look as her hand hovered in front of his tattoo.

This would be the first time he had sex with a woman who knew what the violet over his heart represented. It meant everything that she knew and cared.

He nodded permission, and she pressed her palm to the flowers he'd had inked into his skin six months before Violet died. Rain drummed on the organic roof, but he could almost hear the beat of his heart under her warm palm.

"I could have lost you today."

He lifted her hand and brought it to his lips. "But you didn't." He kissed the inside of her wrist, then trailed down her arm. "And I'm going to show you how very alive I am right now."

He abandoned her arm for her breast, first running his tongue over her nipple, then gently sucking it between his lips. He glanced up to see her expression. Did she like nipple play?

She tilted her head back as her hands came up to cup her breasts, and he got the hint. Yes to the nipples, but she wanted him to cradle her breasts in his hands too.

He filled his palms with the soft mounds, taking turns between kissing and sucking on each nipple. From the sounds she made and the way she moved her hips, she definitely liked that. Lucky him, because he *loved* it.

Her hands cupped his biceps, stroking up and down his arms, then over his chest, down his sides, and up the center, tracing his abs and sliding up over his pecs. "Kiss me, Dean." Her voice was soft, panting a little. A bit desperate.

It was so damn hot.

His mouth left her breast and traced a line upward, nuzzling her neck on the way to her lips. Finally, he reached her alluring mouth with its tormenting freckle and kissed her deeply, his tongue sliding against hers.

She tasted of strawberries and cream and heat and pleasure. He could forget everything in this kiss. The rain outside, the cold, damp, overgrown floor. The attempt on his life. Even the torment of knowing he would eventually let her go.

Right now, he had her, and he was going to possess her as he'd promised. He'd give her the ultimate pleasure, as she deserved.

He shifted as he kissed her, until his body was over hers, his hips between her thighs, his bare chest pressed to hers. They were skin to skin at last.

Her fingers threaded in his hair as he supported his weight with his hands on her pack, rocking his hips in the cradle of her thighs. His erection thickened as they mimicked sex, grinding against each other as their mouths penetrated and tongues stroked.

As hot as the kiss was, he needed to touch her. Taste her. He took her bottom lip between his teeth and gently nibbled, then slowly released as he raised his head. He held her gaze. Her face was fully flushed now. Her lips plump and swollen, damp with his kisses.

It was an achingly erotic sight that was crushed as an important realization hit him. He closed his eyes and cursed softly.

The fingers she'd been sliding between his whiskers stopped. "What's wrong?"

"I didn't bring condoms. I promised myself I wouldn't take advantage of you and wasn't about to . . . tempt fate like that. I was going camping to *avoid* temptation."

Her body stiffened beneath him. "You aren't taking advantage. I am fully capable of making informed decisions for myself."

He pressed a kiss to her lips. "I know. I'm sorry. But the problem still remains."

"No. It doesn't. I have a box."

"You brought condoms?"

She nodded.

"All the way to Ruby Island?" He highly doubted Reynolds or his staff would have provided her with a box.

"I did."

"But . . . you don't do field flings."

She grinned. "When we were on Chiksook, I decided to . . . live a little more. Be open to more opportunities and relationships. I didn't come here looking to hook up in traditional field-fling style, but I wasn't going to not be prepared if something—or rather someone—good came along."

He smiled. "And you put them in your field bag . . . when?"

"This morning, once I knew I'd be spending the day in the field with you."

"Does that mean I'm something good?"

She stroked his cheek. "Hot Bird Man, you are the *ultimate*."

He grinned and nipped at her neck. "I like the sound of that."

"Good. Now, get off me and get naked while I get the condoms."

"Bossy. I like that too." He stood and checked the fire, adding more fuel.

Fiona dug in her bag and produced a full box of condoms, a bit battered from being crushed in the pack but sealed tight in a thick zipper-top bag. She stood upright and handed him the package.

He studied the bag. "This isn't a sandwich bag."

She laughed. "No. It's an artifact bag. Extra-thick. High-grade plastic. You think I'd protect my condoms with anything less?"

"You're adorable."

She smiled. "Thank you. Now, get naked so I can finally admire every inch of you."

He crossed his arms. He liked bossy a lot, but sometimes it was even more fun to push back. "You first."

She raised a brow, clearly guessing at his game.

Even better.

He stepped forward and cupped her hips, his thumbs sliding between her shorts and skin. He dropped to his knees and kissed her belly, then slowly pulled down the shorts, his mouth trailing along her hip and thigh as he lowered himself.

Her shorts hit the floor, and he was face-to-face with her pale-brown triangle of hair. She'd trimmed but not shaved, which was pretty much his favorite thing if given a choice. He ran a hand up the inside of her thigh, and her body shuddered as he neared her center.

He looked up to see her face, and the desire—the absolute *need*—drove him wild. He'd wanted this for so long. His fingers were just below her opening. He could smell her arousal. "Can I touch you, Fiona?"

"Please. Now." The words were almost desperate.

He touched her lips, slipped a finger between, then slid it upward, penetrating her slick heat. Leaving his finger there, he slid his thumb higher to stroke her clit. She jolted and let out a soft sound of pleasure. "Yes. That."

His hard-on strained against his shorts. He moved his finger inside her and pressed with his thumb, pinching her G-spot and clit between thumb and forefinger. She bucked again and braced her hands on his shoulders. Her eyes were closed. She was deep in the sensual zone, pleasing his ego greatly.

"Can I lick you, Fiona?"

"Oh my, yes."

He chuckled and moved his face between her legs so his mouth could join the fun. He licked her, starting where his finger stroked her and ending at his thumb, which he moved out of the way. He laved her clit with his tongue, then gently ran his teeth over the sensitive flesh and sucked on her.

Her legs shook as her weight shifted to the hands that rested on his shoulders. He'd fantasized about giving her this pleasure dozens—possibly hundreds—of times in the last nine months, and it was glorious to finally be in the moment for real as he watched her pant and moan and lose herself in the ecstasy he could give her.

His mouth left her clit so his tongue could slide inside her. The hands on his shoulders gripped him tight as she gasped at the thrust of his tongue.

His cock was at full attention, eager for the exquisite sheath of her body.

"Dean. I want—need you inside me."

He gave her clit one last stroke, then leaned back to look up at her, rubbing the back of his hand across his mouth and beard. "Lie down," he commanded.

This time, she didn't hesitate and dropped down and stretched across the sleeping bag draped over the thermal pad.

He rose and dropped his shorts, his gaze on her face as she took in his fully naked body for the first time.

Damn, if he could bottle that look, pack it away, and take it out to savor when he faced lonely nights on expeditions in the future.

She sat up and reached out, wrapping her warm palm around the base of his penis and stroking to the tip.

Now it was his turn to shudder and moan.

She licked her lips as she stroked him again. He would come way too fast if he let her put her mouth on him, so he nudged her back. She released him and lay down, spreading her legs. He knelt between her thighs and picked up the package of condoms, then fumbled with the zipper-topped bag and box before finally reaching the individually wrapped condoms inside. He should have prepped that part ahead of time.

At last, he had a single condom free of the wrapper and placed it in her hand. She unrolled it down his hard length. He lowered himself and stroked her clit with his sheathed erection.

She rose up on her elbows and whispered in his ear. "Make love to me."

He kissed her, his tongue probing at her lips as his erection probed her slick opening. Slowly, exquisitely, he slid inside her as his tongue took her mouth. He filled her to the hilt; she gasped, and he groaned.

She clenched tight around him as he slowly pulled back, then thrust deep again. He was fully connected to Fiona at last. A part of her, even though temporary. He would remember this pleasure, this joining, with reverence for the rest of his days.

He'd forgotten what it felt like to make love. How the pleasure was richer. The joy higher. He'd blocked that out. But now he was inside Fiona, and his emotions overwhelmed as his body moved in a familiar rhythm.

For ten years, sex had been rote.

But not with Fiona. No. He gave it to her sensuous and sweet, slowly building to fast and hot.

Her hands gripped his shoulders as her legs crossed over his ass. He was up on his arms and looked down at her. Eyes closed and mouth open, she was fully given over to the moment. Basking in the pleasure he gave her. She panted and thrust her chest out as she rocked her hips in rhythm with his.

He reached a hand between their bodies and stroked her clit. All at once, her eyes popped open and she said, "Oh *yes*." And he felt pretty much like a god.

She was utterly beautiful as her face tightened and she let out a cry as she came. He kept stroking, his thrusts fast and deep, and her cries turned into a moan. Certain she'd reached the pinnacle, he threw back his head and pumped his hips, letting go completely. A cry tore from his throat as he came, pulsing into her.

It was a powerful orgasm—worthy of the long dry spell since he'd last had sex with a partner, but also, he guessed, since he'd last made love. All he knew was the pleasure that rippled through him wasn't something he could quantify.

It was simply a soul-deep release.

He collapsed on top of her, then, not certain his arms were up to the task of holding his weight, he rolled to the side, pulling her with him. His penis slipped from her body. He'd need to deal with the condom, but for the next minute or two, all he wanted to do was nuzzle her neck and breathe in her sweaty scent.

Her hand ran over his hip and side; her fingers were warm on his skin. He opened his eyes. They were stretched out with the fire behind her, and her skin glowed in the orange light. He traced her hairline with his fingertips, tucking loose strands behind her ear. "You are so incredibly beautiful."

She flashed a smile. "Thank you. I take that as a high compliment, knowing you've slept with at least one actual supermodel."

He narrowed his eyes as he held in a laugh. From another woman, he'd take the words as a sign of insecurity, but with Fiona, it was a tease. She did enjoy mocking him in this area. "Did I live up to your expectations, given my reputation as a seducer of beautiful women?"

She grinned. "For the most part."

He pulled back. "What do you mean, *for the most part*? I was magnificent!"

She giggled, then pushed him on his back. "That you were." Her voice was breathy and low and damn if he didn't feel his cock stir. She pressed her lips to his chest in a soft kiss, then added, "But I'm not sure if I felt entirely *possessed*. I think we're going to have to keep trying."

He laughed and sat up, pushing her back as she straddled his hips. "Let me take care of this condom, then, so we can try again." He licked her nipple, then said, "We'll start with me finishing my dessert."

TWENTY-FOUR

Dean's sleeping bag was a backpacker's mummy-style bag and not the wider, base-camp-style bag they had shared on Chiksook. This meant there was no way the two of them could share it with the bag zipped, but thankfully they were in the tropics, not the North Pacific Ocean. Between the fire and padding to protect them from the cold brick floor, they would be warm enough with the bag unzipped and draped over the two of them.

The camp pad wasn't really wide enough for two people, but sleeping wrapped in Dean's arms was no hardship for Fiona. They'd managed it when they were virtual strangers. As lovers, it was as sweet as pavlova, and left her feeling just as airy.

She lay facing the fire with Dean at her back, his knees tucked behind hers. She was drifting off to sleep after he'd made love to her a second time, when she suddenly jolted.

Richards. The chaotic day kept stripping the man's presence on Ruby Island from her mind. She'd yet to tell Dean any of it. At first because she couldn't, but then today, after what happened, she'd been waiting for the right time. When slashing through vines, it was hard to have a coherent conversation about spying on a friend.

"What's wrong, Fi?" His voice was sleepy; he'd been drifting off as well.

Goodness, where to start?

She closed her eyes and considered her options. She'd been legally forbidden from sharing anything about the meeting with the admiral, the FBI agent, and the mysterious Mr. Richards, but secret clearance was moot once the attempt had been made on Dean's life.

He had a right to know.

She scooted onto her back, then rolled to her other side so she could face him. "There's something . . . I need to tell you."

He opened one eye, then both, reluctantly shedding his dozing state. "That sounds . . . ominous."

"It's not. I mean, you might be upset I didn't tell you before, but I couldn't. It's Secret."

He placed a hand on the small of her back and pulled her a fraction of an inch closer. "A secret? About Jude? I would imagine he has a lot of secrets."

"No. Not that kind of secret. The security-level kind. Secret as in not Top Secret, but not Confidential either. In between."

"Is this about what happened on Chiksook? Obviously, you can tell me about that. I was in on the secret."

She shook her head. "Yeah. No. Not that either."

"Okay. How about I stop trying to guess and let you speak?"

She brushed her lips over his. "Great idea."

"I'm an excellent thinker. Top-notch."

"You are also loquacious after sex, apparently."

"Not usually, but maybe so with you. I kind of like it. What should we talk about?"

She giggled. He was being ridiculous and adorable, and she loved seeing this side of him. This was who he was when he relaxed. They'd never really had downtime together.

Unfortunately, they shouldn't be having it now.

He smiled. "I'll stop interrupting if you kiss me one more time." She leaned forward to press her lips to his when he stopped her. "I didn't say where."

She narrowed her gaze. "Where am I supposed to kiss you?"

He grinned. "Ohh. I didn't think that would work. Where indeed . . ."

She stretched her neck and kissed the tip of his nose, then pressed her fingers to his lips. "Enough. Okay. I'll just blurt it out. Before I received approval for my leave of absence to work this job, the admiral at the base I work on called me into his office. There were three people in the room when I arrived. The admiral, an FBI agent, and another guy who I thought was NSA or DIA."

"You have my attention now."

"Yeah, I *thought* that would do the trick." She cleared her throat and continued. "So, to say this was unusual is putting it mildly. Furthermore, there wasn't anyone *else* in the room. No one from HR. No union rep. And this was ostensibly for an HR issue—a leave of absence. But at the same time, it wasn't entirely surprising the paperwork for my leave request made it all the way to the admiral's desk. What happened on Chiksook put me on his radar.

"So I'm called into this meeting, and the FBI guy shows me his badge. The admiral, of course, I know. Not well, but he's been in the Pac Northwest for eighteen months, and one component of his job is attending cultural outreach ceremonies with local tribes, which I help coordinate. We're not exactly chummy, but I know him and, well, he's an admiral in the US Navy. He's been thoroughly vetted. So I didn't really worry when the third guy only gave his name, Christopher Richards—'Call me Chris'—no agency affiliation. I immediately started thinking NSA, which made sense because he wouldn't be allowed to say who he works for."

Dean's body was no longer languid against hers; she could feel the rising tension as they lay chest to chest.

"So, to start things off, the admiral said he wanted to grant my request for leave to work on the Ruby Island Archaeological Inventory—I'd included the scope of work with my request—but he had some questions about my association with Jude Reynolds and RAM Freight.

"I told him what I told you. We were friends once upon a time . . . yadda yadda yadda . . . I mentioned the lousy date four years ago, because hey, the NSA guy might wonder why I didn't say anything if he's been listening in on my phone calls with Sadie." She laughed nervously at the memory. "It's weird how you can feel like you've done something wrong, even when you know you haven't. My request for leave was totally legit, but suddenly it felt . . . dirty. Suspicious."

Dean's hand on her back was grounding, something she needed as she looked back on that meeting with a more critical eye.

"So after I told them pretty much everything about my friendship with Jude except the skinny-dipping in the quarry—it wasn't just the two of us, mind you, half the crew was there—"

"Fiona Carver, you went skinny-dipping on a field project?"

She narrowed her gaze. "Yes, and I'm not ashamed."

His hand dropped lower to cup her ass. "Good, because you shouldn't be. I was just surprised."

"I was twenty-one, and it was field school, not a work situation."

"Were you equally daring when you did the underwater archaeology field school in Jamaica?"

"Yes. Now, back to—"

His lips found her neck, and he whispered, "Maybe tomorrow we can go skinny-dipping in the lake. There's got to be some sort of waterfall we can play in. Now, will you stop distracting me with tales of nudity and tell me what's going on?"

"*Tales of Nudity* is the title of my memoir."

She thoroughly enjoyed the feel of his body against hers as he shook with laughter.

When his laughter subsided, he kissed her nose and said, "Talk."

She placed a hand on his chest, over his tattoo, and resumed her story. "So after I spill my guts, the admiral reminds me that I have Secret clearance—necessary for my job—and that everything that is about to be discussed is classified and falls under that umbrella. What he's sharing with me is all he can reveal at my security level, and I may not discuss it with anyone outside the room because they don't have the same 'need to know' that I have. Failure to comply means I would be fired and could be prosecuted for revealing classified information."

Dean pressed his fingers to her lips. "Should you stop right now? I don't want you to get into trouble."

"Well, you see, that's the thing. They never really *told* me anything. They asked me to do something. So how am I revealing classified information when they didn't tell me anything classified? And I've been doing what they asked me to do, so I'm really just revealing my part. And at this point, given the situation we're in, I'll take being fired, *and* if they dared try to prosecute me, I'd call them out for sending me here—endangering me, and you, and everyone involved—without so much as a heads-up."

He kissed her nose again. "I will hire the best lawyers for you."

She laughed and said, *"Awww."*

"So what did they ask you to do?"

"Well, before they asked, the admiral signed my leave request. He said he wanted to be clear that leave to work on this project wasn't contingent on me agreeing to their request. He also said I was free to leave without hearing the request, but if I stayed and listened, I'd have to adhere to my security clearance. There was a ten-second period when I could have walked out of the room free and clear."

"But you were curious," Dean said.

She nodded. *"Soooo* curious. So I stayed. And then the quiet guy who was maybe NSA started talking. He asked me if I could be on the lookout for irregularities on Ruby Island. I asked him what that meant, and he basically said I'd know it if I saw it. I gathered that they were interested in RAM Freight, not Jude in particular. And then I got here, and Kosmo was so very hostile to the project. I wondered if that constituted *'irregular'* by Richards's standards. But Kosmo being hostile didn't seem to rise to the level. And then Jude started telling me about his drone, and I was sure that was it."

Dean nodded. "Yeah, it would make sense for the navy to be interested in that technology."

"When I agreed to play spy—and that's why I was sure the guy *wasn't* CIA, because only the FBI can investigate Americans, and both Jude and Kosmo are American—I was given a login to SIPRNet, which is the Secret Internet Protocol Router Network, and very specific instructions on how to use it, because it's encrypted, but I needed to access it through Jude's network, which has a gazillion fire walls. My job was to email the admiral using SIPRNet and report any irregularities and also provide a list of visitors to the island as best I could."

Dean let out a low whistle. "So really, they could have been monitoring someone who was likely to show up at the party."

"Yeah, that crossed my mind too. So my first report was about Jude's drone. The second—"

"I'm guessing was the helicopter crash."

"Yeah. I figured that qualified as *'irregular.'*" She held up her fingers in air quotes. "And, of course, I sent a list of party guests and told them about the boat explosion and lost drone. And tonight, if I were back at the house, I'd have reported the tampering of your descenders."

"They were right about you knowing odd when you saw it."

She snickered. "Yep. Can't sneak an explosion past me." She pressed her lips to his shoulder and breathed in his scent. Sex and woodsmoke smelled good on him. "There's more, though. And it's something that happened today and is an absolute violation of my Secret clearance, which is why I didn't tell you earlier. Not without context. But someone tried to kill you, and I can't deal with this alone—"

"You don't have to justify it to me."

"I know. I'm justifying it to myself. I take my oaths seriously."

"I know you do, Fi. It's one of the things I admire about you."

She took a deep breath as heat unfurled in her belly from the compliment. "This morning, I saw Chris Richards walk out of Jude's office."

"The NSA guy?"

"If he's really NSA, then I'm going to need your attorney, because unmasking a covert operator is . . . *bad*."

"But you don't think he's NSA anymore."

"No, I don't," she said. "And what I think he is would be worse for Jude. For the situation we're in. We could be in a helluva lot more danger."

"If he's not NSA, I have a guess—"

"Say it at the same time?"

At his nod, they both said, "Drug Enforcement Agency," in unison.

"Shit," he added.

"Yeah. It . . . never even crossed my mind until we were talking as we hacked away at the vines tonight, which seems silly really, but it was much easier to think the government was interested in Jude's drone technology than thinking my old friend could be a drug lord of some kind. And I remembered something tonight as we were drifting off to sleep . . . You know how your brain can throw out random facts that seem irrelevant? The admiral mentioned that his posting prior to the Pacific Northwest had been in the Southeast Command. Which, of course, includes the states on the Gulf of Mexico and Cuba and includes Caribbean waters."

"One of the major tasks of the navy in this area is drug interdiction," Dean said. "Working with the DEA."

"Exactly. As an admiral who'd been commander of a base in the region, if there was even a whisper of drug smuggling connected to RAM Freight or Ruby Island, he'd know about it. And so of course my request for leave would have been flagged. And given what happened on Chiksook, I was deemed trustworthy, I guess. Or maybe gullible, so they wanted to use me as a spy when they had no other entrée to the island."

"They saw an opportunity in you."

"Yeah. But honestly, I don't think they're necessarily after Jude so much as RAM Freight." She paused; here was where it got either absurd or chilling. "It's possible the admiral, the FBI guy, and Richards figured the lidar survey or the underwater survey would uncover evidence of drug smuggling through Ruby Island. We were talking earlier about how much cocaine is moved through the Caribbean and the fact that RAM Freight started as rum runners. The FBI guy asked a lot of questions about the survey and mapping I'd be doing here. And they were more interested in RAM than they were in Jude."

"And if Ruby Island is a hot spot for smuggling," Dean said, "Jude couldn't know about it, or he'd never have hired you and Sadie and Chad."

"Exactly. And that has me thinking that's the reason Kosmo has been so hostile to the project. What if he's been trying to derail us from the start? What if he's behind all the sabotage because he doesn't want us to find his drug operation and tell Jude his business is a fraud?"

TWENTY-FIVE

Every decision Chad had made was wrong. Every idea. Every plan. Every action. From the moment he'd set foot on Ruby Island, he'd made one bad choice after another. But fifteen hours ago, a little after eleven a.m. Atlantic Standard Time, he'd made the worst mistake of his life. And every minute since then had been an absolute nightmare.

He'd never imagined he could screw up so badly, but at the same time, he didn't quite understand how he didn't see this turn of events coming. He'd been so desperate to win Sadie's trust again, he failed to think his plan through.

And now Sadie would be the one to pay the ultimate price for the mess he'd created.

His stomach churned as he tried to figure out what the hell he was going to do.

Where had Kosmo taken her? There were only so many places to imprison someone on Ruby Island.

He didn't for a second believe the executive would let them sail off into the sunset once Chad delivered what he wanted. At this point, the only way to save Sadie was to get help. He couldn't go to Jude. Kosmo would kill Sadie if he did that.

Fifteen hours ago, after Chad approached Kosmo and offered a deal, the man had gone into action, as if he'd seen the moment coming from the start of the fieldwork. But then, Chad figured he probably had.

Kosmo had sent all island staff who didn't work directly for him to Dominica to weather out the storm. As far as Chad knew, the only people left at the estate who didn't work for RAM Freight were Nico, Sadie, and himself. Fiona and Dean hadn't returned from the field that day, which raised even more questions.

Had something happened to them, or had they taken the opportunity for a romantic getaway? Dean had planned to camp in the forest. Maybe Fiona had opted to join him?

Chad had bolted immediately after receiving Kosmo's ultimatum, before the man could saddle him with Walker or one of the others as a babysitter. He couldn't save Sadie if they were monitoring his every move. He'd spent hours after that watching the house, trying to figure out his next steps. Looking for signs of where they'd taken Sadie.

He'd seen Jude pacing in front of his third-floor windows, pausing every so often to look out over the gardens toward the rainforest. Was he distraught Fiona hadn't returned from the field after setting off with Dean? Or had he realized his executive VP was a Judas?

His money was on Fiona's rejection, because how the hell did the billionaire *not* suspect Kosmo?

It must be willful ignorance. Chad doubted the man would intervene if he knew the truth. He had far too much to lose, and Kosmo knew it.

Sadie's only hope now was if Chad got help. She was Kosmo's hostage, and unless the VP got what he wanted, she'd pay the ultimate price for Chad's horrific miscalculation.

But he couldn't do it alone. The minute Kosmo got what he wanted, they were all dead.

His only option was to find Fiona and the photographer.

She was pissed at him, and Slater had probably heard all about Chad's fight with Sadie from his brother. But it didn't matter if they both hated him. Fiona loved Sadie. She'd help him because it would help Sadie, and that was all that mattered.

But where were they?

He'd watched the house until the storm got bad, then took shelter in one of the servant bungalows. They hadn't returned, unless they came back at the height of the storm. Possible, but unlikely.

He needed to find them. He pulled out the map Sadie had made and studied it. Fiona had been tasked with ground-truthing the lidar survey in the area near the lakes to find Sadie's structures.

That could be a refuge if they'd been caught in a torrent. If he wanted to find Fiona and Dean, he had to start with the lake.

———

Waking up with Dean's nude body wrapped around hers was absolutely delicious. It didn't matter that her hip hurt due to only having a camping pad between her and the hard brick floor. Or that her arm was asleep, and she probably looked a wreck after getting drenched in the rain, then going to bed without combing out her hair.

He'd seen her look worse in the morning, that was for sure.

The only thing that mattered was his hand draped possessively on her breast and the morning erection that pressed against her backside. She smiled. Even in his sleep, he wanted her.

Later, she'd worry about how much it was going to hurt when she said goodbye to him, but right now, she'd let herself revel in the intimacy they'd finally shared.

Everything else was going to hell; she needed to hold on to joy when she felt it.

Dean's even breathing changed to a new pattern, and the hand at her breast squeezed softly, his thumb brushing idly over her nipple.

She wiggled her butt in response. He let out a soft groan, and his lips nuzzled her neck.

This was her idea of heaven. He wasn't holding anything back, and it was glorious.

His hands explored her body as she lay facing the extinguished hearth. His fingers slipped between her thighs and teased her clitoris as she rocked her hips so her backside stroked his erection.

They didn't exchange words, but still, his touch, his body was in sync with her wants and needs. It wasn't long before he rolled on a condom and nudged her onto her belly so he could take her from behind. Exquisite pleasure ripped through her as he slowly slid into her. The rhythm of his movement sent her into a languid state of pleasure where she lost track of everything but the feel of him inside her.

He slipped from her and broke the silence. "Turn over, beautiful, I want to see your face as I make you come."

He raised his body to give her room to move, and she did, facing him, seeing his handsome features in the gray light of the rainy morning, with those blue, blue eyes hot with arousal.

Dean. Her Dean.

Mine.

As he slid inside her again, he leaned down and kissed her, his tongue sliding deep into her mouth. Possessing her as he filled her. His beard brushed her chin and cheeks as he tasted and teased. She loved everything about the feel of him on her, in her, even the abrasion of whiskers.

She came before he did, letting out a guttural sound as pleasure rippled through her. His thrusts intensified, and she opened her eyes, watching his face as his body pulsed with orgasm.

He kissed her again, hot and deep, then raised his head and met her gaze. The look in his eyes made her belly flutter, and this was *after* he'd given her an orgasm already. His voice was husky as he said, "Do you feel possessed yet?"

She smiled and stroked his beard. "Not even close."

Dean laughed. She was incredible, and being with her was dangerously addictive. He rolled to his side, taking her with him. He wanted to stay here for a week and do nothing but make love to her until he satisfied her impossible standards. But they would run out of food today and condoms tomorrow at this rate. And there was that little issue of someone sabotaging his climbing equipment and the arrival of the DEA agent and the possible smuggling conducted by RAM Freight.

"We need to come up with a plan for today. I'm not sure marching right back into the house is the best idea."

"Yeah. I was thinking the same thing. I want to talk to Richards, but I can't exactly walk up to him and say howdy."

"*Tempus* is at the dock by Fort Domingo, and I heard that's the safest port during a storm. I think we should head that way." He closed his eyes, seeing the map of the island in his mind. "We're pretty much at the center of the island. But there's more jungle between us and the house than if we hike to the fort. There are large swaths of Mount Asilo that aren't overgrown, but it's a hundred percent rainforest between here and the estate. I think we should head to the fort, convince Chad to pick up Sadie and Nico, and head to Dominica. From there you can contact the admiral and ask about Richards."

"Sounds like a plan."

Given that it was still raining lightly, they decided to build a fire and linger over breakfast, boiling water for instant coffee to go with their PowerBar meal.

As familiar as this was, it was also entirely different now that they'd been intimate. He felt the same desire he'd felt before, but now it wasn't tangled with guilt over lusting after Dylan's girl, among other things.

She leaned against him, her head on his shoulder, and he breathed in the scent of her soft hair—earth- and rain-scented after yesterday, with the added pleasure of the scent of sex—*him*—on her skin. It was a primal feeling. Marked territory.

As a wildlife biologist who tracked animals in the wild, he completely understood *why* this particular scent stirred him on a fundamental level.

Fiona was *his*.

He could smell it on her skin, and it aroused him again. Somehow, she'd managed to turn the tables and possessed *him* now.

He wouldn't keep her, but he'd revel in this feeling as long as it lasted. He'd live off the memories of her hands and mouth on his body for years to come. He twisted in his seat and planted his mouth on hers, just because he could. She melted into him, kissing back with a heat that seeped into his cold, empty heart.

He kissed her long and deep, and when he raised his head, he looked down at her flushed face. Her eyes fluttered open, and she said, "Wow. What brought that on?"

"Do I need an excuse?"

She brushed her lips over his. "No."

Emotion surged as he stared into her beautiful green eyes. Part of him recognized how dangerous this was, but then, wasn't he an adrenaline junkie?

Danger was his favorite drug.

He kissed her forehead and then pulled back, rising to his feet. "We should probably get going if we want to catch Chad before he takes the boat to the estate."

She nodded.

It took a few minutes for them to douse the fire and pack their gear. They set out and worked their way through the tangled vines to where jungle gave way to more mature rainforest where it was easier to cut trail. It had taken forever for them to cut this path, but they retraced their steps in a matter of minutes.

The rain was a steady drizzle that didn't make it all the way through the canopy.

They each donned their emergency rain ponchos that they hadn't bothered with the night before because the vines and branches would have shredded them in minutes as they hacked their way through the vegetation.

At least it was warmer today, as the humidity was high in the wake of the storm, so there wasn't a concern they'd get chilled again, and yesterday's clothes had dried out overnight, since they'd hung them from the branches of the ceiling to dry in the heat of the fire.

The hike had a steady increase in elevation as they ascended the forested slopes of the volcano. At last they reached the clearings, and the sun shone bright, the storm having passed completely. Sunlight baked down and dried the damp, rocky earth, and the air positively steamed with water vapor.

Two hours after setting out, they reached a ridge above the star fort that gave them a partial view of the easternmost bastion, the side of the fort that was entirely covered with thick vegetation.

While the west flank had been cleared of debris and vegetation, the east had been left alone. There'd been talk of clearing it all, and Dean realized he was disappointed that he'd never get to see the fort restored to its seventeenth- or eighteenth-century condition.

It would have been interesting to photograph it from the deck of a boat, giving the world a glimpse of how the island would have looked to pirates as they approached the refuge for the first time. Cannons in the embrasures and all. There were several different flags that had flown over Ruby Island, and with special permission, Jude could have commemorated and honored the people who had lived here over the centuries by flying their flags.

But none of that could happen if it was true that Ruby Island remained a smugglers' haven centuries after pirates had first used it for that purpose. Dominica would never renew the lease, and Dean would personally do everything he could to ensure Kosmo and Jude faced jail time.

Dominica was the most natural of all the Caribbean islands, and the inhabitants wanted it to stay that way. Openly allowing drug trafficking with Colombia or Venezuela would invite the wrong people to make inroads into the power hierarchy of the country.

As much as Dean would like to see the fort restoration and archaeological inventory completed, he was glad the island would revert to Dominican hands after this. The place was too precious to be exploited further. It was an island without golf balls, uniquely pristine in that way.

Hell, even the moon had golf balls littering the surface.

Their view of the cove to the east was obstructed by plants. "I'm going to head farther down the path, see if I can get a glimpse of the dock without exposing myself."

She grabbed his hand. "You think we're in danger here?"

"No clue. You might've seen a DEA agent at the house. Someone screwed with my descenders. We've been away for twenty-four hours. We have no idea what the situation is."

Her brow furrowed with worry. Finally she said, "Be careful."

He leaned down and kissed her. "Always." To fulfill that promise, before heading down the path, he pulled out his camera and used the zoom to examine the parts of the fort he could see.

It took him a moment to realize what he was seeing. "Fi, someone cut a path through the vines."

He snapped photos of the straight line that marked a trail through the foliage and zoomed in to capture images of the cut leaves and vines. The slashes through the vegetation were obvious in the close-up shots.

He showed her the display screen.

Her brow furrowed. "Why would anyone do that? Why not wait until it's cleared?"

Dean's quick reconnaissance mission was a bust. *No boat.*

Damn. Fiona didn't realize how much she'd been counting on *Tempus Machina* being there until it wasn't.

This meant they'd have to hike back through the jungle and go to the estate. There was no other option. The hike alone would take half the day without a boat to provide a shortcut. And what would they find when they got there? How safe would it be?

Fiona pulled out her satellite phone on the irrational hope that they'd imagined the disconnect yesterday and today all would be fine. This point always had great satellite coverage.

But no such luck. It wasn't a bad dream. Their phones had been cut from service.

"Let's go check out the fort," Dean said.

She nodded and followed him down the hill. They passed the path they'd used days ago to climb to the top of the walls and look down on the sea. It felt like a lifetime ago that they'd returned to the crash site with Keili, Gordon, and Isaac and discovered the helicopter debris was missing, but it had been only a week.

When they reached the cut path through the overgrown vegetation, they both doffed their rain ponchos to prevent them from tearing as they plowed through the grabbing, thorny branches and vines.

They'd both donned yesterday's field clothes, which at least had long pant legs and shirt sleeves, providing a little protection, and each wore sunglasses to protect their eyes from whipping branches. Dean went first, and she hung back far enough to not get hit while branches snapped back into place.

At last, Dean came to a stop at a rounded archway that appeared to be the top of a portal. The opening was only about two feet high. The lower portion was filled with large rocks that must have been used to seal the opening once upon a time. Vines and roots threaded through the cracks between rocks. No mortar had been used here.

"This could be a sally port or postern gate," she said.

"This will take us under the fort? Where the cistern is?"

"Most likely. I wonder if the dredge piles came from here."

"No one used this entryway to dredge," Dean said. "I've looked at historic aerial photos of Ruby Island, dating back to the 1920s. The vegetation was thick on this side of the fort even then."

She'd seen the same photos—they were in the packet of information she'd received on the island so she could draft a field methodology plan. "Yeah. My guess is there's an entrance underwater too. Probably to the south." She'd point to the water, but they were so deep in the vines, there was nothing to see but leaves and thorns. "I think Chad was planning to map that area. Or maybe he did it already. I haven't been keeping up with his work. But there are a lot of boulders there that broke off the cliffside in storms. Placed just right, boulders could hide an underwater entrance pretty well."

"Perfect for smugglers."

"Yes, if they know scuba or have a small submarine that can maneuver through a rock maze."

"An unmanned drone would be perfect in this situation too."

She nodded. Did this mean Jude was in on it after all? But why would he initiate this project if it was likely to expose his crimes?

Dean nodded to the small opening. "I'm going in."

"We don't know what—or who—might be in there." For all they knew, someone could be listening in on their conversation right now.

"I have to check it out. I'll take pictures first to scope it out."

"I wish we had one of Sadie's smaller drones. We could send it first as a scout."

Dean's camera revealed a narrow corridor, the floor of which was only a few feet below them. Apparently, this entrance had been meant to be small and easy to hide from its first construction. Getting in and out wouldn't be difficult.

"I'm going with you," she said after they'd gleaned everything they could from the photos.

"I can go alone."

"No. We're in this together. Always."

He nodded and brushed his lips over hers, then dropped his pack on the rocks at his feet. "After I'm in, hand me the packs."

She did, and a few minutes later, she was dropping through the opening feetfirst.

Dean's hands on her hips guided her to the ground, then he turned her in his arms and held her for a brief moment.

He whispered in her ear. "I'm going to put my bow together. I've only got blunt arrows, but it's better than nothing, and I don't want to navigate these corridors without a weapon that will strike from a distance."

She nodded and watched as he quickly assembled his bow and strung it. He unscrewed the ball tip from the arrow, nocked it, but didn't draw the string.

Fiona couldn't help but smile. This fort was constructed to defend against gunfire and cannons, not bows and arrows, and yet the weapon felt in keeping with the historical structure. Like one might expect to see someone charging up these corridors with an arrow at the ready.

"Do you want me to call you Legolas or Hawkeye?"

"Depends which you like better."

"Legolas. Hundred percent."

He grinned. "Whew." He glanced down at his pack. "You want the slingshot?"

"I'll take it, but since I'll be behind you, I won't have it cocked and loaded. Otherwise, the only person I'm likely to hit would be you."

She grabbed a few rocks from the pile at the postern opening and slipped them into her field pants' thigh pocket. The wrist rocket she gripped with her left hand.

Dean slipped his pack on again and picked up the bow with nocked arrow.

"Know anything about where this might lead?" he asked.

"Postern entrances were small and meant to be hidden. They were essential for safe transmission of information and passage between enceinte and the outer parts of the fort. They were made to be easily defensible, which means there might be portals in the walls where hot oil can be dropped on us or we can be shot. The ramp has a slight incline, so there could well be a vantage point where someone in the fortification can see us before we see them."

"You should stay here, then. We have no way of knowing what's beyond the first curve."

"No. We go together, or we don't go at all."

Dean's nostrils flared, and she knew he was feeling the same fear she was. She was terrified for him in the lead, and he was terrified something would happen to her at the rear.

She rose on her toes and kissed him. "Together."

He nodded and turned to face the dark corridor that disappeared up at a curve.

He shone his light all over the walls as he reached the curve, and they moved slowly—as silently as possible—but the light would give them away before footsteps would.

The corridor straightened out after a ninety-degree turn to the left, and they found themselves descending into the heart of the fort. As expected, slits in the wall hinted at corridors beyond where defenders could watch and shoot at intruders, but no shots came.

The fort *felt* empty except for rodents. Not even bats had found their way in here. A fact Fiona was grateful for.

They descended into a rectangular chamber with a bricked-over wide archway on the opposite side. But like the floor of the structure they'd slept in last night, the bricks that filled the doorway had not been mortared. They'd been stacked, and someone—recently, if she were to guess—had punched a hole through like the Kool-Aid guy. It was just wide enough for a person to pass through. Dean shone his light through the opening, and they both peered inside, her crouching down below him to see into the void.

The chamber beyond was massive. Far larger than would have been tunneled out when the fort was constructed. The walls were bedrock in places, indicating they had blasted through solid layers of rock to create the chamber.

She met Dean's gaze. He raised a brow in question, and she nodded. No way would they turn around now.

She pulled a rock from her pocket as he pulled back the string on the bow. He entered first, arrow ready to fly. He stepped to the side, and she placed the rock in the leather pocket of the wrist rocket. She stretched the bands and crossed the threshold, entering the hidden, secret chamber of the star fort.

TWENTY-SIX

The bedrock floor of the chamber sloped down to sea level, and a large pool filled half the space. A grotto like the one Dean had swum in in the Bahamas and was featured in the Bond movie *Thunderball*.

The chamber was empty, but there was a long tunnel that extended to the south and disappeared underwater. An underwater entrance?

Probably.

They were about an hour from low tide, and if there was an entrance, it remained underwater. Scuba or a small submersible would be required to enter this space from that end at all times.

Fiona ran her light over the walls. "This must be the source of the spoil piles. They cleared it out to deepen the pool at low tide." She shone the light upward. "It almost looks like someone was building a missile silo or something but gave up."

He could see what she meant. Half the wall was cut and hewn, but then the work just . . . ended and gave way to natural rock and earth.

"Wasn't the previous owner, before the Reynolds family, a Soviet sympathizer?"

She nodded. "He was. Fedor Mallet. He was American, but his family immigrated from Russia before 1917. They were active in building a US communist party in the 1920s and 1930s. Their wealth grew exponentially selling oil to the Soviet Union."

"What if this was an attempt by Mallet to provide an alternative to Cuba after the Cuban Missile Crisis? The mistake in Cuba was the photos taken by high-flying aircraft. But if you built a silo in an existing fort that was abandoned three hundred years ago and brought the missiles in via submarine . . ."

"They would have had to build a much bigger entrance for the sub, but it could be done, given the size of this chamber."

"But then, for whatever reason, either the USSR or Mallet pulled the plug," he added.

"And Jude's family got the lease sometime after that. A family with a history of smuggling had a perfect operation for moving goods through the Caribbean," she finished.

"The part that confuses me is they had a fleet of ships and containers. My guess is the bulk of the family smuggling operation is done through the containers. So what did they need this place for?" he asked.

"It's not Jude who's running drugs through here," a voice said from behind them.

They both whirled around to see Chad. He had a swollen eye and cut lip.

Dean raised the bow, and Fiona stretched back the rock in the sling.

Chad held up a hand. "Don't. I need your help. Sadie's been taken. They're going to kill her."

TWENTY-SEVEN

Fiona didn't release the tension on the slingshot. Her arm started to shake. She wasn't sure if it was from the pressure or Chad's words.

"Start talking," Fiona said.

"Please put down the rock. And the arrow. I need to show you something. It'll be easier if you aren't holding prehistoric weapons."

Dean lowered the bow but then pulled a beefy knife from the sheath at his hip. "Fine. I'll go with this, then."

Chad nodded.

Fiona dropped the rock into her palm and tucked away the wrist rocket. "And I'll be keeping the rock. Now start talking."

"I found this place the other night. After we dived on the dredge piles. I was alone on the boat, looking at the charts and data, and I figured there would be a postern gate hidden somewhere on the east flank. I got to the interior brick wall, and realized the bricks were loose." He ran a hand over his face. "I removed a bunch, then punched through."

He pointed to the right. "I need to show you something over there."

To get where he indicated, they'd have to either wade through the water or climb a loose pile of rocks mounded to the ceiling and sloping down, trickling into the saltwater pool.

"It's safe to climb the rocks. They're stable."

"You first," Dean said.

Chad nodded and climbed the slope using hands and feet. It was steep enough to require all fours.

He pivoted and went feetfirst down the back side.

Dean followed, and Fiona waited until he was safe on his feet with the knife out again before she took her turn.

She wasn't about to trust Chad for even a moment. She wasn't sure if she believed him about Sadie, but if he was telling the truth, she needed to listen.

What the hell has Chad done?

When she was back on her feet on the other side of the rock pile, she got a glimpse of the back alcove for the first time and let out a soft gasp.

Waterproof bags were piled against the wall. Dozens of them.

But the bags weren't what drew the gasp from her throat. No, it was the sight of Jude's missing drone sitting right there on the uneven stone floor as if it had magically washed up inside a secret grotto.

———

Chad dropped to the ground and put his head in his hands. "When I found the drone, I thought it was my ticket to fix everything. It had to be Kosmo who'd stolen it. He could have redirected its path using Jude's computer. I saw him in Jude's office more than once, at the computer, when Jude was outside working with the drone in the bay. I'm sure he has all Jude's passwords or a back door into the system somehow."

He raised his head and pointed toward the stacks of dry bags against the wall. "And in case you're wondering, yeah, those bags are full of cocaine."

Dean studied the bags. Holy hell. He'd expected it, but that was a massive amount of coke. Several million dollars' worth, he'd bet.

"I figured Jude doesn't know about any of this shit," Chad continued. "I mean, why would he hire us if he did? He had to know we'd find the underwater entrance at the very least.

"I think the entrance we came in was the sally port—not a postern after all." He nodded in the other direction, to the northeast, where they hadn't explored yet. "The postern gate is that way, a tunnel that cuts into the hillside. It's not far from the dock where I've been mooring *Tempus*, and totally concealed by vegetation and rocks, but easy to pass through on foot once you know the route.

"The way I see it, they're bringing the drugs in through the water entrance." He rose and walked to the water's edge. "Yesterday morning, I dived on the south end and found a perfectly constructed serpentine gate made of boulders, spaced far enough for a small submarine to maneuver no problem. But laid out so you can't see the obvious path on a casual dive. I'm guessing the Soviets placed the boulders in the 1960s. Then the coral grew and camouflaged the passageway."

"Get to the part about Sadie," Fiona said.

He nodded. "I will, but there's something else you need to know. I found the helicopter debris." He pointed to the deep pool. "It's all right there. Underwater. They cleaned up the outside of the fort and dumped it in here."

Well, *that* was litter that was substantially bigger than a golf ball.

Dean rocked on his feet. He had yet to begin processing the helicopter crash, really. Somehow, having the whole thing disappear from the crash site had made it seem like it hadn't really happened. The boat explosion was more real to him, because he and Fiona had dived on the wreckage the day after.

They'd seen the anchor.

"Kosmo's been behind everything." Chad swallowed. "I figured finding all this was my ticket out of my mess with Sadie. I needed to pay off the debt on the boat. I thought the investor wanted the boat and us for a documentary series. We'd pay off the equipment loan and land a permanent gig. Win-win. I thought I was signing on to something big. For Sadie."

"For *you*, Chad," Fiona said, her voice burning with hostility. "Admit it."

He nodded. "And for me. But then the guy said he might replace Sadie and me if we didn't click with viewers, but the boat and tech were locked in, part of the show no matter what. Anyway, it was a seedy deal, and I guess I didn't read the fine print. But I could get out of it with enough money." He nodded toward the drugs and the drone. "I figured this was my chance to get Kosmo to pay. I mean, he wouldn't want Jude to know about his little operation, right? Or that he stole Jude's drone."

"So I took the battery housing from the drone. You know, the part Jude keeps bragging about being the game changer. I'm sure that's what Kosmo wanted. With that technology, he could make a dozen drones just like it, and he'd have his own personal invisible drug-delivery vehicle that could zip from here to Miami undetected." Chad pointed to the bags of drugs again. "Jude's drones will be full of the mapping technology and other crap needed to act as scouts for the fleet, and he's months away from perfecting that part of the system. Kosmo doesn't need anything that fancy, just a hollow tube with a big battery and excellent navigation. My guess is Kosmo wanted his engineers to copy the battery and navigation systems."

"What did you do with the battery case?" Dean asked.

"I can't tell you. It's the only thing keeping Sadie alive."

"So you went to Kosmo to cut a deal," Dean said as the last pieces clicked into place.

"Yeah. I told him he'd get the battery and I'd keep my mouth shut about what I found—I'd even erase all the data from the GIS. No secret smuggling chamber, no underwater tunnels. No missing helicopter debris. No postern gate or sally port. I could bury everything so Sadie and you"—he nodded toward Fiona—"would never know what was here. His secret was safe with me."

"But Kosmo wasn't keen on the deal."

"No. He—he—" His voice broke, and tears spilled. "He had one of the staff—Walker—bring Sadie into the room. She'd been down on the pier, filming a segment with Nico about mapping Cannon Bay. Easy to grab. I didn't think of that."

He looked down and added, "I lunged for Walker, but Erik punched me. Held me down while Walker pulled out a knife and pressed it to Sadie's neck. Kosmo demanded I tell him where the battery case was, or Walker would slit her throat."

Chad swallowed. "But if I told him, he'd slit her throat and mine anyway. So I told him I'd get it and bring it back. He gave me twenty-four hours to return it, or Sadie's dead."

TWENTY-EIGHT

"Where was Jude during all this?" Fiona asked. Dean picked up the slight tremor in her voice. She was deeply shaken but trying to appear calm.

Chad shrugged. "I presume in his rooms on the third floor. I was on the first floor, in Kosmo's office. Right after he gave me the ultimatum, he announced that all house staff were being sent to Dominica to ride out the storm. Everything was being locked down. The only people left at the estate are Kosmo, his men, and Jude."

"What about Nico? Was he evacuated?"

Chad shook his head as though dazed. "No. Just the house staff. He would have wondered why Sadie and the rest of us weren't evacuated too, I guess."

"So you don't know where Nico is?"

"No. I took off as soon as I could. Before Kosmo could change his mind, or order Walker to go with me. I watched the house—waiting for you to come back so I could intercept you—until the storm got bad. I figured you wouldn't be out in that. So I took shelter in one of the bungalows behind the house. In the hours that I watched, I didn't see anyone come or go from the house. Just Jude pacing in front of his windows on the third floor."

"So Nico is probably a hostage too," Dean confirmed.

"I think so? I'm sure he figured out something was up when Sadie never returned to finish the interview, and then everyone was shipped off on the ferry. I have no clue how much Jude knows at this point."

"If you give Kosmo the battery compartment, it's all over," Fiona said. "For you. Sadie. Probably Nico too."

Chad nodded. "That's why I came to find you. I've only got a few hours left before I need to turn myself in by their deadline. But I can't bring them the battery. They can't kill me until after I turn it over. I'll warn them that if they hurt Sadie, I'll never tell. I'll kill myself and take the location to the grave."

"You realize these guys don't mess around," Dean said. He pointed to the bags of cocaine. "Someone who moves drugs at this level has people on his payroll who are versed in torture and interrogation."

"They'll have to kill me. I got Sadie into this situation. I won't let her die for my mistakes."

Odds were, Sadie *would* pay the ultimate price for Chad's actions, but Dean wouldn't be the one to voice that thought. It would devastate Fiona. And she needed hope right now.

He remembered how she'd insulated him from her doubts and fears on Chiksook. He owed her the same.

"What can we do?" Fiona asked.

"Get a message out somehow. Kosmo had all our sat phones deregistered. He locked down the Wi-Fi, so internet is out. He seized *Tempus*, so I can't use the radios. All the speedboats were locked up for the storm. But maybe you could get to one of those?"

Fiona cleared her throat. "I could go to Jude. He'll listen to me."

"No," Dean said sharply. Jude might not be part of Kosmo's scheme, but Dean still didn't trust the guy.

"Jude won't hurt me."

"That may be so, but I'm not willing to bet your life on it."

"Jude is just as much a victim here. Kosmo blew up his yacht and stole his drone."

"None of that leaves Jude in the clear. He might be Kosmo's target, but I highly doubt Jude Reynolds is innocent. Kosmo wouldn't have sent the staff away if he didn't have absolute power to do so. He's not afraid of Jude."

"But Jude might be our only hope," Fiona said firmly.

"He's a last resort."

She nodded, then said, "Chad, did you see a man at the house yesterday who wasn't part of Kosmo's team or the house and grounds staff? Anyone who didn't leave with the staff?"

Dean realized she was talking about Richards. She couldn't reveal to Chad who the man was or that piece of info was sure to come out in interrogation.

Chad frowned, thinking. "I'm not as familiar with the staff as you are. I've been living on the boat more than not since Dean arrived."

Did that mean Richards could still be there? If so, the man certainly had a satellite phone or other way to communicate. And the lie about the staff being sent off for the storm would be deemed plausible to tell him—in whatever role he was playing to infiltrate the house.

"Why do you ask? Who is he?" Chad asked.

"Probably no one," Fiona said. Clearly, she, too, was aware of the damage Chad could do under torture. "It sounds like you should go to the estate to meet your deadline. Dean and I will follow, but stay hidden. If I see an opportunity to talk to Jude or anyone else, I'll take it. Otherwise we'll try to seize a boat and enough fuel to get to Dominica."

"If we're going to head back to the estate, we're going to need better weapons," Dean said.

"You're with two archaeologists," Fiona said. "We happen to know how to haft a point to an arrow, and you've got arrows and a bow."

He nodded. "But only four."

"So we'll have to make them count."

"You planning to flint knap projectile points?" Chad asked. "We don't have time for that. If we had obsidian, maybe. But the basalt we've got here isn't easy to work."

"I was thinking we'll both have to sacrifice our trowels. Yours is sharp, yes?"

He nodded.

"We'll break off the tips and haft them to the shaft. That's two arrows right there."

"How do we break them?"

Fiona scanned the chamber and landed on a pile of bricks. She grabbed four and stacked them in a short tower, then slid the tip of her sharp, pointed trowel between the second and third bricks.

"Dean, can you step on the top brick, putting all your weight on it?"

He did as requested, and she pressed down on the handle of her trowel.

Seeing her plan, he said, "I'll have better leverage pulling the handle up with my weight on it if you handle the downward push."

She moved her hand, and he reached down for the handle and pulled it up, bending the metal where it met brick. Fiona took over, pushing it down, and this time it bent farther in the other direction. They worked it back and forth, and in no time, the metal snapped.

Dean removed his foot from the pile, and Fiona extracted the triangle of metal from between the bricks.

She held up a sharp-edged, one-and-a-half-inch-long tip that could kill a person if applied with the force of an arrow.

Chad handed over his trowel, and they repeated the process on the second tip, while Chad notched the sides of Fiona's blade with a small file from his dig kit.

Next they used the tiny saw on Dean's pocketknife to cut a slit in the top of the arrow shaft. "Just like a Tinkertoy," he murmured as he slipped the thin metal blade into the slit. Chad fixed it to the shaft with a small length of leather cord from his bootlaces, giving them two deadly arrows.

"What do we do with the other two?" Chad asked. "Attach knife blades?"

"That would be unbalanced. No way to shoot straight," Dean said. "We can file down the fiberglass shaft to make a sharp point."

Fiona extracted her own file, and she and Chad set to work, while Dean paced the cavernous room, trying to think of other weapons, other ways to approach the house.

What if they killed Chad on the spot when he showed up without the battery case? Or killed Sadie?

But there was no other way around it. Chad had to go back before his deadline expired. Kosmo wouldn't mess around. But Fiona and Dean couldn't be anywhere near him when he walked into the lion's den. And they couldn't tell Chad even a single part of their plan, which meant they couldn't make a plan until Chad was on his way.

Fiona stepped up to his side, her gaze on the smooth wall of the fort behind him. He turned to see what had caught her attention.

This was part of the original structure—built in the mid-1600s by hand, not cut with machinery in the 1960s. She took off her headlamp and laid the beam across the rock face, just as she'd done in the cave what seemed like an eternity ago but was really only a few days. The beam spread across the surface, and just as it had done in the cave, the light revealed etchings in the rock.

"More petroglyphs. The same spiral and something else. A bird, maybe?" she said.

"How did you do that? Just walk right up and find it?"

She laughed softly. "Much as I'd like to claim spiritual intuition or something equally magical, it's nothing like that. When you turned your head, your light spread across the wall, and I thought I saw something. These grooves haven't weathered like an exposed petroglyph, making it stand out even more."

"As cool as this is," Chad said from behind them, "we should probably get going. Just in case Kosmo sends Walker or one of the others this way to find me."

The man had a good point. They'd lingered long enough. Too long really, but it was easier to make the arrow tips here than it would have been later.

They grabbed their packs and followed Chad through the corridor to the sally port. Dean took the rear with Fiona in the middle. No way would he trust Chad to have their back.

Part of him even wondered if the man had made up his wild story, except the UUV was definitely in the chamber, and the battery compartment was indeed missing.

How could Chad let the woman he loved get caught in this situation? What kind of man endangered those he loved like that? Betrayed her as he did?

Dean's best bet was gambling debt or something along those lines had led him down this ugly path. Chad's behavior smacked of uncontrolled addiction, but Dean didn't see signs of drug or alcohol abuse. Both would be difficult to hide with the frequent scuba dives necessary for his line of work.

It was sunny and humid when they climbed out of the fort and into the thick vegetation that had hidden the sally port for decades.

Who had bricked up the interior archway, and why?

But that was a question for another time. Even the petroglyphs were interesting but unimportant to the moment.

Ruby Island wouldn't get her archaeological inventory, but maybe someday, Dominica could use the information Fiona, Sadie, and Chad had managed to gather before the project fell apart.

Outside, they moved into the forest above the fort so they wouldn't be exposed when Dean had Chad make a recorded statement about everything he'd found, said, and done. Evidence to be used against Kosmo just in case the worst happened.

Once the camera was off, Fiona asked, "What are you going to say to Kosmo when you return?"

"I'll tell him I need a boat. Couldn't get to where I hid the battery case without it, even at low tide. I tried, but it wasn't possible."

"You could claim it's in the southeastern littoral cave. Even at low tide, a boat is required to access that one, and when you hid it, you had the tender from *Tempus* available."

He nodded. "That could work. Plus, only being accessible at low tide will buy us time. Low tide is right now, so by the time I get back, the window will be closed, and the next low isn't until eleven thirty p.m."

"Insist on taking a Whaler. The bigger the boat, the bigger the entrance required, making a smaller access window to enter and exit the cave. He won't let you take out a boat like that by yourself, so that would get you and at least one of Kosmo's men out of the house tonight," Fiona said. "It would take you a few hours to go there and back, especially in the dark."

Dean liked this idea a lot. "Yeah, and once you're gone, that's when we can enter the house."

"The cave is really deep," Fiona added. "You could take your time inside, looking for where you hid the battery. Delay until the tide is too high to exit with the boat."

"Or maybe I'll be able to find a way to escape with the boat," Chad said.

Dean doubted it, but it was worth a shot. The guy was otherwise out of options.

Chad met Fiona's gaze. "I'm going to make this right. I know you hate me for what I did to Sadie, but know this: I love her. And I'm going to do everything I can to fix this."

Dean believed him. But he wasn't certain that everything Chad could do would be enough. He studied Fiona, and once again wondered how Chad could have put his lover in danger.

Dean's greatest fear was losing those he loved. But to be the cause of it? It was unthinkable.

If he could, he'd leave Fiona safe in the stone haven they'd shared last night, but he knew without a doubt that Fiona would never sit idly behind while Sadie was in danger. Not when she could help.

Not when she might be the *only* person who could help. Jude Reynolds was in love with her, and even though he had to be tangled in Kosmo's scheme somehow, odds were that he'd do what he could to protect Fiona.

Did the man have any idea how many kilos of cocaine moved through his island? And what they'd seen in the chamber beneath the fort was just what was there this week. How often were drugs moved through?

Was this a normal week, or was it special because of the party?

Dean stopped dead in his tracks. The party. Paige's text about the boat being stopped and searched when they reached an American port, along with two other party-guest yachts.

And Fiona had sent the guest list to the DEA.

Well, that could answer how Kosmo was moving the drugs once they got to Ruby Island. It maybe even explained the massive fuel tanks buried by the dock, which Walker managed for Jude. Everyone who came to Ruby Island got a few thousand kilos with a free refill. And Jude had said his father had been the one who'd installed the tanks.

Was Kosmo carrying on Jude's father's smuggling operation without Jude's knowledge?

"What's up?" Fiona asked Dean.

He shook his head. He couldn't share any of this in front of Chad. "Tell you later," he whispered.

Once they reached the top of the rise, they separated, Chad taking the coastal path they'd used on Dean's first day on Ruby Island. It would be a faster route, but still a long way without a boat to pick him up on the southwest shore.

Dean and Fiona would take the harder, longer, but hidden route, crossing up and over the slopes of the volcano, and cutting across the overgrown center of the island. In places, they'd have to machete their way through as they'd done last night, but they'd be able to traverse the island undetected.

The first part, however, was simply retracing their route from this morning. They reached the clearing on the slope of the volcano, where there was a wide swath without trees or significant vegetation because the wind scoured the rocky ground just so, preventing soil and seed from finding a home for long.

"What's that?" Fiona said, pointing to something high on the exposed slope.

"Probably one of the sensors Dylan is monitoring for Jude."

Her brow furrowed. "Is there any way to use it to send Dylan a message?"

Dean shrugged. "No idea. I don't know how they work."

"Let's check it out."

He nodded and led the way. It wasn't far and couldn't hurt. If nothing else, maybe it had sharp points they could haft to an arrow. Or they could make a spear.

Spears weren't exactly concealable, but then, neither were bows and arrows.

Dean had never been a gun person, but he knew how to use them. He'd been on expeditions where he was required to have armed guards in case they found themselves endangered by the wildlife. The thought of harming an animal like that—even in self-defense—was repugnant. After all, he was invading their territory. Still, he understood the requirement and had learned how to shoot should he need to do so to save someone else's life. But in all his travels, this was the first time he actually wished he had a gun on assignment. Of course, here the predators weren't wild. They were all too human and the worst kind of humanity.

Dean didn't blame the addicted for their affliction, but he did blame those who preyed upon the addicted. So often it was those people who found a way to create the addiction to begin with.

Even Chad, he didn't blame—if, indeed, his downfall was due to addiction—for having a vice. But he absolutely held the man accountable for his actions that had harmed others. Mortgaging the business without informing Sadie. Trying to cut a deal with a drug smuggler that led to Sadie becoming a pawn threatened with death.

It was a repulsive, horrific act, and there was no coming back from that. No forgiveness to be found.

They reached the seismic sensor, a large gray box with a pole planted behind it—Dean assumed that was the antenna—and a solar panel attached to the pole. All self-contained, and nothing sharp and stabby they could borrow.

"Bummer," Fiona said as she must've come to the same conclusion. "What if we shook it really hard? Think Dylan would read that as an earthquake?"

"With no other sensor going off anywhere around us? Doubtful. But even if he did, he'd probably call Reynolds and ask about it . . . and that would just tell Kosmo where we are."

"Good point."

"Sorry."

She gave him a weak smile. "Never apologize for sharing a hard truth. I can take it."

He took a step forward and tilted up her chin. "Fiona Carver, I believe you can handle just about anything."

"Well, except heights and cliffs, and you might not know this, but I'm not a fan of snakes."

He kissed her, fast and hard, then smiled down at her. "Remind me to show you a picture of me snuggling with an albino Burmese python."

"Pass, thanks."

"I'm shirtless."

"Oh, well, why didn't you say that in the first place? Also, who takes the photographer's picture?"

"My guides."

They turned and headed back down the slope, aiming for the concealment of the trees. At least this part of the hike was downhill. As they walked, Dean took her hand in his and threaded their fingers.

A stroll down a hillside while holding hands. It was so commonplace and yet so foreign for him, and such an odd moment to find himself enjoying the simple pleasure.

TWENTY-NINE

Fiona let out a sigh of relief once they were in the cover of the rainforest again. She knew Kosmo wasn't all-seeing but still, she'd felt exposed out in the open, and who knew if there were surveillance cameras set up all over the island?

After all, if the man was moving massive amounts of drugs through Ruby Island, it stood to reason he'd have security in place. But then, she'd studied the walls of the interior chamber as best she could, and there'd been no sign of a camera.

Perhaps because it was so well hidden, there'd never been a need?

"I want to try to find Richards first," she said as these and other thoughts swirled through her mind.

"Agreed. If he's still on the island, he's got to have a way to reach his boss."

"So, I didn't say it in front of Chad because . . ."

"He's almost certainly going to be tortured," Dean finished for her.

"Yeah." She huffed out a deep breath. "I know a way to access the main house from the cellar."

"Surely Kosmo knows about that too?"

"I'm not sure. It was the original storm cellar, but when Hurricane Ella swept through in 1958—a year after the house was built—there was so much groundwater seepage that the cellar flooded. Which isn't great if that's your refuge. Instead of configuring a better drainage system, Mallet had the old cellar closed off and built the current aboveground storm shelter into the hillside."

"Do you think Sadie could be held in the storm shelter?"

"I suppose it's possible. It's basically a fortress surrounded by rock. No windows, only one exit. It has two rooms plus a bathroom with actual plumbing. Posh for a storm shelter."

"Where is it?"

"On the hillside by the runway. Near the power station."

"Yeah. That's probably where she is," Dean said.

"Is it a mistake to go to the house, then? Shouldn't we head there first?"

"She'll be guarded, and if you know a way into the house that's not any of the obvious exterior doors, we should try that first. Tell me more about the storm cellar. Like, how does it help us if it's been closed off?"

"When Jude was ten years old, he found the slanted door in the ground behind the house. He went inside and discovered the old cellar and managed to open the hidden door in the house—it's in a closet, I think he said—in the service area on the ground floor. It became his escape route from the house when he wanted to get away from his parents. He told me about this at field school. He said he'd never told his parents about his secret tunnel. It was a private, hidden place that was his and his alone. He also said I was the only person he'd ever told about it. It's possible he still hasn't told anyone."

"He was in love with you even then, wasn't he?"

She thought back and tried to put herself in the mindset she'd inhabited then and see Jude through those eyes. Did he give off vibes she'd picked up on but chose to ignore?

"I don't know. Maybe? I don't remember. I was hung up on someone else at the time, I guess, so I wasn't sending him any encouraging signs."

"Did Jude show you the cellar when you arrived on the island?"

"No. He's never mentioned it at all, and I haven't either. I didn't want to remind him I knew his secrets. It just . . . would have invited a kind of intimacy I was trying to avoid. I really wanted to keep him firmly in the boss box, and worried that he'd take any reminiscing as a sign that I was open to receiving his advances."

"But that changed. You went out on the boat for a date."

"You were here. It was field school all over again. My interests were elsewhere, and he knew it. Also, you *told* me to go for it with him, I might add."

"I regretted that the moment the words were out of my mouth."

"Good."

He raised her hand to his lips. "You didn't want to see me with Paige. I didn't want to see you with Jude. But it didn't feel right to demand that, since I was the one who wasn't offering you anything."

"So we'll make a deal. In the future, if we cross paths, if neither of us is seeing anyone at the time, we won't mention or pursue others in front of the other person."

It was a convoluted offer, and her heart squeezed as she made it, because it meant she and Dean wouldn't be a couple in the future. Plus, she knew damn well that meant their paths wouldn't cross if he could help it.

"Uh. I guess. Sure."

"And there's the suave playboy I remember so well." When all else fails, resort to teasing to hold it together.

Dean came to a stop and pulled her to him. "You still questioning my skills as a ladies' man?" He was taking her tease as the lifeline it was and running with it.

She smiled, opening herself up to the faint flutter of heat that would keep the game going. It was there. It was genuine. Just hard to conjure in the situation. "Well, you have my verdict on that front. Not *quite* satisfied."

He unbuckled the hip belt and chest strap of her pack, then pushed the padded front straps over her shoulders. The backpack hit the ground with a thud, and he scooped her up and pressed her against a tree. His mouth covered hers, and he kissed her deep.

Banked fires roared to life, and heat flooded her. This wasn't a game to hide from future heartache. This was here and now, and in this moment, she was Dean's and he was hers.

She kissed him back, tangling her tongue with his as branches shook above them and dropped water from last night's rain upon their heads. She ran her fingers through his beard. She loved the feel of his whiskers against her cheeks. It reminded her of how his beard had felt against her inner thighs.

Dean had given her the best sex she'd ever had—hands down. And maybe that was due to how she felt about him, but she figured the playboy thing had some merit. He was magnificent in the sack. But there was no point in telling him that or he'd stop trying to prove to her that she pretty much melted at his touch.

And she liked a determined Dean Slater.

He raised his head, his eyes all hot and smoldery. Her knees would be weak if he wasn't holding her up against a tree. "So how did that rate?"

She bit his bottom lip gently, then said, "Solid eight."

"Out of five, I presume."

She giggled. The kiss had been a thousand on a scale of one to five.

She whispered in his ear. "You're the best time I've ever had . . . *Jack*."

His eyes narrowed. "That's from *Romancing the Stone*."

She batted her eyelashes. "I might have watched it again after we talked about it."

He leaned down and whispered in her ear. "So did I. And Kathleen Turner is a beautiful woman, but she's got nothing on you." His lips brushed over hers. "You're the full package, and I'm always in awe."

Her heart surged. It was a sweet, heartfelt compliment, and the way he said it—the reverence in his tone—turned her to jelly. Last night, when he'd called her beautiful, she'd deflected with a tease. She owed him better today. She stroked his beard. "You're amazing, Dean." She

closed her eyes and took in the joy of being with him, blocking everything else out, then opened them again so she could look into his eyes
as she said, "And I hate everything about how this all came about, but
I'm so thankful we got this time together."

"Me too." He held her gaze, and there was something in his eyes
she hadn't seen before. "I've been thinking, maybe when we return—"

She placed a hand over his mouth. She didn't want to talk about
the nebulous future right now. Didn't want to hope for more when he
might change his mind. Didn't want to know there was no hope either.

"Now isn't the time. Let's go rescue Sadie."

He gave a slow nod, then gently lowered her feet to the ground.

She donned her pack, then took his hand. Their fingers threaded,
and they set out once again. They had hours of jungle to traverse and
needed to come up with a plan.

"What do we do once we're in the house?"

"Look for Richards."

"And how are we supposed to do that? We don't even know who
he's pretending to be."

"Or if he's even there."

The trek was a slog; in places they had to hack through vines, but
cutting a path was the safest approach, as it kept them off the literal
beaten path. That meant traversing jungle rather than rainforest—where
there was no high canopy, so sun and rain had no trouble reaching the
floor and the understory was thick to the point of being impenetrable,
much like the plants that had crowded in upon the stone structure the
night before.

With Sadie's maps that indicated where the vegetation was the
thickest, they had a route to avoid, but that was only avoiding the
worst of it.

Welts marked both their faces and arms after the first twenty minutes of serious hacking. After forty-five grueling minutes, Fiona called
a break. "My arms need a rest."

She'd still been sore from yesterday's machete workout.

They sat on their packs in the hole they'd created in the green prickly ocean of plants. Humidity was high and mosquitoes swarmed. It was hard to believe she'd been chilled the night before in the cool, enclosed stone house, as she sweat in the sultry jungle heat today.

Her skin was drenched both with rainwater that had collected on the broadleaf plants and sweat. Her clothes soaked through as if she'd gone swimming in the lake that supposedly harbored Spanish coins.

A swim in the lake sounded really good right now, but they'd passed their haven more than an hour ago. She guzzled water from her hydration pack. No need to ration when there was water all around. Dean handed her a bag of trail mix. The good kind, with M&M's.

"You look like you could use a sugar hit."

She nodded, took a handful, then held the bag out to him.

"No. Finish it. I've got a granola bar that will hold me."

"You sure?" It wasn't right to take a guy's only M&M's. His granola bar wasn't even coated with chocolate or peanut butter. It probably wasn't even sweetened with honey. It was sad and healthy-looking.

"You can't possibly enjoy that."

He let out a soft laugh. "I used to be vegan, remember?"

"I thought you were vegetarian and your wife was vegan."

"She was full vegan. I indulged in dairy and eggs occasionally, but most of the time we ate according to her diet. Until that last year, of course, then all rules were off. The goal was to get food in her, period."

She couldn't imagine what that last year of Violet's life must have been like for Dean. But she knew from the little he'd said, and from what Dylan had shared later, that Dean had been his wife's primary caretaker for two and a half years. There'd been multiple brain surgeries and extended hospitalizations, but also many months when she was home with Dean, confined to a hospital bed in their living room, and he took care of her twenty-four seven.

When she considered how that experience must've been, watching her slowly die while being her primary caregiver, she understood why he would never love or marry again.

She couldn't fault him for his need for self-preservation. For the heartache he must feel every single day since her passing.

Pain she knew, from Dylan, he'd locked up inside. Dylan said Dean never spoke about Violet to anyone. Not even to him, if Dean could avoid it.

Until the press delved into his life after Chiksook, Fiona had been one of the few who even knew he'd been married. But then Chiksook happened, and the media dug into the life of the wildlife photographer who had risked everything to save his missing brother, and they'd discovered a dead wife and her bitter relatives who asserted he'd married Violet for her money.

Forget the fact that he'd spent two and a half years taking care of the woman and it was so very obvious Violet Slater had been the love of his life.

Only Violet's sister and grandmother denied the claim that Dean had been after Violet's trust fund when he married her right before her first brain surgery.

It was another salacious detail that made Fiona so angry at the coverage they'd received after Chiksook. It was why she'd been repulsed by questions from Jude's friends at the party. Why she'd been bitter that her and Dean's reunion was to be part of the documentary at all.

He'd been treated as if he had no right to privacy, all because what happened to Dylan had been deemed newsworthy.

"I'm so sorry for what the press put you through," she said softly. It was something she should have said days ago.

While Dean had been dragged through the mud, Fiona had largely been left alone. Sure, the press had mentioned her sister's death and Fiona's allegations that her fall had been no accident. And there had been that awful statement by her brother, Aidan. But that part of the story had quickly been eclipsed by the supposed scandal of Dean's marriage. It didn't help that there were plenty of photos of Dean partying it up in Hollywood with beautiful women.

Fiona hadn't read any of those stories—it felt like a violation to do so—but her friend Cara, who'd been on Chiksook at the start of the expedition, had given Fiona a summary.

Just enough to let her know not to search for the stories.

Thankfully, after that first month, the stories faded away as new scandals captured media attention.

"Thank you. Except for engaging a lawyer to pursue both slander and libel cases against my in-laws, I ignored it."

"Are those cases moving forward?"

"They settled out of court after being informed I would make public the notarized written statements and a recording by Violet, in which she detailed her parents' abuse and why she wanted me as her primary caretaker. She knew from the start that they might come after me someday and made sure I had what I needed to protect myself. They publicly recanted—not that the press bothered to report on that."

"She sounds like an amazing woman."

"She was."

"I'd like to see a photo of her sometime."

"There were plenty in the stories last fall."

"I didn't read any of them. I wasn't about to give them the clicks."

He nodded and reached into his pack, unzipped the front organizer pocket, and pulled out a laminated photo. "I bring her with me on every project." His voice cracked as he added, "She made me promise I'd travel and live my life to the fullest after she was gone. That I'd live the dream we planned to share. So I bring her with me every time."

Fiona took the photo with shaking fingers. It was thickly laminated and the size of a credit card.

Violet Slater had dark hair and delicate, pixieish features. She looked a lot like her younger sister, Becca, who Fiona had gotten a glimpse of in September. Becca had been tiny compared to Dean, and without a scale in the photo, Fiona imagined Violet was similarly petite to go with her delicate features. "She's lovely."

She started to hand it back but then realized there was another image on the back and turned it over.

There was a tiny Violet in the arms of a tall and very young Dean. "Our wedding day," he said.

Dean's face was lean and unlined. No beard, so she could see a hint of Dylan's chin in the jawline. His blue eyes were clear and bright and beaming with love for his bride.

She knew Violet had just been diagnosed with brain cancer and the wedding was days before her first surgery, but even then, Violet was radiant.

Both faces were beaming with joy and hope. This couple was deeply in love, and it showed. In spite of the circumstances of their hasty marriage, the union was joyful for them both.

She smiled, feeling a rush of affection for both people in the photo. Happy that they'd had that joy, that love, to see them through the coming pain. "Dean, this is so beautiful." Her eyes teared as she handed the photos back. "I'm so glad she had you. That you had each other."

She swiped at her tears and noticed he did the same.

"Thank you, Fi. I was lucky to have her, even if it wasn't long enough." He tucked the photo away, then ripped open the granola bar that had triggered the conversation. Fiona ate her trail mix in silence.

When this project was over, she would have to let him go. She'd known that from the start, but seeing the photo served to underscore why.

At least understanding why would ease some of the pain of their goodbye.

———

They reached the outskirts of the estate, and Dean climbed a tree to get a better vantage point to watch as darkness settled in. Once it was dark, they'd be able to circle around and use the defunct storm cellar entrance.

They were in the overgrown woods adjacent to the circular garden. Dean settled in a tree about twenty feet up, where he had a good amount of natural camouflage. In addition, he pulled out a small jungle camo sheet he kept in his pack and draped it in the branches before him. He then pulled out his best zoom lens and attached it to his camera and scanned the windows on the south face of the house. The lower floor had the four sets of french doors that opened into the ballroom. The ballroom was dark without movement on the other side of the glass doors.

He also had a line of sight into Kosmo's first-floor office. The executive sat at his desk.

A noise in the garden had Dean releasing the camera and taking up the bow and nocking an arrow. Fiona was hidden in the vegetation beneath him and unable to see potential threats. If anyone came after her, he would have a split second to decide if he should loose an arrow.

After a moment, he spotted a red-rumped agouti, a large rodent that lived primarily in northeastern South America but which had been introduced to a few islands in the Lesser Antilles, including Dominica and Ruby Island. He'd been on the lookout for one from the day he arrived. Figures he'd spot one now when he was holding a bow and arrow, not a camera.

He let out a soft sigh of relief and quivered the arrow, then raised the camera to his eye again. He snapped pictures of Kosmo at his desk. Thirty minutes passed with little activity. Dean's legs cramped, braced as they were between branches. He knew Fiona must be anxious as she hid below, but she remained silent, as they'd agreed.

He breathed deeply, trying to capture the headspace he occupied when he waited in a blind for the perfect shot. Patience was perhaps his greatest skill, but with Sadie's life on the line and Fiona in danger just by being here, it was a hard mental zone to find.

Forty minutes later, full dark set in, following a short twilight. The moon was but a tiny waxing crescent in the sky, giving off next to no light, and would be setting in less than an hour.

A door opened in Kosmo's office, and Walker and Erik dragged a bloody and battered Chad into the room.

How had he not pegged these guys for a drug runner's henchmen from the start?

Because you were distracted by Fiona. And thrown off by Reynolds's open interest in her, dickhead.

Truth was, he'd never given Kosmo's team a second look. He'd done the thing he'd knocked others for in the past—not seeing the bigger picture, not noticing the help.

When he went on assignment, he was one with the help. He hired guides, consulted with locals, and always paid attention to the members of the community because their culture was part of the natural world the wildlife he wanted to capture lived in. But here on Ruby Island, he'd done none of that. Plus, he'd never been with Walker in the field like the others had.

He'd been so caught up in his head, he'd missed the signs that things weren't right—even after he'd been in a damn helicopter crash.

He'd been certain something was up after the boat exploded, but his focus had been directed at Jude, the potential victim. And, of course, Fiona, the other survivor.

Now he snapped pictures of the two beefy white thugs who dropped Chad on the floor. After a long moment, Chad rose to his feet. It was clear he was hurting. Dean guessed he had a few broken ribs. That meant he'd gotten off easy so far.

Conversation went back and forth, Chad and Kosmo both in profile to the window as they faced each other across Kosmo's desk.

Another person was dragged into the room, and Dean's bile rose at the sight of Nico, his face swollen and nose bleeding.

Fuck.

He'd wanted to believe Nico had somehow managed to escape being swept into the drama, but that really had been too much to hope for.

Dean snapped pictures to show Fiona.

After an interval, both men were led from the room, and ten minutes later, he spotted both Chad and Nico exiting through a ballroom door, Erik and Walker following as they headed toward the dock.

Dean hoped this meant they were heading to the cave in an attempt to find the battery case. They hadn't counted on Nico being tapped to go with Chad. Would that be better or worse?

Chad could have an ally. Well, except Nico would probably be ready to kill Chad himself at this point, and no one could blame him. And Dean doubted Chad would get a chance to tell Nico any kind of plan.

On the plus side, both Erik and Walker were accompanying Chad and Nico. Was there anyone else in the house, or was it just Jude and Kosmo?

Someone must be guarding Sadie. Was she locked in the storm shelter?

Lights on the third floor came to life. Jude's suite. What else was up there? Did Fiona know?

The billionaire passed by a window in the upper floor. Dean snapped a photo. While Sadie was being held hostage somewhere, Jude was pacing his room, doing absolutely nothing to save her.

How deep in this was Jude? There was no way he remained ignorant of Kosmo taking over his island.

Dean stayed in the tree thirty minutes longer—seeing nothing that answered any of his myriad questions—then descended to share with Fiona what he'd seen. He consulted his watch. "We're still an hour out from low tide. Chad and the others won't be back for two hours at least.

If Chad can delay them and they're trapped by the tide, they won't be back until noon tomorrow."

"There are lots of hiding places in the caves," she whispered. "But with Nico there—if they aren't able to talk and come up with a plan, someone will get hurt."

Dean nodded. His thinking exactly.

Chad's screwup could well cost Nico his life.

THIRTY

"The doors are inset in the hillside on the far side of the pilot's bunga-low, on the end," Fiona said.

Dean paused and frowned. "The pilot. Philip. I haven't seen him since before the party. Did he leave?"

Fiona shrugged. She didn't think she'd seen him since the lidar demonstration on the veranda. Had he been at breakfast any of the subsequent days? "He's from Puerto Rico. Maybe he went home for a spell? There wasn't much for him to do without a helicopter. And even if Jude managed to get a replacement quickly, I can't imagine he'd want Philip to pilot it until the cause of the crash was determined. And Philip might not have been keen on flying."

"He was a good pilot," Dean said. "We'd all be dead if he hadn't been clearheaded in the moment. But I get why he'd be grounded for a while."

She placed a hand on his arm. "I'll forever be thankful to him. Maybe we can track him down when we leave. We'll probably have a layover in Puerto Rico. We can tell him about the helicopter debris being hidden inside Fort Domingo. Plus, the DEA will want to inter-view him." She looked in the direction of the row of bungalows. All eight were dark and quiet. "I vote we hide in Philip's bungalow and watch the house for a while to make sure it's safe to open the cellar door. It's so exposed, in the open as it is, and we'll need time to move the bench that covers it."

Every move they made on the house had to be done carefully. They had only one shot at this.

He nodded. "Works for me."

They made their way through the vegetation that grew behind the line of bungalows, both in a low crouch as they moved through the broadleaf plants, making far too much noise.

Special Ops they weren't.

They reached the rear of the last bungalow.

Dean emerged from the cover of the plants and darted to the back door. She watched from the shrubs as he tried the knob, to no avail. He took a moment to search for a key on the upper doorframe and under rocks, but when he came up empty, he used the slingshot and one of the rocks Fiona had grabbed in the fort to break the windowpane in the door. He donned a leather glove and wrapped his hand in the camouflage sheet he used for photo blinds and smashed out the jagged shards that remained.

After removing the cloth from his hand, he reached through the broken window and worked the knob. A moment later, the door swung inward, and he waved to her to join him.

She darted across the open space and in moments was inside the house, finding herself in a small kitchen.

Dean pushed a heavy butcher block from the center of the room against the back door. At least they could feel secure while they were here, knowing no one could sneak in on them.

They searched the small two-bedroom house quickly, ensuring the pilot wasn't in residence and looking for any kind of weapon they could scavenge.

Unfortunately, since the pilot didn't cook his own meals, there were no knives or even dishes. Just glasses and mugs. It appeared the only item ever prepared in the kitchen was coffee in the coffee maker.

There was a dirty mug in the sink and used grounds in the filter.

His clothing remained in the bedroom, which indicated the man expected to return.

Fiona studied the RAM Freight logo on his flight uniform. He hadn't worn the uniform to pick up Dean and the others, but she'd seen him wear it when flying Jude or Kosmo or picking up business associates to bring to the island, as he'd done a few times those first two weeks.

If she remembered correctly, none of the Dominican workers' uniforms had the logo; only RAM Freight employees, like Walker and Erik, wore it. Were those all Kosmo's men?

"How many of the workers here wore the RAM Freight uniform?" she asked.

"No clue. I didn't pay attention."

"Me neither. I have regrets."

"Yeah. Me too."

She moved on to the nightstand, and her heart hammered when she spotted a satellite phone. She hit the power button, but nothing happened.

"Probably dead," Dean said.

She rifled through the drawer. "No charger. And mine is in the house."

"Mine too, but Philip and I got our phones at the same time—we both lost our old ones in the crash—same phone, same battery. And my battery is full."

He swapped out his battery for Philip's, and the phone powered up.

Fiona grimaced at seeing the request for a passcode.

Dean typed in 1-2-3-4, and it opened. He laughed. "He never bothered to change it."

She felt a surge of hope that quickly died when she took in the words on the screen: No Service Provider. "I guess that would have been too good to be true."

"Yeah. But it was worth a shot. Back to plan A."

"Which one is that?" she asked.

"Find Richards."

"We can't be sure Richards is still here, and Jude is on the third floor. He might help us."

"That's plan B. Or C. Maybe finding Sadie should be plan B."

"He won't hurt me, Dean."

"No. But he might turn you over to Kosmo, who *definitely* will hurt you. You're as much a pawn as Sadie is to Kosmo. Probably more so, because Jude is in love with you." He took a step forward and cupped her face between his palms. "I *can't* let Kosmo near you. Do you have any idea what it would do to me if you got hurt? Promise me you will *not* endanger yourself by trusting Jude."

She flashed back on the photo of his incredible blue eyes bright with love as he stood with his bride. He'd watched Violet suffer, and all these years later, he refused to love again.

She cleared her throat. "Okay. I won't seek Jude out. But if things go sideways, you'll let me do the talking. He is extremely jealous of you. You'll just inflame the situation."

His nostrils flared, but then he nodded. "Fine. I'll defer to you in that situation, as long as you promise not to seek him out. When we're in the house, we're looking for Richards and Sadie. Period."

"Deal."

It was just past midnight when they made their way through the inky darkness to the cellar doors. A large, woven-fiber mat covered the inset doors with a heavy wrought-iron bench placed on top. Given the slant of the doors, the bench had shorter legs in the back. Custom-built for this exact spot. Fiona supposed this was Jude's way of disguising his secret tunnel, but the heavy bench also meant he likely hadn't used it in a very long time.

Days after she arrived, she'd noticed the mat under the bench and remembered Jude's stories at field school. She'd lifted an edge and spotted a panel and hinge, then dropped it back into place, keeping Jude's childhood secret safe.

As quietly as possible, she and Dean moved the heavy bench, then rolled back the mat, exposing the double doors.

She placed the mat several feet over, and together they moved the bench again, hoping that no one would notice the altered position and exposed doors should they pass by here in the next few hours.

At last, they were ready, and the moment of truth came. She hoped the doors weren't locked from the inside, but couldn't imagine Jude would close off his childhood escape like that.

Dean tugged on the recessed handle, and at first, nothing budged. Fiona's heart sank.

He gave another tug, and this time, there was movement. "Hinges are just rusted, I think."

She pulled out her trowel that was now missing the tip, slid it in the gap where the two wood panels met, and attempted to use it as a lever to pry up one side. "Based on the condition of the wood, I think Jude had the doors replaced before he hid them with the mat and furniture."

"Looks like it. He doesn't need a secret escape route anymore now that the house is his, but he didn't want the doors to rot and the entrance to be found."

The trowel lever did the trick, and the hinges loosened until the door popped open, revealing brick stairs set into the earth.

Dean insisted on leading the way, and she didn't argue. He had the bow, and from what she'd seen, he was a good shot. But then, she was a terrible archer, so he was bound to be better than she was anyway. She followed him down the stairs, closing the door above her head as she descended.

Armed with the wrist rocket in one hand and a rock ready to be dropped in the sling in the other, she studied the cellar in the red glow of her and Dean's headlamps. The first room was what one would expect from a 1950s-era storm cellar, but there was a passageway that led to the house, so the cellar could be accessed from inside if necessary, a luxury many storm cellars didn't offer.

Was there a possibility that there was a tunnel to the newer storm shelter? It was a much farther distance from the house, but both the previous owner and the current one could easily afford it.

She knew the location of the storm shelter, but had never been inside, and Jude had never shared any of those secrets with her.

The passageway to the house was long and dank and had taken on water during the recent storm, as expected for a storm cellar that had been abandoned due to flooding.

The corridor led to a larger rectangular room with cinder-block walls, and Fiona figured they were now under the main house. Specifically, the northeast corner of the mansion, where the kitchen and service areas were.

She'd had only a cursory tour of the service areas—Jude didn't want the interior of the house to be part of the inventory—but he'd agreed she could at least see it.

She was glad for that tour now, as she had a vague idea of the layout of the area they would be in when they climbed the steps on the far side of this stiflingly humid room.

An inch of water covered the floor, and she wondered if the sump pump had failed or if they manually pumped out water after the bigger storms. There were small windows—dark, reflective rectangles at this time of night—on the long wall. She guessed it was those windows that had intrigued Jude at ten years old and led him to seek out an entrance to the basement.

She and Dean both dialed down their headlamps to the faintest setting in an effort to prevent a red glow from emitting from the windows.

She tried to imagine Jude as a boy, discovering this basement with its secret passage to the outside world, and even though it was empty and humid, it must have been a magical moment. Who didn't want to find a secret passage in a mansion on their very own private island?

Her heart ached at the thought that the ten-year-old who'd found magic might have grown up to be just like the parents he'd been desperate to escape.

Jude at twenty-three had been awkward and brainy and wonderful. Jude at thirty-four had been pompous and entirely unlikable. She'd had hopes for his thirty-eight-year-old incarnation, but there was no denying he was involved in this mess one way or another. Even if he was a victim of Kosmo's scheming, he must know that his executive VP had taken over the island. Yet all he did was pace his room, failing to intervene on Sadie's behalf.

They crossed to the steps, splashing sounds accompanying their footsteps as water soaked into her already damp boots.

There was a small landing and a door at the top of the stairs.

Dean pulled her close and whispered in her ear. "I'm going in first. You stay on this side of the door until I determine it's clear."

She wanted to object, but this wasn't a time to argue, and it made sense not to rush in foolishly.

She nodded, and he kissed her, hard and deep, his tongue stroking hers. There was fear in his kiss. And protectiveness. And another emotion she refused to name.

He pressed his forehead to hers. "If anything happens to me, get out and hide in the rainforest." He straightened and lifted the camera strap from around his neck and placed it around hers. "Go to Fort Domingo and use a flare to signal a boat heading to or from Dominica. In addition to the photos I took inside the fort, the memory card has Chad's statement and photos of Chad and Nico in Kosmo's office. Proof of what's going on here."

She nodded even as her eyes burned.

He brushed his lips over hers again, opened the door, and slipped into the dark closet.

A moment later, he opened the door and whispered, "Room is clear."

She entered the house to find herself in a very large pantry. The door to the cellar was in an alcove in the back, not readily visible to the casual observer who might not realize the shelf was offset from the wall by about a foot and a half. Just enough for a person to scoot sideways through. She had to doff the backpack and pull it along at her side to fit through the tight space.

She ran her flashlight over the dry goods stored on the well-stocked shelves and was reminded that she'd subsisted on trail mix and beef jerky since the afternoon. Anxiety had cloaked hunger, but the bin of potatoes set off a longing for mashed potatoes and gravy—the ultimate comfort food her mom had made for her when she was in elementary school.

With a pang, she wondered how her mother was doing in her memory care facility in Seattle. But she knew the answer to that question. Time only went backward in the world of her mother's mind.

She was fine, completely unaware that her daughter hadn't visited in several weeks. But then, she was completely unaware she'd ever had a daughter, let alone two.

Fiona focused on the shelves. It wasn't a big mystery why she craved her mom's version of a food hug in this moment. The reality of being inside the house, where Kosmo lurked and ruled, terrified her in a way she hadn't expected.

Her light landed on a pair of thick stainless steel doors on one side of the room. Each door had a built-in thermometer at eye level. Walk-in refrigerator and freezer, she presumed.

Her belly rumbled. Maybe she could ease both her anxiety and hunger with a brick of cheese or a vat of ice cream. She pondered freezer versus refrigerator and decided that in this climate, apples might be stored in the fridge as well, and she needed something more portable than Ben & Jerry's.

She tilted her head toward the doors and raised a brow. Dean nodded and grabbed a bag of onions from a shelf as they crossed the room. He pushed open the door with the thermometer set to four degrees Celsius and dropped the bag on the floor by the doorsill, ensuring the refrigerator wouldn't close and seal them inside.

A bright white light turned on the moment the door opened, and she blinked against the sudden glare. Dean stepped back from the inward-opening door to allow her to precede him. She stepped inside, then slapped a hand over her mouth to stifle a scream.

Philip, the pilot, lay on the floor. His skin was a grayish color that could only mean he'd been dead for some time.

Dean stared in shock at the body on the floor. His face was battered, indicating he'd been beaten before he died.

How long had he been here? Surely not before the kitchen staff was evacuated before the storm?

Had he been alive but a prisoner between the time they'd seen him last and yesterday?

If that was the case, why had they killed him?

"I need my camera," Dean said, nodding to the DSLR that hung around Fiona's neck.

With shaking hands, she lifted the case and unsnapped the cover, which flipped down to expose the lens. She raised the camera and powered it on. "I can do it," she said in a voice as quivery as her hands.

He was glad he'd taught her to use this one the other night, but this was not how he'd expected her photography lesson to pay off.

After snapping a few photos, she turned the mode dial to video and hit the red-dot record button. She did a slow scan of the fridge. He followed her progress, turning as she did.

She let out a gasp, and he saw the foot sticking out from behind the open fridge door in the same instant.

Dean swiped at the door. It swung until it hit the bag of onions and revealed a white man Dean had never seen before. He sat with his back to the wall, head slumped down. Blood covered the gray hair at his temple, his ear, and the collar of his shirt. A whole lot of blood.

But still, his pallor wasn't the same grayish color as Philip's, and Fiona dropped to her knees and pressed her hand to his throat.

"I think he's got a pulse. But it's hard to tell. My heart is pounding so hard, I'm not entirely sure I don't feel it in my fingertips."

He dropped to his knees on the opposite side of the man and touched his neck. He thought he detected a pulse too. "Is this Richards?"

"Yes."

He touched the man's cheek. It was cold, but then the man had been sitting in a refrigerator for who knew how long.

Dean gave him a gentle slap. "Richards?" he said, keeping his voice low. With the door open, anyone near the pantry might hear.

Richards's head lolled.

Dean could swear he twitched.

He slapped again, slightly harder this time.

The man let out a low groan, and one eye opened a slit.

"Richards!" Fiona's voice was a whisper, but still urgent. "Remember me? Fiona Carver? What happened to you?"

The man's eyes opened wider. "Carver?" He looked like he was trying to focus but failed. "Is it really you?"

"Yes. We met in Admiral Martinez's office. What happened?"

"Kosmo. His men jumped me. Hit me with something. Dragged me into Kosmo's office. He questioned me as they beat me until I passed out. Woke up here." He nodded toward the body. "Found my missing informant too late to do him any good."

"Philip was an informant?"

With closed eyes, Richards nodded. He grimaced, as if even the slight movement triggered agony. But with that head wound, it probably did.

Dean pulled out a T-shirt from his pack and gently pressed it to the wound, but he had a feeling it was a lost cause.

The cold fridge might have slowed the bleeding, keeping him alive longer, but from the pool of blood and the size of the gash, Dean would bet he'd lost too much blood to survive much longer.

"You came here to find Philip?" Fiona asked.

"We lost contact with him two days after the crash. Then you reported the boat explosion. Reynolds never reported the helicopter crash or explosion to the NTSB or FBI. My boss decided I needed to come in. Find Philip and extract you both."

"You were here to get me off the island? Why didn't the admiral notify me?"

"He tried, but Jude's server wouldn't let any messages through. Blocked the IP address. Nothing in or out. Don't know how he did it, but Reynolds must've been able to skim the content of your SIPRNet messages. No encryption when they passed through his server."

"I logged in and emailed the admiral an hour before I saw you in Jude's office. The system was working then."

"Reynolds likely set it up so it would look normal on your end."

"Jude? Not Kosmo?"

"Jude's the tech guy. Kosmo wouldn't begin to know how to spoof the system to fool you, let alone unencrypt your SIPRNet emails. We figure he was tipped off when the boats were detained by customs, and he started looking for a mole."

Richards confirmed what Dean had suspected. Jude was involved, but there was still something very off about the man hiring Fiona, Sadie, and Chad. No way would he do that, knowing they'd discover Ruby Island was a smuggler's haven.

"Are you DEA?" Fiona asked.

Richards nodded.

"What was your cover in coming here?"

"DEA spent months setting it up. Business associate. Not my first time on the island. I wanted to talk before you left yesterday, but Kosmo's men were watching me."

"I wish I'd been told all of this before you sent me here and asked me to spy for you."

"We were certain you would be safe. Your history with Jude checked out. Reynolds has never been violent."

"But Kosmo is."

"We didn't know he'd be here the whole time. He's never spent more than a few days on the island before. We think he wanted to keep an eye on the fieldwork."

All at once, Richards opened his eyes and grabbed Fiona's wrist. "Film me. Now. Then leave. Kosmo will kill you if he finds you. Like he killed me."

"You aren't—"

"I'm already dead, Fiona. My brain just hasn't caught up with that truth yet. Turn on the camera."

She raised the camera, giving Dean a glimpse of the screen on the back. It was still recording. She hadn't turned it off when she'd spotted Richards.

Now, with shaking hands, she turned the lens to face Richards. Silent tears streaked down her cheeks as she knelt before the dying man. Dean could see his face centered in the screen. He spoke directly to the camera.

"My name is Christopher Richards. DEA agent working under-cover on the Ruby Island case. For the last year, we've been investigating a report that cocaine was being distributed via luxury yachts. Their crews have a pattern of sailing to Ruby Island as a refueling stop while their owners are not on board. The crews then deliver the coke to various other destinations in the United States or Caribbean."

Fiona let out a soft gasp and said, "That explains the massive fueling tanks."

Richards nodded. "Yes. Under the direction of Jude's father, Kosmo Andreas had them installed ten years ago. We believe that's when the private-yacht smuggling started and the senior Reynolds was fully on board, possibly even the instigator of the scheme."

Richards kept his gaze on the camera. "I came to Ruby Island to extract informants Philip Gomez and Fiona Carver. Hours after my arrival, the house staff was evacuated, and my comms went out—I suspect some sort of signal blocker was employed. Kosmo must have learned of my identity—possibly from Gomez under torture—because hours ago, I was attacked from behind and woke in a refrigerator with the dead body of Philip Gomez. I believe the helicopter crash eight days ago was an attempt on Gomez's life, likely because Kosmo suspected or found proof he was a DEA informant."

Dean turned to the body on the floor. Philip Gomez—he was only now learning the man's last name—had saved his life that first day, and now he'd paid the ultimate price for attempting to shut down a major smuggling operation.

He'd been incredibly brave and a hell of a pilot. Dean desperately hoped the man's sacrifice wouldn't be in vain.

"I will die here," Richards continued. "You need to go now. Both of you. Get this video to the DEA. With this evidence, they can raid the island. Leave. Now."

"We can take you with us," Fiona said. Tears resumed streaking down her cheeks.

"No. As I said, I'm already dead. You try to take me with you, and you'll be dead too." He closed his eyes.

Dean guessed he wouldn't talk anymore. Conversation would just keep them here, and they had to leave.

Now.

"C'mon, Fi."

She nodded and rose to her feet even as more tears fell. She preceded him out the door. He scooped up the bag of onions and let the door close. Leaving the man to die alone.

THIRTY-ONE

Fiona leaned against the closed door and held her breath to suppress the loud sob that wanted to escape. She barely knew either man, but that didn't lessen the horror of the moment.

Dean wrapped his arms around her, and his warm body after the cold fridge was welcome.

"I'm sorry, Fi, but we've got to keep moving. I'm going to check out the kitchen, make sure it's safe, while you gather yourself. I'll come back when I'm sure the coast is clear."

He released her, and she nodded, swiping the tears from her cheeks. "I'll wait behind the pantry door."

He brushed his lips over hers and headed to the door. She took her position behind it as he slipped silently from the room.

Minutes ticked by, and she knew he must be moving slowly as he confirmed there was no one in the service wing.

She heard footsteps in the corridor and felt a rush of relief that he was coming back. Except Dean was being careful to make sure his footsteps didn't make a sound.

She heard voices.

Fear spiked so hard, she was nearly dizzy with it. The sound of blood rushing through her head nearly blocked her hearing. She took a silent breath and focused on the voices. They were getting closer.

"We need Carver and Slater. I don't believe for a minute that Baylor is going to return with the battery case, but once he sees us carving on

Carver, he'll deliver, especially knowing his girlfriend won't be spared any longer." That was probably Kosmo's voice.

"Fiona is not to be touched. I told you that." That was Jude, she was certain.

"You lost the right to object when you invited a DEA informant to spend two months on Ruby Island."

Any thought that Jude might somehow be innocent was obliterated by that comment.

"She's not an informant."

"She is. She sent the *guest list* to the admiral. Every boat she named was detained and searched. My guys onboard managed to dump the shipments before they could be found. Do you have any idea how much money we just lost?"

"*You* lost. Not me. I didn't make—or lose—a dime from that."

"Maybe not since your dad died, but before that, you sure as hell did. Why the fuck do you think he had so many damn parties over the years? You think he *liked* those assholes? You will never be the business-man your father was."

"I don't want to be. I never wanted that aspect of the business."

"Too bad. It comes with the inheritance. Came with the island. You always figured as long as you didn't personally get your hands dirty, you were above it all. Pretend you don't know what's in those special containers. But those containers have paid for everything you own, including this island."

"That may be true, but it doesn't change the fact that you're the one running coke through Ruby Island, not me. I didn't know a thing about it."

They were in the kitchen now, right outside the pantry door. Where was Dean? Had he found a place to hide?

She heard cupboards open and then slam closed. "Next time you send the chef away, make sure he leaves us some fucking food first."

Jude's voice was irritated and churlish, reminding her of the man she'd had dinner with at Canlis.

"'*I didn't know*' won't get you very far in court if this gets out. For that reason, Fiona Carver suffers the same fate as the rest of them. You're in this as deep as I am."

More cupboards slammed.

"Play along," Kosmo said, "and we'll get your battery case back and you can play with your drone and we'll pretend this never happened."

Glass shattered. "I'm not your fucking pawn, Kosmo. This is *my* company."

"I know. And with the amount we move in the containers, you're CEO of one of the biggest drug-smuggling operations in the world. Try to '*I didn't know*' your way out of that conviction."

"You can't do this to me."

"You should have walked away from the CEO position when you had the chance. I told you you'd regret it."

There was a long silence, broken by Kosmo. "Well, well, well. Mr. Slater. Nice of you to join us. I guess you and Ms. Carver were feeling peckish too."

———

Dean knew it was only a matter of time before they spotted him, so he chose to take control of his capture and stepped out with the arrow nocked and string pulled taut. He could shoot only one of them. Jude might not hurt Fiona, but Kosmo had threatened to cut her.

It was an easy choice, but Jude stood in front of Kosmo, blocking the shot.

"Starving, really. I'll take a sandwich. Light on the mayo, extra tomato."

Kosmo's eyes flicked to behind Dean's head, and he gave a short nod. Dean wouldn't fall for it. Oldest trick in the book. No one else was here. Walker and Erik were off in a cave.

"Reynolds, move and I'll take care of your rat infestation."

The moment he got a clear shot, he'd loose the arrow. A mere ten feet separated them. Kosmo was as good as dead.

"You think you're safer with Jude? You're banging the woman he's in love with. He'll kill you faster than I will."

"No he won't, because if anything happens to me, he'll lose Fiona forever. And she's not sleeping with me. She gave me the heave-ho last night. Said she wants to give this thing with Jude a shot. She wanted to come back last night and tell him, but someone stole our canoe after trying to kill me. Then the storm hit, so we were stuck in the jungle."

Jude turned to Kosmo, but didn't move to the side, *dammit*. "You tried to kill him?"

"My gift to you. To make up for stealing your drone. It would have been a perfect accident. I'm sure Ms. Carver would have turned to you in her devastation." Kosmo's smile, visible above Jude's head, was chilling.

It was too bad an arrow wasn't as precise as a sniper rifle for small targets.

The hairs on the back of Dean's neck stood up, and a moment later, he felt the barrel of a pistol pressed to his temple.

"Lower the arrow," Kosmo said.

Slowly, Dean released the tension on the string, then pushed the nock so the arrow detached and clattered to the floor.

"Do I waste him anyway, boss?"

"No," Kosmo said, leaving no doubt as to who was in charge. "We need him if we're to find the lovely Ms. Carver."

Jude had turned to face him again. His gaze assessing. Was he wondering if Dean had told the truth about Fiona, or did he see right through the lie?

Either way, Dean's only protection was Jude's desire for Fiona. "Not a scratch on me, Reynolds, or she'll never speak to you again."

"I have no doubt on that point. Fiona is loyal to a fault."

"She was informing on you," Kosmo reminded him.

"She was informing on *you*. Not me."

"Can someone kindly tell this asshole to lower the gun from my head?"

Jude nodded—apparently the thug took orders from both men—and the gun was lowered.

"Where's Fiona?" Jude asked. He held Dean's gaze, and his eye twitched. Not a wink but a sign nonetheless. Dean guessed he knew exactly how they'd entered the house and probably figured Fiona was still in the pantry, and the last thing he wanted was for Kosmo to find her.

In this one area, he and Reynolds were allies.

"I don't know. She's probably looking for Sadie."

"Well, isn't it convenient, then, that we'll take you to her," Jude said. He nodded to the guard. "Jerry, bind his wrists and take him to the storm shelter."

Much as Dean hoped she'd already fled the house, he also hoped she'd heard Jude confirm Sadie's location.

———

Fiona bolted for the shelf that hid the cellar door. She would hide by the door until she was certain the coast was clear.

Then what?

She needed a working phone. Or computer. Or anything that could communicate with the outside world.

She could maybe find something in Jude's office, but everything would be password protected by a man who'd managed to spoof an encrypted government network. Jude had complete control of all data that passed through his server.

How else could she get a message to the outside world?

Dean's suggestion of using a flare was too risky. Kosmo would see it, and a passing boat might radio the island to ask what the issue was.

The sensors on the volcano came to mind. Those were operational, but they'd already examined one, and there was no way for a person to send a message using the satellite link. Dylan wouldn't understand it even if she could get it to register seismic activity, or whatever it was he was monitoring.

Dylan. If only she could reach Dylan.

With a jolt, she remembered Dean's game cameras. Dylan was monitoring the feed and flagging photos that showed different bird species, giving Dean a summary of the data.

The game cameras had their own satellite hookup and solar panels to power both the satellite link and camera.

If she could get to a camera, she could hold up a sign. An SOS.

The only problem was, the cameras were a hundred feet straight up a tree. Fiona didn't have climbing equipment, and she had a paralyzing fear of heights.

THIRTY-TWO

Chad was out of options, but he still needed a little more time. The tide was coming in, and the window to escape the cave was rapidly closing, but they weren't at the sweet spot yet. They were more than an hour past low tide, but the Whaler could probably still scrape through if need be. If Walker was desperate enough and didn't give a damn about the boat.

Getting trapped in the cave was only one way to buy time so Fiona and Dean could get help for Sadie. If Chad returned now without the battery case, they'd torture her to get him to talk. And he would talk to save Sadie.

And then they'd all die.

"Where is the fucking battery case, Baylor?" Erik asked.

Chad guessed it would be another ten to twenty minutes before the cave was completely sealed off. The next high tide would be at six a.m., and the next low would be at one p.m. They'd be able to take the boat out sometime before noon, maybe eleven if they were lucky—and again didn't give a damn about damaging the boat—after all, they were just a few days past the new moon, and high tides were higher and low tides were lower.

Until then, if they wanted to leave the cave before the tide was far enough out, they'd have to swim. If they did have to swim, Nico would probably be able to get free. Like Chad, he was a strong swimmer. He had to be to film underwater. Swimming out of a cave at night without scuba was a different beast, but desperate times . . .

Maybe they'd both get lucky and Kosmo's men weren't swimmers at all. Except these were probably the guys who'd collected the helicopter debris and planted it in the fort.

No. They had to stay put until the next low tide. That would buy Fiona and Dean a lot of time to find a way to steal a boat or make a call for help.

Twenty minutes more. That's all he needed. Which meant going deeper into the dark, rank, bat-shit-filled cave. He silently apologized to Nico, but then, he'd been doing that ever since the guy was marched before him with a battered face.

If looks could kill, Nico would have done Erik's job for him.

Chad breathed in the guano-filled air and said, "It's up in this tunnel a bit farther." He hoped to hell the tunnel went deep, and he could keep leading them deeper and deeper into the heart of the island before they realized they were trapped by the sea.

———

Fiona stuck to the shadows and back passageways as she made her way to Nico's room on the second floor. The house was silent as a tomb, but that didn't mean a nightmare wasn't lurking around every corner.

Had they all gone to the storm shelter, or had Kosmo and Jude remained on the premises? Were there more henchmen she didn't know about? She only vaguely remembered Jerry, reminded when Jude had said the name. He worked on the dock with Walker most of the time.

Had he been the one to put the bruises on Chad's and Nico's faces?

Knowing they'd killed Philip and Richards was dying—*is he already dead?*—her fear for Dean and Sadie nearly took her breath away as she skulked along the corridors.

Was Dean being beaten even now? Was Sadie's face swollen with cuts and bruises?

311

These horrors were what spurred her to take one scared step after another. She had to get to Nico's quarters.

At last, she reached the interior staircase. There would be no place to hide from here until she was in Nico's room. She had to move quickly but silently.

She'd removed her boots before she left the pantry, and now she trod on bare feet up the tall flight of stairs. She reached the landing and breathed a silent sigh of relief at finding the corridor empty. She darted down the hall and twisted the knob for Nico's room. Thankfully it wasn't locked.

Inside, she found the room a mess. It had been thoroughly tossed. His camera equipment broken. Computers smashed.

Thankfully, those items weren't the reason she was here. She imagined her room looked much the same.

She spotted the pile of climbing gear and pounced on it.

She found harnesses and carabiners and tucked them in her pack. She grabbed extra rope. Panic started to rise when she didn't see the last thing she needed. She dug through the ropes, her breathing shallow as she found it hard to fill her lungs.

Her hand gripped something, and she yanked it from the pile. Hope bloomed, and she shoved the ropes aside, looking for the rest. She'd found them. Two ascenders and two descenders.

She burst into tears even as she crammed them into her pack.

She had what she needed.

———

Sadie jolted at the sound of the lock turning. She didn't know if she was glad or terrified that Kosmo or one of his henchmen was back.

It was sweltering in the room, and she'd run out of water hours ago, so on the one hand, they could bring relief. But they also always delivered terror.

Light from the outer room spilled in through the open door, and she closed her eyes against the intrusion after sitting chained to a claw-foot bathtub in absolute darkness for hours.

Her back ached from the cramped position she had to maintain on the hard tile floor. She had only two feet of space to sit in the gap between the end of the tub and the wall. Her range of motion was even smaller.

Trapped in a damn storm shelter bathroom and desperate for water was not how she'd envisioned her death, but over the last day and a half, she'd come to accept this could very much be how it all ended.

At least her captors had seen fit to give her a jar, which she could empty in the tub, so she didn't have to sit in her own urine. Yippee.

She forced her eyes open and faced the glare, seeing the silhouette of a man.

She recognized Dean immediately from his size and shape as he was shoved into the room. Too tall to be Nico or Chad. She didn't figure anyone else would get the prisoner treatment.

The light landed on his face, confirming her conclusion. His cheek was swollen and bottom lip split, but he looked fine otherwise. He hadn't been put through the paces like Chad. But then, he wasn't a traitor like Chad.

Her belly churned at that. She'd loved that man with all her heart for the better part of a dozen years, and he'd caused this. Her, cuffed to a fucking bathtub in a storm shelter, on an island where her ancestors had probably sought refuge.

It was a nightmare to be in this situation, but utterly galling to have it happen here, after being betrayed by the man with whom she'd planned to spend the rest of her life.

Years ago, she and Chad had faced his gambling problem head-on. He'd gotten help, and as a couple, they'd been stronger for the journey. She didn't know if he'd fallen off the wagon or not, but he'd spent time alone on Aruba and in the Dominican Republic this spring when Sadie was taking care of her mom in LA following hip surgery, and both countries had big, tempting casinos.

The entire situation could be because he'd gambled away their savings and didn't want to admit to her what he'd done. If he'd just *told* her, they could have found a way to work it out.

Dean was dragged to the other side of the tub. He didn't make it easy, but he also didn't make it hard. She recognized a man going through the motions of resistance.

He'd accepted his fate, but he wanted Jerry to believe he still had some fight in him. Was he buying time?

Where was Fiona?

Where was Chad?

And what had happened to Nico?

Dean's handcuffs closed around a leg on the other side of the bathtub with a click of metal on metal, and he was bound as surely as she was.

Jerry left, and she and Dean were alone.

Silence passed between them for a long interval. He breathed heavily, as if he were gathering himself, conquering the pain of blows to the face. She knew that sound. Her half brother had made it more than once after he got involved in things he shouldn't have.

Dean wasn't that type, though. She guessed his brother wasn't either.

Dylan Slater had crossed her mind more than once these last few days as Chad spun out of control and she longed for someone—anyone—to step in and make the nightmare go away.

She wasn't the type to pine for some man to save her, but Dylan hadn't hesitated to intervene in the heat of the moment, and the rush of relief and burn of appreciation had caught her by surprise.

She could take care of herself. She always had.

But it was a fine experience to have some tall, handsome stranger step up and offer protection he had no obligation to provide.

It was hot, frankly.

But she'd have to save her lusting after a man she'd met only briefly for another day. Right now she had to speak to his brother. "I will refrain from asking questions, because odds are, Jerry is listening on the other side of the door. But I can answer your questions, as long as the answers are what Jude and Kosmo already know."

"Exactly how deep is Jude in Kosmo's scheme?" he asked.

The door pushed open, and Kosmo entered. "He's in far too deep to save you, if that's what you're thinking."

———

Once again, without a boat, it was a long hike back through the rainforest. The island was familiar now, but this was her first time traversing it alone. At night. And terrified for Dean and Sadie.

And Nico.

And yes, even Chad.

Fiona's headlamp lit the way as she slashed at vines with her trusty machete. Rote actions, all she was capable of as fear threatened to consume her.

Her compass gave her direction. Navigating in the dark wasn't easy, but the physical exertion and need to track distance and direction kept her from falling apart. One foot in front of the other. Don't think about what was happening behind her or what was in front of her.

Don't think about the climb. Don't think about the height.

And definitely don't think about Dean's last descent.

Just slash. Take a step. Push branches and leaves out of the way. Walk. Check the compass. Adjust trajectory. Slash. Walk.

Her arms ached, but she was past the point of really feeling.

She'd have time to rest when she reached the camera. She wouldn't begin her ascent until full daylight. No way could she climb a hundred feet straight up in the dark.

Plus, the batteries could be low and need charging with the solar panels. She'd sit in the damn tree all day if that's what it took to send a message to Dylan.

For the hundredth time, the machete stuck in a trunk, and she paused to pry it out. She pulled too hard and when it released, momentum sent her backward. Her heavy pack upset her balance, and she landed on her ass on the wet forest floor.

She sat there and breathed heavily, tears just beneath the surface.

Dean was counting on her.

She closed her eyes and remembered the feel of his lips on her neck. The look in his intense blue eyes and the way his blond hair glowed in the firelight as he made love to her.

The laminated photo of his wedding day, and his words about the promise he'd made to Violet that he would live his life to the fullest and do all the things they'd planned to do together.

She swiped at tears that were wrung from terror.

She couldn't let Violet down. After all he'd done for his wife, the pain he'd suffered, he deserved a long life filled with adventure. He deserved joy.

But right now, he was Kosmo's prisoner, and the whole reason he was on this damn island was because of her.

She pushed herself to her feet. Slash. Step. Brush aside branches. Keep moving.

She wouldn't let Violet down.

THIRTY-THREE

Dean waited in the seat that faced Jude's desk in his first-floor office. It was all very civilized for a middle-of-the-night meeting, except both of his arms were handcuffed to the ornate, heavy antique chair.

Jerry had escorted him from the storm shelter to the house on, apparently, Jude's orders. Clearly the billionaire was flexing his power for Dean's benefit, but really it made him wonder if Jerry was the only muscle at the estate.

If so, Chad must've gotten them trapped in the cave—otherwise they'd be back by now.

Dean could handle Jude until the moment the guy was backed into a corner. He had no doubt that when the time came, Jude would sacrifice Fiona to save his own ass. Which meant they were all dead because they all knew too much.

The question was, how was Kosmo going to explain the deaths or sudden disappearances of Nico, Chad, Sadie, Fiona, and Dean? They were running out of boats to blow up.

He jolted upright—*shit*—he could see the plan now. Chad and Sadie's boat. The documentary gave them all a reason to be on the boat at the same time, no questions asked.

He'd bet his new favorite camera and all the cannons in Cannon Bay that Kosmo would find a way to get Jude on the boat too. Take care of all his problems in one fell swoop. Or rather, explosion. Kosmo probably even had a plan to make it look like Jude's obsession with Fiona was the cause of the blast.

Too bad there was a dead pilot and dying DEA agent in the refrigerator. Their murders would be harder to explain.

But then, putting refrigerated remains on the boat, along with an explosion that would blast them all to bits, would obscure time and cause of death.

Motherfucker. Kosmo could get away with it, unless Dean found a way to get Jude to balk.

Jude entered the room carrying Dean's backpack, which he set on the right side of his desk before settling in his seat. There was no way Kosmo didn't know of this meeting and a good chance the guy was listening in, so what was the game here?

"For a photographer, your backpack is strangely lacking in cameras."

Dean nodded toward the bag. "There are extra lenses."

"But still, no camera or case."

He shrugged. "It must've fallen out."

He was certain now that Kosmo had put Jude up to this. His questions in the storm shelter bathroom had also focused on Dean's missing camera. The man must've guessed Dean had incriminating photos and video. But then, he'd left his T-shirt with Richards in the refrigerator. They knew he'd talked to the DEA agent.

Time to redirect. "I have to say, this assignment isn't at all what I expected. But then, I'm guessing it hasn't gone as you planned either."

Jude didn't say a word as he rose from his seat, crossed to the wet bar, and poured himself a shot of whiskey and downed it all at once.

"None for me?"

"My apologies. I figured you'd want to stay sharp."

"So how's your plan to woo Fiona going?"

"Touché." Reynolds grabbed a second tumbler and carried both along with the bottle to his desk. He sat and poured a shot in each, then set one glass in front of Dean and drank from the other, slower this time.

Dean eyed his drink, then cleared his throat. "I'm afraid I'll need a straw. Or a free hand." He raised a wrist and rattled the metal cuffs against the wooden arm of the chair.

"Oh. Sorry. Of course. Couldn't let you take off when no one was in the room." Jude pulled a handcuff key from his breast pocket and unlocked the right cuff that was attached to the chair, so the metal dangled from Dean's wrist.

He raised the glass and took a small drink. He wasn't about to dull his reflexes, but he did want both a free hand and to know if Jude even had a key, let alone where he kept it.

"I'm presuming the bit about Fiona dumping you because she changed her mind about me was bullshit."

"And yet here you are, asking."

"I've been in love with her since I was twenty-three. Of course I have to ask."

"But will you trust my answer?"

"No."

Dean knew what it was like to be in love at twenty-three. He even knew how people discounted strong emotions felt at that age. Multiple people had questioned his decision to marry Violet. Only Dylan had never wavered in his support.

He imagined Reynolds had gone through something similar, but also worse, because his love had been unrequited.

"For what it's worth, I think you did have a chance up until Sadie was taken hostage." A lie, but it would give him a reason to protect Fiona to the end.

"I didn't take Sadie hostage."

"But you also haven't freed her. Don't think Fiona doesn't realize that."

"She was in the pantry, wasn't she? You came in through the storm cellar?"

Dean looked around the room. "You really want Kosmo to hear all this?"

"Kosmo noticed the bench and mat had been moved and saw the exposed cellar doors."

"Busy night."

"Very much so, yes."

"I'm guessing he wasn't pleased you kept that secret," Dean said.

"Well, I have my own issues with his secrets, so we're even."

"You mean like using your island to run drugs via mega yachts?"

"Yeah. That."

"But really, how surprised were you? I'm guessing not as much as you should've been."

Jude's glare was hard enough to cut glass. "Did you fuck her?"

Dean picked up his tumbler and downed the rest, then set it back on the desk. "No. But I did make love to her."

Reynolds's face bloomed red, and Dean felt a deep and incredibly immature satisfaction. He wanted to *hurt* this man whose willful ignorance had endangered Fiona.

He believed Reynolds hadn't known about Kosmo's extracurriculars, but that had been a choice on his part.

"You've always known your family's business was based on drug smuggling. But you figured if you looked the other way, it was all peachy?"

"My parents' choices were not mine. I didn't ask to be born."

"But you didn't shut down the smuggling on the container ships when you stepped into the CEO role. How do you justify that?"

Jude waved his hand over his desk. "Do you see any papers regarding drug smuggling here? I run a legitimate business, Mr. Slater."

"You *knew*, even if you didn't give the orders. You knew. And that money paid for this island. This house. The helicopter and yacht. Even the archaeology project you hired Fiona to do. It was—and is—all drug money."

"Not *all*. And my drone was going to cut fuel costs, bringing our profit margins up so the drugs wouldn't be needed. RAM Freight is going legitimate under my leadership. I'm investing in streaming TV networks too. All legitimate. Legal."

"Your drone invention is going to be used by Kosmo to smuggle drugs, and you know it. What's the battery range? Fifteen hundred miles—or rather, twelve hundred nautical miles? That's just slightly farther than the distance from Ruby Island to Miami. Convenient."

"I didn't know that's why Kosmo put that in the specs."

"So you're saying you . . . lack intelligence?"

Jude's nostrils flared, and Dean knew he was on the right track. He'd known. He'd followed Kosmo's specs to the letter, building the guy his dream smuggling device to please Daddy's right-hand man and shut him up. And then he'd even guessed what had happened when the boat blew up. He'd chosen not to report it to US authorities because an investigation would only lead to questions he didn't want answered.

"You knew the explosion was a grab for the drone. And you did nothing."

Reynolds poured himself another shot and waved the bottle in the air as an offer to Dean.

"Pass, thanks. One of us needs our wits to deal with your boss."

Reynolds's eyes burned with anger. "I am the CEO of RAM Freight."

"And yet, you answer to Kosmo Andreas."

His fist hit the desk. "I am CEO of RAM Freight!"

Dean changed his mind and picked up the bottle, pouring himself another shot. "I'm sure that's very exciting for you, to finally be the big boy and sit at Daddy's desk, but Kosmo is running the company and has been for years."

"I can handle Kosmo."

"You couldn't handle a sloth on downers." Dean leaned forward and held Reynolds's gaze. "I don't like or trust you, so I'm going to make something very clear. If anything happens to Fiona, if she's harmed in any way by you or Kosmo, I will kill you."

"You would kill for Fiona?" Reynolds asked.

He settled back in his chair. "I already have." He took another drink, then set it calmly on the desk. "I would die for her."

"I can arrange that."

———

Sunlight struck Fiona's eyes, and she startled awake with a jolt. *Shit,* she'd fallen asleep? And then she'd . . . *overslept?*

She'd reached the tree an hour before dawn and had slumped into the cradle between two buttress roots and closed her eyes to gather energy. She'd never thought she could fall asleep, not when she was so worried.

But exhaustion must've won, because the sun was now high enough in the sky to penetrate the canopy and find her face.

A hole-in-one shot by Mother Nature.

Bitch.

She was always cranky when she was short on sleep, and her entire body ached after all she'd put it through in the last forty-eight hours. How was she going to muster the strength for the coming climb?

She tilted her head and gazed upward, taking in the tall, straight trunk and dangling ropes.

She had to climb that.

It was the only way.

And she was at least a fucking hour late in getting started.

What price had Dean paid because she'd fallen asleep?

She was on her knees, pulling climbing gear from her pack before her mind had cleared of the dregs of sleep.

Best to start climbing before she was completely conscious. A fully awake brain would only get in her way.

She found the ascenders and harness. She could do this. She'd been a climber once. It had been one of the great thrills of her life to climb with her father.

Then the accident happened, and both she and Regan developed a fear of heights. Ropes. All of it.

There was no way Regan had stood on that cliff's edge the day she fell to her death. Her fear of heights never would have allowed it. Which meant Regan had been dragged there. Pushed.

Fiona knew this, but she was all alone in the knowledge. Her mother couldn't remember. Her brother didn't believe it.

She shoved those thoughts away and breathed through the fear that had only ratcheted up since Regan's death.

She'd enjoyed climbing, but she'd been a teen the last time, and she'd never been an expert. Her dad had always told her what to do. And then one day, his rope had failed.

Deep breath.

She knew what to do. She knew how to rig all the lines and which loops her legs went through in the harness. She'd watched Dean do this multiple times in the last week.

She remembered her last climb. With Regan, Aidan, and their dad. Like Dean, Regan had been an adrenaline junkie, even then.

Regan and Dean would have been besties, no doubt. Fiona and Dylan would have sat in the corner, drinking wine as they watched her baby sister and his twin brother bait each other into wilder and wilder dares. As long as it didn't involve heights, Regan was all over it.

She swiped at a tear as she stepped through the loops of the harness, the tangle of straps making sense as her lizard brain provided guidance and primal memory when she needed it most.

She could do this.

She adjusted the harness to fit her form. She and Nico were a similar height and build, giving her confidence. It was like the equipment was made for her.

But more important, each cinching of the straps reminded her she knew *how* to do this.

Muscle memory. Lizard brain.

She could do it.

She *had* to. For Dean. For Sadie. For Nico.

For Violet.

And yes. Even for Chad.

She attached the ascenders to the rope and clipped the carabiner on the line.

Each action was rote—like smashing through vines with a machete. This was what she had to do. For Dean. For Sadie.

For Richards, who'd probably died at some point in the night as she beat her way through the forest. He deserved justice.

Sadie deserved saving.

Dean deserved love.

Climbing this terrifying rope was justice, salvation, and love for everyone.

She gripped the ascender and put her foot in the loop attached to the bottom ascender and started her climb.

She wouldn't think about anything but one hand reaching up, one foot pushing down until she reached the damn top of the line.

Her muscles burned, and she had a new respect for how quickly Dean had ascended each time.

But then, he was in far better shape than she would ever be. Probably helped that he put effort into it.

For her, it was a slow slog. Not looking up. Not looking down. She rose like she was in an elevator with closed doors and opaque walls. But with a lot more exertion, because she was climbing the cable without any kind of assist.

Damn arm muscles had to do the work without aid from electricity.

As terrified as she was, focusing on the line in front of her seemed to work. No up. No down. Just steady movement.

Her hand hit the branch the rope was tied to, and a glance to the right and she saw the camera and cables that linked to the satellite hookup, and above were the solar panels.

She'd done it. She was a hundred feet in the air with a live camera and satellite feed.

Salvation was at hand.

She braced herself in the cradle of two thick branches and hooked multiple tethers to the safety lines Dean had set up. Then she hauled up her heavy pack, which she'd clipped to the end of a long rope before climbing. She slipped the other end of that rope through the pulley Dean had rigged and pulled on the line, clipping it off at intervals so if it slipped thanks to her tired arms, it wouldn't drop far.

Her arms had gotten quite a workout in the last two days. When she got home, she was going to make a commitment to going to the gym more to build arm strength. It was closing the barn door after the horses escaped, she knew, but goal setting was important when life was terrifying and could end at any moment.

At last, she had her pack. She clipped it to the tree with several carabiners.

She then took a long drink of water. She was sweltering in the morning sun. Humidity was high, and the breeze wasn't reaching her through the canopy right then.

She clipped the hydration nozzle back to the side of her pack and took a deep breath, facing up toward the sun as a ray slipped between the branches and touched her face. She was doing this. It wasn't elegant or pretty, but then, she'd never seen herself as either of those things.

With a deep breath, she turned her attention to the satellite hookup. It would help if she had a manual to tell her what all the cables and ports did, but no such luck.

She waved to the camera with its two owl-looking eyes, each a separate lens. It was motion activated, so she needed to make sure it got multiple pictures in case the text on her signs was blurry. She wasn't certain what depth of field the lenses would focus on, but Dean had said it was different for each, so she could probably count on one getting a clear image.

All the cables were plugged into ports, so she figured they were working, considering Dean had gotten good results before the storm, and nothing had changed since then. She reached for her Rite in the Rain notebook. She would write messages to Dylan, and he would call in the cavalry. Easy peasy.

Exhaustion and nerves had her hands shaking. But that was nothing new. Her hands had been shaking practically since they'd run into Chad in the fort yesterday.

She dug in the backpack, her fingers finding the yellow plastic cover of the spiral-bound notebook. She would sit up here in her perch for as long as it took to be certain the camera had taken shots of every sign. Dylan would contact the DEA. Help would come.

She tugged on the notebook, and it caught on something. The unexpected resistance threw off her balance, and she slipped a bit.

She gripped the branch with one hand in the moment the notebook cleared the snag, popping free.

She wobbled on the branch, her gaze dropping to the ground below.

The distance made her dizzy. The fingers gripping the slippery plastic cover went slack, and the notebook slid away, hitting branch after branch as it fell a hundred feet to the forest floor.

"The tide is low enough now. We should swim out," Nico said.

"You jump into that water and we'll shoot you before you break the surface. We were told not to go back without the battery case or two dead bodies. We leave here on the boat and go straight to where he really hid the case, or we shoot you both now." Walker turned to Chad and placed the barrel of his gun against his head. "Time to talk, or time to die. Where. The fuck. Did you hide. The battery?"

Time was up. They had less than an hour before the boat would clear the cave entrance. Surely Fiona and Dean had had enough time to get help? If they didn't, all was lost anyway.

His only option now was to buy more time by telling the truth. "It's in the forest. Where Slater strung up one of his cameras."

"Why there?"

"I wanted to make sure it would be found by Slater or someone else if something happened to me."

———

Fiona would not panic. She'd made it this far and didn't need to climb down for the notebook. She'd write on her shirt. Or her arm. Whatever it took.

She dug in her bag, feeling her heartbeat all the way to her fingertips. Was it the adrenaline of fear because she was a hundred feet high in a tree? Terror for Dean and Sadie? Or concern this plan wouldn't work?

It had to work. There was simply no other option.

Her fingers landed on the roll of one-liter, four-mil thick, zipper-top bags she always carried in the field for soil samples and artifacts. *Who needs paper when you've got plastic bags and a Sharpie?*

She pulled out a bag and a thick-tipped black marker and wrote in block letters: DEA AGENT KILLED BY KOSMO—SADIE & DEAN TAKEN HOSTAGE.

Out of room, she pulled out a second bag and wrote: CALL DEA. RICHARDS IS DEAD. CALL ADMIRAL MARTINEZ—PAC NW COMMAND. CALL FBI.

On a third bag, she wrote simply: Help Us, Dylan!!

She clipped the first bag to her aluminum clipboard. The black letters stood out in bold against the silver background, just visible through the thick layers of plastic.

She held the sign at chest height and positioned herself in front of the pair of lenses. She knew she wouldn't hear the snick of a shutter. The sound might alert animals to the camera and scare them. Likewise, there was no light on the front to indicate if it was working.

She adjusted her position on the branches to get a better look at the camera without upsetting its placement. She didn't dare touch anything in case she screwed it up.

She inched sideways, leaning on a branch until she could see the back of the camera by craning her neck. There, she spotted the tape Dean had used to cover the lights on the back. She gingerly peeled off the tape and saw the green dot that indicated it was on. The satellite uplink was strapped to a branch and protected by a small camouflage rain cover. She lifted the cover and peeled the tape off the control panel, revealing green LED lights that signaled it was transmitting.

Satisfied, she resumed her position on the branch and held up the clipboard with the first sign again. She held it closer to the camera, then farther back, waiting several seconds in each position to give the camera time to work. It was probably snapping rapid photos, but she wasn't about to take chances.

She changed signs and repeated the process. She cycled through all three a second time, then pulled out another blank bag and wrote: Locked Out Of Internet, Cell, And Sat Comms. No Boat. Trapped.

On another bag, she wrote: Kosmo Is Running Drugs Through Island. Hidden In Star Fort.

Next she wrote: Tell DEA Helicopter Pilot Philip Gomez Was Murdered.

She then rotated through those signs several times. What else could she tell Dylan? What did the DEA need to know?

She didn't know how many men guarded Kosmo. Didn't know Jude's exact role other than he was complicit.

She pulled out another bag and made one last sign: DEAN & SADIE ARE PRISONERS IN THE STORM SHELTER.

She hoped that was accurate.

She ran through her series of signs again and again, until she'd been up in the tree for more than an hour. Surely enough photos had been taken and uploaded?

Dylan would see them at some point. Did he check the feed in the mornings? Evenings? It could be hours before he saw these.

She'd head back. Spy on the house and try to figure out how to free Sadie and Dean from the storm shelter. But to do that, she had to climb down the rope. She feared descending even more than she'd feared the climb. But she'd inspected Nico's descenders. They hadn't been sabotaged. Nico had never been one of Kosmo's targets.

She closed her eyes and remembered the pictures Dean had showed her of Nico's swollen face. He'd been forced to go with Chad. He had nothing to do with any of this, but he'd been dragged in just the same, sent off with Chad to collect a battery case that wasn't there. It had been a suicide mission for Chad, but what did it mean for Nico? Would he be killed when Chad failed to produce the battery?

Where the hell had he hid it, anyway?

The chirping of the birds—a cacophony of sound that had become white noise to her in the weeks she'd been on the island—suddenly ceased. Fiona stiffened, alerted by the abrupt halt of sound that she was no longer alone in this small little patch of rainforest.

She did the thing she hated most and looked down.

The bright yellow cover of her notebook lay at the base of the tree, not far from where the ropes dangled, just touching the ground.

Unlike when Dean had been up in the canopy, she wasn't in camouflage. She didn't have his camo sheet to wrap around her. No, she wore a bright orange top, the color of safety vests that could be seen even in the worst weather. It was her go-to field shirt, and as four men approached the base of the tree, she knew her safety shirt might be the thing that got her killed.

THIRTY-FOUR

Chad spotted the notebook before the others. *Shit.*

No way did Fiona leave that behind when she and Slater were last here, which meant she'd come back. And was still here.

He didn't look up. Wouldn't look up. Couldn't give her or Dean away if one of them was up in the tree.

Had to be Slater, though. No way would Fiona be able to handle that height. If it was Slater, he'd be in full camo. Not easy to spot.

Fiona must be hiding in the shrubs and dropped her notebook.

Erik nudged Chad in the back with his gun. "Where is it?"

There was no way he could get to the notebook before someone else saw it, but maybe he could buy time. Redirect. He just had to hope he didn't lead them right to Fiona, wherever she was hiding.

"I think it's to the left," he said, steering them away from the notebook, pointing to the network of buttress roots under a neighboring tree in the opposite direction.

Nico made a sharp turn, telling Chad he'd spotted the notebook too, and he also knew what it meant. "This way?" the cameraman said, climbing over the roots.

"Yo, Erik, what have we here?" Walker said.

Shit.

Slowly, Chad turned to see Walker bending down to pick up Fiona's notebook. The guy lifted his gaze, peering up the rope and into the canopy. Chad followed suit as dread slithered along his spine.

Erik let out a low whistle, and Nico cursed under his breath.

There was Fiona, her light-brown hair lit by a sunbeam that sliced through the canopy, her orange field shirt a beacon shining bright.

"Well done, Baylor. We come back with the battery case and Carver, and we'll get a big fat bonus," Walker said.

But the rest of them would be dead.

For a moment, Chad hoped Dean was hiding in the shrubs, an arrow pointed at Walker. But no. That was impossible. If he were here, he'd be the one in the tree. That Fiona had made the climb could mean only one thing: Slater had been captured.

Erik nudged Chad in the back. "We'll deal with her after you recover the battery. No stalling or we'll shoot you here and now. Carver is worth more than the battery case to Reynolds, so your life just became worthless to me."

It was true that Jude didn't need the battery case as much as Kosmo did. He would probably cut a deal with Kosmo to build a new prototype to save Fiona's life, which did make her more valuable than the case and Chad's one bargaining chip moot.

"It's over here." He turned to a different tree, adjacent to the one Fiona had climbed. He'd placed the battery case in a spot where Dean— or anyone in the photography blind—could see it from above, should they bother to look down.

Erik followed Chad as he climbed over the high ridges of roots that buttressed the tall tree. He spotted his backpack, tucked among the roots, and lifted it from its hiding place.

The case was heavy, but lighter than one would expect for something that could power a drone to swim twelve hundred nautical miles. But then, it wasn't the batteries that were important so much as the recharging action that harnessed the flow of water through the propellers to generate electricity as it burned it. For every mile it swam, it generated enough power to go an additional three-quarters of a mile.

It wasn't a perpetual motion machine, but it was damn close.

An invention like this could change the world, and Kosmo wanted to use it for drug smuggling and Jude to cut fuel costs for ships.

Not that Chad could stand on any moral high ground. He'd tried to use it to get out of a dangerous gambling debt.

Instead he was going to die, and he'd probably take the woman he loved with him.

He handed the pack to Erik, who opened it and peeked inside.

"We've got it," he said to his partner. Then he looked up into the canopy. "Time to climb down, Carver, or I'll shoot Baylor."

———

Fiona had used the minutes when attention was focused on Chad to remove the memory card from Dean's camera and slide it into the game camera's empty micro SD card slot.

The camera wasn't a traditional game camera, which required cellular service to operate. This was a high-end surveillance camera with its own satellite uplink and solar power source. Because of this, it was connected to USB storage wired into the satellite box, so there was no need for a memory card. But if Fiona descended this tree with Dean's camera and card, Richards's recording was certain to be destroyed, so in the empty micro SD slot the card went. She prayed Kosmo's henchmen didn't think to climb the tree to see what the hell she was doing up here.

She tucked the plastic bags with her urgent messages to Dylan under a rope that held the satellite uplink to a sturdy branch.

As she prepped for her descent, she wondered if Jude or Kosmo knew Dylan was checking the canopy camera feed. She doubted it. The times Dean had mentioned it at breakfast, neither man had been present, nor had any staff.

If asked, she'd claim she'd been trying to hook her phone to the satellite, but without a carrier, it had been useless.

"Climb down, Carver, or I put a bullet in your buddy Chad." This time it was Walker who made the threat.

"I'm trying!" she yelled. "I need to rig the descenders, and my hands are shaking."

She wasn't lying about having shaking hands, but she hadn't tried to attach the devices to the rope yet. She needed to make sure she had nothing else on her that would tip off Kosmo or Jude.

She pulled out the satellite phone and checked her text messages to Dylan. Nothing about him helping out Dean. She deleted the ones that referenced where he was staying on Dominica, just in case someone decided to target him, then tucked the phone away and reached for the descenders.

Her hands really were shaking as she clamped them on. Oh God. She had to climb down this rope and face two men with guns. Both parts were terrifying.

"Get moving, Carver."

"Give her a break. She's terrified of heights," Chad said.

"If that's so, then what the fuck is she doing at the top of a damn tree?"

Don't answer that, Chad.

"Beats the fuck out of me. Why don't you ask her when she gets down?"

Without warning, a shot rang out. The loud bang echoed through the forest. Birds let out alarmed squawks and scattered from their perches throughout the canopy.

The tree shook, and Fiona gripped the descender she hadn't finished attaching to the rope.

She didn't dare look down. If sheer terror didn't get her, vertigo would.

"What the fuck, man?" Chad's voice was pained. But he was speaking. He was alive.

"I'm tired of you talking, and the bitch needs to hurry up." The voice projected upward. "Get your ass down here or the next shot will be in his brain. And if you still don't come, the cameraman is next. But he won't get a shot in the arm as a warning."

She managed to get both descenders on the rope and clipped her harness to them as well as a safety tether, should the descender fail.

"I'm coming. I need to send my pack down first, though."

She unhooked the pack from the branch and quickly lowered it, letting the rope slide between her gloved hands. Once it was safe in Nico's arms, she let go of the secondary rope and tree and gripped the descenders.

It was just her on the rope now, no other support. She didn't look down. Didn't look up. She looked straight out at the branches that stretched across the high canopy.

She pressed down with her foot on the rope, triggering the lower descender, then pulled down with her hand on the upper one, a rhythmic motion that felt like climbing down a ladder if she didn't think about it being nothing but ropes and air.

Slowly and methodically, she descended. Slower than the average climber because each movement required full concentration, like she was holding a one-legged yoga pose, and the slightest stray breeze would upset her and send her tumbling.

She forgot about everything and everyone. Her world was reduced to the rope under her hands and the one under her foot.

She was so focused, she didn't realize she was only feet from the ground until she felt a hand on her ankle.

She kicked out, startled by the touch. Her heel caught Walker in the face. He growled and yanked on her, but the descenders locked, and he only managed to break her grip on the rope so she fell backward, dangling, her back parallel to the ground as she hung by the carabiner that hooked to the center of the harness.

Tears streaked down her cheeks as she faced the canopy, staring straight up the rope she'd just descended.

"Bitch! Get the fuck down!"

She reached for the rope, but her hands flailed. She was too damn tired. Drained. She spun in a slow circle, the leaves above a blur through teary vision.

"I'll help you, Fi," Nico said, and she felt a hand on her back, pushing her up so she could grip the rope.

Once it was in her hands, Nico placed her foot on the bottom rung of her invisible ladder—the loop that connected to the bottom descender. "Just a few more feet and you'll be on the ground."

She worked the ropes and descenders, and her feet found soft earth. She unhooked herself from the rigging before turning to see Chad. His face was an ashy gray in the places that weren't swollen and purple.

Yesterday's beating must've been a doozy, and the gunshot wound to the arm wasn't helping his pallor any.

His eyes were pained and sorry, but the words didn't need to be said. She blamed him for this situation, but at the same time, it was inevitable. Even if he hadn't stolen the battery case, the moment they found the drugs in the fort, it all would have been over.

Kosmo had done everything he could to sabotage the project to keep them from finding his hiding place, but they were bound to find it. And as horrible as Chad's act had been, it had bought them some time.

Maybe, just maybe, her SOS had worked, and help was already being mustered.

If Chad hadn't been greedy, they might have all been rounded up and killed without warning. She and Dean could have returned to the house and walked straight into a trap.

Sure, they were being cautious because of the attempt on his life, but that didn't mean they'd have escaped harm. Philip had probably already given up Richards as a DEA agent at that point. Kosmo already knew she was an informant.

So in a way, Chad's rash move might have saved them. If they lived, that was.

She wasn't big on hope in this moment.

"We need to get a bandage on that arm," she said. Was it her fault he'd been shot? Because she'd been slow to descend, or had Walker just been itching to pull the trigger?

"No bandage. He's fine," Erik said.

"Radio Kosmo," Walker said. "Let him know we've got the case and the girl."

"The radio won't work unless we're close to the shore, out of the forest," Fiona said. There was a reason they'd never bothered with radios on this project.

"Then get walking."

Before they set out, Walker handcuffed Chad's wrists behind his back, causing his face to turn a new sickly shade as his wounded arm was wrenched backward. "Cuff Nico," Walker ordered Erik. "No one is getting any ideas of escaping before we get to the house." He faced Fiona. "We don't have cuffs for you, so know this—you make a single move, and your buddies are dead. We don't need them anymore anyway."

But they did need *her*. Nico and Chad would live as long as they could use them against her.

If she had food in her stomach, she'd be retching right now.

They set out; the path straight to the water was well worn at this point. Chad led the way, his steps faltering as he lost blood. She doubted he'd slept last night or eaten since Dean had given him a handful of PowerBars yesterday.

Would the bullet wound be the death of him after all?

She and Nico walked side by side. She was well aware that any conversation between them could get Nico shot, so she said nothing at all.

What could she tell him anyway, other than she was sorry?

Dean was back in the bathroom, handcuffed to the claw-foot tub opposite Sadie, where they'd both spent an uncomfortable night. On orders from Reynolds, Jerry had delivered Dean back to the awkward prison immediately following the strange conversation in the billionaire drug smuggler's office.

Reynolds was certainly determined to impress Dean with the meager power he wielded.

Dean spent his hours locked up in darkness wondering what purpose the meeting had served for the man, considering he must've guessed it was all over when it came to Fiona the moment Sadie was taken hostage. So what had Reynolds been trying to glean?

Dean shifted positions to relieve stress on his leg. Pins and needles pummeled his foot as blood flow resumed.

Sadie had been chained this way for nearly forty-eight hours now, with only a single hour of respite after Chad had returned without the battery case. She'd told Dean that she'd been brought to the house to watch as Jerry and Erik had beaten Chad, before he was delivered to Kosmo's office. Dean had seen—and photographed—what followed through Kosmo's office window, while Jerry dragged Sadie back to the storm shelter.

He'd heard her sobbing softly at one point in the night, and he'd wished he could reach across the length of the tub and take her hand. Give her some assurance that help was on the way, except he had no idea if that was true.

If Fiona could find a way, she would. Of that he had no doubt. But he was at a loss for how she would do it. Sure, she could build a big bonfire in the center of the fort, send smoke signals to Dominica, but that would just alert Kosmo to where she was.

He'd told her to use the flare gun—something he always carried in his pack after Chiksook—but the flare had the same problems. Plus, there would have to be a boat to spot it, and he knew damn well that any boats near Ruby Island right now were likely to contain more henchmen or more drugs and not be filled with friendly strangers casually sailing by.

Dean suspected Kosmo had the waters patrolled by a team, and the only reason they hadn't been ready to swoop in when things went down two days ago was because of the storm, since all boats had been ashore.

"Tell me about your brother," Sadie said, her voice cutting into the silence.

"What do you want to know?"

"Is he in love with Fiona?"

That question caught him off guard. "Why do you ask? Did Fiona say he is?"

She let out a soft laugh. "No. He told me *you* think he is. Do you still believe that?"

"No. He set me straight months ago."

"Why did you believe it to begin with?"

"When he was coming out of surgery, he said some things. He was loopy—drugs heavy in his system. I figured anything he said then was the truth. He didn't remember any of it later, though. Said he'd always found her attractive, but he wanted me to meet her. What he said in the hospital was just rambling because he thinks she's great and wanted me to see it too."

"Do you see it? See *her*?"

He closed his eyes, not that it mattered in the unrelenting darkness of the windowless room. But still, with closed eyes, he saw Fiona, beneath him, on top of him. Some were memories and some fantasies. He'd always seen her.

Especially when his eyes were closed and he could let his rules go and desire run free.

Right now, he was terrified of being apart from her but also eternally grateful she wasn't here with them. As long as she wasn't here, he could believe she was safe.

"Yes. Always."

"Good." She shifted on the far side of the tub. He couldn't see her, but he heard the handcuff clank on the metal leg. "Now, tell me about that hot brother of yours."

He let out a soft laugh as he leaned against the wall, his arm in an awkward position, but it was the closest thing to sitting up he could manage. "What do you want to know?"

"Anything that will distract me from this shitty situation. Is he seeing anyone?"

"No. He divorced over two years ago and hasn't gotten involved with anyone since then."

"He ever cheat or sell assets without his ex's permission?"

"No and no."

"Good to know." She sighed. "He's too nice to use for revenge sex, though. I should probably steer clear until I've gotten that part of my process out of the way."

"Yeah. I'm afraid Dylan doesn't do casual. Never has."

"For twins, you aren't a lot alike."

"Not in that area anyway."

"I'll keep that in mind."

He knew she wanted to ask if he was going to break Fiona's heart.

And the truth was, he had no idea. Right now, they just had to get out of this nightmare.

The door opened, letting light in from the room behind. Dean squinted and tried to sit up straighter at seeing Jerry.

"Looks like you're going for a little boat ride," Jerry said.

He bent down and unlocked Sadie first. Dean couldn't see because of the big damn claw-foot tub in the way, but from the sound she made, the moment she was unlocked, the guy put his hand to her neck. "Now, listen here, sweetheart, you're going to stay right here, not moving a muscle until after I get Slater unlocked and on his feet with his hands cuffed behind him. You make one move while my back is turned and I'll snap your pretty little neck. You hear me?"

"Yes." Her voice was a rasp of air.

Dean was going to kill this man. Somehow. Someway. He would get to him.

"Good."

The man released Sadie and rose. He crossed to the opposite side and stayed on his feet. With one hand, he pulled his gun and trained it on Dean's chest. Then he dropped the handcuff key. It bounced on the tile floor and landed underneath the tub. "Unlock the cuff around the tub. Move real slow."

Dean placed his free hand under the tub and patted around, searching for the small piece of metal.

"I can't get it, not at this angle."

"Then get on your belly and find it. I don't have all day."

It took some effort to stretch his body out in the confined space, but he managed to get his chest on the floor with his knees bent as he folded over and searched for the key. He spotted it and stretched, his arm nearly too thick to reach that far beneath the basin.

He got his fingertips on it and managed to scoot it just under his palm and slide it from beneath the tub. He unlocked the cuff from the leg as instructed.

"Now what?"

"Stand up real slow. Arms raised. Key in the hand not cuffed."

Pain shot up and down his legs as he extended them fully for the first time in hours.

Jerry grabbed the key from his hand, then said, "Turn around," with the gun still pointed at his chest.

Dean obeyed and a moment later, his hands were cuffed behind his back.

Jerry ordered Sadie to rise, and the three of them left the bathroom single file, with Sadie at the front.

Dean guessed the guy had been warned Dean would try something, but really, what could he have done? He'd never risk Sadie getting hurt.

They left the large, comfy storm shelter, in which they'd been housed in the most uncomfortable way possible when there were beds and couches available, and stepped out into the bright, humid, perfect sunny day. They followed the path that led them down past the house and to the dock, where Dean could see *Tempus Machina* tied in *Rum Runner's* spot at the end of the low pier.

Sadie came to a dead stop as a speedboat sounded in the distance, approaching the sheltered bay. Dean halted to keep from bumping into her, even as the guy behind him pushed the pistol barrel into his back.

"Keep going."

The boat drew nearer. Dean counted five people.

"No!" Sadie said, and her voice might've broken on that one word.

Dean's heart shattered as his gaze landed on light-brown hair that glowed with red highlights in the noon sun.

THIRTY-FIVE

The speedboat sidled up alongside *Tempus Machina*, and Fiona was ordered to climb over the railing to board the dive boat, followed by Chad and Nico, for whom the maneuver of climbing from boat to boat wasn't so easy, given their hands were cuffed behind their backs. Last came Walker with her backpack, which he handed to Kosmo while Erik steered the Whaler to tie it farther down the dock.

"Good work," Kosmo said. He unzipped the pack and pulled out Dean's camera, snapped tight in its case.

He removed the case and studied the camera, then pressed the side button to open the panel. With another press of a button, a memory card popped out from the slot. Kosmo flashed Fiona a nasty grin, then pinched the small card between a pair of long-handled pliers from a table that was laid out with various tools. Next to the pliers was a propane-powered blowtorch, which he lit up and used to destroy the memory card in a burst of acrid blue flame.

She was damn glad she'd found the pack of unused memory cards in the attached camera case and dropped one in the slot, but she had to remember to appear distraught even as satisfaction filled her.

It wasn't hard to generate tears when her gaze landed on Dean and Sadie being marched down the dock by another of the so-called maintenance crew. Jerry.

All the RAM Freight employees were Kosmo's men, it seemed. She was just glad that the regular household staff and groundskeepers—including Oliver—had been sent to Dominica before the storm and weren't witnessing this, or their lives would be in danger as well.

Tears rolled down her cheeks as Sadie's swollen eye came into focus. Her steps were unsteady, and Fiona ached at what the woman must've been through. She'd been a prisoner for what . . . forty-eight hours?

Dean's gaze met hers. His eyes were hungry. Sorry. And pained. His face, too, was battered, but not as bad as the others'.

She wished she had telepathy to tell him what she'd done. That the memory card Kosmo just destroyed was blank. That there was hope.

All she could do was mouth, *I'm sorry.*

And she was. So sorry she'd been caught. If Walker and Erik hadn't found her, they wouldn't be gathering on this boat. They wouldn't all be facing their execution.

If she'd just climbed down the tree fifteen minutes earlier . . .

After Sadie and Dean were aboard, Kosmo gave the order for the bodies from the fridge to be retrieved.

Yes, this was definitely their execution, and they had two more bodies to get rid of.

Jerry stayed on the boat while the other two trudged up the dock. When they reached the shore, one grabbed a two-wheeled cart and pushed it up the path to the back of the house.

A few minutes later, both men and cart reappeared, but this time the cart contained the bodies of Philip Gomez and Chris Richards.

Sadie's cheeks were streaked with tears as the cart rolled toward them.

Chad, who had slumped down on the deck and been silent after climbing aboard, let out a pained curse.

She glanced down and saw the horror on his face. His pallor was worse than it had been five minutes ago. His bleeding went unchecked, and the pain had to be unbearable.

She doubted he'd survive without medical attention soon.

She glanced in Sadie's direction. Her friend was staring at Chad too, and from the look on her face, she recognized the depth of his injuries. As angry as she was, this man had been her lover and best friend for over a dozen years. She had loved him with all her heart.

Fiona looked away in a feeble attempt to give the couple privacy in their silent communication.

The boat rocked as Walker and Erik hauled the dead pilot and dead DEA agent aboard and deposited them at the stern as if they were cargo and not human beings.

Once again, if she had food in her stomach, she'd be losing it right now. As it was, she held back dry heaves. She didn't want Kosmo to see weakness or pain.

A shout sounded from the mansion's upper balcony, pulling her attention away from the silent dramas that were playing out on the boat.

Jude streaked across the third-floor balcony and down the outside stairs.

On the boat, Kosmo cursed. "I thought you drugged him?" he said in a low voice to Jerry.

"He must not have finished the drink," came the whispered reply.

But as Jude stumbled down the cobblestone path to the dock, she guessed he'd had most, if not all, of it. His movements were awkward. Sluggish.

A man who'd been pulled out of a deep sleep and whose body hadn't caught up yet.

He tripped on the lip of the dock, and Walker sniggered.

Bastard.

Jude pushed himself up to his feet slowly. Once upright, he placed his foot carefully, walking with deliberation down the long dock.

His footsteps echoed on the wooden planks. His eyes burned with fire as his gaze fixed on Kosmo.

"This is my fucking island. My fucking company. What the fuck do you think you're doing?" His words were surer than his footsteps.

"Cleaning up your island and fixing a company problem."

"It's not a company problem. It's *your* problem."

Jude reached the boat, and he grabbed at the rail, missing on the first try.

"I've been with this company longer than you. You were off playing at being an archaeologist and *I* was working for your father, learning the business. He wanted *me* to take over when he died."

"The board disagreed."

"That's because they think your stupid drone will bail us out with rising fuel costs."

Jude grabbed for the rail again. Gripping it, he pushed down with his hand and raised his foot to climb aboard at the same time Jerry shifted his weight and slammed into the portside railing, causing the boat to rock.

Jude, unsteady to begin with, slipped. For a breathtaking moment, he clung to the rail with one hand and looked like he would fall in the water between boat and dock. He managed to get his foot on the gunwale and hauled himself up with his one hand. He lurched through the gap in the railing and fell forward onto the deck. He stumbled sideways, slamming into Dean, and both men went down.

Unable to catch his fall because his hands were cuffed behind him, Dean's face took the brunt when he slammed onto the deck.

Fiona winced, feeling sympathetic pain. To make matters worse, Jude fell on top of Dean and floundered to rise.

After a moment of flailing limbs on Jude's part, Erik pulled his boss to his feet. Jude straightened his spine, mustering what she guessed was the cold, stiff dignity his father had browbeaten into him from an early age, then faced Kosmo.

"I don't care what you do with the rest of them, but Fiona and I are getting off this boat before it leaves the dock."

THIRTY-SIX

Something was in Dean's pocket, placed by Jude when he flailed on the deck. The man wasn't as sluggish as he appeared to be, but then, Dean had gotten a whiff of vomit on the man's body and suspected that when Jude realized he'd been drugged, he'd forced himself to vomit to expel what he could before all of it could be absorbed into his system.

New respect bloomed for the man. He wasn't the fool Kosmo thought him to be, and he wasn't the puppet Dean had assumed.

There was no doubt he was complicit, and he'd employed willful ignorance to ease his conscience, but he wasn't on par with Kosmo.

Dean dropped down on a cushioned seat that lined the rear deck where they all had gathered. With his hands hidden by the backrest, he felt around in his back pocket.

Something sharp scraped his skin, cutting his thumb.

What the hell was that?

He felt around again, more carefully, and realized it was the wire saw from his backpack. In a flash, he remembered Jude dropping the pack on his desk. With this new information, everything about that meeting shifted in Dean's mind.

The pack. The key. The questions.

"You would kill for Fiona?"

"I already have."

And now, Reynolds had given him a weapon.

A weapon that wasn't much good with his hands bound, so he kept digging, keeping his face blank and movements small. Thankfully, everyone on the deck was focused on Jude and Kosmo.

And that, too, was a master move by Jude. He knew Dean would need time.

He had no illusions that Jude was trying to save him. No. Jude had simply determined that Dean was the best bet for saving Fiona, should Jude fail to get her off a boat that was destined to be sent out to sea and explode.

Dean was Jude's plan B.

His fingers landed on the handcuff key, and he didn't care which letter plan it was, because Jude had given him the first real hope he had that they might survive this.

"She can't walk away, she knows too much," Kosmo said, disgust evident in his voice.

Dean had no doubt the man would kill Jude if he could get away with it, but he needed him. For the drone battery technology and probably for other reasons related to the company. Kosmo could count on Jude's silence no matter what happened, so that wasn't a risk. Jude was in way too deep to report the executive. Hell, he'd let the man slide after his boat exploded.

Sadie settled on the seat next to Dean, and he wondered if his movements had been too obvious. All at once, she lurched forward and launched herself toward where Chad lay on the deck, slowly bleeding out with no one paying him any mind.

"Chad! Can you hear me?" She turned tearful eyes to Kosmo. "Uncuff me so I can bandage his shoulder."

Dean was certain now she was also drawing attention away from him, as there had been no discernible change in Chad's condition.

He took her offering and fumbled with the key, at last finding the hole.

Fiona, who was unbound, dropped to her knees next to Chad, across from Sadie. "They wouldn't let me bandage him. Even when we were on the boat."

Fiona doffed her shirt and pressed it to Chad's arm. She knelt in her sports bra, the bright afternoon sun beating down on the teak deck, her orange top pressed to a bullet wound in a dying man's arm.

Jerry yanked her backward by her hair, but she fought him off and reached for Chad again.

She was jerked back a second time as the first of Dean's cuffs clicked open. He wanted more than anything to launch himself at Jerry, who had his hands on Fiona, but he held back. Kosmo was the power here.

Fiona struggled as Jerry gripped her arms at the elbows from behind.

Jude commanded the man to let her go while Kosmo said to hold her.

Dean worked the key into the other cuff.

On the deck, Chad's eyes opened, and he raised his good arm to touch Sadie's tear-streaked cheek. This wasn't acting or distraction. The man really was dying.

He mouthed *I love you* and *I'm sorry* as she sobbed silently.

And now it was clear Sadie wasn't acting either.

How long ago had Chad been shot? How much blood had he lost? He'd been beaten and likely had broken ribs. He probably hadn't slept in two days, and it was unlikely he'd been fed in the last twenty-four hours.

He had a survivable wound, but not in these circumstances.

"Uncuff Sadie!" Fiona demanded.

Jude turned to Kosmo and repeated the demand.

That was the moment Jude made his first mistake. He deferred to Kosmo. Let it be known he saw who was really in charge. Any chance he had of asserting control over the others was lost in that moment.

Dean could only hope Kosmo didn't realize the request also meant Jude no longer had a cuff key in his possession.

A silent exchange passed between the two men, and Dean saw the moment Jude accepted his error. "Uncuff her," he said. "Give them that at least. They're both going to die anyway." The only thing that was missing from the plea was the word *please*.

"No," Kosmo said. "He gets no aid or comfort. He stole from us. Lied to us. Play deadly games, win deadly prizes."

Both cuffs were off, and Dean slipped the wire saw from his pocket, sliding a thumb through the hole of one end loop.

Jude turned his back on Kosmo and yanked Fiona from Jerry's hold.

"Fiona and I are leaving now."

The sound of a gun cocking got Jude to turn his attention back to Kosmo as the executive VP and drug smuggler said, "No. Just you. She stays."

"She'll keep her mouth shut," Jude said. "We'll live on this island. She can't tell anyone if she can't contact the outside world."

Was Jude mad enough to think he could keep Fiona hostage in his paradise forever? That she'd grow to love him and accept her imprisonment?

No. He wasn't that naïve.

"Do you really think I'm that stupid?" Kosmo asked. "She will die. Today. And if you stand in my way, so will you."

Silence filled the boat as the two men stared each other down.

Off in the distance, Dean heard a rising sound, too rhythmic to be the wind. It came closer, and Dean recognized it for what it was: a helicopter.

But what did that mean? Reinforcements for Kosmo?

He didn't for a moment believe Jude had called for help. No, the man was *in* this conspiracy too deep to take that risk.

Kosmo's gaze jerked to the sky as not one, not two, but three helicopters came into view. And now, in the distance, Dean could see a boat racing across the waves at top speed.

This had the earmarks of a full-on raid.

But how?

Who had managed the SOS?

Dean looked to Fiona and caught the satisfied smile on her face.

His heart thrummed in his chest. He had no idea how she'd managed it, but his beautiful, amazing Fiona had done the impossible.

But Kosmo must've seen her smile too, because he switched his gun from Jude to Fiona and said, "You bitch."

Dean lunged for the man, whipping out the wire saw and catching it with his other hand as he brought it around Kosmo's neck just as he pulled the trigger.

Dean watched in horror as Jude threw himself in front of Fiona. The bullet hit him square in the chest. The force sent him backward, into Fiona, and they both went tumbling through the gap in the rail into Cannon Bay.

Kosmo bucked against the wire as Dean pulled the ends, working the blades across his throat, opening shallow wounds before he pulled the saw tight, cutting off Kosmo's air. "Don't fight me or I'll cut your fucking head off," he said as he cinched the barbed garrot.

The three RAM Freight henchmen looked from the water where Jude had disappeared, to their boss being strangled, to the helicopters in the sky, and as one, they bolted from the boat, running the short distance to where the Boston Whaler was tied.

Kosmo struggled against Dean's grip. The gun slipped from his fingers as Dean sawed at his throat. Kosmo reached for the wire, only to get cut by the sharp barbs.

Nico looked from Dean to the water, then showed Dean his cuffed hands. "I can't go after her. She hasn't come up."

"Get my cuffs from the bench."

Nico did as instructed, grabbing them with his cuffed hands and bringing them to Dean, who quickly slapped them on Kosmo, then shoved the man forward. He slammed down on the deck, coughing and sputtering, blood seeping from the line across his throat.

"There's a key on the bench somewhere," Dean said to Nico, then launched himself across the deck and dove into the water to find Fiona.

THIRTY-SEVEN

The shock of the water combined with searing pain below her collarbone was disorienting. Fiona never had a chance to take a breath. Didn't have the wherewithal to hold it. Her nose burned and lungs ached as she took in saltwater.

A heavy weight pressed on her, making it impossible for her to kick to the surface.

She struggled even as water choked her.

It was Jude. Jude's body was pressing her into the sandy bottom of the bay.

He didn't fight against the water, didn't struggle to breathe.

Was he unconscious or dead?

The clear turquoise water was cloudy with red, taking on a purple hue in the sunlight that penetrated the salty sea.

Jude had been shot. Fiona's upper chest hurt. Had she been shot too?

She pushed at Jude's body. She needed air. Then she could come back for him. But one arm refused to move.

With her other arm, she managed to push Jude away enough that her chest was free. In the same moment, hands reached for her. She panicked.

Was it Jerry?

But it was Dean who grabbed at her and pulled her to the surface.

How had he gotten free of the handcuffs?

She broke the surface and coughed, then swallowed water as she slipped down again.

Dean caught her to his chest and swam on his back, supporting her like a raft as he pulled her to shore.

She coughed and sputtered and watched the sky go by. Puffs of white clouds were overtaken by helicopters that hovered in the air above the dock and beach, kicking up water and sand that sprayed her face.

She closed her eyes against the chaos, her brain swirling as wooziness engulfed her. Her shoulder burned. Her lungs ached. And she was so damn tired.

When was the last time she slept? Ate? Didn't ache?

She was lifted from the water. The whirling blades of the helicopters wiped out all other sounds.

In her mind, she saw the flash and heard the bang of Jude's helicopter so many days ago, and she gripped the wet shirt of the man who held her and said, "Dean."

A mouth next to her ear responded. "I'm here, sweetheart. I've got you."

She was placed on the warm sand. She lay faceup with her eyes closed. The sound of the copters faded. She guessed they were landing on the airstrip.

A boat engine roared into the bay.

The DEA had arrived.

"Thank you, Dylan," she whispered.

"Dylan?" Dean said.

She nodded and risked opening her eyes, now that the sand wasn't swirling and stinging. She blinked against the bright sun above and let out a grunt of pain as Dean pressed his wet shirt to her shoulder.

"Bullet must've gone right through Jude," he said.

She pushed against his hand, trying to sit up. "Jude—"

"Nico dove in after him."

She tried to see around his broad bare chest to the water, but he leaned down, blocking her view. "Don't look. Focus on you."

"He—?"

"He slipped me a key and my wire saw. He helped save you."

"He took the bullet for me."

Dean leaned down and pressed a soft kiss to her lips. He wouldn't say what she wanted to know most, so she asked the question. "Is he dead?"

Dean nodded. "I think so."

To be fair, none of them would have been in danger in the first place if Jude hadn't looked the other way while Kosmo smuggled and stole. But still, his last act had been selfless.

She remembered the young man she'd used as a pillow during field-work naps in the sun a lifetime ago. She would grieve the loss of that Jude for the rest of her days.

———

Medics pulled Fiona from Dean's arms. Her fingers slipped from his, and he sat back in the sand and watched them transfer her to a stretcher, then clean and staunch her wound.

"She's gonna be okay," a medic said. "A C-130 medevac was scrambled from Key West as soon as we got the call. It's less than two hours out. She's stable, and we'll take good care of her until then."

The men lifted the gurney and started walking up the beach.

"Where are you going?" Dean asked.

"Taking her in the house. Out of the sun. Marines gave the all clear."

He nodded. He had no idea how much time had passed. Long enough for marines to clear the house, apparently.

He rose to follow but was intercepted by a guy who had to be DEA. "Mr. Slater, we have some questions."

"I need to be with Fiona."

"She's in good hands. And we need information."

Dean watched the men carry the gurney up the path, then glanced around, seeing Nico talking to another man. Sadie was on her knees a few feet from where two medics worked on another body on the dock next to *Tempus Machina*.

They were performing CPR, which wasn't a good sign for Chad at all.

Sadie let out a sob, and Dean remembered all too clearly what it was like to watch a loved one die.

No matter what Chad had done, he was still the man with whom she'd spent the last twelve years of her life.

A short distance down the beach, Jude was being placed in a body bag. He was past saving.

Dean looked for Kosmo and didn't see him. "Where is Kosmo Andreas?"

"He's in custody. He's got some nasty cuts on his throat, but he'll live. And he'll go to prison for what he did here, but only if you tell us everything you know. We need evidence to lock him up tight."

"He had the DEA agent, Richards, killed."

"We know. We have Richards's statement to that effect."

Dean frowned. "What? How . . . ?"

"It seems Ms. Carver held up signs in front of one of your game cameras. Your brother saw them and contacted us."

So that was how she'd done it. His gaze returned to the house. A tear spilled down his cheek. "She's afraid of heights."

The man looked at him in confusion.

"The cameras, they're a hundred feet high. In a tree."

"Oh," the agent said.

Dean couldn't begin to guess how terrifying that climb must've been.

"Well, it seems that while she was in the tree, a hundred feet high, she placed a micro SD card in the camera slot. The app your brother was using to monitor the camera registered that a disk with recorded data had been inserted. He played the video as he was contacting the admiral and DEA. He gave us the URL and password to access the feed. We have Richards's recording and all the other photos you took of Kosmo's operation. The drone, the drugs inside the fort, Baylor's statement. Everything."

Damn, Fiona was amazing. She'd not only sent out an SOS, she'd also gotten their irrefutable proof out there.

Kosmo would have paid for this even if he'd managed to kill them all.

A boat approached the bay, and the agent got on his radio. A moment later, he turned to Dean and said, "That'll be your brother. I told them to let him through. But I still need to question you before you can talk to him or anyone else. Let's go sit on the veranda and get comfortable. This is going to take a while."

Dean nodded.

He wanted to talk to Dylan. Hug Sadie. Thank Nico. And hold Fiona.

But first he had to talk to the DEA to make sure Kosmo Andreas never saw freedom again.

THIRTY-EIGHT

Fiona was in a haze that she suspected was drug induced. It took effort to open her eyes, and she couldn't quite figure out what the humming was. It reminded her of the last flight to Chiksook. The one when she'd met Dean. But he'd been Bill then. Hot Bird Man with blue, blue eyes.

She finally managed to get her lids to open, and she realized why she'd thought of that day. She was on a military transport plane. Not the one she'd been on last September, but the sound was similar.

She tried to sit up and found she couldn't. She was strapped down, and also her shoulder was bandaged. She couldn't feel her shoulder. Like it wasn't even there.

That was a bit freaky. Was she paralyzed?

A face floated into her line of vision. A medic, she supposed, but not familiar.

But why would a medic be familiar?

She searched her brain for what was going on, and a memory surfaced of being on the beach and then in Jude's house as medics tended her wound.

She'd been shot.

Or rather, Jude had been shot, and she'd gotten the rest of it.

Jude. Was he alive?

Everything after the shooting was hazy. They'd gone into the water?

"What's happening?" she asked, her throat dry and croaky, and she doubted the man would hear her over the noise of the plane.

But he did, because he said, "You're being airlifted to the military hospital in Jacksonville."

"Military? Why military?"

The man shrugged. "We had orders from some admiral to pick you up. Said if you were critical to take you to Puerto Rico, but if you were stable, the closest, best military facility is Jacksonville. So that's where we're going."

Well, at least that told her she was stable.

They landed thirty minutes later, and the next hours were a blur. She went straight into surgery to have the bullet removed.

Sometime later, she woke in a recovery room, groggy and loopy. The doctor and then some nurses said things she didn't understand. The next time she opened her eyes, she found herself in a private hospital room.

It took some effort to read the clock on the various monitors, but it was after two a.m.

How long since she'd been shot? Or had she technically been shot by proxy, since the bullet went through Jude?

She lay in the dark, a dull ache in her shoulder. She tried to remember what the doctors had said post-surgery, and wished she had someone with her to give her an update.

But Sadie . . . she was probably with Chad, wherever he was. Dean was probably being grilled by the DEA.

Dylan was probably stuck on Dominica.

Would the navy fly Dean here, or was the military transport just for the wounded navy employee who'd been spying for the admiral and DEA?

Dean was none of those things. Would he even come at all?

It might be easier if he didn't.

Another clean break.

She tried to banish the pain at the thought of not even getting a goodbye this time. The dull ache in her shoulder bled over to her heart.

She closed her eyes and waited for the drugs to do their job and return her to sleep.

Hours later, she woke to daylight streaming through the window and a nurse checking on her vital signs. "You're awake," he observed.

"Awake-ish," she muttered.

He smiled. "I'm guessing you're hungry."

"Now that you mention it, starving. I don't think I've eaten in days."

"The doc said you can have liquids this morning."

"I don't remember anything I was told after the surgery. And don't have friends or family to relay the details. Can you tell me?"

The nurse nodded and tapped keys on the computer terminal. "I need you to confirm your name and date of birth."

"Seriously? You think I switched bodies in the night?"

"Sorry, security protocol. Plus, it tells me how you're doing in your recovery. Who is the president?"

She answered all three questions, and he pulled up her medical record. "According to this, you were shot."

She let out a soft laugh. "Is that what happened?"

"Medical records never lie." He turned to face her. "The bullet passed through someone else first?"

She nodded.

"Okay, so what we have here is the bullet passed through the first victim, and it did what bullets do, which is expand to cause major damage to the target. But the bullet that was used in your case was an all-copper trocar bullet. What makes a trocar bullet different is the base continues on while the rest of the bullet essentially explodes in the initial target." He gave her a look of concern. "I'm guessing, if the person was standing in front of you, as they must've been for you to be hit at that angle, it hit them somewhere near the heart. It's pretty hard to survive a trocar to the chest."

"I don't actually remember. But I think that's right."

"I'm sorry." He paused, and she knew he meant it. But he also had information she wanted, so he resumed. "The good news for you is the base lost most of its steam as it hit your upper chest. There was no explosive energy in the base, and it didn't go too deep. Your surgery was an easy extraction of the base and cleanup. Doc says you should be fine for release within twenty-four hours. You'll need the stitches removed in ten days, and you'll want to baby that arm and shoulder for at least a few weeks."

"So you're saying rock climbing is out for a while?"

"Definitely. You like climbing?"

"I hate it, actually."

"Well, that's good luck, then."

She smiled. He was a nice nurse.

"Have there . . . been any calls for me?" she asked.

"I don't know. I can check. We can't let anyone know you're here without express authorization from you. Can you give us a list of names?"

She nodded. "It's short. Only three people."

"Great. I'll add them to your record right now."

"Sadie Tate, and Dylan and Dean Slater."

"Are they family or friends?"

"Family," she whispered, because they were the only family she had left.

Her mother was lost to her illness, and Aidan didn't count.

———

Dean was frantic to get to Jacksonville. It took far too many flights—Dominica to Puerto Rico. PR to Fort Lauderdale. Should have been fine from there, but everything was booked solid, so they flew to Tampa and then finally got a hop to Jacksonville.

It was evening the day after the shooting on Ruby Island when Dylan and Dean's plane finally touched down on the runway.

They made a beeline for the rental car desk. As they waited in line, Dylan said, "I've been thinking you should see her alone first. Drop me at the hotel, then continue on to the hospital."

"You sure?"

"Yeah. I can take a taxi later if you don't want to come back and get me."

"Good plan."

Forty-five excruciating minutes later, Dean was dropping Dylan off at the hotel and heading to the hospital.

At the security gate for the base, he ran into another snag. Arriving after hours and being nonmilitary, he was supposed to have arranged for entrance twenty-four hours ahead of time. He showed the guard the emailed authorization from Admiral Martinez. "Please. I need to see her as soon as possible. The admiral authorized it."

"We'll need to call the admiral to confirm this. It's highly irregular."

Dean swiped a hand over his face and reminded himself these marines were just doing their job to keep military personnel and bases safe. Fiona worked on a similar base, and he sure as hell wanted her protected to the maximum extent.

He texted his contact at the DEA and asked him to reach out to the admiral. It was after five in the Pacific Northwest, and the man wasn't likely to be in his office.

He also texted Dylan and told him his plan of taking a taxi would never work. Odds were, they wouldn't be able to get a pass for Dylan until morning, as his name wasn't in the admiral's email.

It took thirty additional minutes and was nearing ten p.m. when Dean was finally issued a pass and allowed on base.

He drove to the hospital, his heart pounding. Could he really do this? Ask her for more?

He'd been so firm in his rules, maybe a fling on Ruby Island was all she wanted from him. After all, she'd been the one to shut down that conversation when they were in the rainforest.

When he finally got to the front desk, he found himself as nervous as he'd been on his wedding day.

"I see from her file you are an authorized visitor." The woman behind the desk had him sign in and gave him a visitor's pass and her room number.

He went through another round of security when he reached her ward. The nurse confirmed he was on the authorized visitor list before saying, "I believe she's sleeping, but since she hasn't had any visitors, you should go right in. I'm sure you'll be welcome."

He ached thinking of her alone here for the last twenty-four hours. "Thank you."

He realized he should have picked up flowers or something, but that would have only cost more time, and it was nearing eleven p.m. now. He felt like he'd run three marathons to get here.

He reached her door and pushed it open.

And felt a massive punch to the gut.

There she was, asleep in a slightly elevated hospital bed. Her finger hooked up to an oxygen sensor and the heart monitor moving across the screen with steady spikes.

Seeing her, he was zipped back in time over eleven years. Violet's last surgery. The one that broke her. Broke them both. There was no way to extract the mass from her brain.

She wasn't going to have a miracle recovery.

The doctors gave her less than six months.

And she'd lain there sleeping in a hospital bed so much like this one, her face a gaunt shadow of her former features and still the most beautiful woman he'd ever known.

Now he was facing another woman he cared about in a similar bed. Her eyes hollowed with shadows after a series of brutal days.

She could have died.

She'd been inches from taking that bullet. If Jude's reflexes had been slower, or if Dean's lunge for Kosmo's throat hadn't thrown off his aim . . .

Dean stared at the beautiful woman in the hospital bed, and every fear he'd carried with him since Violet's last year came rushing back.

The love and the nightmare, intertwined.

He couldn't do this again. Couldn't love and lose.

He gently closed the door and continued down the hall. He found a door to a stairwell and stepped inside to catch his breath.

He slid down the wall, placed his head in his hands, and let out a sob he didn't even know he'd been holding back for nearly eleven years.

———

Fiona heard the snick of the latch on the door and knew what it meant. She'd been half-asleep when she heard the door open. She hadn't opened her eyes, but she'd felt the flush of joy. If it were a nurse, they'd walk in with no-nonsense strides.

This was a visitor. And she was going to let him kiss her awake. Or just take her hand. Or quietly sit in the visitor's chair. She wasn't picky, she was just glad he was here.

But there were no footsteps at all. Just a long pause followed by the door closing.

He left.

He left.

She waited. Maybe he'd be back. After twenty minutes, she pressed the call button.

The nurse appeared after an interval.

"Did I have a visitor?"

The woman on the night shift smiled. "You did. I'm surprised he's not still here."

"I was sleeping. I guess he didn't want to wake me. Can you tell me who it was?"

"He was on your list. One of the men with the same last name."

"Did he have a beard or no beard?"

"Beard."

"Thank you," Fiona said. "Am I going to be released in the morning?"

"Yes, first thing if you want. The doctor signed off on it after rounds this evening."

"First thing is perfect. I want to catch an early flight to Seattle."

"We'll do what we can to get you out of here fast."

"Thank you."

THIRTY-NINE

Dean didn't show up at the hotel until four a.m. He'd spent hours driving aimlessly and had gotten lost a few times until he remembered GPS was a thing. It was good to have a phone and normal cellular reception again.

Dylan texted a few times to see how Fiona was, but he didn't answer. Finally, his brother said he was going to bed.

Dean was almost to Tallahassee at that point and turned the car around and headed to the hotel. He picked up his key from the front desk and tiptoed into the room, then he kicked off his shoes and crawled under the covers fully dressed.

He closed his eyes against the pain in his chest and placed his hand over the violet tattoo, remembering the pain of the needle as the reminder of the love of his life was inked into his skin.

He finally fell asleep as the first light of dawn peeked around the room-darkening curtains.

———

Dean woke with a start when his brother barged into the room, none too quietly.

"What the fuck happened, Dean?"

Dean rolled over on the bed. His eyes had been pasted shut—a hazard of crying—and he was pretty sure his face was creased with a mark from the embroidered throw pillow he hadn't bothered to remove from the bed.

He tugged a different pillow over his face to fight the bright light as Dylan pulled back the shades and welcomed the shitty day.

"I'm trying to sleep."

"What the fuck did you do?"

"I didn't do anything."

"What did you say to her?"

"Nothing." That was true enough. He pulled the pillow from his eyes. "Why? What did she say?"

"She didn't say anything because she was gone. Released from the hospital. She *left*."

Dean sat bolt upright. "What? Why would she do that?"

"I don't know. That's why I'm asking you. What the hell happened last night?"

He flopped back against the pillows. "I didn't see her. I got as far as her doorway."

"*What?* You were gone for hours."

"I—I couldn't. I just . . . I saw her there, sleeping in the bed, and it brought it all back. Violet. The last surgery. The last months." He kept his gaze fixed on the ceiling as a tear streaked down his cheek. Dammit. He didn't want Dylan to see this.

He didn't want anyone to see this.

He swiped at his cheek and forced himself to face his brother. A dozen emotions washed over Dylan's face. Anger, outrage, frustration. He finally settled on pity, which just might be the worst one of all.

"I couldn't do it, Dyl. I just . . . I found a way to work through the pain. And part of that is not leaving myself open to it again. When Violet died, I made a promise to myself. I was in the fucking middle of nowhere and living off grubs and grasshoppers, and my heart hurt so bad because she was gone that I promised myself if I found a way through that pain, I'd never open myself up to it again."

He closed his eyes, causing the pooled wetness to overflow. "And I *did* get through it. I survived and I was *happy*, dammit. After years of agony, I was happy."

"You were lonely."

"But I was still happy. It's possible to be happy and alone, you know."

Dylan gave him a wry look. "Yeah. I know. You've been pushing me to screw around with everything that breathes, but that's not happiness for me. I can be happy by myself. I don't need mindless sex to fill a void."

"I'm not filling a void with sex."

"Maybe not, but that's what you were trying to do."

"I was *happy*," he repeated obstinately.

"Dean, you made Violet a promise."

"And I kept it. I promised her I would live the life we'd planned for both of us. And I am living it. Better than she and I ever dared to dream."

"That's not the promise I'm talking about. I'm talking about the one where she made you say you would live again. *Love* again. That you would open your heart and fall in love and also have *that* part of the life you didn't get to have with her."

"How do you know about that?"

"She told me. Made *me* promise to hold you to it."

Dean's tears fell unchecked now. "She didn't know what she was asking of me. She wasn't the one who had to get out of bed every day after she died and try to figure out how to live without the most important part of her world. She didn't know what it was like to face dawn after dawn with a hole in her heart. She asked too much. I can't risk losing like that again."

"Not even for Fiona?"

Dean flopped his head back and stared at the ceiling again. "I can't do it, Dyl. I just can't. I saw her in that hospital bed, and it brought it all back. I lost it."

"You're going to let the best thing that's happened to you since Violet slip away."

"Yes."

"You're going to let the woman who has a nearly paralyzing fear of heights but who still climbed a hundred-fucking-foot rope to save your sorry ass get away?"

Shit. Dylan wasn't fighting fair.

"I want you to give this thing between you and Fiona a chance. I love you and love being your brother, but I don't want to be your *only* family anymore. I don't want you to be *my* only family. I'm fine with being alone while I work through my divorce baggage. But I'm going to get through it and move on, because I want what our parents had. I want us *both* to have it. What you almost had with Violet."

"Almost," Dean said.

"I know, man. And I have seen how much it hurts. I'm not telling you to forget her or let her go. I'm telling you to do what Violet wanted you to do. Keep her in your heart but still make room for someone else. Maybe Fiona isn't the one, but you'll never know unless you give her a chance. She deserves that chance."

FORTY

Exhaustion pressed on Fiona like a weighted blanket. She was sure even her toenails were tired. She leaned her head against the cool glass of the taxi window as the lights of Tacoma went by. She'd never in her life splurged on a taxi from SeaTac airport to her Kitsap Peninsula townhouse, but the last thing she wanted to do was call a friend for a ride or share a shuttle with strangers.

The drive took an hour and a half thanks to traffic in Tacoma, but it could have been worse.

It was early evening by the time she reached her rental home, which was bright as candy, a fact that led to the neighborhood being referred to as "Skittleville" by locals. Laying eyes on her home for the first time in weeks, the place did look sweet enough to eat.

She was ever so grateful for the medics on Ruby Island, who had taken the time to collect her belongings from the mansion. She had her purse and phone and keys and ID and credit cards, all the major ingredients for getting home after a traumatic week that had culminated in shoulder surgery.

Tomorrow, she'd take the ferry to Seattle and meet with the FBI agent who'd been part of the initial meeting in the admiral's office and start the interview process. Or maybe the man would come here. It had all been a blur in the arrangements she'd made during her layover in Denver because she'd been so desperate to get home, she'd left the hospital before the FBI or DEA could interview her.

She remembered Paige's long, pearly white fingernails as she pressed her hand to her lips and offered an unrepentant *"Oops."*

The moment had been meme-worthy and summed up Fiona's feelings exactly.

She'd managed to avoid talking with the admiral, sending all his calls directly to voice mail. She did not have the bandwidth. All she wanted was to get home.

Now, here she was. Home at last. It was worth it.

She tipped the taxi driver generously, and he carried her full suitcase to the front step, which was good because she wasn't entirely sure she could have managed that feat at her level of exhaustion and with only one arm.

She unlocked the door and dragged the bag inside with her good arm. The townhouse smelled like home and that, all by itself, brought tears to her eyes.

Well, maybe something else triggered the tears, but she wasn't ready to admit to it. After all, she didn't even have the right to be mad. Or hurt.

He'd never wavered in his rules. She'd agreed to them. She'd straight-up told him she wanted sex, knowing it would end there.

And when she'd held his wedding picture, she'd understood his rules. His need to keep his heart walled off. He'd broken the rule to a degree by making love to her. But it hadn't changed the overall deal, and she'd known it then. Felt it in her soul now.

She was home at last. It smelled like comfort. Gone were the scents of tropical flowers and the salt sea. No birds filled the house with sound.

It was a crisp, late June night. The house was cool even though it had been closed up for over three weeks. The refrigerator hummed. A car drove by on the street.

It was all so . . . normal. She leaned against the door and began to sob.

She'd held in the tears throughout the long night and day. Through three airports and two flights. One very long cab ride.

At last, she was alone in her own space. She was safe. She could let the tears flow.

And she did. She let it all out.

Her tears came in every flavor. The exhilaration of making love by the fire with him. The horror of hearing him become a hostage. The separate terrors of the helicopter crash and his near-fall from the tree.

And then there was Jude. Her two-faced friend. Janus would be a better name. She could mourn one face while being devastated by the other.

And Sadie, who'd lost Chad, but her mixed grief went a thousand leagues deeper. Chad had been her whole life.

It was too much, and it made her silly heartache ridiculous.

So what if Dean didn't want more than a jungle fling? Rules were rules.

Her fault for getting burned.

She pushed off the door and entered her home, turning on lights.

Everything was the same. She'd had a similar feeling when she returned home from Chiksook. How could everything be the same when everything had changed so deeply inside her heart and mind?

But it was. She didn't have plants because that would mean needing a house sitter when she was in the field. Same for pets, but she regretted that now. It would be so wonderful to be greeted by a cat at the end of a traumatic trip.

Tomorrow, after she talked to the FBI, she'd go to the Humane Society and see if they had a cat she could lavish love upon. Tomorrow, she'd make all the changes that would take this pain away.

But tonight, she'd curl up on the couch and binge-watch something on TV as if her life hadn't been totally upended.

She entered the kitchen. She didn't have much in the way of food and didn't want to run to the store. But then, she wasn't really hungry. She found a fancy hot chocolate mix she'd received from Cara at Christmas and heated the water in the microwave.

She settled on the couch with her warm mug and began searching her streaming service for something to watch.

Nat Geo popped up in the feed, and she did the thing she'd promised herself she'd never do and found both of Dean's one-hour documentaries he'd filmed for the network. She hit play on the first one.

Five minutes in and her tears were too thick to see the screen. She shut it off and selected an old sitcom she didn't have to pay attention to instead.

She needed to pace herself in working through the heartache. No point in upping the dose to the max the first night.

She fell asleep with her head on the arm of the couch as the show streamed without her.

Tomorrow, she'd get a cat or seven and fully embrace her new, less lonely life as an eccentric cat lady.

For the second time in twenty-four hours, Dean found himself at a rental car counter. He wasn't even entirely sure how momentum had gotten him here, but Dylan's words had finally penetrated, and he knew he had to make things right *now* or he risked losing the first shot at true happiness he'd had in over a decade.

And so he was at an airport rental counter paying the massive markup of getting the car at the actual airport and not an off-site facility. Not that he cared, he just needed to get to Fiona.

Two nights in a row, he was desperate to see her. Would he freeze this time?

Would she slam the door in his face?

He couldn't blame her if she did.

He was on the road and taking the exit for the Tacoma Narrows Bridge when his phone chimed. A female voice helpfully read aloud Dylan's text: **Don't blow it or I'll kick your ass.**

Dean rolled his eyes as he kept his fingers tight on the wheel. Forty-five minutes to Fiona.

Forty-five minutes to the start of the rest of his life.

A computerized voice provided direction in the darkness as the miles passed by. He rounded a bay and spotted lights on the ships of the Puget Sound Naval Shipyard. This wasn't the base Fiona worked on, but it was nearby.

At last, he reached her exit and wove through neighborhood streets to find her townhouse.

It was well past midnight. He could go to a motel, but he was pumped with adrenaline now and had to see her.

To hold her.

If she'd let him.

He found her home and parallel parked in front. He left his bags in the vehicle. There was a high probability she would kick his ass to the curb, so he would leave his bags there instead of making presumptions.

A dim glow shone from behind the front window curtains—like a TV or other light had been left on—but otherwise, her home was dark.

He took a deep breath and rang the bell.

A cool breeze drifted over him as he stood on the porch, and he wished he had a coat of some kind. The Seattle area in June was a whole lot chillier than the Caribbean.

He knocked on the door, a softer sound than the bell, and waited. Another minute ticked by. He screwed up his courage and rang the bell again.

This was a mistake. He should have waited until morning. Brought her flowers this time. And coffee and a pastry.

Fiona loved coffee, and she'd never skipped indulging in the pastries laid out in the breakfast buffet. He should have come up with a plan to woo her. Brought her chocolate peppermint LUNA bars. A new trowel to replace the one she'd sacrificed.

There were so many better ways to do this. What had he been thinking, showing up at her door after . . . He checked his watch and wanted to groan. *Oof.* How did he not realize it was two a.m. already? And here he was, empty-handed. Standing on her doorstep like a ubiquitous golf ball, spoiling her paradise.

He didn't even have a clue what he was going to say.

All at once, the porch light came on, bathing him in yellow light.

The door was yanked open, and there was the woman who'd haunted his dreams for nine months. The woman he'd made love to days ago. The woman he'd walked away from in a moment of scared weakness.

She looked at him warily. Her right arm was in a sling, the only sign she'd been in the hospital just that morning.

"Can I come in?"

"That depends."

"On?"

Her expression remained guarded. "Is this hello or goodbye?"

All at once, he knew exactly what to say. "Neither." He leaned against the jamb and smiled. "I came here because I need to make sure I've fulfilled all my promises."

A spark of humor flared in her eyes, but she quickly doused it even as she stepped back, widening the door to let him enter. "I'm listening." Her tone remained serious.

He crossed the threshold. "Did I teach you how to use a DSLR camera?"

She tapped her lips as if giving the question great consideration. "Well, I'm not sure if one lesson really covers all I need to know."

He frowned. "That's what I was afraid of. Clearly, I owe you more lessons." He closed the door behind him and leaned back against it. "And then there is that other promise."

Her voice turned breathy as she said, "Which one is that?" and stepped closer.

His hands found her hips, and he pulled her to him. Her eyes were slightly puffy. She'd been crying. Because of him. Because he'd lost it last night when he saw her in the hospital bed.

He would make it up to her. A thousand times over.

He cupped her cheek as her head tilted back to hold his gaze. He felt the tension in her body release by slow degrees as she molded against him. He'd been aching to hold her like this for days.

With his thumb, he traced her bottom lip and its enticing freckle. "I think you remember it. The one I made on Chiksook, when I promised to make you feel utterly possessed when I made love to you."

Her eyes were warm, and this time she allowed a slight smile. "Oh. That one. You know, I don't think you really had a fair chance to pull that off. I mean, we only had one small camping pad between us and the cold brick floor. Not the most comfortable setting. Probably we need to try again, in a bed. And this time you can bring your A game."

His body shook with silent laughter.

This woman was it for him.

He brushed his lips over hers. "There's another promise I need to keep. This one I made to someone else."

She pulled back an inch. "Oh?"

"Yeah. To that end, I need to ask something. I know we both agreed that what happened on Ruby Island would be a fling, but . . . would you be willing to reconsider? Maybe . . . try a relationship?"

She rose on her toes and pressed her lips to his in a gentle but still somehow utterly sultry kiss. "Well, Mr. Slater, that's really going to depend on how good your A game is."

"Sweetheart, I was a jock for a long time. I promise you, I've got game."

She grinned and took his hand in her good one, pulling him toward the stairs to the right of the entryway. "You make a lot of promises. It's time to see if you can deliver."

AUTHOR'S NOTE

As stated at the beginning, Ruby Island and all the cultural, historical, and geological features described in this book are fictional. This, of course, includes Fort Domingo and its secret interior chamber, along with the caves and other structures.

In the summer of 1999, I was extremely lucky and spent a week in Sint Maarten with a dream team of archaeologists recording Fort Amsterdam, a fort built by the Spanish and Dutch over the course of two decades starting in the 1630s. We measured, mapped, and dug test pits in and around the fort, and some aspects of the fort described in these pages are based on that experience, but as already stated, there was no fort interior (other than cisterns) documented.

There are Caribbean islands that did have runaway slave settlements. For more information on that subject, look to the work of Syracuse University professor of anthropology Theresa Singleton, whose lecture "An Archaeology of Marronage: Mapping Slave Runaway Sites in Hispaniola, 1521–1822" was very helpful when I began researching this book.

The lore of pirate gold in the lake is entirely fictional, but the 1567 sinking of the Spanish treasure fleet and rumors that the Kalinago hid coins in Dominica's littoral caves is not.

When writing characters whose cultural history and affiliation are different from my own, my goal is always to provide respectful and meaningful representation. Not surprisingly, I share Fiona's goal of wanting people to know the history of colonization and enslavement in the Caribbean and want the people whose history it is to be the ones to tell the story. To that end, readers interested in knowing more about the Kalinago should visit the Kalinago Archive website at www.kalinagoarchive.org. The website is a repository for ancestral knowledge of the Kalinago people of Dominica, and is the first time their history, traditions, and culture have been written by themselves.

ACKNOWLEDGMENTS

Huge thanks to Darcy Burke, who was always there for me when I needed help plotting this book. She helped me work through the problem when I was hitting a wall and provided inspiration in several areas that helped me figure out how to bring Fiona and Dean together.

Massive thanks are also due to my husband, Dave, who was patient and listened and helped me talk through plotting holes and find a way to plug them. As a navy archaeologist with a master's degree in nautical archaeology, he has an understanding of Fiona's job and the world she navigates that is vital to the plausibility of this and all my books, but as always, inaccuracies due to fictional license or errors are on me.

I also need to thank Zoom, for giving me the ability to spend time with author pals Toni Anderson, Jenn Stark, Julie Kenner, Annika Martin, Gwen Hernandez, Manda Collins, Jayne Ann Krentz, Christina Dodd, Serena Bell, Kate Davies, Kris Kennedy, Courtney Milan, Erica Ridley, and of course Darcy Burke in the midst of a pandemic. I don't know how I would have navigated the last year without my author community!

Huge thanks to my editor, Lauren Plude at Montlake Romance, for trusting me to write this story, and to my agent, Elizabeth Winick Rubinstein at McIntosh & Otis, for helping make this dream come true.

I need to thank the dream team I worked with in 1999 recording Fort Amsterdam on the island of Sint Maarten: Janet Friedman,

Heather Crowl, David Blondin, and Kevin Mock. Janet was my boss, mentor, and dear friend who passed away in 2002 and is dearly missed. She was instrumental in my work on the Thermo-Con project, which inspired my debut novel, *Concrete Evidence*. Heather, David, and Kevin, working on Sint Maarten with you all was and will always be one of my greatest field experiences. I'm thrilled to finally get to use it in a book!

Thank you to my son, who was navigating the most disappointing senior year ever as I drafted this book. I am so proud of you and know you and your fellow members of the class of 2021 will thrive, given how you've learned to adapt and understand sacrifices made for the greater good.

Thank you to my daughter, who also has learned to adapt and excel as her college classes all went online only. And thank you for sharing your office-supply store employee discount with me. (Discounted office supplies! I'm living the DREAM.)

Lastly, as always, thank you to my husband, not for the writing and plotting help, but for being my life partner and sharing this dream with me.

CONNECT WITH RACHEL ONLINE

Follow Rachel on Facebook
www.facebook.com/RachelGrantAuthor

Follow Rachel on Twitter
www.twitter.com/rachelsgrant

Find Rachel's books on Goodreads
www.goodreads.com/rachelgrantauthor

Email Rachel
contact@rachel-grant.net

Visit Rachel's website
rachel-grant.net

ABOUT THE AUTHOR

USA Today bestselling author Rachel Grant worked for over a decade as a professional archaeologist and mines her experiences for story lines and settings, which are as diverse as excavating a cemetery underneath an historic art museum in San Francisco, surveying an economically depressed coal-mining town in Kentucky, and mapping a seventeenth-century Spanish and Dutch fort on the island of Sint Maarten in the Caribbean. In all her travels and adventures as an archaeologist, Rachel has found many sites and artifacts, but she's only found one true treasure: her husband, David. Rachel Grant lives on an island in the Pacific Northwest with her husband and children. For more information visit www.rachel-grant.net.